Billy Christ

Michael Cameron was educated at Cambridge University, became a theatrical director and later worked in television and radio drama. Under various guises he has written drama for television, stories, plays, several audio books and hundreds of radio commercials. For a while he worked as a ghost-writer on books as diverse as life-coaching manuals and the history of a German car parts manufacturer. His book *In Harm's Way* about the life of Sean Hogan who was a victim of Irish child abuse, was critically acclaimed and became a best seller. Michael lives in Farnham, England. He is married with two grown-up children. He has a passion for old cars and electric guitars – which he plays badly but loudly!

Billy Christ

Michael Cameron

BILLY CHRIST

Published by
THE OTHER PUBLISHING COMPANY
www.otherpublishing.co.uk

ISBN 978-0-9573191-2-7

Cover design by Deana Riddle
Author's photo by Georgia-Rae Sacre
Book design by Maureen Cutajar

For

Alison, Jess, Will and Duncan

Without whom…

Contents

Prologue

I think I've made the right decision. Explanations could only confuse things. Who's going to believe that I don't remember what happened, that I'm confused between reality and what happened in my head – so I don't know if I am guilty of... well, of what's happened, or not.

My guess is she was strangled – I mean it's hard to tell, she was pretty beaten-up but there are bruises on her neck and I might have done that – I just don't remember. I'm pretty handy, I suppose – I have strong wrists – in fact, I reckon I can hold my own with most people when it comes to... to things like taking the top off a bottle, for instance.

As I say, I think I've made the right decision. Better not to say anything, not even to suggest that I know where she is, because my only alibi is that at the time I was... Well, where I was...

I mean let's face it, who's going to believe me? Anyway, the whole thing's difficult and frankly, confusing. It could have been me, I suppose: I was jealous. And, truth to tell, I have never really understood girls. I mean, I haven't exactly had any 'experience' of them. Have I?

So as tragic as this is, I'm going to keep this to myself because I don't really know what happened and I do not have the sort of alibi that I probably need for the police to be satisfied with my innocence. I keep a lot of things to myself. I always have. I've always had to.

Control. Everything is about control, isn't it?

'...Now I want spirits to enforce, art to enchant; and my ending is despair...'

Shakespeare, The Tempest

Sometime in the 1970s
A Saturday Night

Billy's Private Memoir:

There are two worlds.

Sometimes I think I belong to one world and all the other boys at school and some of the teachers belong to another.

Take the drama club. Some of the older boys and some of the boys in my year and even some who are below me and who are not in the drama club look at you funnily when you go to rehearsals and they nudge each other if Father Martin asks you to rehearse privately up in his office.

I once heard Roger Inkman in the 1st year sixth say to another sixth former, 'Oh, they call it rehearsals? – That's a new name for it!' And he put a sort of funny emphasis on 'new' and then they both giggled and gave me an ODD look. I didn't understand that, especially as most boys in my school have been in the drama club at one time or another.

Yes. They're in another world. That's quite clear.

* * *

~~Diana Watson's Secret Diary~~
~~Miss Diana Watson's Private Diary~~
Diana Emma Katherine Watson's ~~Secret Di~~ Personal Diary
Property of Diana Watson
3, The Brewers' Cottages
The Maltings
Breddon
Near Leeford
England
The World

7

MY Diary – Private – that means you brother dear!! Dear Paul – if you think it is worth reading this then go ahead but I will tell Mum about you and Roger Hammond being caught shoplifting in W H Smith and Son!!

* * *

To begin at the beginning... which is from that dead good Welsh play we have been doing in English (which is an odd thing to do in *English* if you think about it). I've decided to keep a diary – to write down my thoughts and personal stuff. I have reached *that* age!

There are some things I can talk about to Mum and there are some things I can talk about to Vicky and Karen – because they are my best friends (though Vicky is the bestest). But there are some things that you just need to write down for yourself. IMPORTANT THINGS.

I'd hate it if I had to *say* some of these things to anyone else – but I need to say them somehow. So I'll write them here and who knows when I am dead older (or even just dead) they may not be so important or dead embarrassing and other people will read them and see what I was thinking.

(Spooky thought – I may have kids one day and my daughter might read this!!!! Blooooodyyyyy frightening!!!)

Nothing on telly tonight, unless you call '*The Two Ronnies*' funny – which they really, really aren't! '*Jim'll Fix It*' was on when we had tea and Paul said, 'Perhaps he can fix it for you not to be so spotty!' So I said, 'Yeah, and perhaps he can fix it for you not to smell – there is such a thing as a bath in this house,' which was a pretty quick *reposit* or whatever the word is, repo something anyway.

So, because there is nothing on I have come up to my room and started this diary. I've left the curtains and windows open and now it is nine thirty it is practically dark and through the window I can smell that country night smell. It's from the fields and the woods I suppose. Damp, with a little chill to it and kind of musty. I'd never smelt it before, not in London. Now it's here every night when it gets cooler after the sun's gone down. I wonder if I'll ever get used to it and not notice it, like the smell of the Thames.

I am being reflective I think, like Shelley or Wordsworth or some other dead poet we read last term. It is because I'm sad. I should write an ode. Not like that Cyril Fletcher, he's a complete wazzack, I mean proper sad odes to Grecian urns and all that malarkey – like Shelley or whoever it was (Byron??)– An *ode to a sad London girl in the countryside* would be loads better than an ode about an old pot.

I'd like to go on *'Jim'll Fix It'*. I mean I don't want to jump out of an aeroplane or eat my dinner on a big dipper or any of the daft stuff like that. I just wish Jim could fix it for me to meet a boy. I mean a decent boy, you know, a half good-looking one with half a brain. I mean I deserve a snog at the very least after all I've been through. I reckon if we were still in London (another thing Jim could fix for me) I'd have a boyfriend by now. Lynn Smith from my old school wrote to me last week and even she has got a boyfriend and she was *really* not attractive. I mean I don't want to be rude or personal or anything but she had blackheads on her blackheads and there was always that, well, you know, slight smell...

I mean if Lynn Smith can get a bloke, and apparently they have got as far as groping one another at the back of the

Young's Brewery – then anyone can. Even me! It's just not fair, is it??

Of course, there are loads of boys at my new school but I mean you wouldn't want to go out with any of them, not really *go out*! I mean compared to Wandsworth and Putney the boys here are all a bit spazzy. I reckon it's 'cos they all come from farms and they're only used to being with animals – in fact some of them probably are animals.

Di – are you turning into a snob?? Must watch out for this...

* * *

So lots of people are in the other world that I am not part of.

I think it is to do with MATURITY. I don't think maturity has anything to do with being old, I think it means you are in the other world – the 'not my world.' Take my brother Pete. He is only eighteen months older than me but he understands about *certain things* and he formed a secret club with his friends called *The X Rated Readers Club*, which he thinks I do not know about – but which is to do with the magazines he hides on top of his wardrobe and swaps with his friends. So he is MATURE. They are all MATURE. Except me. I am still IMMATURE.

I know I am immature because last summer we went on holiday in a caravan and two tents to a campsite in Spain and my brother's friend Mark came with us. I thought Mark and me were just as good friends as he and Pete were. Then one night while my parents stayed in the caravan with a bottle of red wine ('Rough but drinkable and you can't knock it at three pesetas a litre,' my father had said) we three boys went for a walk into the nearest town with the two sisters who were in the tent next to us.

They were all in the other world – the second world – right from the time we started to walk along the dusty track out of the site. It was warm and the sound of cicadas was really loud and my brother and the girls were talking. It all seemed really nice. It wasn't too hot and I was pleasantly tired from swimming in the sea and my skin was glowing from the sun (as they say in the colour supplement holiday features) and I felt really grown-up as we mooched about the town and sat in the square and had ice creams. I thought, this is the life! I am an English gentleman abroad, a sophisti-cated explorer of foreign cultures. And I thought I might write an essay when I got home and submit it to the *Sunday Times* Travel pages – or to the *Sunday Express*, both of which my parents get – 'one for the news, and one because it's a good read,' they say. Then we walked back to the site.

The next morning Mark said to me as we went to the shower block, 'You didn't get it last night, did you?' I didn't understand what he meant and I told him I didn't.

He said, 'You just wanted to eat ice cream, but me and Pete had other fish to fry!'

I still didn't understand and he looked at me and he said.

'Billy, you're so immature.'

And then he said.

'You'd better stay in the caravan with your parents to-night.'

I don't know why it was but I felt desperately sad then and very left out and I knew that everyone, even my brother and Mark were in this other world and I couldn't join them.

It is a bit like dying I suppose. You are in heaven and you are alive in eternal life and you can see all your friends and family but you can't join in because you are in another place – a place with a view but without a door to go through.

I liked Mark very much and he used to make me laugh. Though he doesn't laugh so much now, not since the unfortunate accident last Autumn on the school geography trip involving the steep hill and the barbed wire fence. My father says, 'Plastic surgery today can do wonders, and it's all thanks to the guinea pigs in the last war.' My mother says, 'God moves in mysterious ways and for such a thing to happen there must have been a reason.' There was of course, but I'd rather not think about that.

Things that mean things to me:

'That you were once unkind befriends me now,
And for that sorrow, which I then did feel,
Needs must I under my transgression bow,
Unless my nerves were brass or hammer'd steel.
For if you were by my unkindness shaken,
As I by yours, you've pass'd a hell of time,
And I, a tyrant, have no leisure taken
To weigh how once I suffer'd in your crime...'
Shakespeare, Sonnet 111

I think that's dead gorgeous. I quite like Shakespeare. I mean he can be quite modern. He says 'hell of a time' which is pretty well swearing and the sort of thing you'd say today, isn't it? I've found loads of good bits like most of *Romeo and Juliet* and the mechanics in *A Midsummer Night's Dream,* who can be dead funny.

Other things that mean things to me:

The Monkees, especially Micky Dolenz.
Brian Jones
Roger Daltry.
Dustin Hoffman and Paul Newman and Robert Redford.
Tea and toast by the fire with Mum and Paul on a wet Sunday afternoon.
The park at the back of our house in Putney and the river.
My new black mini-skirt.
Being in school plays (I am going to be an actress, like mum was).
The hippy beads and the purple sunglasses like Yoko Ono's that I found in that boutique in Leeford.
Sweep, our cat
And my Dad, of course.
Oh, and that boy I see from the bus every morning. Seeeeexy! (Wish *he* went to my school).

I have just heard Paul coming up stairs, so it must be getting late. Even though he is a pain, it's nice to know that he is in the room next to me. It is comforting to know there is still a man in the house, even if Paul isn't really a proper fully grown man. I mean at least he's quite strong since he started doing weight-training after school – though not as strong as dad who could lift me up with one arm – even when I was quite big.

Sometimes when I wake up in the night after one of my dreams, shaking and feeling like I can't breathe and everything around me is very dark and I feel all cold and sweaty at the same time – like I always do after my dreams, if I press my ear to the wall I can hear Paul breathing – and that's dead good. I know that if I needed him he'd come and rescue me. Not that I'd tell him that because he'd say I was a 'bleeding wazzack' – which is his fave expression right now.

I can also hear Paul through the wall when he is doing other things apart from sleeping – which is DISGUUUUSTIIIING!

* * *

I'm lying here in bed and I should be happy – I should be looking forward to the rest of the weekend; I bet Niall Mahoney is looking forward to tomorrow and Patrick Flynn and Ian Shane. They'll be in their beds too I expect – well, perhaps not Patrick, because his parents have a 'modern' attitude to child rearing or so my mother says, and they let him stay up later than he should.

'Later than is good for any young, growing person,' my mother says and she adds, 'But what do you expect of them? Have you seen the length of her skirts?!'

I wish my mother wore short skirts. If the length of skirt is relative to the lateness of your bed time then I wish the hem of her skirt would touch her bum. I should not say 'bum.' Nor should I think of hems and skirts, so I will have to cleanse myself.

I rise from my bed and kneel beside it and beg God to forgive me. But HE is a harsh God. 'Do you think God gave us free will, so that we can do what we like?' Father Hennesey said in R.I., 'I think that would be presumptuous, don't you?'

He said that on Thursday. I remember him saying that because he also said that we should lie in bed every night and 're-run the film of our day on the screen of our minds' and we should remember all our sins and misdemeanours before we beg forgiveness of Our Maker.

I don't like films much as they involve going out and you will certainly end-up in a seat next to someone who has a cold or other infectious DISEASE. I saw Bambi when I was six and it gave me 'flu, in my opinion, though the doctor said I could have got it at school – but I suspect he was wrong, despite him having trained for the PROFESSION of Medical Practitioner.

Anyway, I run the film of the day in my mind right now – let's face it, as a Priest asked me to do this I have no choice, they *are* GOD'S representatives on earth (priests that is, not films). I'm surprised to find that the film has a title, which appears in my head in big letters with a picture of my school behind it. The film is called '*My Day*' – which frankly doesn't sound like it's going to be an Oscar winner. Still, with a title like that you know where you are. Another title tells me that it has been '*Filmed In Technicolor*,' which is always a good thing I reckon.

I beg forgiveness for my sins as I watch the film and I have just got to the bit where we go into school lunch when suddenly the film is interrupted by a scratchy white sign on a black background that says '*Intermission*' and then another one that says, '*Playing at this theatre next week… SCHOOL-BOY MOTHERS…*' and I find myself looking at a film of my mother and Mrs Flynn walking along Leeford High Street in mini-skirts, and my mother's is so short you can actually see her knickers underneath it.

I am quite shocked.

Actually, I'm appalled.

* * *

Monday...

It's been a dead hot sunny day today. Even this morning when I went to school the sun was blazing. My face and arms and even my legs are getting a tan. Perhaps people will think I have been abroad – like to the South of France or something where all the rock stars hang out. Me with *The Rolling Stones* and all that. Me and Mick sipping cocktails in a bar in St Tropez and Keith begging me to sit with him instead – 'Sorry Keith I'd love to, but Mick just won't let me…'.

We've all hitched our skirts up dead high, well, as high as you dare with old Ma Hawkes on the prowl checking us all as we go in the gates – you should see all of us girls round the corner where we get off the bus, pulling our hems down before she spots us. The boys have taken to wearing their shirt sleeves rolled up and a few of the sixth formers have taken off their ties and slung their blazers over their shoulders. They might look quite sexy, you know, like Frank Sinatra, only they're all complete mongs who want to be football players or car mechanics or tractor engineers or whatever it is you do in the countryside. I doubt if they're going to get an O-Level between them unless they do ones in the life and times of being Bobby Moore and how to service a combine harvester.

Sat with Vicky and K as usual on the bus. I keep the seats for them as they get on a stop after me. V had got a pair of sunglasses on – they were huge with bright red rims and she didn't take them off even in the bus, though she tripped over some old woman's shopping basket as she walked up to the back where I was and she pretended she hadn't but she went really pink 'cos she knew I'd seen it.

Some of the boys from our school got on and they were so disgusting. One of them made a loud farting noise and they all giggled and looked around and pretended it was the old woman whose shopping bag V had tripped over and the old woman went pink too and gave them a really filthy look.

Like I said – they're all mongs.

Karen was dead grumpy and she has been all day – she's 'due' in a couple of days and she always gets like this. I am sooo glad I never get P.M.T. (Whatever Mum says!).

We went by the big posh boys school just outside Hurstwood like we always do and as usual I looked at them going through the gates. HE (the sexy boy) wasn't there to-day, which was a bit of drag – or perhaps he didn't walk to-day and his mum drove him to school in one of the posh cars all the mums seems to drive in that place.

The sexy boy's already browner than anyone I've seen this summer – so I reckon he probably does walk in every day and I just missed him. Anyway, he clearly likes the out-door life. Oh, God I hope that doesn't mean he's a bloody farm boy too! Well, I suppose if he is and he goes to a posh school his dad probably owns the farm – so that's all right.

At assembly Mick Figgis farted so loudly that Mr Evans

heard him and stopped reading the notices and sent him out
of the hall in front of everyone and gave him a detention.
Good. That's all the boys here ever do it seems to me – fart
and burp.

* * *

I am in school early as I had something to attend to in the
woods. Assembly was very good. We sang, '*Ave Maria*' and I
have to confess that I hit the top notes quite well. In fact the
headmaster definitely gave me a look as if to say, 'Well done,
at least someone is putting in the effort!' Though Diarmuid
O'Callaghan standing next to me nearly spoilt everything as
for some reason he had a fit of the giggles. He may not be *all
there,* I reckon.

English and History were followed by Biology. This is
good. I like all three and I think I impressed with my
knowledge of the anatomy of the frog. Well, I have a lot of
practical experience in this subject, when all is said and done.

I am walking along the corridor towards the lunch hall
with Ian Shane when Father Martin appears around the corner and smiles at us both, which is NOT a very pleasant
sight, let's be honest. Suddenly the day which had been so
good takes on an unexpected gloom.

Father Martin takes us up to his room, which is high up
in the school, right at the v. top, where the old attic was
when the building was a stately home, before the diocese
bought it and turned it into our school. His room is dusty
and crammed with books – which in my opinion is v. v. un-
healthy and likely to lead to DISEASES of all kinds being
spread around the place.

The room is large and he has divided it into two by pulling a book case half-way across the middle of the floor. One half is his 'bedroom' with the old iron bedstead and a greasy mattress, dirty-white sheets and a pillow with a stain on it from his hair (totally disgusting, in my opinion and I apologize if I cause offence by drawing attention to these sordid details).

The bed stands on a threadbare rug and there are piles of books and magazines all around it. The walls are faded cream and a crucifix hangs above the head of the bed. The crucifix is covered in dust and cobwebs and, if we're being brutally honest, it is dirty – which in my opinion is heaping insult on injury to the Lord Our God who has suffered quite enough as it is with the nails and the crown of thorns.

Everything in this room is v. dirty and everyone knows that he never (well, hardly ever) changes the bed sheets. (Perhaps he has something to hide?) You can smell the stale odour from the bed even where we sit on the sofa and it is disgusting & horrid.

I am sorry to be so explicit – there is a danger that we will enter into the realms of the 'kitchen sink' in this story – like they do in the *Wednesday Play*, which is, according to my Mum, 'pornography by another name, from the likes of Dennis Potter – who went to a good university and should know better.'

The other half of the room is used as his office. (That's Father Martin's office, not Dennis Potter's). Some of the teachers have 'studies' but Fr Martin prefers the term 'office'.

He has an old roll-top desk along one wall of this 'office.' It is leaning crookedly where a caster has come off it. The roll-top desk is never closed because the desk is too full of letters and books and test papers waiting to be marked and old registers and pens and pots of ink and pieces of paper and some other things that I cannot see because they are hidden behind the aforementioned items.

Along the opposite wall is a big old red sofa with bursts in it where more stuffing is appearing and coffee and other stains (which I would rather not think about) mark the fabric. It is very dirty of course but it is quite comfortable.

When Father Martin invites boys to his room to discuss the school play (he is head of drama) or to look at their English essays or to discuss the film society (he is president and founder of the film society) or for some other reason, he likes to sit next to them on this sofa. Although the sofa is very big he likes to sit right next to them on it and if there are two boys up there to discuss the school play, film society etc. then he likes to sit between both of them and pull them both quite close to him.

Father Martin has a big hooked nose, he is going bald but he combs what is left of his hair back over his head and he wears gold rimmed glasses, also he takes snuff so he has a stain under his nostrils. Regretfully, he has disgustingly bad breath and clearly he has not discovered the advantages of 'Pepsodent' nor has he taken advantage of the '*Colgate ring of confidence*' as demonstrated in the TV adverts.

It is true to say that I do not like Fr. Martin for various reasons but mainly because his personal hygiene is wanting! It is a sin not to like someone and especially if that someone is a priest but I can't help it, I do <u>not</u> like Fr. Martin.

I am now sitting on the sofa next to him and on his other side is Ian Shane. Father Martin lifts his arms and drops them round our shoulders, round mine and Shane's and he draws us in close to him. I can smell sweat from his under arms and even feel the damp patch in his cassock, his sweat has actually soaked through his cassock and now it is soaking through my school shirt. '*It's nice to know, you're nice to know*,' must be another advert that he has not seen!

'Boys,' he says, 'Dear boys. My stalwarts of the film society and of the drama club. My little actors...' (He says 'actooors'). '...My stars in the making. I have such plans for us. In a few days we break-up, but whatever you have planned for the holidays put it aside, make space in your crowded schedules. I have planned a project!'

And when he says 'project' he squeezes us more tightly and I can feel the wet trickling down my back – it is the wet of his sweat, not mine and I feel sick.

He grins at us, turning his head from side to side, showing us his brown teeth and I try not to take a breath or I will smell his as he speaks again and puffs in my face.

'I have an idea for a film – a film we must make and make at once for it calls on the hot, indolent days of summer to be a success.'

I make a note to look up indolent in my Chambers 20th Century Dic. as it isn't a word I am completely familiar with.

'I have devised a little script,' he goes on, 'which is based upon the Greek Gods...'

Ian Shane groans and quickly turns it into a cough.

'The story is an allegory – it shows us how modern man has left behind the mystical and the spiritual and abandoned the great gods of nature... but they are not gone, they are only sleeping!'

He beams at us and I want to groan too but I don't. I have been in three of Father Martin's '*little films*' and in all of them it seems to me that the ancient gods are sleeping, waiting to be woken or they are in exile and waiting to return from Hades or Heaven or wherever it is Father Martin has sent them, and part of me wishes they could just stay away or come back and get on with something but they never do – they just keep hanging round like they are waiting for the bus. But that isn't what really worries us, me and Ian Shane, what worries us is more down to earth, and it is Ian S who finally asks the BIG Q.

'What'll we wear father?' he says in his soft Irish lilt (as it says in my book on Oscar Wilde) and there is more than a hint of what I think you might call *trepidation* in his voice.

Father Martin beams at us again. 'Shane you will be the great god Pan...' Ian blinks nervously under the priest's gaze and I think if he did not have his arm round us Ian would shrink to nothing, a pile of dust in the corner of the sofa, '...And you will wear a little white tunic, a blond wig and a laurel crown. You must be sun tanned and your eyes will need heavy black liner – *a la mode* – I will help you do the make-up!'

I can see the pain in Ian's eyes. Perhaps he doesn't understand the French – I know I don't, but it is not that of course – it's the, what's the word? *Humiliation* of it.

Shane swallows hard and when he speaks his voice cracks a little. 'I...I won't be able to make it Father... I can't do it...'

Father Martin opens his eyes wide and stares at Shane.

'Won't..?' he begins but his voice tails off.

'No, Father... I won't be here. You know... It being the holidays 'n all... I'll... I'll be home in Dublin.'

Father Martin stares at him, not understanding – perhaps he has never heard of Dublin.

Desperately Ian carries on. 'I'm a boarder Father. I go home to Ireland in the holidays... to see my family.' Father Martin does not blink, still staring at him. 'They'll be expecting me...' Shane finishes hopelessly.

Father Martin throws back his head and laughs.

'Oh, that,' he says. 'That won't be a problem. I've already called them. You can stay at school for another week. Wonderful news, eh?'

Shane doesn't look as if he thinks it's that wonderful. In fact, he looks rather annoyed – perhaps he is angry that Father Martin called his parents without asking him first or perhaps he is annoyed that his parents said it was all right for him to stay behind. Mind you, as Shane's parents are Irish he never stood a chance – they would never say 'no' to a priest. That's how it is. I am not Irish – but nearly every boy in school is, so I know their ways. (To be completely honest, apparently my great grandmother on my mother's side did have a brief flirtation with a builder from Galway but we never talk about that at home and I don't think it left anything permanent in the genes – at least I hope not).

Father Martin is saying to Shane, 'Of course the boarding house will be closed but no need to worry, you can sleep in Mr Terry's room right here, right next to mine... That way I can keep an eye on you.'

And he grins a brown tooth grin.

Ian Shane is cringing as I twist round to look at him and he is definitely much smaller than he usually is and there is deadness in his eyes.

'Now on the subject of costume,' Father Martin says and he turns to look at me and I am not quick enough to dodge the drop of spit that lands on my cheek and I am too embarrassed to wipe it away. 'For you my dear boy,' he says to me. 'For you there will be no choice, for you are to be The Nymph Syrinx, the beauty with whom Pan has fallen in love...'

So that's it then. I will be a goddess and he has found a long flowing dress and another blonde wig in the school theatre's wardrobe for me to wear. Someone always has to dress up as a woman in our school plays and films because we are a boys' school and it's usually me, though at my school most of us have spent a good deal of time in skirts and tights.

I sigh. I wonder if I will ever play a man – I had hopes I would when my voice broke but Fr Martin seems not to have noticed.

I really don't want to make the film. I want to ride my bike and walk in the woods. But I don't say anything. It would make Fr Martin unhappy if I say anything. So I look around the little office while he goes on and on about the script and the kind of cine camera he will be using. I look at the piles of books and his old radio gram and the stack of 78 rpm records beside it which are not nearly as good as the 'thirty three and one thirds' that me and my brother have with *Sergeant Pepper* and things. And he is saying it will be fun for us all to spend some time together in the empty school and in the fields around it and in the woods and by the little stream, which will be what he calls our 'locations'.

And looking at his dirty, untidy room I think it is odd that he likes films and plays but he doesn't have a telly. Everyone has a telly. My father has even got us a colour one this year from Radio Rentals, 'I'd never *buy* one,' he said, 'modern technology is too unreliable – and that's a fact!'

But Father Martin hasn't got a telly, not even a black and white one. Perhaps it is a sacrifice he makes to honour the Lord our God or perhaps he'd rather watch the cine films of all the different productions he has made over the years with generations of school boys. There must be a lot of them, after all he has been here since 1959.

Just as I am thinking how awful it would be not to have a telly and to have to watch lots and lots of films of school-boys in dresses and other costumes, the bell rings for the end of break and Fr Martin has talked all this time at us and I've missed my school lunch and I'm hungry and worse, he has not taken his arm from our shoulders and we both have wet patches on our school shirts which makes me feel nauseous.

So Shane and I go miserably back to class and some of the other boys snigger at us as we walk down the corridor, they can tell from the wetness and the smell we drag with us just where we have been.

* * *

As we walk along the corridor towards our Latin class Teddy Edwards in the year above me, who is a bully and a gang leader, pushes past us. As usual he is surrounded by his gang of obnoxious and frankly distasteful followers. I am sensible enough to press myself flat against the wall and let them pass and I ignore their comments. 'Oh, look out,' says Teddy. 'Bum boys in the corridor!' And his friends giggle like the pathetic morons they are.

He often calls me and other members of the drama club 'bum boys'. I assume it is some reference to the way we look i.e. that we have faces like bums – which we do not, but I suppose this is about the level of Teddy's idea of cutting sarcasm.

I said this to Mark once and he looked at me really oddly

and said, 'Wise-up, mate!' Then he shook his head. 'It's slang you, pratt.' But I still have no idea what sort of slang and what it means. It might be like cockney rhyming slang (Teddy definitely has the air of a London gangster about him) but I can't think what 'Bum boys' would rhyme with.

When they've gone, Ian Shane turns to me and says, 'I hate the fockin' drama club...' and although that word is not one I would ever allow in my vocabulary, somehow in an Irish accent (brogue I think they call it, though why it should be named after a shoe I don't know) it doesn't seem quite so bad. 'It's bad enough having to lose some of the holidays but it's bleedin' awful being thought of as one of *those* all the time.' He adds.

'One of those what?' I ask and Shane stops walking and looks at me.

'Those!' He repeats as if maybe I was deaf. A couple of second-formers brushed past us and one of them holds his nose. Cheek. In my day we treated our elders as our betters, as my father often says.

'Come on,' Shane says. 'We'll be late for Latin and then Rogers will be the second Priest to ruin my day.'

I don't like him saying that because as much as I don't want to be in the film in the holidays, I don't think a Priest can ruin anything and we shouldn't really criticise him. As a general rule Priests are being guided by God, so what they decide we should do, we must follow obediently. Of course they are not infallible like his Holiness Pope Paul VI, but they're not far off it in my book. But I don't say anything because I can see that Shane is looking quite hot and grumpy and I do not want to put him under undue stress. I have had quite a lot of experience of being under undue stress myself, in fact I lead quite a lot of my own life in that state and it is not something I would wish to inflict on anyone else.

Still Shane does have a point. These are our holidays and really it's unfair that we should have to perform in the film during them, instead of in term time.

I suddenly think that perhaps I could go and see Father Martin privately – I believe that being what you might call a 'trusty' and naturally something of a favourite with the clergy he might listen to me and bring the filming dates forward to the last week of term. And then I realise that could never happen as he would probably be too busy marking end of term exams and because, quite frankly, as bad it is having to wear a dress and a wig in the holidays, doing so while all the school is still here watching us would be even worse.

* * *

Dreary tea with Mum and brother. Dreary homework – *The Norman Conquest was as much a new beginning as the end of a previous era – discuss –* Yes it was. Actually I suppose you could say for King Harold it was the end of an '*eye-r*' not an 'era' but I didn't write that as Miss Cowley has absolutely NO sense of humour whatsoever!

Am in my room. All windows open – it is sooo hot even at night. Have put on *Bridge Over Troubled Water.* It's so sad. I like *The Monkees* mainly and also *The Beatles* of course, but sometimes at night, you just *need Simon and Garfunkle.*

Thing is, Mum and Paul have got used to the country life. I haven't. I'm more sophisticated than them. I mean I know Mum was an actress when she was younger but she is not 'in touch' like she used to be. She seems to have lost her, you know, *sparkle*! I guess it could be the thing with dad. I think we all lost our sparkle 'cos of the thing with dad.

* * *

Having been quite shocked last night by the film of my mum in her short skirt, which ended in a way it is better not to describe, tonight I need to restore some of HIS faith in me. To do this of course, I must punish myself. If I don't the consequences could be serious.

It's dark now. My floor is covered in the cold lino that my parents found in The John Lewis partnership – 'Good value and you know you can't get cheaper. Believe me, when they say they're never knowingly undersold, they really mean it,' my mother said.

So, I have to kneel on this cold floor in my pyjamas and pray. But as I pray, I know that kneeling is not enough and that being quite cold (which I am) is not enough. I am only kneeling and that is UN-satisfactory in my book and almost certainly in HIS! No, it is DEFINITELY not enough. I must do more than this if HE is to forgive me and we are to avoid his terrible retribution against us all.

I bend over backwards for God... literally. My knees stay on the cold lino floor and I arch against the natural curve of my spine trying to touch the floor behind me with my forehead but without lifting my knees from the floor – it is awkward, a clumsy manoeuvre. Then it becomes more than that, it is now slightly painful. My back is telling me to stop but I can't stop – God does not want me to stop. I must give myself pain in order to gain his forgiveness, in order to be in HIS presence, to be acknowledged by him.

I push myself further back. It is now hurting quite a lot. I push again, forcing my knees down, pushing my back against itself, so that my vertebrae (I am quite good at Biology and at anatomical terminology) are screaming at me. I push and push. White lights flicker behind my closed eyelids. I push myself again and my knees want to lift from the floor. But they mustn't! If I do not complete this manoeuvre without my knees staying on the floor, then I must start it all over again... And I must keep on trying to do it until I have gained forgiveness. That's the rule and I believe in following the RULES.

Once – a week ago I think it was – or maybe it was longer – I did this all night and it was dawn before I finished. I couldn't walk properly for three days afterwards and I told my mother and father that I had slipped in the playground. I shouldn't have done that of course, it was a lie and that night after I had told them the lie, I had to punish myself all over again for the sin of mendacity, which is one of the worst in my b.

I think it takes me only an hour or so to find forgiveness tonight, the pain isn't really so bad after all. But I wish I was asleep like Niall Mahoney or Patrick Fynn or Ian Shane, looking forward to tomorrow. But I don't look forward, instead I'm worried... I think I am always worried.

* * *

Mum came up stairs a few minutes ago. You could hear she was walking dead quiet so as not to wake us but she heard the music and tapped on my door and stuck her head round. I was lying on top of the bed in my nightie, reading my library book. (The Railway Children. Well, you are never too old for The Railway Children!)

She said, 'Are you all right, darling?'

I told her I was just going to go to sleep and I was fine. But she gave me that odd look she does sometimes, like she can see *into* you and not just see you. She came in and sat on the edge of my bed and put her arm round me and I could smell her – my mummy smell, perfume and cigarettes and the gin she drinks before she has her dinner (and quite often after her dinner as well). And I felt all warm and cosy like I always do when she hugs me – and all the things like not having a boyfriend and missing home (I mean real home, Putney home) and Dad and everything, didn't seem so bad...

'It'll be ok, you know...You'll get used to it, to being here.'

It's amazing how she kind of knows what you're thinking without you saying anything. So I grunted. I'd like to have said something but you can't always say what you want or be bothered or something, and anyway she was only partly right, I mean I couldn't exactly say, 'Yeah but it's not just the poxy countryside, I mean I wouldn't mind snogging a bloke and getting my tits squeezed, as it happens.'

Actually, you probably could say that to my mum because compared to other mums she is amazingly groovy and I know she had loads of blokes in the theatre and some big ding-dong with someone like Albert Finney or Terence Stamp or someone like that back when she was young – so unlike most mums she's lived a bit – but I didn't say anything 'cos it was just easier to grunt and not to have to get 'involved' as it were.

She hugged me again.

'Get some sleep, poppet.'

I threw my book on the ground and she let go of me so I could slip into bed. She went over to the record player but I said to leave it, I'd just hear side two before I went to sleep.

She was going through the door when she said, 'Is it your dad? Or is it just being a teenager?' And she said it really nicely and softly.

'Both,' I said and turned to face the wall.

'It will get better. I promise you it will.'

And then she went into the landing and closed the door. I lay there and I felt kind of bad that I hadn't said much to her and that I turned my back on her. But it's so hard with parents, isn't it? Inside I know how lucky I am. I mean, I can always rely on Mum and even on Paul in his funny boy way. And as much as I miss Dad, as much as I ache when I think about it, right down in my heart and in my head and even in my toes and teeth, I'm dead lucky really and I am getting happier all the time, even here, even in The Brewers' Cottages, somewhere in the countryside, in the back of bloody beyond near a stupid town called Leeford. I am happier now.

And so I think about the boy I see from the bus and other good things like tea and toast after school and the new Laura Ashley skirt Mum said she might get me for my birthday.

* * *

Although it is summer the room is quite cold at this time of night but even so I take off my pyjamas. I throw my bed clothes on the floor and open the bedroom window so that a cold draft blows through the room and then I go back to the bed and lie on it. I reach over to where the jug of water is that I keep beside my bed in case of night-time thirst.

It is full and I lift it up and pour the water all over me – over my body and especially over my testicles and penis. I am soaked, the bed is soaked. I put down the jug and the wind from the window blows over my wet body, and the cold is like a terrible ache that goes right through me.

I don't know if I have done enough to please the Lord and I must be careful not to think that I have, as vanity is a sin – Father Connelly said so.

I shiver and freeze until dawn… I am sorry God. And it isn't just my body that aches. I realise that I ache inside, I ache in my soul.

The whole house is dead quiet now the record's finished. Not just quiet but restful, peaceful – and that's nice. I think I am turning a corner. I don't know why but I think things are going to get better. I'm going to finish writing this and go to sleep.

Brill…

* * *

'Forsan et haec olim meminisse iuvabit.'

The sun is hot, beating through the classroom windows. The windows that will open, are open. But there is no air and it is very hot.

I am drowsy and so are all the others.

'Forsan et haec olim meminisse iuvabit,' Father Rogers

repeats. He isn't drowsy. His bald head shines in the hot sun and sunlight flashes off his little gold rimmed glasses and the reflections of the class – the boys, the windows, the white sheets of paper on his desk, make it impossible to see his little, steely eyes behind the shiny panes.

Father Rogers teaches us Latin and also maths. There is a rumour that he trained as a Jesuit and this explains why he is so hot on discipline and why he has perfected the art of making us feel terrified. He never seems to smile and no one has ever heard him laugh and he talks in a low, precise way that you have to strain to hear. Even when he is angry he never shouts at us. He doesn't need to. No one ever talks when he is around, because not only does Father Rogers have steely eyes behind his steely glasses but he has a steely attitude to match.

As if that is not enough, Father R. is, to be blunt about it, a big man – what you might call an *imposing figure*! He is perfectly built – broad shouldered and tall and he is in what you might call *proportion;* everything about him is neat (except his teeth which are crooked and yellow because he smokes a pipe for pleasure in the evenings apparently) – and this neatness makes him even more frightening to us boys.

I heard Mrs Hayes talking to my mother about him once when they didn't know I was listening and Mrs Hayes said, 'What a waste. A body like that on a Priest.' And my mother laughed, but you could tell she was uncomfortable at what I can only call a minor blasphemy. Then Mrs Hayes said, 'So it's not true then, the devil doesn't always keeps the best for himself.' And she fell about laughing. I was appalled, I don't mind saying. A man of the cloth deserves better than this, especially from lay people. Still, God moves in mysterious ways – a few days later all the paintwork on Mrs H's new car (a blue Austin Maxi) was scratched while she was in Sainsbury's and apparently it cost a fortune to re-spray. I'll say no more...

Personally, although I would never say this to anyone in case they laughed at me, I too admire Father Rogers' perfectly proportioned body. I do not like people who have some parts of their bodies that are out of proportion with other parts. I would not like to have been Richard Merrick – or a dwarf, for that matter. I'm glad that like Father Rogers I cut a pretty dashing figure myself. I've been known to lift weights in the school gym and I do press-ups most evenings before I say my prayers. So father Rogers and I have something in common and I hope to grow-up very like him.

I once heard my father say that Father Rogers was, 'Clever, controlling, and commanding,' and he added, 'Which is not a bad thing in a religious man, if you ask me.' My father has strong opinions about the clergy, many of which I tend to share.

Fr R. easily exerts his will over us. He can do this because he has learnt to freeze us with a look, and send us reeling across the room when he shouts at us and he can hit your head with a flying board rubber at twenty feet. He only has to look at us and we shut up.

Now he is a dark figure on a hot Monday afternoon, encased in his cassock which is perfectly buttoned and with a glistening white and crisply starched collar. His Mum has definitely taught him the benefits of using Persil, I reckon. I can't help but notice that there is not a hint of sweat on him. He, unlike another I could mention, definitely does not have wet patches under his arms. It occurs to me that he might even control his own body temperature – he is so perfectly in command of everything.

Father Rogers only occasionally shouts, usually he makes whispered threats at us with tightly drawn lips as he flicks his red pen across our exercise books. There is never a smile on his lips. He has probably never laughed, not even been a little amused by anything. Fred Dymond says he would like us to be as miserable as he is... Except that I do not believe he is miserable; he is happy in his humourless, but neatly ordered world, in which he is in command, in which he controls everything and everyone. I suppose his tough stance will make us boys become men in the one true Catholic Church – which is his vocation, when all is said and done.

'I say again,' he says, and I think his voice is like ice cubes of speech in the hot weather.

'Forsan et haec olim meminisse iuvabit. The source and translation, please.'

His eyes sweep around the room and he settles on Flaherty. I breathe a sigh of relief. Not me today, then, thank you dear Lord.

'Mr Flaherty, will rise to his feet,' he whispers.

Fred Flaherty, shuffles awkwardly to his feet behind his cramped desk. We have fixed seats so it is always hard to stand straight, the bench seat presses into the back of your knees, making you want to double up and Flaherty is, q. frankly, fat – his hair is disgusting and he has never taken advantage of the double action of Vosene. His face is dirty, (no creamy Camay, used there!) his shoes are unlaced and scuffed and his shirt hangs out of his shorts. One school sock is half way down his leg, the other has given up completely and lies in limp folds around his ankle. His knees are dirty, his hands are dirty and his face is dirty. It is all quite shocking.

He stands with one shoulder lower than the other and his head turned away from Father Rogers, looking at him with a sort of sideways look, from under lowered eyelids, as if he has something to hide or carries some great shadow on his conscience – which he probably does, as he tends to release wind on inappropriate occasions and not apologise for it.

He is not nice to look at and most of the time I try NOT to look at him as he is REPULSIVE but now I do look at him and Father Rogers looks at him too – a cold, level, icy look. Fr. Rogers' upper lip twitches very slightly and curls into the faintest of sneers.

There is a silence, while Flaherty shuffles uncomfortably under his gaze. What must Father Rogers – neat ordered, controlled – be thinking when he looks at Fatty Flaherty as he is known or 'Farty Flaherty' as he is also known? Fr R. shudders slightly and there is, what you might call, an imperceptible shake of his head.

'Forsan et haec olim meminisse iuvabit!' He says at last and there is a terrible menace in his voice. The warm air around his words becomes frost and Flaherty turns his head still further from his gaze, so that he looks at the wall to his right.

Then Father Rogers speaks again.

'Translate it, boy! Translate it and tell me where it comes from... the source. What is the source?'

He doesn't know. Old Fatty doesn't have the foggiest i. And we all know that he doesn't. Even Father R. knows that he doesn't, which makes you wonder why he keeps staring at him and waiting for an answer.

There is a long silence. Flaherty shuffles and Father Rogers gazes at him, like a scientist with a sample on a slide.

And then he says, almost like he was talking about the weather or next week's cricket match, 'You are a useless cretin. You are worthless. You are no good to yourself or to this school. You are a mess in your clothing, in your personal hygiene and in your attitude. You will go outside and stand in the corridor until this lesson is over as I find your very presence in this room an insult to me and to the cross under which we all labour.'

He glances up at the crucifix that dominates the room above the blackboard and he bows his bald head in deep reverence as do I because the Lord must always be shown reverence, and then he continues.

'You will write out fifty times: *The odd quarter of a day in Julian reckoning was accounted for once in every four years by the addition of an extra day.*' Which is his current favourite set of lines. '...And you will take this chit to the strap room tonight, where you will ask the discipline master to carry out this wholly deserved punishment.'

He writes something on a small scrap of paper which he carefully folds and hands to Flaherty who has shuffled up to the teacher's dais, hand held out. Everyone knows that the chit is for four strokes of the thick leather strap used by the discipline master, two on each hand. It has all been done neatly and correctly in red ink, the chit written and signed in the prescribed manner – even though there is no need for such a note as the discipline master is Father Rogers himself. Then Flaherty shuffles to the door and leaves the classroom. Humiliated. Punished.

As the door closes behind him Father Rogers looks at us all, sweeping his gaze around the room.

'Forsan et haec olim meminisse iuvabit!' He says. 'From Virgil, the Aeneid, Book I. Line 203. Meaning?'

He raises an eyebrow and fixes us with his stiletto eye. 'Meaning,' he explains. 'Maybe one day it will be cheering to remember even these things!'

* * *

At last the lesson is over and Father Rogers strides out of our classroom, satisfied with his afternoon's work and the chant of the endings of the second declension are still ringing in our ears as he closes the door behind him: '...Us... E... Um... I... I... O... , I... I... Os... Orum... Is... Is...' (as in: 'Annus, Anne, Annum...')

He leaves us, waiting in silence he hopes, for Mr Terry's English Lit lesson. Ryan Smith, known as Smudge to his friends – of which I am most definitely not one – throws his Latin exercise book across the classroom and it lands with the pages flipped over in the dust on the floor next to Flaherty's desk.

'Anus, anus, anus or up your bum,' he chants danger-ously loudly (and revoltingly) and peels some gum that he has been chewing earlier from under the lapel of his blazer, picks some cotton thread off it, puts it in his mouth and chews it noisily.

Flaherty puts his big dusty boot onto the opened exer-cise book and wiggles his foot around on it so that it leaves a dirty heel mark right across Smudge's scrawling writing. I can see the words 'Amo, amas, amat...' being obliterated even from where I sit.

'Well, how will you get out of that one?' I think to my-self. 'What will Father Rogers say when he comes to mark that book next week?' But I don't say anything out loud because I learnt ages ago that the others don't listen to me – they just giggle and turn away whispering when I say anything, especially when I point out their obvious misdemeanours and short comings.

In the past when I was a lot younger, if I made any comments about them they didn't just giggle they would beat me up and I have even been near to being 'posted' -which is hideous, and involves being carried by several boys at high speed with your legs held apart, down an alley way at the side of the school. At the end of the alley is a thick steel post set in the ground – I'll leave the rest to your imagination!

I sensibly decided in the third form that I would take drastic measures to make sure that 'posting' would never happen to me and I invested in a 'Bullworker' as recommended by Muhamed Ali (formerly Mr Cassius Clay), which was advertised in the back pages of the 'TV Times' Christmas edition. (Christmas is the *only* time my parents will tolerate having the 'TV Times' in the house. Usually they restrict themselves to the much more sophisticated Radio Times as it is a well known fact that commercial television is not necessarily for people like us).

Anyway, as I was saying (or to be more precise writing) I bought this 'Bullworker' device with my savings and practised long hard hours alone in my bedroom with it. As a result, I developed a fairly good set of pectoral and abdominal muscles if I say so myself, which had the effect of catching the attention of the PE Department and getting me into the rugby squad (C-team reserves) and putting off would-be assailants. I don't mind admitting that the last time one of the school bullies cornered me at the back of the tuck-shop he had a pretty bad time of it. I do not necessarily condone violence unless it

is sanctioned by the Lord – which I think it was in this case
(and in some other cases I could mention but won't just now).

So now, as a riot begins in our classroom, I sit tight and
keep quiet. This is my policy with the rougher boys. I may
have the means at my disposal to deal with them – but I prefer to *keep my powder dry!*

The noise in the classroom is rising to what you might
call (and I do, as I am quite musical) a *crescendo* and there is
now, as my father would say, a great deal of unrest among
the natives. In fact one of the creatures with whom I am
forced to share my education, has gone so far as to put a
waste-paper bin over the head of Niall Murphy, who is small
for his age and quite frankly obviously somewhat retarded,
and several other boys are taking it in turns to beat the bin
with their rulers. Flaherty has even taken off his dusty shoe
and is using that to beat the bottom of the bin and possibly
he is causing Murphy even more brain damage than he already has.

Fortunately, just as it looks as if things are getting out of
hand, the door opens and Mr Terry strides into the room.

'What are yous all doin'?' he shouts and it's like someone turned down the volume on a record player and everyone stops where they are and stares at him.

Mr Terry is from Northern Ireland and he is clearly quite
mad. He is also an alcoholic I reckon, judging from the fumes
he breathes over you when he leans across to look at your exercise book. He is short and has wiry red hair that sticks up oddly in different places and he has broken glasses that are always
repaired with Elastoplast and are higher on one side than the
other. He has a bristly ginger moustache or it may not be ginger at all, it might just be stained by nicotine because he

smokes all the time – even when he is teaching – despite the fact that teachers are not supposed to smoke in class.

Actually, he doesn't teach us very much as he prefers to sing. He sings us Irish rebel folk songs in a loud tenor voice that shakes a little like his hands do.

Mr Terry could be a good teacher if he didn't sing so much or if he'd stop telling us about the politics of Northern Ireland and what he calls the 'Struggle' or the 'Troubles.' I mean, he certainly knows his English Lit and quite a lot of American Lit too and he obviously knows loads and loads of Irish Lit – not that there is much Irish Lit in my opinion that is any good, apart from the sublime O Wilde who is miles wittier than the tedious G B Shaw, if you ask me.

Now Mr Terry stands by the door and he looks at the chaos and he goes pale with anger. He splutters, lost for words:

'You...You... Kerrumph...'

At least it sounds like 'kerrumph' but think it's just a sort of explosion in his mouth as he can't speak. So he tries to light a cigarette instead but his hand is shaking so much the match goes out before it gets near the tip of it. He takes the unlit cigarette from his mouth and pushes his broken glasses which have slipped down his nose, back onto his face and makes them even more crooked then they were before and then he finds his voice again and shouts: 'Will yous all sit down and shut-up... At once!' And there is a threat in his voice that chills the blood.

Flaherty puts his shoe back on and runs across to his desk, Nial Murphy pulls the bin off his head and everywhere desk lids slam shut and seat backs crash down. Mr Terry stands staring at us, licking his dry lips and finally he manages to light the cigarette. 'It's like a riot,' he says angrily. 'It's like a bloody riot on the Falls Road – what are you, a bunch of proddy Orange men?'

You can feel the insult strike home. A lot of these boys have fathers and mothers who have what you might call *connections* with certain factions in the South of Ireland. Sean Daragon for one, has a black beret and a military jacket that his father gave him, which he tells us he will wear with pride in a few years on his eighteenth birthday and Sean Malahide is a distant descendant of Michael Collins and his entire family still have what he calls a 'relationship' with Sinn Fein.

'These are violent times' it says in my father's copy of *The Daily Telegraph* and they are definitely right. You only have to visit my school to know that. And Mr Terry knows it better than most. There was a picture of a riot in Belfast on the front page of *The Telegraph* last December and it featured a Civil Rights marcher whose eyes glittered with anger and whose lips were twisted back in hatred. He was throwing a brick at the police. None of us were particularly shocked to see that it was Mr Terry himself as he has often told us that he likes to go over at weekends and do his 'bit'.

You never know how Mr Terry will react in any situation. It is said he once threw a boy out of a window – and it wasn't open at the time – because the boy had said Ian Paisley may have a point if you looked at things from a Protestant point of view. He'd barely finished speaking apparently, when 'crash' he was gone! Of course, this story may not have been true. On the other hand, having seen the photograph of Mr Terry with his brick, I would rather not take any risks myself and I have always treated him with a great deal of cautious respect and in his presence I have even been known to say how much I respect the works of Sean O'Casey and how I despise the British 'occupation'.

So Mr Terry stands here now looking at us, puffing on his cigarette and I notice that he has a grubby, battered paperback copy of Brendan Behan's '*The Quare Fellow*' sticking out of his jacket pocket. He stares at us through dirty glasses and he doesn't move at all, apart from his shaking hands and his twitching left eyelid – both of which move all the time because he can't control them.

I definitely think looking at his wild and glazed eyes that he may now have gone completely mad and I am expecting the worst. So when he crosses over to one of the classroom's big sash windows my heart starts to beat dangerously fast in terrified anticipation – we are two floors up and the victim won't stand a chance – but he only flicks his cigarette through the window into the playground below and then he turns to us and shakes his head. He sighs.

'Look at you.' He says. 'If only you boys knew what was going on over *there.*' He stares at something through the window, the Falls Road perhaps. 'You should all be in the streets fighting for your country, not fighting each other...' and then he looks at me, '...Or fighting for your faith, if you have no country,' he adds – he pities me for not being Irish, he has said so.

'I've seen a boy,' he says, 'After the police had beat him on the head with a baton...' He pointedly looks at Murphy and he shudders, '...The blood, the brains... Everywhere!'

Niall Murphy swallows and goes quite pale. 'Young lads,' Mr T goes on. 'Not much older than yourselves, fighting for their country. For what's right...'

He lights another cigarette holding the shaking match in

two hands and exhales a cloud of smoke. He looks past us again, out of the window at the blue sky and there is a misty look in his eyes. The whole class goes still, no one dares to move. There is an endless wait in dreadful anticipation and then he turns from the window to face us. For a moment we hold our breath. 'It's war lads,' he breathes. 'It's bloody war and we must step up to the barricades… all of us.'

He turns to look at us now, his eyes sweep over us, sparkling, challenging, angry.

'Come on lads. Rally to the cause. Be men. Be men among men…! This is no time for fighting each other. We've a greater cause…'

Then he takes a deep breath and throws his head back and I wonder if he is going to shout out some blood curdling Irish battle cry but instead in a quaking voice, he starts to sing: he sings us '*The Minstrel Boy*' and he is suddenly a wild minstrel himself rallying his troops, his motley bunch of rebel soldiers before him, and as he sings he is no longer looking at us, he looks beyond us, he looks through us at some distant sight as if we aren't there – presumably he is seeing the war he is fighting on our behalf, fallen comrades and the great heroes of the struggles – Pearce, Collins, Parnell – and now he is straight backed, chest thrust out, conducting us with an orange stained index finger, his voice rising in shaky emotion.

By the time we get to, '…*One sword, at least, thy rights shall guard, One faithful harp shall praise thee!*' he is singing so passionately that the tears are streaming from his eyes, his fists are raised in triumph and he is shaking them at the imaginary British enemy and now the whole class is standing-up to join in. Truth to tell, even I am singing along… just like any good rebel.

* * *

The bus was dead crowded coming home tonight and we had to stand because all the seats were full. It was really hot and because of all the boys it smelt revolting. Karen kept wrinkling her nose and mentioning the word 'deodorant' really loudly but most of the boys just laughed at her and then one of them deliberately pushed his armpit into her face, pretending to grab hold of the rail. She shrieked and told him he was disgusting and he said if she really wanted to smell something disgusting she could sniff his crotch. I thought she would die from anger and embarrassment and all the boys shrieked in hysterics like the animals they are.

So Karen and I stared out of the window and tried to ignore them.

We went by the posh Catholic boys' school and although I'd said to myself that I wasn't going to look out for him, I did of course. Why, Diana? Why? I hope I am not getting 'fixated!'

He wasn't in front of the school or anywhere along the lane and I'd just about given up any hope when I saw him in the distance. He was in the fields near the stream and although he was a long way off I could tell it was him from the way he was walking. He had his bag over his shoulder and his head was down, like he was looking at the ground.

I wonder where he was going and what he was doing? Perhaps I'll go and find out. Maybe, one evening, I'll follow him.

Physics homework. Yuck. Also English essay. We have to write about 'nature'. I am going to write about a wild boy who lives in the woods near here and has been brought up by the wolves, like Tarzan. Stupidly, I told this to Paul at teatime and he said, 'Don't be daft, we haven't got any wolves in England.' So I said, 'Well, by foxes then.' And he laughed and said, 'Oh, yeah! He'd be chased by the local hunt and torn to pieces by the Fox Hounds.' Sometimes I hate my brother. He always wants to make my ideas sound stupid.

I wrote the essay anyway and I reckon it's jolly good. The boy has ended up being like THE boy – but that's inevitable, I suppose.

Played *The Monkees* before bed and also the new single Paul bought at the weekend – *Spirit in The Sky*. Weird record – it's religious I think, but I'd quite like to dance to it. Actually, it might be more hippy than religious, I suppose. These things are hard to tell apart. We live in a spiritual age thanks to India and the Maha do dah, what's-his-name. I think the hippy thing is so cool. I hope I haven't missed the boat and got into the fashion too late – still it won't matter down here in Leeford – they're still into Mods and Rockers I reckon – So I'm way more fashionable than they are. Right on! I'll tell you how out of date they are, I actually saw a Teddy Boy near the bus stop at the posh school. It's like time has stopped here. It must be all the fertilizer they use on the fields – I reckon it makes them a bit backward.

* * *

I am worried that the light is not switched off properly...

...I know it is dark. I know there is no light from the small, white bedside lamp but supposing I have not quite properly clicked off the little switch on its cable; suppose that in the night, while I am asleep, some hidden spring within the mechanism of the switch suddenly releases itself and the light comes on again. Or worse, suppose it does not come on all the way but the little contacts inside the switch become close enough to each other that sparks fly between them and then the light switch starts to melt and finally catches fire and drops in hot, scorching plastic dollops onto the lino floor, which then also catches fire and burns our house down and kills us all in our sleep... And then I will have murdered my family.

This is a fantasy. You might call it a wild flight of my imagination but it could come true.

So I open my eyes, I reach out of bed and I switch the light on and then off again to make sure that it is working safely. And I do this four times, slowly and deliberately, to be certain. But then I think, supposing our neighbours can see the light going on and off through my curtains? They might think it is an emergency of some kind and ring the doorbell or phone us and my parents will be disturbed while watching *Softly Softly*. (Which, in my humble O., may not be a bad thing, as some of the language in it, is quite shocking and I do not know what my parents can see in it!) My Dad will come upstairs and ask me what I am doing and that will be a DISASTER because I will have to tell him and he will think I am mad and then they will think they should send me to the man with the bow tie again and whatever he says or does will be v. v. awkward for me.

* * *

'He looks peaky!' my father says to my mother. 'You look peaky,' he says to me.

And I feel it. After all, I've been awake nearly half the night with the light switch situation. But I can't say, 'Yes, Dad. I am feeling peaky. I was up all night trying to stop my bedside light from burning the house down,' because he will think I am mad and that is my GREAT fear – that someone will think I am mad and they will make me see someone to help me again – like they did all those years ago.

Because that's what happened then – in 1966 I think it was – and it was breakfast time then too...

BACK IN '66

My father was sitting at the table in the kitchen in his suit having a quick breakfast as he always did before rushing to catch the nine oh-eight to London from Leeford Station. He looked up over the rim of his reading glasses as I walked into the kitchen, staring at me over the top of the *Daily Telegraph*.

'Mother,' he said, looking at me, (he always calls her mother, even when I am not in the room – I know because I hear them through their bedroom door or when they think they are alone in the garden. Not that I like to eavesdrop but sometimes you just can't help it, can you?).

'Mother,' he said. 'This boy does not look right to me. He looks peaky!' My mother looked up from the stove. She was cooking my brother and me breakfast – she believes in sending us off with a hearty start to the day and bacon, eggs, fried bread and tomatoes are fuel for active minds and bodies, she reckons. Cereal is all very well, but her family has never been afraid to put a pan on the stove and make the effort to cook something.

She looked at me. 'You look pale, Billy. Are you feeling ill?'

I was actually.

My head had been spinning all night from too much prayer, too much worry and too much annoyance that things wouldn't go right.

This is what had made my head spin then:

To pray, I had to press my hands together and say 'Amen'. But I had to say 'Amen' *exactly* at the time that I clasped my hands together. This was ESSENTIAL. Not to say 'Amen' precisely as I clasped my hands together was unacceptable to God and whatever prayer I said would not be listened to, unless my hands met at this precise moment and met in faultless alignment.

Now, you might think this is madness and at times in 1966 and even today I do wonder if I am perhaps a little, what you might call, unbalanced – but this is often the way for those who have great faith; the strain of it can give you doubts about yourself and others usually fail to recognise your holy state for what it is and think you might just be bonkers...

Anyway, I had to join my hands together in this perfect gesture of prayer because I believed, and I still do even today, that perfect alignment is the way to a BETTER understanding of the Lord Our God and his perfectly SYMMETRICAL universe. GEOMETRICAL harmony is everything in my opinion – so why <u>not</u> insist that one little finger has to be perfectly lined-up with the other little finger and the rest of the fingers have to match each other, tip to tip, joint to joint? It is not unreasonable, if you ask me. And also the thumbs – these have to cross over each other. Left over right. Because in prayer these represent a cross. A symbol for *the* cross. For HIS crucifixion, for the death of God made man.

Fingers rising in prayer. Thumbs bent in death...

...Now that's what I call iconic!

My mother put the frying pan back on the stove and came over to me. She pressed a hand to my forehead which was quite greasy with bacon fat (her hand, not my forehead) and I tried to twist away but she wouldn't let me go.

'No temperature,' she said and went back to cooking the breakfast. With my mother temperature is everything. If your forehead wasn't as hot as the frying pan she was using for breakfast, then quite frankly in her book you simply weren't ill.

My father grunted, 'Nevertheless...' he muttered but he went back to reading his paper, though he gave me an odd look.

I have to admit that over the next few weeks things got a little out of control. I have learnt in the ensuing years to keep myself to myself, but at that time being A) much younger than I am now and B) less experienced at the business of being one of God's chosen ones – I was not so effective at maintaining my privacy.

The hand joining situation began to play on my mind quite a lot. Up until then most of my sacrifices and prayers took place (as they do today) at night in the privacy of my own room or in the clearing in the woods at the top of the hill (which is in many ways my second home) but about this time I found out that my prayers needed to be said regularly throughout the day, even at times when I was, shall we say, in the public eye.

Obviously in my position you need to pray quite a lot and this was as true then as it ever has been and I don't mind saying it could be very awkward at school. There were a number of occasions after that breakfast with my parents, when I had narrow escapes walking along the school corridors with my hands joined or when I was standing at the urinals in the toilets making the sign of the cross.

The terrible Teddy Edwards once found me outside the physics lab, down on my knees, hands clasped in front of me. He clumped towards me in the silly pointed boots he always wore.

'What you doin', spaz?' He grunted at me and his mates leered at me from behind his back.

'I lost some money,' I said, quick as a flash and pretended to pat the dusty ground. 'Fell out of my pocket. A shilling…'

He grunted and then he grinned at his mates.

'Well, I've got a thruppeny one, you can have,' he said and he kicked me hard in my rear. They all fell about laughing then as I lay sprawling in the dust.

Grogan Flynn who is a Neanderthal creature with the body of an ape, found this particularly funny and he kicked me again as I tried to get up and then he grabbed my cap from my pocket where I had carefully folded it.

''Ere Teddy,' he said. 'Fancy a game of footie?'

He threw my cap onto the floor and kicked it. Then they all ran along the corridor playing football with it and shrieking with laughter and I had to kneel there like a complete idiot.

It was also the terrible Grogan Flynn who a few weeks later found me kneeling, bent low in prayer, at the back of the bike sheds clasping and unclasping my hands, trying to get the hand joining to be as effective as possible. He only saw me from a distance as he came round the far end of the sheds for what he and his mates call 'a crafty fag' but seeing me kneeling, bent over, he made up his mind that I was doing something else entirely – something which certainly had nothing to do with prayer and he told me in a very loud voice just what he thought I was up to.

I was mortified and not just at the disgusting word he used to describe it. This was the sort of thing that would get round the school like wildfire. It was the end of mid-morning break and fortunately there was no one around for him to tell just then but I knew that at lunch-time my whole life would be ruined and I would be cast into the pit of shame while the whole school gathered round me baying like hyenas.

Fate has a funny habit though of looking after the just or as Mrs Hayes would put it, 'God *does* keep the best for himself'. Less than an hour later Monsignor Magellan, the head master, walked into Father Kelly's Chemistry class and demanded that Grogan Flynn open his desk. Inside it he found several packets of cigarettes and to everyone's surprise a packet of condoms – and even Grogan Flynn looked surprised at *that*.

It is hard to know which item of contraband upset Monsignor Magellan most but they say he had to sit down for an hour and the school matron had to bring him some brandy from her first-aid cupboard before he got his colour back. Grogan Flynn was expelled on the spot and his father collected him there and then.

Apparently there had been an informer...

Having been spared what you might call 'the spotlight' on this occasion, I fell more deeply into the need for prayer and this took concentration and it also took a lot of practise to get the prayers just right and inevitably I would get them wrong again and again. This caused me a lot of GRIEF.

I should say that I did not want to be doing this. I had no enjoyment in clasping my hands together repeatedly in an effort to attain perfection. But by now it was the school holidays so I had a lot of time to myself to think about these things and to worry about them, alone in my clearing in the woods, at the top of the hill.

I took to saying to myself 'Now… Now…,' meaning now it would work, I would get my hands to clasp correctly and it would be all right to stop praying. This became a complete obsession. Apparently I didn't talked to anyone for a week while I tried to sort all this out in my head and then, after the eighth day, I started to say 'Now…Now…' out loud.

Whenever my family came near me or spoke to me and I knew it would be good to speak to them, and I wanted to speak to them, all I could do was say, 'Now… Now…' I went on saying 'Now… Now…' hoping to get things right but somehow it was never QUITE right, so I went on saying it anyway – 'Now.. Now…' 'Now… Now…' 'Now… Now…' repeatedly, endlessly. And people stood and looked at me and listened to me and got v. v. worried about me but I didn't care because I just wanted to get this alignment of hands and prayer perfectly correct and end my agony.

'Now… Now…'

'Now… Now…'

'Now… Now…'

In the end they took me to the doctor and the doctor made a phone call to someone while we sat there in the surgery, and my father said, 'Well, yes all right, we'll pay of course, if it means he'll see him sooner.'

* * *

So I went with my mother and father to see someone in Harley Street. My parents said he was a child psychologist.

He wore a pinstripe suit, a bow tie, a gold watch chain and a lilac coloured shirt and he smelt of after-shave but not the Old Spice that boys in the sixth form had taken to wearing since the advert had been on telly with the ship and the music. He smelt sweeter and more like lemons and oranges and in an odd way I thought of the women who came to my mother's ladies' evenings, where her friends from the Bridge Club gathered in our living room and drank sherry and ate cheese and pineapple chunks on sticks – that smell always seemed to linger after they had gone.

The Man In The Bow Tie had funny skin – it was sort of orange coloured and shiny, his hair was very carefully combed into place and oiled flat and when he talked he raised his left hand, spread his fingers with the palm turned out and rested his second finger, on his chin just below his lip – it was as though he was worried that his mouth would open too far. As it was, it opened enough for me to see that he had very white teeth, the whitest teeth I had ever seen.

He was sitting behind a large oak desk in a leather covered revolving chair. When my parents had gone out of the room saying they would just wait outside until they were called, he waved a hand at me to show me to sit in another leather covered chair opposite him. But I didn't realise this at first and I thought the dangling hand he held out was for me to shake and because I was a bit nervous about the whole thing and not thinking very straight, I grabbed at it with my right hand. It was q. damp and felt a bit like the cod my mother sometimes gets at The Leeford Macfisheries.

He seemed a bit taken aback as I plunged across the desk and grabbed his hand and he gave me a startled look – perhaps he thought I was trying to kill him or something. His fingers sort of slipped through mine as he pulled them away and he said, 'No. I meant do sit down, over there...' and he pointed at the chair.

'Sorry,' I mumbled and I sat on the chair which was very slippery and I found I shot all the way back into it so that my legs stuck up in the air, which made me look like my Action Man when you fold it up to fit it in its box. I tried to perch on the edge and ended up with my feet just off the floor and my hands gripping the arms to stop me skidding around but I decided it was better to sit like that, even though it was v. uncomfortable than to keep squirming around, even though it put me at what I believe they call an 'immediate disadvantage'.

He looked at me and then he picked up a small case from his desk and took a pair of half moon shaped glasses out of it, perched them on his nose and stared at me some more. At last he said, 'Well, hello Billy? Or do you prefer William?'

'Billy,' I said. And then, remembering my manners, which are after all the mark of gentleman with good breeding my father always says, I added, '...Sir.'

He nodded slowly as if I had said something very important, which q. frankly I had not and then because he didn't seem to be saying anything else. I said, 'But I don't mind. You can call me William, if _you_ prefer.' Which I thought was dead polite, let's face it.

'No,' he said. 'Billy will do.'

Then there was another silence while he looked at me through his glasses and then over the top of his glasses and then through them again. It was dead uncomfortable being stared at and I suddenly realised that the shiny leather seat was making my legs and bottom sweat and because I was wearing a short sleeved shirt my bare arms were sticking to the chair's arms because of how hard I was gripping them. I had this sudden thought that if I moved them too quickly all the skin would come off and there would be blood all over his carpet and bits of gobby flesh glued to the arms of his chair, probably forever.

At last he said, 'I gather you're worried, Billy. I wonder if you want to tell me what about?'

'Falling off the chair,' I said.

He looked a bit put out at this, so I added. 'It's quite slippery.'

'No,' he said. 'I meant... other worries...'

I had to think about this. It was possible, of course, that he was referring to my role vis-à-vis God and prayer but as I had never spoken to anyone about this it seemed unlikely. There was of course the 'now...now...' business but I had moved on from this a few days ago, and I could now hold quite normal conversations. This was because one evening in my clearing I attained the perfect joining of my hands. I know this because I was definitely told by a voice that I no longer needed to worry about how my hands were joined in prayer and I had done all I could to please God. Which was quite a relief, I can tell you. The voice was, of course, my guardian angel and on this occasion I was particularly relieved that he was watching over me, as you will appreciate.

So I said to the man in the Bow Tie, 'Actually I don't have many worries...' And then I remembered something else my father had said, 'I'm upper-middle class you know, so I have very few worries. Let's face it, you don't get much better than being upper middle-class in Great Britain. After all, that's why it's called Great.'

He swallowed and stared at me so hard that I thought his eyeballs might pop straight out of his head over the top of his half moon glasses. Finally he said, 'I see.' And he wrote something with his fountain pen in the notepad he had on his desk. Then he said, 'And what's your favourite subject at school?' Which was a bit odd, perhaps he couldn't think what to say next.

Anyway, I didn't have to think long about it. 'R.I., Biology, Latin and Music – but Biology and R.I. best of all.'

'And why's that?'

'Because it's only when you look at how things like frogs and birds and animals work, you know, inside, that you realise just how great God is. It all goes together, doesn't it, R.I. and Biology?'

He didn't answer my question and I suppose he didn't have to really but he did make another long note in his book and then he looked up at me.

'Do you spend a lot of time thinking about God?' He asked.

This made me feel v uncomfortable. Of course, I spent most of my time thinking about God but I reckoned that was private and something was sort of telling me that if I started to talk about this side of things, as you might put it, we would be in what I can only describe as dangerous waters. So I shrugged my shoulders (which was a bit rude I must admit) and I looked away and out of the window...

* * *

He talked and talked at me after that but I told him nothing.

I did not answer any of his questions because as a general rule I never tell anyone about myself and now I definitely thought I'd said more than I should – for all I knew, he may have been something terrible such as an atheist. Only GOD knows my inner self. And this bow tie man was not GOD. Though my father had said when he got his bill a few days later, 'The amount this bugger charges, who does he think he is? God?' My father did not know I was in the room a the time, or he would not have sworn, of course.

We went back to see the man in the B. T. a few weeks later. Everything was just the same except this time he wore a pink shirt and he looked a bit more orange than he had done before.

On this visit we sat at a little table on the far side of the room, which was a relief I can tell you, as the seats were quite normal and made of non-slippery material. He had given me some sheets of blank paper and he read out a list of words to me and he asked me to scribble down things after he had said them, either words or drawings. But I thought, I shan't defile the name of the Lord by putting anything religious, so I drew a ray-gun or a machine gun or a fighter plane after every word he said.

It was while we were doing this that I had one of my little daydreams – you know, where I see things. I was sitting opposite him and he was chuntering on asking me Qs and asking me to w. my ideas down on the piece of p. and I remember he said, 'If I say *scaffolder* to you, what would you draw...' And then he quickly added, '...but it can't be a ray gun... or a machine gun...' and I had just started a fighter plane when he said, '...or a plane...'

As soon as he had said this and while I was thinking what to draw instead, he stood up and kind of danced over to the window. I mean he really did dance, like a ballet dancer does, such as I have seen when they show the arty bit on the Royal Command Performance and Rudolph thingy comes on and does something from *Swan Lake*. The man in the bow tie actually leapt across the room in big dancing strides, his legs flicking apart, his toes perfectly pointed. And when he got to the window he pirouetted round on one foot and stared across at some scaffolding on the other side of the road where they were putting up a new building.

There was a builder there in a tin hat and he had his shirt undone to his waist. He was really big and muscular and his skin was tanned dark and leathery. You could see all that even from where I was and he was whistling a tune as he climbed up the ladder.

The man in The Bow Tie began to sway to the tune and then he started to dance again just like Rudolph thingy, light and dead graceful and all the time he was dancing in front of the window, like he was dancing for the builder. Though why a doctor in a bow tie would possibly want to dance for a big leathery builder, with his shirt undone to his waist I have no idea. But that's what was happening or so it seemed to me.

Then suddenly he came back to his chair, picked up his papers and said, 'So, if I say 'happiness' to you, what would you draw.'

'Oh,' I said a bit confused. 'I thought you said *scaffolder!*'

He looked puzzled. 'No,' he said slowly. 'I'm sure I said happiness.' But he didn't sound too sure and he suddenly looked very hot and bothered and he glanced over at the window but the builder man had gone by now.

I realised then that this was one of those things that often happened to me. I often see things that other people don't notice or pretend they don't. I think it is one of the gifts I have been given.

I went on seeing him for a few more months and every time I came out of his office my Mum and Dad would rush me down to the car and then, as we drove home, they would ask me what had happened, and what he had said.

I told them we drew a lot of pictures and that he asked me questions like what was my favourite colour, who would I most like to be when I grew-up, did I have a favourite teacher, who was my best friend at school and what did I do for a hobby and so on. And they always seemed a bit disappointed that there wasn't anything else.

One day I told them that he had asked me what I knew about the facts of life. My father who is normally quite a good driver suddenly wobbled the steering wheel and we almost went over onto the wrong side of The Hogg's Back. 'Sorry,' he said. 'A cat ran out...' Which was a bit weird as I didn't see it, so it must have been running dead fast.

I was getting pretty bored with these trips to London, especially as I hate going out at the best of times and I especially hate London as it is dangerously overcrowded from my point of view and nowadays very, very dangerous with the threat of IRA bomb attacks from the likes of Sean Daragon and his father and quite possibly Mr Terry. Sometimes we didn't go by car but took the train and that was even worse as then there was also the added risk of picking up a disease from the person next to you. What's more, I couldn't work out why we were seeing the man in the Bow Tie, anyway. He was dead boring and I know it was something to do with my having said 'now…now…' a few times but I had been told not to do that anymore by my angel, so what was the point? I reckon my Angel was a lot better doctor than the man in the Bow Tie, that's for sure, and also he didn't send the brown envelopes to my father every month with his 'compliments' that made my dad swear in a way that would have upset them on the Golf Club committee.

Finally it all ended, the going to London and the brown envelopes. We were driving back home after one of the, what my parents called, 'sessions' and they were asking the usual questions. 'So what happened this time, Billy?' my mother said. 'Not much,' I told her. 'He asked me to draw some more pictures and then he asked me if dad had ever touched me in a way I didn't like…'

This time we very nearly did go right across the Hogg's Back into a lorry and when my father got the car back under control he didn't even mention a cat.

'What…?' He spluttered.

And my mother said very quickly. 'Father, I think we'll talk about this when we get home…'

'But…' I said. 'You asked me what happened?'

'And now we know,' she said.

And we spent the rest of the drive in silence. When we got home they went into my father's study and closed the door quite firmly. I went outside to play and I decided to sit in the sun as it was a lovely day and I sat under the study window as that was the warmest spot and also because the study window was always left open on a hot day.

I couldn't hear everything but I heard my mother say,

'Well, we won't be making that journey any more.'

And my father said, 'I think he needs to see someone himself… It's outrageous. Good God! I'm a churchwarden!'

And my mother said, 'And that first time we met him – I mean he tells me how to bring up kids. I doubt he's even got a wife. Have you seen his shirts? *If you know what I mean!*

And my father said, 'It's the bow-tie, you can always tell…'

And after that I stopped seeing the Man In the Bow Tie – which was relief I can tell you.

The 1970s CONTINUED...

From then on I learnt a valuable lesson that has stood me in good stead ever since. I learnt to:

A) KEEP MY SECRETS.
B) KEEP MYSELF, TO MYSELF.
C) KEEP ALL MY SACRIFICES AND PRAYERS PRIVATE.

This makes things easy for my parents especially as they don't want the embarrassment of having a loony son. Who would?

My mother and father are very neat and tidy and they like a strict routine. My behaving normally is much neater and tidier and fits in much better with their routine and it is much less upsetting than visiting Harley Street again. Everyone is happy and embarrassment is spared all round.

So when my Dad says this morning, a few years later, 'He looks peaky,' just like he did before, we all know what he is worrying about. And even though my mother has gone back to the stove I can tell that even she is concerned.

So I say, 'Don't worry. I haven't been sleeping well. I've got things on my mind, that's all.' And then for some reason

I add, without really thinking about it: 'After all, I am of a certain age – when all is said and done.'

My father looks v. awkward when I say this and my mother sort of freezes as she hands me my plate of breakfast. And then my father mumbles something about 'that time of life' and 'things changing' and a boy 'needing his privacy' and then he leaves for work without finishing his cup of tea and as he goes through the door he says, 'Control. Umm… you'll find, you need some degree of control, old son. It's best in the long run. You'll see.'

And he forgets to take his umbrella, which he has never done before. And my mother does the washing up, with her back to me.

I will burst and the pain is a terrible ache that throbs all through my body, except that it is coming from only one part of my body – down there between my legs – well, just above the base of my penis, inside, below the flesh and the muscle – sweeping round to my bum hole and then into the cheeks of my bum, because I am clenching them against the pain. I have not peed for fifteen hours. It is a sacrifice. If there is one thing I have learnt from my religious upbringing, it is that God appreciates a sacrifice and having been chosen to do his work I have to make more than most.

It is a hot day again. This summer is full of hot days but I am in the cool of the school chapel, right at the back and I am alone. I have gone in there because I have a free period at the end of the day and instead of study I have chosen private meditation in the chapel, which we can do once a week. I am kneeling at the back of the chapel and even though I am out of the heat, I am sweating loads because I am in so much pain from not peeing.

Then there is a bang and a side door quite near me opens and light thumps into the dark chapel – golden and hard, filled with the specks of dust made from the dead cells of the bodies of all those people who have worshipped here before me and the shaft of light falls onto the station of the cross above my head. I look up at it and Christ is being hammered to his cross; his head is bleeding where the crown of thorns pierces his skull and there is a pool of blood seeping from the scourging of his back and above him the ceiling of the chapel rises in an arch and reaches out to God.

I stare in surprise and Monsignor Magellan, the head master, tall and broad; 'built like a boxer', my mother says, glides past me. 'Light on his feet, for a big man,' my father would say, and Mgr Magellan's cassock flutters in its own breeze.

He does not even notice me or if he does, he decides he should not interrupt my silent prayer and he moves quickly towards the door of the vestry and disappears inside it. I look down and there is an ugly wet patch on the floor and down my shorts. For a split second I think Christ has bled over me from above my head, but it is only that I have paid the price for being distracted from my prayer.

I make my way 'wetly', you might say (if that is a proper word) to the other side door, behind the lady chapel because I know it opens onto the little patch of scrubland between the chapel and a grassy hill and I will be able to run unnoticed up the hill to a little patch of woodland with a clearing in the middle of it which only I know – my secret place, where the evening sun will dry my shorts and shoes and socks.

It is a relief to be in the daylight again, even though it is so hot and it is a relief to have an empty bladder but I must pray that no one kneels in the pew until it has dried.

And I hope it won't smell. And understandably, The thought of the pew reeking like the Gents' lavatory in the Leeford central car park, fills me with dread.

* * *

It is only 4 pm, so the sun is still hot enough to dry my shorts – I've taken them off and hung them with my socks on a bush and I have left my shoes on the grass to dry.

I throw my bag on the ground and I fall down beside it and take out my homework books and an Osmiroid cartridge pen, which is the one the school recommends for best handwriting at the price – available from W H Smith and Son. I lie here with my inky pen and my maths homework, which has to be done in the squared exercise book that Father Rogers issues all his pupils because Father Rogers teaches us maths, as well as Latin.

I stare hopelessly at the exercise book in the bright afternoon sun. I have to draw a margin with a ruler in pencil exactly one inch wide on the left side of every page and exactly one inch wide on the right side of every page – which I do, and that's about as far as I can get.

In the margin on the right of previous pages Fr Rogers has marked my work with his very neat, very small precise ticks and crosses. (Which is a good thing because personally I cannot stand sloppy h. writing and I always work hard to make mine as tidy as poss.) In his very neat, very small, precise hand-writing he has written his comments:

'You have fundamentally missed the point of this equation.'
'This is doodling, not trigonometry!'
'Your algebra is about as good as your calculus – dire!'
'Your arithmetic would be good if you could only add, subtract, divide and multiply.'

Apparently, I have some minor problems with maths but I like Father Rogers. I shouldn't like him, I suppose, as he's quite rude about my work but he has qualities I admire – neatness, order and tidiness which are all GOOD things.

As I lie in the sun doing my homework I am being watched. I am always watched here in my clearing. Eyes are burning into me, into the back of my head. I try not to look around when his eyes burn into me because I know who is looking at me and I don't want to frighten him away. I have, over the years, learnt to be what you might call subtle. That's why I don't look up.

The owner of the eyes often watches over me in the woods and sometimes in other places, though I have never seen him because he hides behind the trees and saplings or on the far side of the clearing. That's the annoying thing about Angels, they prefer anonymity and like to be in the background – they tend to *shun publicity* as it says in the Daily Mail.

Perhaps my angel is waiting for me to enter a deeper HOLY STATE and then he will reveal himself to me, like the B.V.M. did to Bernadette Soubirous.

So, I lie here in my special place in the afternoon sun, wrestling with my maths but really my mind is filled with the thoughts of my Angel watching over me. I try to imagine his face; what he wears and how he would speak. But for some reason I always get confused between what his face should be and Illya Kuryakin in '*The Man From Uncle*', who has blonde hair and who my mother says is 'angelic'. So I find myself wondering if my Angel has a Walther P-38 special with extended stock, silencer and telescopic sight. Which would not be v. Holy but would be q. exciting!

I shake my head.

I should really try to concentrate on my homework. But it is hopeless. The figures swim before my eyes and I can't understand what they mean. Anyway, I console myself, you do not need maths to be a success in life – look at Dickens or Beethoven or Einstein.

So I abandon maths and I get out my biology homework. This is easy. I like biology. I like dissecting best and then drawing pictures of what I have dissected. The first thing we ever dissected at school was a bull's eye. Not the sort you suck of course but a real one, from a dead bull. Some of the boys hated it. It was tough and smelt disgusting, rotten and musty and of pickles all at once. Also, you had to hold it tight in one hand and stab at it with your scalpel to get it open and then gooey stuff (the aqueous fluid, to be technical) would burst out and some of the boys got it in the eye. (Their eyes – not the bull's!)

I didn't. I cut it open very carefully. I sliced into the thick shell of it and peeled it apart very slowly. I was the only one to extract the retina complete and the lens. I was able to cut the lens in half and draw a picture of the layers that made it up – like a small, hard onion. I enjoyed this and I enjoyed cutting up the frog and the rat that we were given later in the term.

And having got a 'taste' for this (as my father, would say) I decided that I wanted to cut-up a lot of other things

too and see how they work. I think this is a very HOLY
thing to do, because I am learning how God made the world
and all the wonders in it. Also, I have a natural hand for a
blade – steady and cool.

To date I have cut up a rabbit, that I found dead in the
lane, and a squirrel that was shot by a farmer and left to die
in the hedgerow and I have cut up a blackbird, pigeon and a
crow. But best was the hare that was run over late at night
and which I found when I was walking Buster, early in the
morning.

It's head was what you might call pulp but the rest of it
was certainly in what they call, in some of the rougher TV
police programmes, 'good nick!'

I have cut-up all these creatures here, in my clearing in
the woods. I borrowed a scalpel from the school biology labs
and a small sharp kitchen knife from my mother's cutlery
drawer and I have used my own sheath knife, with the tartan
handle that I bought on holiday in Crieff in Scotland. I have
also got a piece of tarpaulin from my father's workshop and
some grease. I have greased all the knives to keep them free
of rust and I have wrapped them in the tarpaulin and I have
put them, along with a bread board that my mother was going to throw out, in my old satchel (from Kindergarten) and
I have buried the satchel in a hole I made at the foot of the
sycamore tree on the edge of the clearing.

Now when I find a suitable SUBJECT I bring it to the
clearing and I dig up my satchel and I dissect the SUBJECT
on the bread board and I draw the parts of the subject carefully in an exercise book and label them. Then I bury the
knives and the board again under the Sycamore and I leave
the BODY PARTS in the woods for other animals to feed

on: 'Ashes, to ashes and parts of animals to other animals,' that's what I say.

Here I am then. I am lying here in the woods, in the clearing doing my dead easy Biology homework with my angel watching over me and my clothes drying nicely and everything, apart from the unfinished maths, is v. nice.

Then I think, 'Yes, it is v. nice. In fact it is v.v. nice so I must thank God for giving me such a v. v. nice evening to be enjoying.'

I put down my biology book and I haul myself to my knees and I begin to pray. I say 'In the name of the Father and the Son and the Holy Ghost,' as I make the sign of the cross and then I realise that I have not said the words with equal emphasis and that I have rushed the name of the Holy Ghost. I am always doing this and it is something that really worries me. God is three in one. One in three. Therefore, I must say the three NAMES with equal weight and respect. This is called LOGIC, in my book.

I make the sign of the cross again and I say the names slowly with equal stress but this time I am trying so hard to say the name of the 'Holy Ghost' correctly, that I do not say the name of 'The Son' properly because my mind has leapt ahead, as it were, to the 'Holy Ghost'.

So, I must start all over again. I am sweating, my knees are stinging from being pressed against the hard ground and the spiky grass and my back is aching from being held rigid as I kneel bolt upright. I open my eyes. I cannot concentrate anymore and it is all hopeless, so I open my eyes. And then it happens... the moment that changes my life...

...Forever...

There is a flash of gold in front of me, in the bushes on

the other side of the clearing and a glimpse of something pale blue appears below the gold and then the leaves move a little and the gold and blue vanish as quickly as I saw them. There is stillness for a moment and I stare hard at the spot in the bushes where I saw the flash of gold and blue. Then, suddenly, the leaves move again – a secret little rustle and it is not the breeze but it is something moving in the undergrowth.

It is my angel of course. He has come to me, made visible because he knows that I have been trying to pray and that it has all gone wrong and he has come to me in his physical form to take me to my God or possibly to escort me to Hell and I don't care which at this moment, because A) I can seen him and he is real B) My legs ache C) My back aches and D) My head is spinning.

For the first time I can actually see my angel and he has golden hair and a pale blue garment, like a priest's vestments. Then the leaves move again and the bushes are pulled apart and he is walking towards me, with a puzzled look on his face – only it is not a him. It is a she.

My angel turns out to be a girl about my own age or maybe a little older. (Girls are, in my opinion, quite hard to put an age to – it is to do with the development of their chests, and other secondary s----l characteristics, which happen at v. different times from us boys).

This girl has a medium sized chest and she has golden blonde hair and wears a pale blue blouse with a red tie and a dark blue pleated skirt (which she has hitched up to what you might call an immoral shortness) and white socks – one pulled up to her knee, one hanging loose about her calf and black brogues. She is carrying a satchel in one hand and a straw school boater in the other. She stops a few yards away from me. She looks at me with her head on one side.

'What are you doing, you silly wanker!' She says.

This is DISGUSTING language. Fit only for the gutter and the likes of Grogan Flynn in my view, but I am embarrassed at being caught on my knees, so I struggle to my feet but my knees are stiff and sore and I stand upright like an old man and I feel dizzy and the world is spinning a little in my eyes.

'Bloody hell! You look rough. Are you pissed?' She says.

I stare at her.

I cannot understand why my angel is speaking like a '*Wednesday Play*' and then I slowly adjust to the real world and to the fact that this is a real girl, a real schoolgirl, not my angel, and that she is in my clearing and that she has seen me praying. My heart sinks. On top of all my other miseries she has seen what I have been doing and she will think I am mad and she will tell everyone that I am mad.

So I stare at her and my mouth opens but I can't think what to say – so I just carry on staring, with my mouth open, – which probably makes me look like a complete idiot.

'You are pissed, aren't you? Or are you on drugs? ...Are you on drugs?' She repeats urgently.

She has stopped a few yards away from me and I realise that she is wary of coming too close to me.

'No,' I blurt out. 'Certainly not. I was… was practising for a play.'

Forgive me Father for I have lied. But I have no choice. She will think I am mad or a drug addict if I don't say anything.

'What play?'

I will have to lie some more. I will get deeper into this than is good for both of us. I shuffle uncomfortably but she carries on.

'Seems like a funny play. You were kneeling on the ground, waving your arms about.'

I stare at her and swallow. My mouth is dry though, and it hurts to swallow. Girls are, you might say, v. persistent when they want to know something.

'A torture play,' I say.

Which is quite quick witted I think and shows an ORIGINAL mind on my part. 'I was being tortured... By Nazis,' I continue. 'In the war. I'm the prisoner in it.'

'Is it your school play?' Says my ex-angel, relaxing a little and coming a step nearer.

'No,' I say. 'It's my own play... I'm writing it,' I finish triumphantly. She looks at me. Her head on one side and she drops her satchel on the ground. 'Oh. You were playing a game. Like my brother used to. War games.'

'No,' I say a little insulted. I am NOT a child, when all is said and done. But then I hastily say; 'Yes, I was,' as appearing childish on reflection, may be better than appearing to be mad.

She looks at me with level, cool blue eyes – an unblinking, relaxed stare. 'You're mad,' she says and I can't think what to say. 'Bloody mad!' she says, which is frankly rude in my b. and not the way to speak to a stranger and even worse, makes all the lies I told her a complete waste of time.

'Still, that's quite interesting, I suppose.'

She sighs, dropping to her knees. Then sitting back on the grass she arranges her skirt carefully over her legs and flings the boater to one side. She turns her face towards the evening sun and closes her eyes, letting the sun warm her. Eventually she speaks again without opening her eyes, which I again consider to be quite rude.

'Does your dad own a farm?'

Now this is a weird thing to say in any one's book. I look carefully at her. Girls are of course quite odd but as I have no experience of them this may be normal behaviour. I really don't know.

'No,' I say. 'He's a Civil Servant.'

She laughs. 'Oh. Do you mean he's a polite butler – like Jeeves.'

I have to admit that's quite quick witted and as an admirer of the v funny works of P G Wodehouse I am quite impressed, which is really annoying. So I say in a cold voice, 'No, of course not. He works for the Government…' And then to put her in her place I add, 'Like James Bond.' I'm not sure if the Leeford Ratings Department really counts as the secret service but my father does often bring home files marked, 'Official, H. M. Government,' so it might be.

She opens her eyes and shrugs. Then she looks around.

'Nice here isn't it? I mean, I've walked in the woods a lot but I never found this spot before.'

My heart sinks. Up until now, no one apart from me, has found this 'spot' as she calls it. I suddenly have a sinking feeling that this won't be my secret, private place anymore.

She smiles at me and I know I was right. With that smile she has taken occupancy and made me a visitor to my own world. I will have to share with her now or move out.

Or something else, I suppose.

She leans forward. She speaks to me in a sudden and what you might call, conspiratorial tone. I think she is going to tell me some great secret but she says: 'Why are your socks on that bush? And why are your shoes over there?'

I think I must blush because my face feels hot and I

know that I am going to have to lie again, but before I can say anything she carries on. 'Are they wet? Are they drying out in the sun?'

She sees too much. She knows too much, this girl with golden hair! She is accusing me of me of behaving like a baby.

I swallow dryly.

'I had...' I begin and I was going to say 'an accident' but I knew that she would laugh at me, so I say, 'I slipped into the stream, over by Butler's farm... I was looking for frogs.' Forgive me God. I should not have added the bit about the frogs. The stream was bad enough but I have EMBROIDERED the lie. She looks at me. That cool, level look again. She knows I am lying but then she smiles.

'My brother's always doing that.'

Falling into streams or lying? I wonder. But either way, we are off dangerous territory at least.

'What's your name then?'

I tell her.

'Well, Billy I'm Diana but you can call me Emma.'

I'm a bit confused about this.

'I don't like Diana but I do like Emma. I like Sophie too. I did call myself Sophie for quite a long time but then a few months ago I changed to Emma. I have been Katherine, with a 'K' but I think I prefer Emma.'

She closes her eyes again and lies back in the sun. I think I am supposed to say something but I can't think of anything, so I don't. I just stand there looking down at her and wishing she would go. Wishing she had never arrived in the first place; that she had never found my clearing, my private place that she calls a 'spot'. (Some people are so 'common', as my mother would say.)

She lies back, her head in the grass and looks up into the blue sky.

'You go to that posh school don't you?'

'St Joseph's,' I say. I prefer to give it it's correct name.

'Yeah. And it's posh, innit?'

She still doesn't open her eyes and I can't think what to say, because it is and we don't say 'innit' there, if we can possibly help it! So I just say: 'It's Catholic. Roman Catholic.'

'I know,' she says. 'My mum said – when we drove by it on the way to Leeford once. I don't go to a posh school or a Catholic one. Me and my brother go to Leeford Secondary Modern.'

Again I can't think of anything to say but she carries on anyway. 'We used to live in London until… Well, until my dad died last year…'

And her voice has suddenly become very sad and she looks away from me. Then suddenly she looks back at me, 'Anyway, Mum decided we'd move down here after that. Into the countryside. 'Cos it was cheaper.'

She pauses. It is a long pause, so I say:

'That's nice.'

She sits up and opens her eyes to look at me.

'What's nice? That my Dad died?' She says with a sudden edge in her voice.

'No,' I explain, blushing again. 'I didn't mean... I mean that's horrid. I'm really sorry.'

'Oooh! So, you're really sorry are you!' She sneers. 'Oooh! Mr. high and fucking mighty's really sorry that the poor little girl has no dad.'

I am completely confused by her sudden change of manner AND at her using the F. word, which I CANNOT tolerate. Her eyes are flashing and there is a red glow on her cheeks.

'Look. I'm sorry. I didn't mean…' I say and I try to sound a bit indignant as well as apologetic.

Suddenly, she is laughing and the red cheeks have gone and her eyes are blue and cool again.

'I know,' she says. 'I was only taking the piss out of you. I'm good at being angry aren't I? I can be sexy too or really cruel or soft and mumsy… I want to be an actress. So I practise. I watch telly and then I do the voices and things. I like adverts best. Do you like adverts?'

I nod and I think about the Persil adverts which actually show quite exciting ladies' underwear on a clothes line, which is quite interesting and a change from the large pants my mother hangs on ours.

'*One thousand and One cleans a big, big carpet for less than half a crown..*' She is singing and then she puts on a really deep voice. '*For less than half a crown.*'

I stare at her and then laugh because she really has got the voices dead right, just like on the telly. I sit down on the grass in front of her and stretch out my legs which are still sore as she is obviously going to go on and on. I notice that her white socks are a bit grubby, not just muddy, like they would be from being worn out and about but quite definitely not properly white. In fact they are more white/grey than white…

…So I am not surprised to find that she and I are dancing together in the woods and holding hands and that I am in a slightly grubby white school shirt and she has really dirty socks.

Also there are people singing all round us. Really yucky looking men and women in white blouses and sun glasses.

They are a kind of singing group, like you might see on the
B & W Minstrels on the BBC – only they are all white and
not black at all. In fact, they all have smiling white teeth and
beautifully done hair and they sway as they sing and remind
me of the entertainers I have seen in travel brochures for
cruise liners. Then one of them steps forward and he starts to
sing v.v. loudly and very brightly and he looks a bit like
Andy Williams (who is my mother's favourite singer). He
sings to a light, loud, bouncy, bright, sparkly tune with lots
of brass. And it seems perfectly OK to me, to find that we
are in the middle of the *Persil* advert that is always on the
telly:

'*Someone's Mum thought that was white..*' Sings the
cheesy singer pointing at my shirt.

'*And someone's Mum thought that was white…*' He sings
pointing at the girl's socks. '*But when someone's Mum really
knows what's white…*' He goes on '*…New Persil, washes even
whiter, even whiter!*'

And then my Mum walks into the woods, wearing an
apron over her best evening dress and she stands next to a
washing machine and a clothes line full of really nice lady's
pants and bras that someone has placed in the middle of my
clearing. She turns to face an imaginary camera and she is all
smiles and holding her head slightly to one side and to my
amazement she says, quite seriously and in a voice like the
Queen's: '*It's wonderful, a soap powder that leaves no scum,
even in our hard water, and it washes even whites.*'

She points at the white underwear on the clothes line and
then she bends down to the washing machine and from inside
it she produces a packet of New Persil and she looks at it long-
ingly and for some reason I feel my Dad would be jealous.

'*New Persil, washes even whiter, even whiter. New Persil washes even whiter... New Persil!*' Sings the cheesy man, dancing round my Mum...

'...So we came down to the countryside to be near my Aunt and Uncle.'

It takes me a moment to realise that this isn't part of the advert but that the girl is still telling me about herself. My Mum has gone, and so have the singers and the cheesy man and it is just this girl and me, sitting on the grass. I have a quick look round for the washing machine and clothes line but of course it is not there and nor is the interesting underwear and I realise that I may have been seeing things again.

'...That was three months ago and we live in one of the Brewers' Cottages just outside of the village,' she is saying and I realise she is telling me where she lives.

I know the Brewers' Cottages. They are a dingy row of terraced houses that stand on their own, just off the main road as you come out of the village. They had been owned by Sampson's Brewers once when they grew hops here and they had two breweries and a malt house. But that was hundreds of years ago and now the breweries are little factories and the Malt House is a trendy theatre that has classical plays and Shakespeare seasons in the summer and jazz concerts in the winter.

Then I realise that she has stopped talking and she is staring at me. I must clear my head of Persil and cottages and breweries and theatres and say something.

'Well?' She repeats. 'Where do you live? Wake-up dozy.'

I tell her.

I don't want to because actually I just want her to go away and I don't want her to know anything about me but I can't help it – there is something about her that I cannot explain and whatever it is, it makes me want to tell her, to share things with her and that is something I have never done before.

I tell her about my parents and how my mother is a part time librarian and president of the Catholic Women's Guild and my father is a civil servant (which we have already established, only this time she doesn't make a silly joke)and I tell her about my brother Pete and about Buster, because she asks about all of them but I don't tell her much about myself because I never tell anyone much about myself:

A) because it is NOT an interesting subject and
B) because it is only for GOD to know what goes on in my inner self.

Even so, I talk for longer than I mean to until I can't think what to say next and I feel dead uncomfortable about what I have said so far and we end up staring awkwardly at each other but fortunately she opens her satchel and pulls out an apple and an orange and holds them up for me to choose.

I think this is some kind of bribery, to make me become her friend but I am hungry when all is said and done, so I point at the apple and she tosses it to me. As we bite into our fruit I start to relax. The worst is over.

We eat in silence and then she throws her peel into the long grass and I throw my core into the bushes. Which goes against what I think about litter but at least these things will rot, not like some of the things you find in the woods. I can tell you!

We just sit there then and don't say anything. Then she straightens her skirt, smoothing it over her legs again. I try not to look at this, as it is a sin of the flesh to ogle a girl's legs, especially when they are quite brown and you can see quite a lot of them ABOVE the knee. She sighs, a long slow sigh and then she stands up and says:

'Well, I've got to get home or my mum'll be worried about me. I'll see you round then.'

I'm not sorry to see her go. I want my place back for myself and I want it be nice and peaceful and full of my thoughts and prayers and of God – like it had been before she arrived. Then, as if to make my heart sink, she says. 'I expect we'll meet again then. I'll come here quite a lot now, I expect.'

She picks up her bag and her hat and she strolls to the edge of my clearing but when she gets to where the narrow entrance is, between the beech tree and the brambles, she stops and turns back to me.

'By the way,' she says. 'Did you know you were being watched?'

I stare at her.

'When I found you, there was someone looking at you through those bushes.' She points to the other side of the clearing, where my angel's eyes had been burning into me.

'I couldn't see who it was.'

She gives me a funny look.

'I should watch out if I was you. You get funny types in woods. Especially when you're dressed like that.'

And she gives me an odd stare. Then she hitches her satchel onto her shoulder and walks off through the leaves towards the evening sun. If only I could have told her, if only she had realised she had seen an angel – she has been blessed and she doesn't know it. And then I thought, what does she mean 'dressed like that?'

And then I realise that I am still in my underpants.

* * *

I avoid 'Teddy' Edwards at all costs. He is definitely in the other world, the NOT my world. He is, what my father calls, '...A Rebel!'

'A rebel, without a cause!' My mother says.

He is tall and very strong. He has huge shoulders and a deep voice and he has long hair that he combs into a greased-back quiff like they had in the fifties. (Q. disgusting!) Although he is only a few months older than me, he has long sideburns. Also, he wears his blazer too tight, his tie too short and his top button undone – which is against all the school rules. His appearance does nothing for our reputation with the local community, if you ask me.

Teddy has black shoes but they are really boots with high heels which he bought in Chelsea apparently, as he calls them Chelsea boots and his trousers are drain-pipe thin at the ankles. This is, to my way of thinking, scruffiness, but apparently he wants to be a teddy boy. The fact that there are no more teddy boys seems to have escaped him. The whole 'summer of love' (as the popular press, such as my Mother's Daly Mail, have called it) has gone right over his head. But thee way he dresses is also a form of defiance – of which I do not approve.

Edwards has followers; boys who leer and sneer and even try to dress like him. It is said that they all carry flick knives – once Father Rogers searched their desks and nothing was found but I think this is because they had 'prior' warning and hid them in the toilets.

These are the boys who blew up condoms during Mr. Fogerty's geography lesson (which is UTTERLY disgusting) and who named their pretend businesses in economics lessons, *'Two Acres'* and *'Jones's tents – Erection Specialists.'* (Which is also disgusting and which I had to think about, because at first I could not understand why everyone else was sniggering).

They are dangerous. Cynical. Spiteful – and I am beneath their contempt. They can't even be bothered to beat me up or bully me because I am too silly, too weird, too 'immature' in their book for them to bother with. But they invented my nickname. For which I find it hard to forgive them, although forgiveness should be in us all. It was like this...

I don't have my hair like them nor like the boys who have grown it long. My hair is not even vaguely fashionable, let alone fashioned like the fifties. 'Smart and hygienic,' my father calls it. 'I want my boy to look, like a boy,' says my mother. 'Why boys want to look like girls is beyond me – I blame those pop groups,' my father adds.

Other boys push the school rules to the limit and let their hair get a little longer every day; they have taken to wetting it and slicking it back behind their ears so that after school it will dry and fall long over their necks, but I have my hair cut short.

'Nothing wrong with a short back and sides,' my father says. 'It was men with short back and sides that defeated Hitler.'

So, I am condemned to look like my father – which is unbearably not cool. Unbearably square in the eyes of the other boys, especially in the eyes of Edwards and his gang. I know that anyone seeing me will know just what kind of sad, pathetic person I am and they will put me away in a box with all the other boys who are a waste of space, with short back and sides and Aertex vests like mine. I don't care. But in a way I do, because I know I will never get to enter their World, their 'NOT my World' – not while my hair is like this, anyway.

Fortunately, Edwards's gang have only 'milked' me once – that's all. I was in the playground and they led a charge around the fences and hedges and every boy they bumped into, they grabbed hold of and grasped his testicles through his shorts, pulling them hard and squeezing them. This is called 'milking'. It is something they do occasionally when they are bored or when they want to show us who is in charge.

And it gets worse.

Teddy Edwards saw me in the corridor one day and he pushed past me and as he did so he said. 'Get out the way bog brush!'

Just like that, in passing, 'Bog Brush.'

And so he invented my nickname.

That was all he said. Just once. But by the end of school, anyone who saw me or asked me something or wanted something – called me BOG BRUSH.

I am Bog Brush.

'Bog Brush, lend us your ruler.'

'Bog Brush. You going to the chapel, again?'

'Bog Brush. – Father Henessy wants you.'

'Hurry up Bog Brush. You'll be late for PE.'

Bog Brush. Bog Brush. Bog Brush.

I am Bog Brush.

So I avoid Teddy Edwards and his gang at all costs.

* * *

There has always been sacrifice: Jesus himself; the martyrdom of St Peter – crucified upside down to show his humility before Christ; the forty martyrs of England and Wales – cut down by the bon-believers, burnt and quartered by the sinful and arrogant protestants – 'Dirty proddies and liars,' Mr Terry calls them.

There will always be sacrifice. There must be sacrifice...

* * *

The cat is at the side of the road. There's not a mark on it but it's definitely dead, dead as a doornail (If that's the right expression – seems a bit odd to me but then the English language is full of odd things, or so Mr Terry says).

It must have happened recently as it isn't even stiff and its eyes haven't glazed over. There is warmth too, below the fur, close to the skin. It is a black and white cat and there are blobs of black in its white fur that make odd shapes.

It's the weekend and there's no school, so I have plenty of time to... What's the word, 'experiment'. So I put the cat in my old kit-bag with my lunch and my binoculars that I bought with me because I was going to spend the day exploring and... well, you know, watching things going on, and then I make my way quickly to the clearing in the woods. I have to hurry because it's getting warmer and the cat will soon go stiff and then it will start to smell.

When I get there, I take the body from the bag and hide it beneath a pile of last year's leaves, under the bushes near the oak tree, in the shade. Once it's in, what you might call, my make-shift 'Frigidaire' I run back to my house. More precisely to my father's tool shed, which is right at the end of the garden and can't really be seen from the house. Anyway, it is not yet six o'clock and no one is stirring on this drowsy morning – I reckon I'm the only person awake and up and about for miles around. Even Butler's Farm seems still and quiet and for once you can't hear the sound of a tractor or a combine.

The shed is locked. It's always locked because my father is a keen DIY-er and he keeps power tools and finely sharpened chisels and all kinds of hand-tools in there. But I know another way in...

...At the back of the shed, close to the brambles, in the shadows, there are some loose planks and it only takes a moment to pull them to one side and to wriggle into the cool, sawdust laden interior with its smell of glue and varnish.

I know exactly what I want: a handful of one and a half inch nails, a small hammer, a chisel and an off-cut of plywood about three foot square that I saw him place under his workbench last weekend.

'... Never throw away a good off-cut if you can help it, just in case. That is my advice to you young man,' he'd said. Which is a sound piece of advice and one which I hope to carry with me through life.

Then I'm back into the daylight, running through the fields up to the woods. By now the sun is beating down and the timber is awkward and heavy, and the hammer and nails bang around uncomfortably in my bag – but I've got a job to do and there's no time to slow down.

Back in the clearing, MY clearing, with my heart racing and still panting for breath, I lay the wood on the ground and take out the hammer, the saw and the nails and then I walk over to the old sycamore tree and move aside the rotten log beneath it that marks the spot. I carefully pull back the turf and dig down with my hands into the soft, damp soil. The old satchel is still there and like I always do when I dig it up, I breathe a little sigh of relief. You can never tell, you never know, when someone may breach your security arrangements – as they say in the James Bond films, of which I happen to be a great admirer.

As I lift the old satchel from the ground I can feel the knives inside it, comfortably hard and reassuring. I carry it over to where I left the plywood and the tools and carefully open it. I don't bother with the breadboard that I also keep in it – that's for much smaller species like frogs, mice and rats – today I'm into bigger things. So, I extract the rolled up tarpaulin which I open up, then the kitchen knife, the scalpel, the sheath knife and an exercise book and two sharp pencils which I place on the sheet of wood.

The knives are clean, greased, and completely free of rust. I have always taken a pride in keeping the blades keen, so they are razor sharp – they will slice through cat sinew, muscle and flesh as if it were soap, that's what I reckon.

I arrange the tools on the piece of wood with all the precision of a ward sister preparing for the surgeon – I have learnt a lot from viewing *Emergency Ward Ten*, not to mention *Dr Kildare* with the amazing Hollywood heart-throb Richard Chamberlain, of whom my mother says you just cannot speak too highly. (She always blushes when she says this and sometimes my father grunts and looks annoyed with her – which seems a bit unfair if you ask me, coming from a man who says *The Tiller Girls* have a unique charm).

Next I get the cat from under the leaves where I left it. The body is cold now and beginning to turn stiff but I lift it gently and carry it back to the wooden sheet. Then I arrange it carefully on the wood, laying it on its back.

I decided when I first saw it in the road, that I would enter it through its stomach. I run my hands gently over the fur of its belly and I think I could be stroking it, petting it in front of the fire on a winter's night. Only it doesn't purr, it doesn't close its eyes, roll over and hunker down on my lap in blissful contentment – it just stares up at me, and there is a slight mistiness in its gaze.

I know that it will be difficult to hold it in position when I open it up. Really I need another pair of hands or a helper. But there isn't anyone. There is never anyone. Let's face it, I have always been alone.

That's why I brought the hammer and the nails.

Planning. Planning has always been my strong point. I've always planned well. I'm sorry to blow my own T. but looking ahead and foreseeing problems is what I do best.

So, now I bend the cat's front paws awkwardly up towards its ears and then sideways so that they are spread out wide, as if reaching to the sky. I put a handful of nails in my mouth, in the way that I've seen my father do when he is nailing down an awkward floorboard or something similar and then using one hand to hold a paw flat on the wood, its soft pads pointing up at me, I use the other hand to remove a nail from my mouth and push the point of it into the flesh between the pads. Then, nail sticking upright held by the flesh, I reach for the hammer.

Bang! Bang! Bang!

It only takes three swift, good blows to drive the nail

through the cat's paw, pinning it to the wooden board.

Three more paws. Nine more blows. (Yes Father Rogers, three times three is nine – your teaching has not been in vain).

I rock back on my heels to survey my work.

The cat is spread out paws nailed to the board; front and back legs stretched apart, its stomach laid out for me, waiting for the knife. Its head has rolled slightly to one side and the tip of its pink tongue is sticking out from the side of its mouth, a little bubble of saliva runs from its nose. It lies there, like it's been crucified, I think, nailed by its hands and feet to the wood.

I take a deep breath and try to steady myself. My heart is beating really fast now and I can feel sweat trickling down my back.

Then I take up the scalpel in one hand and a pinch of fur and skin from its neck under its jaw in the other and I gently probe the pinch with the point of the scalpel. The I make my first incision, carefully cutting through the skin, leaving the underlying muscles intact. I slice down towards its belly and over the stomach towards its genitals and anus. I lift the skin where I've made the cut and begin to pull it away from the body to reveal the muscles which are still attached to the skin by a white fibrous tissue. I cut the tissue away and pull the skin apart, back towards either side of the cat's body, sliding my fingers under the skin, to help lift and peel it away.

Now the cat lies half-naked, partly skinned from neck to arse. Its muscles are shiny and damp in the morning sun and then I begin to slice through them.

I cut and probe and pull them all apart, neatly and carefully. This takes a long time because I stop every now and then to make notes and sketches in my exercise book. I don't want this to be simply pleasurable. It must also have what you might call a scientific purpose.

The drawings are good. I like drawing but the book quickly becomes marked with the blood from my fingers and the untidiness of this is annoying but inevitable.

The internal organs are covered in a thin membrane – this I know is called the peritoneum and I cut it and pull it away until at last the cat's insides are laid out like a map before me.

I am mainly interested in the digestive system, separated from the lungs by the diaphragm. But I do notice that the liver is larger than I expected, as is the gall bladder which is attached to it. I have to think hard about what I know from other animals and from the books I have read to help me identify the pancreas and the spleen. But eventually I find them. In fact, I find all the essential organs and I carefully remove them with my scalpel, laying them out on the board and drawing each one in turn.

And then it suddenly hits me...

...What all this is about. What I am doing...

I look down at the cat, with its stomach gaping bloodily open, at the organs I have carefully removed and laid out on the board, at the gaping void of its abdomen and I marvel at the intense beauty of it. The intricacy and delicacy of it.

In this moment I realise why it is that I like cutting-up animals. Why it is that Biology is the only subject, I truly, deeply love at school, apart from RI and possibly music. It is because of the intense Godliness of it. Looking at the flesh, the organs, the shiny moisture of it all, I don't see death or smell the stench of its guts – I see – I marvel – at the brilliance of it. I see life and smell creation. What cunning, what beauty, how incredible it is that this system could exist – so intricate, so clever.

Here is a perfect system based on something as delicate as flesh; a system that looks so unappealing in its shades of dull brown and pink, that smells repulsive, is unpleasant to the touch, and yet this mess of what looks like butcher's refuse, can or could, up until this morning, take in air and water and food and convert it into life and well, into being – into *existence*.

It was only a cat but in this moment I know it is the most beautiful thing in the universe. It had life and independence and individuality because of this structure of coiled tubes and reddened organs and slimy moisture. It is such a brilliant thing, so dazzling and.. and... I can't find the words. What did I want to say?

I want to say:

'If you doubt the existence of God, then look at this. This is all the proof you need!'

But that is so inadequate and not really what I wanted to say; it is just a part of some greater understanding that I have almost achieved, have almost grasped at that moment kneeling in my clearing, under the hot sun with blood on my hands – but even now it is slipping like sand, through the fingers of my mind and it'll soon be lost.

And I know now that I have to worship; to pray and thank HIM for this v. v. brilliant thing called creation. This most extraordinary act where GOD took matter – in this instance the elements that make up flesh and blood, and turned it into something that breathed, that survived, that moved and reacted and was fed and watered and nurtured by the elements around us. Yes, that lived. That WAS ALIVE.

For a moment, as I sit there on my haunches, I can't think properly and the words that come into my head are not a prayer at all but a forgotten poem from some English lesson:

'...*what immortal hand or eye*
could frame thy fearful symmetry?
What the hand dare seize the fire?
And what shoulder and what art,
Could twist the sinews of thy heart?'

And then I know that in this moment of revelation, in this moment of clarity, when things are suddenly becoming obvious to me, more understandable than they ever have been before – at this moment I am not alone...

My angel is there; somewhere very near. I can feel his eyes boring into my back and so strong is the sensation, that I actually turn quickly to look behind me, in case I can catch a glimpse of him. But of course I can't. But he is here. My angel is here to guide me and hold me at this moment, as he should be.

And so I kneel before the cat and I begin to pray...

...I try to say to God that I understand. That I am truly grateful for what he has created and that I am part of it.

But the words go round and round, like a stylus stuck in the worn groove of a record, like the end of *Sergeant Pepper*; words that go round, incomprehensible, yet nearly comprehensible.

And I think, I am part of it. I am part of this great mystery of creation. I too have slimy organs, pink and brown – that change water and food and oxygen into the thing that is me, that is my life, that is the 'Billyness' of being Billy.

I open my eyes. The cat is still there of course, its empty abdomen gaping up at me obscenely. What is left of its fur is bloody and matted and there is a horrible reeking pile of organs arranged around it. Then I pick up the saw and clasp the head of the cat in my left hand to steady it and I saw through its neck.

Removing the head is surprisingly simple. It takes only a few strokes of the sharp toothed saw. I place it carefully on the board. Its nose towards me, the bloody stub of its neck on the damp wood. Then I pick up the hammer and chisel and position the sharp end of the chisel along the centre of the head, between the ears, one white and one black, where there is a natural line along the skull, like the parting in your hair.

I strike the hammer onto the handle of the chisel. Just once. A short, sharp, controlled blow. The skull splits open, neatly, like cracking a walnut at Christmas. Then I drop the hammer and chisel and clasp the head in both hands, thumbs pressed into the crack in the skull and I pull the head apart, splitting it neatly down the middle.

The brain inside is very small. No bigger than the insides of the Christmas Walnut. It is dull grey. There is a smear of blood around it. So small, I think, for something that held all the life of a running, jumping, hunting creature, like the cat.

I'm unsure what to do next. I know the ultimate goal but how to get there? What ritual shall I follow?

And then I know.

So, like the Priest in a mass, I raise the cat's head, with the gaping split and the brain still in it, above my head and look down at the ground.

'*Offerimus tibi, Domine, calicem salutaris tuam deprecantes clementiam...*' I chant as the priest does every Sunday and every Wednesday in term time.

The head I hold up is a chalice. The sacrifice that is required by the Lord our God in order to ensure my salvation is held within it.

Then I lower the cat's head, so that I am holding it out in front of me, so that my Angel over there in the bushes, may take part in the sacrament as well.

'*Gloria Patri, et Filio, et Spiritu Sancto. Sicut erat in principio, et nunc, et semper: et in saecula saeculorum. Amen.*' I say, the Latin tripping off my tongue with long and easy practise.

My angel in the woods, inclines his head, he is lost in some secret prayer and I too pray silently. Then looking up I say, gravely:

'*..Per omnia saecula saeculorum.*'

And my Angel responds at once.

'Amen.'

'*Dominus vobiscum,*' I say to him – may the Lord be with you.

He replies again, sharing the intimacy of the moment with me.

'*Et cum spiritu tuo.*'

And with your spirit, he says.

'*Sanctus, Sanctus, Sanctus,*' I begin. '*Dominus Deus Sabaoth. Pleni sunt coeli et terra gloria tua. Hosanna in excelsis. Bendictus qui venit in nominee Domini...*'

And so on until I say, '*Hosanna in Excelsis.*'

I have said all that I need to say. The moment is come. I raise my eyes and look at my angel. In my mind our eyes meet, we are linked in faith, joined in spirit.

'*Accipite, et manducate ex hoc omnes.*'

Take and eat of this, all of you, I say to my angel.

'*Sed libera nos malo,*' – deliver us from evil.

Deliver us indeed.

I put a thumb and finger inside the broken skull. The brain is soft, it would be easy to put your fingers through it. I feel underneath it, with my fingers, to where it is fixed to the spinal cord. It takes very little effort to pull it free with a little twist, like plucking a mussel from its shell. For a second I hold the brain between thumb and finger – I raise my eyes to heaven and then I close them tight.

I part my lips. I open mouth a little to accept the sacrament and then, reverently, slowly, I place the little brain on my tongue.

Don't chew... Don't be sick... Hold back the bile that is rising in your throat, bubbling up, unwilled from your stomach. Don't be sick. Don't be sick...

I swallow. I swallow back my own vomit and I swallow back the small, cold, slippery goblet of brain...

I swallow it...

Swallow it...

And the Angel is suddenly there, right in front of me, right in my face, staring at me and screaming at me. But I can't hear the words. I can see his mouth moving but I can't hear the words. And his face is changing colour and shape. He is like a picture on a television that is not properly tuned.

My angel is there and then he is fading away and then he is back again and all around me and all around him, the world is spinning and there is a terrible, terrible feeling of falling over deep inside, as if I was tearing down a helter-skelter and the helter-skelter is a part of me and not part of me at the same time, so that I feel dizzy and sick.

My Angel is leaning over me now and holding onto me and his face is so close that I can taste his breath, smell it in my nostrils, stale and unpleasant, like the sulphur we burnt in the chem labs one lesson – and there is another odour – sweat, fear. And oh, is he wearing a dog collar?

But this can't be my Angel. His fingers are digging into my shoulders and his nails are like talons. I can feel them through my shirt, piercing my flesh. He is gripping me so hard that he is hurting me. He is trying to drag me down... Down... Down... into his hell. So I struggle and try to shake him free but he grips me even harder. So I scream the name of the Lord my God at him because the devil cannot stand the name of the Saviour. But he still will not let go.

He still pulls at me, trying to twist my shoulders and screw me into the ground, trying to break the bones in my arms and sear the flesh from them. This Lucifer is strong, he is determined and he will bring me down if he can.

Beelzebub! Beelzebub!

And now the Devil/Angel's face is changing. What was a beautiful, comforting, Angel's face is becoming something else – something filthy and soaked in sweat, with hair bristling from its nostrils and its ears and a smooth, scaly head. His eyes are flashing, little steely angry eyes, his teeth are yellow and he spits in my face as he struggles with me.

How absurd. How awful!

Is this happening? Is any of this real? But of course it is only in my mind, just a trick of my brain, or of the cat's brain as it poisons my body.

Now the Angel/Devil is getting the better of me and shaking me by the shoulders until my teeth chatter. Then, unexpectedly, the World begins to shut down. It shuts down from the edges, and the blackness closes in like the iris of a tightening camera lens, until the only picture I can see is a small blob of light in the middle of what used to be my vision and the Angel/Devil is bouncing round in the blob, mouthing at me and reaching out to me and then he too is shut out by the closing lens and there is darkness.

I feel my knees begin to buckle and my legs going weak. I am feeling suddenly cold and sleepy. Now I am sliding down, slipping through the hands that had been holding me and shaking me. Now the darkness is all around me. So, the last thing I see is the angel but he has the face of a devil. Which is odd, I think. Very odd. It does not make me angry any more, nor does it frighten me, I just think it is odd. Then I slide into unconsciousness and the peace is quite welcome.

* * *

When I wake-up I am lying on my side, with my head tilted slightly back, one leg bent. I have done my First Aid course at school and, if I say so myself, I got a pretty impressive 92%, so I know what I am talking about and I recognise the recovery position when I see it.

Blinking at first I can only see blades of grass which are very close to my face but when I turn my head a little way I can see the sunshine and the leaves on the trees and little patches of blue sky.

I get to my feet very slowly and I think stupid thoughts, like how did I end up so neatly on my side with one leg drawn-up in genuflection when I had been standing-up? I must have been pushed over backwards by the Devil, I think.

'*The mind works in mysterious ways...*' my father would have said.

I am shaken by what has happened, by the visions of good and evil I have experienced, and I wonder if any of it has happened – the cat, the sacrifice, the angel who became the devil... but as I look round slowly, as I feel the sun through the leaves of the oak trees warm on my back and as I smell the English summer, I see the wreckage of the cat on the ground and I can feel dried blood on my chin and I realise that it has been real – though I have presumably imagined the angel/devil part.

Nothing is as it seems. Nothing is as it was. And nothing is real...

My struggle with the devil was a dream brought on no doubt, by the incredible sacrifice I have made – by what I did as a necessary prayer to my God. I am secretly pleased with myself, as well as being repulsed by what I have done.

It was, I know, terrible and I know that if anyone was aware of what I had done I would be in dead serious trouble. They would send me to more doctors, to more men in bow ties, they might even lock me away. All the people in the other world, the not MY world and in this instance that includes my mother and father and even my brother, they could never imagine doing the disgusting thing I have done, nor understand why it had to be done. I am quite sure of that – but equally the very awfulness of it was what made it so good. I have done as much, if not more, than could be expected of me by God. I feel virtuous and I think I feel the glow of what I believe is called '*moral rectitude.*' However, now I must concentrate on the important business of removing the bits of the cat and generally clearing-up.

That is all I have to think about now. What had to be done, has been done – and that is an end to it.

So, I must get on because my wrist-watch says that it is O-eight forty five and that means that someone may be walking their dog and stumble on my clearing. That of course would be a very bad thing in itself but if they found the cat and saw what I had done to it, then there would have to be EXPLAINING and I hate explaining about the things that I do. Ever since the man in the B T who was supposed to help me, I have hated explaining what I do.

I pick up the cat's body and push it into my old satchel and I scoop up all the other bits and carry them bloodily into the woods. There is a place I know which has been trodden flat by the foxes that gather there at night before they go scavenging. I drop the pieces of cat and the cat itself around the fox holes. They will get a cheap dinner tonight I think, as I make my way back to the clearing.

I pack-up the knives, bread board, scalpel and exercise book and wipe them clean with leaves and damp grass before I rub a little oil on them from the can I keep in the satchel and then I carefully re-bury them in their hiding place. Next I take the piece of plywood, and my father's chisel, saw and hammer down to the stream that runs through the field to the south side of where I live.

The plywood is a problem. Despite my planning, I hadn't realised how bloody it was going to get and I can't possibly put it back in the state it is now in, but I think that I will be able to wash the blood off it in the stream where I can also clean the saw and chisel. I do this kneeling between cow pats at the side of the stream with the hot sun on my back.

When I have finished, the board is still streaked with

blood and, of course, it has gone dark with wet but I am confident that as long as my Dad doesn't pull it out from under the workbench for a few days then it will dry up all right.

Now I have only to sneak into the back garden of my house and in through the loose planks at the back of the shed and replace everything to complete the job. This I do and ten minutes later I sling my old kit-bag with my lunch in it over my shoulder once again and I set off, as I had done earlier this morning, to explore and roam around the fields and woods.

I feel good now. It has been hard work, an eventful start to the day you might say, but I have done what is required of me by God and by my Angel and now I can relax for a change. For once I have earned my freedom from the agony of prayer and from having to make my small sacrifices. Thanks to my 'very big effort of the day' I can enjoy the weather, roam free and have fun. The air tastes sweet. The sky has never looked clearer and the sun on my face has never felt warmer.

I make my way to the meadows below Butler's Farm, because there is a shady place there, near the stream. It is one of my favourite places and I plan to sit under the willow tree, my willow tree, and eat some of my food because suddenly I am very, very hungry. But as I think of food, I remember my sacrifice. I remember what it was that I ate less than an hour ago.

I should be able to forget. Normally I can blot things from my mind, if I want to. I expect that over the years I have blotted out a lot of things...though, of course, now I have no idea what they were. But this time the memory won't go. I am nearly at the water meadow and I am walking along the side of the stream towards my willow tree but I have to stop; I cannot get the picture of what I did out of my head and there is a terrible feeling of sickness in my stomach – it is bubbling and churning and I am starting to retch q. dreadfully and q. uncontrollably.

The cat's brain had no taste. I hadn't chewed it anyway – but even so, I can taste the salt taste of blood again and my whole body and mind is suddenly filled with revulsion at what I have done. I feel terrible. and desperately I lean over the stream and begin to throw-up into the clear water. Massive, huge uncontrollable waves of nausea rush through my body and there is an icy finger dragging its way down my spine. My stomach feels as if it will turn inside out and great waves of muscular retching pass through it, that I cannot control.

Will I ever stop being sick, I wonder, as I throw bile and fluid and some other grizzly thing from my guts?

And then it is over. There is nothing more to throw-up and the awful spasms have passed away. I kneel by the stream, shaking and gasping for breath. I am what is called in modern novels, 'completely wiped-out.'

I wipe my mouth with the back of my hand and I wipe the tears way from my eyes. There is a terrible taste in my mouth and snot hangs from my nose and I feel incredibly weak and tired.

'You've either been on the piss or eaten something rotten!' A voice says.

Through my watery eyes I look up but I know who it is already. Diana, Emma, Katherine or whoever she is, stands just next to me and looks down her nose at me. I look up. My gaze passes over her white socks, over her brown knees, her thighs, her pink skirt, her white blouse and up to her tanned face and blonde hair tied back with a spotted scarf. She has freckles, I realise. I hadn't noticed this before.

She puts her head to one side and a hand on her hip, moving her feet slightly apart so that she leans more on one brown leg than the other, and she smiles down at me; so comfortable, so amused by me.

'Well?' She demands. 'What have you been up to? Did you raid your dad's booze cupboard? My brother did that once and he threw up for a whole day.'

I shake my head. Inside I am begging her to go away, wishing she wasn't there. I hate her. I am angry with her for being here, finding me in another secret place, in another secret moment and seeing me like this.

'Something I ate,' I say hoarsely, through my bile burnt throat.

'Here, dip that in the stream and wipe your face.' She says and throws me a little spotted hanky, that matches her head scarf.

I don't want to but I know it is a sensible thing to do. So I take the hanky and soak it in the clear, cold water and press it to my hot brow and wipe my face. Even though the hanky has been dipped in the water I am surprised to find when I wipe my face with it, that I can smell something sweet on it. Perfume. Proper girl's perfume.

When I have finished wiping my face I stand-up. I'm still a little shaky but I do feel better now. I think, 'Better out than in!' As my father would say. She laughs. 'Not for the fish in the stream it isn't,' and I realise that I must have spoken out-loud.

'Come on,' she carries on. 'You shouldn't be in this sun.

It's nice and shady over there, under that willow tree.'

She leads me over to MY tree. My tree, where I was going to eat some of MY food. This is the second time, I think gloomily, that she has come into a private place of mine without me wanting her to.

She settles herself comfortably under the tree and I notice that once again as she sits on the grass she arranges her dress over her knees, like she did before, coyly pulling the hem over her firm brown thighs and I am quite surprised to find that I find this rather exciting and I feel my testicles tightening a little inside my jokey Y-Fronts and I think, 'That's a first! They've never done that before.'

Then she pats the ground next to her.

'Well sit down, wazzack!' She orders. 'Before you bleedin' fall down!'

NO. No. I don't want to sit next to her by a stream in the shade on a hot summer's day. I want to enjoy my one day of freedom, my few brief hours free of prayer and sacrifice.

So I sit next to her. There is something in her face that says I must.

She looks at me in disgust as I flop down beside her and rest my head wearily against the trunk of the tree. She shakes her head pityingly.

'Gawd! What a state.'

She's right. I am in a state. I feel v. v. tired and my stomach muscles are aching and I think that I must look v. pale. I feel v. pale, so I guess I must look v. pale.

'You look green,' she says.

Not pale? Green, then. Green is probably worse, I figure and I close my eyes, because it is bright and my head has started to ache.

'Well, what have you been up to?' She persists, ignoring my closed eyes that I think should be telling her to leave me alone in my misery.

I'll have to lie again. I hardly ever lie and I've met this girl only twice and already I've told her worse lies than I could ever imagine. She makes me do it. I'll end up in purgatory for *years* because of her questions.

For a brief mad moment I think about looking her in the eyes and saying. 'Well, actually I found a dead cat, cut it up, cracked open its head and ate its brain!' I wonder if she'll scream and run away or will she just pass out? Either way I hope it will stop her asking me questions. But instead, I look at her and I say, 'I told you. Just something I ate. I had some fish last night. It must have been a bit off.'

Lying again! Embroidering and making the lie bigger – again! But perhaps the cat had some fish for its tea and so indirectly I had fish too and then the lie isn't so bad.. Perhaps..!

She gazes at me, with those clear blue eyes. Does she know I'm lying? Or does she just think I'm an idiot? Then she looks away. She looks around at the sunny meadows and at the stream bubbling along nearby.

She sighs. 'It's luvverly here.'

She stretches out the word in a contented sort of way. Then she tips her head back and speaks in a different sort of voice from the one she usually has:

'*I know a bank where the wild thyme blows; where oxlips and the nodding violet grows, quite over-canopied with luscious woodbine, with sweet musk-roses and with eglantine.*'

I stare at her.

'It's Shakespeare, stupid.' She says. '*A Midsummer Night's Dream.*'

'Oh.' I nod and try to look clever but I have never read *A Midsummer Night's Dream*. 'Are you doing it in school, then?' I ask.

'Nah. I just like it,' she says.

I'm a bit confused at this. I like Biology and I quite like music but I have never met anyone who LIKES Shakespeare. We have done *Hamlet* with Fr Martin in English and I played Ophelia when we acted it out in class and it was, in my opinion, dead boring. Father Martin said it was the greatest tragedy in the English Language and O'Flaherty said it was, 'Bloody tragic in any language!' Which made everyone laugh, though I certainly did not as I have more respect for both my teachers and our national heroes.

And then there nearly was a REAL tragedy, because Edwards played Laertes and he managed to fix a compass point into the end of the ruler he was using as a sword and he nearly blinded Smith with it, who was playing Hamlet. Fr Martin, mopped up the blood and told everyone to keep quiet about it as there was no point in making a FUSS 'about a little classroom accident'.

Father Martin is, in my opinion, afraid of Edwards.

So, as I say, I couldn't say that I liked Shakespeare – though Hamlet has stuck in my mind – and when she said 'LIKE' she obviously meant it in the sort of way that you mean that you *really* like things, such as *Top Of The Pops*, and *Dr Who*.

'Well,' I say. 'It takes all sorts.' Which is the most pathetic thing to say and is actually quite rude but she doesn't seem to notice. She's still not looking at me and she just sort of carries on as if she's talking to herself.

'In Putney, where we lived before,' she says. 'I used to go

to the park. Not the big one, which is called Putney Heath but the little one near our house. I used to walk through the park and there was the Thames at the back of it. It's the biggest river in England and it was there, right at the back of my little park, next to my house, where there was a little children's playground that I used to play in when I was very small. There was this big, big river with concrete banks and at low-tide there were wide mud flats going out to the water. But even at low tide when there was hardly any water, it was still about fifty times wider than that...' And she nods at the little stream.

'And it smelt. It was a funny smell. Sort of musty and muddy at the same time. Not like shit or anything, though my Dad used to say that the Thames was just a bleeding sewer and I wasn't to paddle in it ever, but it had its own special smell. It wasn't sewage, it was a Thames smell.'

She looks at me at last – I don't know what on earth she is talking about but I try to look interested which is PO-LITE, though I suspect that I don't do it very well. She carries on anyway.

'I used to think that I hated The Thames because it was dirty and horrid and I used to think that one day I would like to find a really clean, little river and paddle in it all day, 'cos I couldn't paddle in the Thames.. And now look,' she says. 'Here I am!'

'Yes,' I say.

And then I think I had better say some more, so I say, 'And that's good then?'

'Only partly. 'Cos I wouldn't be here if my dad hadn't have died, would I?'

I look closely at her and sure enough her blue eyes are filling with tears and she's sniffing a bit.

'The stream's lovely,' she goes on a bit croakily, 'and all these fields and the trees and everything... but I wish my Dad was here to see it.'

This is really bad. She is making me feel v. v. uncomfortable. I don't know what to say to people with dead dads. I can't think what to do, so I look down and close my eyes once more.

'My head aches,' I say.

Eventually, when there has been quite a long silence, I open my eyes again. She isn't sitting next to me anymore. She must have stood up v. v, quietly. Like the proverbial m. She has taken off her shoes and her white socks and she has walked over to the side of the stream. She looks over her shoulder and laughs at me, I am relieved to see that there is no more sign of the tears.

'You coming in to paddle, wazzack?' She says. 'I reckon your puke will be well washed away by now.'

She steps into the stream and gives a little scream as the water rushes over her feet.

'Bloody 'ell. That's bleedin' cold,' she shouts.

You can hear her shrieks of laughter echoing all round the fields and off the hills. I think girls are funny. One moment she's crying about her dad and the next she's laughing and paddling in the stream. I get up and go over to her.

'Come on then. Get your shoes off,' she orders me.

I don't want to do this, not just because the water's cold but... well, I can't explain really. It's something to do with taking my clothes off even though it is only my shoes and socks, in front of a girl. It seems so... so 'intimate', for want of a better word, and I find myself v. v. embarrassed, which I know is silly. Dead silly. But I am and that's all there is to it.

So, I'm standing there trying to make up my mind what to do and fidgeting around on the bank when suddenly a great sploosh of icy water hits me hard in the face and chest. There is so much of it and it is so cold that for a second I stand there gasping, the breath knocked right out of me. Eventually, I open my eyes and see her. Her hands are dripping wet from where she has gathered the water, her eyes are flashing and she is laughing her head off at me.

'What d'you do that for?' I say eventually, my fists clenched, my arms rigid by my sides with the shock and cold. My aertex polo shirt (my favourite one, red with a white collar) is dripping wet and the front of it sticks damply to my chest, I am blowing water from my mouth and my hair is plastered to my head.

She laughs – hysterically, in my opinion – and she bends down to the stream to gather another scoop of water in her hands.

'Don't!' I say. 'Bitch!'

There is something in my voice which startles even me. It is loud and harsh and very angry. I have never used the word 'Bitch' before and I have certainly never spoken to a girl like that before – not that I know many girls but even if I had, I would never have spoken to them like that. What have I done? Where has this anger come from? I don't usually get angry. I am NEVER ANGRY!

She stops, her hands cupped, still stooped over the water. She looks up at me and I see a little spark of surprise (or is it even fear) in those blue eyes. She slowly straightens her back, lets her dripping hands drop to her sides.

'Sorry.. It was only a lark,' she says, quite subdued now.

I look at her and I am really ashamed of myself.

'It doesn't matter,' I say, 'Look, I didn't mean... you know... what I said. It was the shock. I am really sorry. I shouldn't have said that.'

We stand there, me on the bank dripping wet, her in the fast running, freezing stream looking at each other both surprised by each other.

Then I say, typically pathetically, 'You can throw water on me now if you like!'

She eyes me up and wipes her hands dry on her dress.

'No. It's all right thanks. I won't if you don't mind.'

Then she wades very primly through the water to the bank, clambers out and comes right over to me. She is a little bit taller than me I notice for the first time, so she stoops a little as she puts her face very close to mine and stares at me, and when she speaks it is in a low, cold voice as cold as the water had been.

'Don't ever call me a bitch again, Billy. Just don't ever!'

'I w...won't,' I stammer. 'I didn't mean to. It just slipped out.'

She looks at me and I think she is going to say something else but suddenly her face relaxes and she smiles at me.

'Come on. We're going into town.'

'Town?' I echo.

'Yes. To Leeford. You know *the big* town.. shops, cinemas, places to eat..'

'But I can't,' I say. 'I haven't told my mother and father.'

She looks at me as if I am crazy. 'Told them what? What do they need to know for? What did they think you was doing today?'

'I said, I was going out to explore the woods and things...'

'All day?'

'Yes.'

'Well, there you are then. Woods. Towns. What does it matter? You're out for the day. The bus goes in half an hour, so we'd better get cracking.'

'But I can't...' I splutter.

She is already striding away and she doesn't seem to notice that she has no shoes on. She speaks to me over her shoulder.

'We'll go to my house first, 'cos I want to get a cardie in case it gets colder and we'll borrow some cash off Mum... bet you haven't got any have you?'

'A bit,' I say, trotting along beside her like a little dog, trying to keep pace with her long stride, 'But not much. Won't your Mum mind?'

'Mind what? She owes me about three weeks pocket money and we'll get a bit more off her, don't you worry.'

'No. I mean about going into the town?'

'Don't be stupid. We're only going into Leeford..'

And then she adds mysteriously.

'Blimey. I used to go into Wandsworth on Saturday mornings. I mean... Wandsworth!'

'But what about my shirt? It's wet and I'll freeze.'

'It'll dry and you can look on it as your punishment.'

She has a point and with that she leads me over the fields and up to the lane that takes you all the way to Brewers' Cottages.

* * *

It doesn't take long to walk to the Brewers' Cottages. We are on the right side of the village and the lane is all down hill.

The cottages stand just on the outskirts of our village, opposite the Maltings Theatre. It's an odd place to look at because the theatre is covered in trendy art work and bright posters advertising Keith Michelle and Dorothy Tutin in *Othello* (I have seen them in the BBC's mega historical series – 'The Six Wives of Henry VIII' and my mother and I both agree that their acting is exceptional – by anyone's standards.) There are other posters telling us that Topol and Diana Dors are also there, in *A Midsummer Night's Dream* – which I guess the girl must have been to see, as she was quoting it at me not long ago.

The theatre car park used to be a field but it's been tarmacced over now and it's got a smattering of really expensive and trendy cars in it, like Triumph Stags and Jags. (I know about cars. I build Airfix models of them – especially sports cars, and one day I will own a Ferrari Dino. I have decided that this is my 'car of choice', as the Sunday Times Colour Supplement puts it.)

On the other side of the road, opposite the theatre, The Brewers' Cottages stand on their own. They are really scruffy and dingy by contrast, with a couple of rusty Escorts and an old Austin A40 in front of them.

'It's where the old meets the new,' my father says.

'It's the juxtaposition of art and artisan in a place of rural culture that makes the venue so exciting…' the reviewer in *The Guardian* said, when the theatre opened last year. 'Now we've got the theatre, they should knock those ruddy cottages down. It's bad for our image!' my mother says. 'And that's that!' She adds.

There are six cottages in the terrace, red brick, run-down and grimy. They each have a small front garden surrounded by a picket fence – the fences are in varying states of repair and number three's is particularly broken down and shabby.

Diana/ Emma or Katherine opens the gate and it swings dodgily on one hinge. The little garden is just long grass that needs cutting and a few daisies that might have been part of a flower bed before it got lost under the grass. The front door is painted green but it has been bashed around a lot and bits of yellow paint show through the chips and scars. It has a frosted glass window which is dirty and I can see a yellowing net curtain through the grime.

She opens the door, which is not locked and we step into a tiny hallway with cream walls and brown woodwork. A bike leans against the wall and someone's dirty P.E. kit is heaped on the floor. There isn't any carpet and the floorboards have been polished at some time – but now they just look dirty.

I am appalled. My mother would be in a state of shock. 'How some people live!' She would say. 'I mean cleaning costs nothing.'

A steep staircase is in front of us and at the end of the hallway is a door that is half open. Emma/Diana or whatever, leads me through this into the kitchen, which is very small compared to the big one I'm used to at home.

A tall dark haired woman in a red dress is standing at the kitchen sink with her back to us. She turns as we walk in and I catch my breath. I realise Diana/ Emma/ Katherine's Mum is a beautiful woman. I don't know much about judging women by their looks but I know she is really beautiful – not like I have seen on television or in the Sunday Times Colour Supplement but a real beauty, something that I cannot put into words – something that touches me and makes me want to keep looking at her.

She is not even like the beautiful women I have seen in the telly ads for *Gossard Cross Your Heart Bras*, she is soft and warm and… and amazing. Her beauty seems to be coming at me from somewhere inside her and it seems to be reaching out to something inside me.

She is smiling and somehow she makes me feel really good – just being there in the kitchen with her and seeing her smile at us makes me feel great. I can't explain it – she hasn't even said anything but her looking at me makes me feel all warm and happy.

Forgive me Father, I have lusted after an older woman and I will do penance!

'Hello darling,' she is saying to Diana /E or K. 'I thought you were out today... And who's this?'

She looks at me. She has D/E/K's eyes or at least this is where D/E/K etc. has got hers from – only these eyes are even more blue and they smile a lot. She has freckles too, but they are better freckles than her daughter's – they are smudgy and make her lips and eyes and nose more interesting. They kind of blend into her face in a dreamy way. I feel a little sick again or at least my stomach is churning. It might be the smoke from her cigarette which is burning in an ashtray on the kitchen table... Or it might be something else.

'This is Billy,' D/etc. says. 'And we *are* out. At least we will be in a minute. We're going into Leeford, but I need some cash please, Mum. You owe me three weeks and we could do with another quid if you can spare it.'

'What am I? Just a bank, or something?' Says her Mum, but she is laughing and I notice that she has the same accent as her daughter but it is more gentle and there is something else, a sort of husky sound that makes me feel a little odd when I hear it but I don't know why.

She takes the cigarette out of the ashtray and puffs on it while she finds her handbag on the dresser. She clamps the ciggy in her mouth as she looks through her bag and smoke curls from the end if it so that she has to half close her eyes as she searches for the money. There is something about this that makes me think of old posters of the war and people under street lamps but again, I don't know why. Also, as she is looking for the money, I can't help but notice that her breasts press against her dress and that I can see the shape of a nipple pressing through the fabric.

I don't want to look but I do. I can't help it..

Forgive me! Forgive me!

And as I start to pray inside my head I find that I am looking at the cigarette smoke and it is curling up towards the ceiling and winding its way around the kitchen light which is not much more than a grubby bulb hanging from a greasy wire, with a dirty, fly blown plastic lamp shade. My mother would be even more shocked I think. 'Shouldn't be anything dirty in a place of food preparation,' she would say...

But looking again, I see that actually the light is an old fashioned street lamp made of cast iron with an ornate, hooked top and an orangey bulb inside a glass globe and it is throwing its light onto a foggy street below. It sends amber beams of light eerily through the fog and I can see that a woman stands in the dark street below the lamp, her hat pulled low over her eyes, caught in the cone of light in what is otherwise a damp and dusky road.

She is dressed in an old fashioned raincoat, that is pulled tight round her middle and her coat collar is turned-up against the wet night air. She has a trilby hat pulled low over those dark eyes and I can't help but notice that below the raincoat's hem, she has long calves, encased in black nylon stockings and that she is wearing v.v. sexy black stiletto heels. Somewhere in the distance I can hear a Glen Miller record playing. Then there is a sound of footsteps echoing against walls and approaching briskly along the street. The woman looks up when she hears the footsteps and I can see her black hair below the hat and blue eyes and pale skin.

This woman is Emma's mum. She has a cigarette between her lips and she wears bright red lipstick and looks like the sort of film star heroine I have seen in old films about the war.

The figure who is approaching her is a man. He too wears a 1940's style raincoat and he has a black hat pulled low over his eyes. He walks with a swift assurance and he radiates confidence and what I think is called sex appeal. He stops by her in the light of the street lamp and he looks her over from head to foot slowly appraising her. Then he reaches inside his coat and pulls a packet of cigarettes from his breast pocket and a box of matches. He places a cigarette slowly in his mouth, barely opening his lips to receive it.

She watches him, giving him a sultry, sexy look that says, 'I'm too good for you but I still want you – on my own terms...' Then he strikes a match and I can see his face for the first time in the bursting flame of it...

...and suddenly she is smiling at me, looking right through me, through the haze of smoke and into my mind. I am back in the kitchen and she is still holding the handbag and watching me, giving me what I think is a slightly odd look and I think she is going to say, 'Looking at my nipple then, are you Billy?' .

But she says, 'I haven't seen you around before, have I Billy? Are you in the same class as Diana?' And she puffs smoke at me as she speaks.

'No...' I begin but my mouth is dry and I feel my cheeks are burning.

'He's not at Wilmot Lane, Mum. He's a posh boy from St Joseph's.'

'Oh,' says Diana etc's Mum. 'Fancy that.'

And I wonder what she means? Does she mean, fancy our Diana meeting up with a posh boy? Or does she mean, don't you come in here with your airs and graces? Or does she mean, I don't like the look of you young man, standing there with your mouth hanging open, your cheeks all red and staring like that at my nipple! But she smiles at me again and I feel that same churning sickness once more when she does so.

'So how did you two bump into each other, then?' She says.

'I found him in the woods but I'll tell you about it later,' says the girl.

I feel a bit like a lost dog.

'Look, we'll have to rush. We're going to have a Wimpy and see a film. Should be back about six. Alright?'

This is the first I have heard about any of this and I suddenly feel very apprehensive. I also suddenly feel very grown-up. In fact, it all seems *so* grown-up, I don't know if I want to do this. I don't want to go out with a girl and see a film. I don't even go into town with the boys in my class at school, let alone girls I have only known for five minutes.

But she, Diana's mum, the goddess with the black hair and smiley eyes, cigarettes and nipples and smudgy freckles is laughing and saying what a smashing idea and find a call box to phone if you're going to be any later and we are suddenly being bundled out, through the door and the little garden and I am in the lane with Diana/Emma etc.

I find myself sitting on the bus next to Diana etc. etc. and when I look through the window, the countryside is flashing by in a blur and my thoughts are doing the same thing only in my head.

I feel a panic beginning to creep through me and I know that my day without sacrifice and prayer is about to end because everything that is happening is something OUT OF THE ORDINARY and when things OUT OF THE ORDINARY happen I need to pray especially hard, so that GOD will keep things under control and protect me from any of the dangers and sins that might be associated with something OUT OF THE ORDINARY such as this – a trip on a bus into town, with a girl of many names and blue eyes who seems intent on having something to eat and seeing a film. All of which, are things I have never done before and never even imagined that I ever would do, AT ALL.

So I am sitting there, staring rigidly ahead and trying to pray.

'Hail Mary, full of grace...' I pray inside my head, 'The Lord is with thee. Blessed is the fruit...'

'D'you fancy *Rosemary's Baby*?' She says.

I am shaken out of my prayerful state and I turn to look at the girl sitting next to me. She is pawing over the entertainment pages that she has torn from her mother's copy of the local paper.

'What?' I say. 'I don't think I want to see a film about babies.' And I add politely, 'If it's all the same to you.'

'It's by Roman Polanski.'

An Italian I think. I don't like foreign films. You always miss what's going on when you read the sub-titles.

'It says it's about a woman who gets involved with a group of devil worshippers.' She explains.

I am shocked. How can she mention devils, when I have been trying to pray to the most blessed..?

'Or there's *The Graduate*.'

I suppose I look at her blankly, torn between her film world and my spiritual one.

'I don't mind either,' she goes on. 'Actually, I've seen *The Graduate* before but it's really good and *Rosemary's Baby* is new but it's supposed to be dead good too. Y'know sexy and frightening and that. You choose.'

How can I choose? I don't know anything about either of them. I haven't been to the cinema much, not since the *Bambi* event and I don't read much about films. Then I think to myself, 'I don't want to see anything about Devils. It might ruin my HOLY STATE.'

She is giving me a funny look and suddenly I worry that I might have spoken out loud, in which case she would think she was on the bus with a complete nut case, who was chuntering on about being in a HOLY STATE but then I realise that she is just waiting for me to say something. So I say, '*The Graduate*'. Because that doesn't have devils in it. And I add, 'Thank you.' Because that seems quite polite.

'A pleasure, kind sir,' she says laughing.

I don't understand what she means.

I try to get back to my prayers but she has folded-up the newspaper and she obviously wants to talk. So I mutter a quick 'AMEN'.

She looks at me and says:

'What? What d'you say?'

'Nothing!' I reply

Which is a sort of a lie but not too bad a one I reckon and anyway I don't get any time to think about it because she is off on another conversation straight away.

'I like Dustin Hoffman,' she is saying. 'I mean he's a dead good actor, not that he's sexy or anything, though I suppose he is a bit sexy but not so sexy as Paul Newman, now he is sexy. Who d'you think's sexy then?'

I stare at her. What does she mean? Do I find anyone sexy, I wonder? Then I realise that I find her mother sexy. I hadn't thought of that before. I thought she was beautiful just now when I met her in the kitchen, but now I realise that she is more than beautiful, she is SEXY and this is a big thing because I've never really thought about anyone like that before. In fact I have never really thought about sex or being sexy in any shape or form. I never even use that word, the 'S' word, if I can help it.

'So,' she says. 'Tell me.'

I have been asked a question and I must give an answer and I do not want to tell another lie. But I realise that I will have to tell a lie, because if I tell her that I think her mother is sexy then she will probably get upset and quite probably be dead 'beady' with me and I do not think I can face that. So I will have to tell another lie after all – ah well, it is only a little more time to be added to my stay in Purgatory.

'Yes,' I say. 'I think Paul Newman is sexy too.'

She looks at me, a little surprised at first, and then she starts to laugh. I realise that my answer is silly in the extreme but I cannot think what to say to get out of it. So I say. 'And

Dustin Hoffman...I think he's sexy too...' I flounder around for the name of another film star I may have read about in the Sunday Papers, 'Oh, and so is Oliver Reed and Donald Sutherland... and... and Jack Nicholson.'

Why is she laughing so much?

She is choking as she says. 'Oh, Billy. You kill me. You really do. You say such bleeding funny things.'

So we sit on the bus together and make our way into town and we get off in the High Street.

I don't go into Leeford much. To be honest I don't like towns at all. I don't like all the people and the noise. Of course, Leeford is only a small country town but it is quite bad enough. People jostle you and crowd you and there is terrible din from the traffic. Sometimes I try to imagine what it must be like to live in London, or Manchester or Birmingham or some other big city. I don't know how anyone can live in a place like that.

We don't go to big cities very often but occasionally my parents decide that they have to go to London and I will do anything to try not to accompany them. Ever since my visits to Harley Street, I have really hated the place. I cannot stand the noise, the smell, the crowds, the tube trains, the buses or the shops. Everything is awful and too big and too dangerous and as soon as we arrive at Waterloo and I get off the train I start to panic. When I was younger I could hold on to my mother's hand but when you get older you look dead silly if you do this, but I admit that last time we went (which was last school holidays) I really desperately wanted to grab hold of her and say, 'just hold me and don't let me get lost among all these people!' But of course I didn't. She would think I was mad.

Needless to say, London is a place where I have to pray a

great deal. I start praying from the day before we are due to go there and I pray all night and all morning and on the way to Leeford Station and all the time while we sit on the train to Waterloo. And I pray when we go on the tubes or on the buses and I pray when we have lunch in the café at *John Lewis* and I pray when we are nearing the end of the walk round the *Science Museum*, because I know that I will soon be back in the busy street and on the bus or the tube and then back on the train.

I have to pray because I am worried that the train will crash or that the tube will be stuck in a tunnel between stations and that it will be crowded and very hot and that I will be pressed up against other people and be forced to become very 'intimate' with them. And on the bus I am worried that it will try to go under a bridge, at speed and the whole of the top deck with us in it, will be ripped off and peeled open like a sardine tin and that our heads will be ripped from our necks by the impact.

Because I worry about all these things, I have to pray an AWFUL lot and it is v. v. tiring and v. v. stressful to do that and also to cope with my fears and hatred of the place.

Leeford, of course, is not so bad as London because it is much, much smaller and there are no tubes – but as I get off the bus with the girl of many names, I must admit that I feel a sense of panic creep over me and for a second or two I feel quite dizzy and I have to stand still by the bus stop and take a couple of deep breaths. The girl seems eager to get going and strides away into the crowd and she doesn't notice at first that I am not with her. When she does, she turns back.

'Wassa matter?' She asks, loudly over the noise of the bus pulling away.

'Nothing,' I say. '…just feel a bit wobbly, that's all.'

'Yeah?'

She comes back to me.

'Probably hungry. I mean you was sick and you hardly ate anything after. Let's go to the Wimpy and we'll have something to eat and make our plans.'

She grabs my hand and pulls me onto the pavement. Then she puts her arm into mine and she steers me along the High Street. She has her arm entwined round mine. I CANNOT believe it. I have a girl's FLESH actually PRESSED onto mine.

A GIRL.

I am starting to panic. Not just because of the people and the noise and the smell of the town but because I have this girl on my arm and I can feel her warm naked flesh on mine and I can smell her perfume mingling with the smell of traffic fumes and the greasy smell of the Wimpy bar down the road. Is this a sin? To have this girl pressed against me like this? No. I think it is OK. This is not like S-X or any-thing like that, but nevertheless we are being INTIMATE.

I am very confused about girls and about what Father Martin calls the 'sins of the flesh.' Last year I thought that my confusion about 'S-X' would be sorted out as we were promised lessons in, well you know in… shall we say, the ' F of L'. We were told that in these lessons things would be explained to us if we didn't already know them or if we had questions to be asked. But in the end it all went wrong.

One day Mr Terry came into our English lesson and his hands were shaking more than they normally did, his glasses were more skewiff than usual and the smell of old beer on his breath was stronger than it usually was. On this particular day he said in his Belfast accent, 'Sex? I'll tell you about sex.

You get yourself all worked up about some girl and then you sit next to her and she farts!'

With that he took a long drag on his cigarette and I noticed as he removed the fag from his mouth and exhaled, that there was a sticky goblet of spit dangling from his top lip down to his bottom lip. And that was Mr, Terry's s-x lesson.

Next Father Hennessey had a go. He sent us all out of the classroom. 'I am going to ask you back one at a time,' he said. 'And I shall ask you, if you know about the facts of Life. If you don't, I shall explain. If you do, you may return to the playground.'

So if you stayed in the classroom for more than one minute you didn't know about s-x, then? That was the message that went round our playground and Teddy Edwards said he would beat the SH-T out of anyone who didn't know about the F of L and he would grab their cocks and show them just what to do with them. So everyone of us, even me, said, 'Yes Father, I know all about the facts of life.'

But I didn't. Not really.

Then came Father Martin.

He sidled into our class one morning, tapping his silver topped snuff box, his hair greasily slicked back, filling the room with his particular odour. He wiped his nose flamboyantly with his red spotted handkerchief and, like an actor, he stood on the teachers' dais with one hand behind his back and he tossed his head as if he had long curls (which he doesn't). 'Boys… Boys… Boys…' He began and I thought of the production of *Henry V* we had seen at Stratford, earlier in the term. 'Boys... Dear, dear boys...' He declaimed. 'Sex is sinful. That is all you need to know. You may have heard of something called the permissive society. But for you, dear boys, there will be no society in the immediate future and if we teach you well and in the true ways of the Lord, there will be no permissiveness, either.' He paused for effect and tapped his snuff box again. Then he took a pinch of snuff but didn't put it up his nose – he just stood there holding it and I could see the fine dust of it falling to the floor in a shaft of sunlight through the window.

'You may have sex in marriage and this is tolerated because it is procreation. You may not have sex at any other time, because so to do is a sin. *A sin*! I re-emphasise that – *a sin*! You may, before you marry find yourself wanting to indulge in some forms of intimacy with one of the other sex. You can I am sure decide for yourselves what I mean by 'forms of intimacy'. Now, I would suggest that the more pleasurable and the more *urgent* your need for such an intimacy – the greater is its degree of sin. Therefore, you will be able to create a scale, a table if you like of how sinful certain actions may be. I should avoid the top of that table at all costs and quite frankly the bottom is not to be desired either. Finally, you may ask where SPILLING the seed by personal manipulation lies in our table of sinfulness?'

Here he paused but he did not answer the q. Instead he placed what was left of the pinch of snuff in his nostrils and stared out of the window. Then he seemed to shake his head and he looked round at us and focused on me.

'Do I make myself clear?'

He did not. I did not understand. So, I nodded, which was the easy way out.

So there was a table of intimacy by which we were supposed to live, that much I had gathered but after that no more was said about S-X.

Over the last few months I have taken the trouble to make certain enquiries and to read certain books. Also my observations of the local wildlife and my dissecting of same have now led me to be fairly confident about what is meant by procreation or the F of L and even by 'personal manipulation', which is, in my humble o. a fairly messy and unpleasant business and I cannot really understand why people like Edwards get quite so worked-up about it.

To date I have not really been troubled by any unnecessary or uncontrollable urges and the quantity of intimate fluids that my body has shed has been quite minimal, I think, compared to some of the stories I have overheard in the changing rooms. Yes, I can truly say that the fluids I have shed have been shed largely by accident and usually while asleep.

But what I am still not sure about, is that table of intimacy. How far down the line of perdition, as it were, are we going when this girl holds onto my arm, like this? This is why I pretend that my shoe-lace has come undone, so that I can pull away from the girl's arm when I bend down to tie it and why, when I straighten up again, I do not re-engage her arm but walk stiffly at her side to the Wimpy Bar.

* * *

I have a strawberry milkshake and a wimpy and chips. She has wimpy and chips with a coke.

We sit at a small greasy table and I can feel some old, squashed chips on the floor under my foot. People are V. V. messy. It is, 'the curse of the modern age,' as my mother would say. 'Dirty little B's want to remember the poor B who has to clear-up after them!' My father would say.

I hate dirtiness and things like squashed chips. It is one of the reasons why I hate going into towns and why I hate coming into places like this, full of smelly people eating their smelly chips and dropping their rubbish on the floor.

In fact the more I think about it and look around me at what I can only describe as UTTER SQUALOR, the more I wonder why on earth I have come here with this girl? I was happy in the woods and fields and I had a really nice day planned on my own in the places that I love, under the blue sky, with my pack of sandwiches in the fresh air. God's air!

What I am doing here? That is what I am asking myself. What am I doing here?

She smiles at me over her Wimpy, which is half way to her mouth with a little bit of grease dripping off the end of it and a dill pickle poking out from under the bun and her blue eyes glitter under the light of the fluorescent tubes and her freckles look dead nice and it is then that I sort of understand why I gave up my day to be with her.

I cannot really explain it but there is something in her smile that makes it almost OK to be here, despite my hating the place and the people and my fear of it all. She makes me feel calm again. It is not like the calm I have when I have said a prayer really well that I know God has heard and really appreciates but it is something like it and it is an EXPLANATION for what I can only call my v.v. erratic behaviour in coming out with her in the first place.

'You don't say much,' she says, wiping the grease off her lips with a little paper napkin from the silver holder on the table. I wipe my mouth with the back of my hand. It does not look too elegant, I think, but it is better than risking an INFECTION from one of the paper napkins, the origin of which and who has handled them we have no idea.

'I don't speak a lot unless there's something to say,' I explain. Which is true and quite rational I think.

'I like that,' she says and she squirts some more ketchup into her bun from the repulsive plastic tomato, that is encrusted with old sauce.

'You meet some boys who just never shut-up,' she says and flicks some of the crusty ketchup off the green spout thing – which is really gross!

'They spend their whole lives,' she goes on, 'telling you how clever they are or how strong or how tough... you know?'

I don't actually, because the truth is that not a lot of boys who are clever, strong or tough bother to speak to me, so I don't know what they might say. She is definitely describing, I reckon, those sort of boys who are in the OTHER WORLD the NOT MY WORLD.

As I don't know what to say at this point I ask her if she has been out with a lot of boys then.

'You've got a cheek!' She says. 'Do I look like a tart or something?'

I'm not sure what a tart is, so I say. 'No. I suppose not.'

'Thanks!' She says.

I think she looks a bit offended but she may be joking. I'm not sure, though and I don't want to upset her. I have done that before and it is not a nice thing to do and also I am still embarrassed at calling her a B. when we were by the stream and... and a terrible thought occurs to me – if I offend her I won't see her again and she might storm off and if she does that A) I will never find my way home on my own, having never travelled alone on a bus or on anything else for that matter and B) I will not see *her mother* again and the thought of that makes me feel v. v. miserable.

I think fast. I can usually make a quick decision when required and get myself out of any spot of bother, like being caught kneeling to say my prayers in a public place (I either plead a stomach ache that has made me collapse or I do up a shoe-lace, as you will have seen).

'Can I buy you an ice cream?' I say, remembering the pound note I keep in my rucksack. 'I would really like to. You know, to say thank you for looking after me by the stream and giving me your hanky when I needed it and also for having the idea of coming here. It's brilliant. I like to get out into town. But it's no fun on my own.'

This is probably the most I have said to her so far. In fact, as it goes, it is one of my longest speeches ever to anyone, anywhere outside of God and the Blessed V. M. The fact that it is full of lies worries me quite a lot but I realise that it is necessary to lie in this URGENT situation and I am pretty sure that I will be forgiven, in the circumstances.

She immediately brightens up and smiles at me.

'Why Billy,' she says. 'That's so nice. What a nice thing to say. I'd love an ice cream. Thank you.'

So I go and get her a glass dish of dead, brown chocolate ice cream with a wafer stuck in it and I put it down on the table in front of her and for good measure I pick up one of the manky paper napkins and flourish it in the air and flap it open like I have seen waiters do on the telly and I spread it out on her lap.

'Pour vous, Mamselle,' I say, dead corny. But she loves it and she gives me this really big smile as she grabs her spoon and starts to load the ice cream in her mouth. This is quite possibly what is called FLIRTING I think or it may be that other mysterious thing that I have heard Mark and my brother talk about called CHATTING-UP.

I do not mean to be a hypocrite and I hope that what I did will not cause me to be seen as such. But it was necessary for the well-being of everyone. I would not want to upset her and in the light of what will HAPPEN TO HER in the next few weeks, I am glad that at that moment I made her happy.

When she has finished sucking the disgusting brown stuff down her face and when she has wiped her filthy lips again with another germ caked napkin, she sits back in her plastic seat and sighs.

'Great,' she says. 'And they've got *The Monkees* on the juke box.'

It's true. '*The Last Train to Clarksville*', is playing in the background and while she has been eating her ice cream I have been tapping my foot to it and in my mind I am singing all the lyrics.

'That's nice,' she says, smiling. 'You've got a nice voice.'

I've done it again. I must have been singing out loud in the same way that sometimes I say things out loud that were only meant to be in my head. I can feel my cheeks beginning to burn again and I can't think what to say, so I give her what is probably a cheesy grin.

She says, 'I like *The Monkees*. I think they're my favourite group. Probably...'.

I stare at her.

'Your favourite?' I say, dead amazed. 'How can you say that? What about *The Beatles*? *The Rolling Stones*? *The Who*? *Pink Floyd*? What about all those proper groups?'

'Well, I like *The Monkees*. I like Peter Torke. He looks

sort of lost.'

Yes, I think, and I bet she prefers to Paul to John, Brian Jones to Mick Jagger and Roger Daltry to Pete Townsend.

'When you listen to *Sergeant Pepper*,' I say to her slowly, because I really want her to understand this. 'When you listen to *Sergeant Pepper*, you go somewhere. I mean GO. You know, like when you go into a Church, like when you think about God, like when you see the sun in the morning or when you look at the moon over the meadows from your bedroom window. When they play that big piano chord at the end, it's like all your prayers and all your fears and everything bad you have ever done is rolled up into a little ball and thrown up into outer space and lost forever. It's... It's... '

I am struggling to explain what I mean.

'...It's like what God intended, why he gave us a soul, why he gave us singing and why he gave us music. It's why we have to suffer and why we have pain... so that, so that we can have moments like that... like that chord.'

I stop. I cannot believe what I have done. I have said more than I ever say.

Worse, I realise that I have stood up and that I am leaning over her, my hands pressed onto the greasy table to support my weight as I speak into her face – very close, too close – almost threatening her.

She is looking up at me. Her mouth is slightly open, her eyes are open v. wide.

'Blimey!' She says quietly. 'I only said I like *The Monkees*.'

I flop back into my plastic chair.

'I'm sorry,' I gasp. 'I'm really dead sorry. I... I... I get a bit passionate about music.'

'I'd never have noticed,' she says.

She is being ironic I think. We have just done irony in English and it is not sarcasm, though some will confuse it, Mr Terry says. But this is definitely IRONY.

'You do get carried away!' She says suddenly. 'One moment you're quite normal. I mean a bit quiet. A bit weird maybe, but not too bad and then you have these outbursts – like about the priests and calling me, well, what you called me by the river and now... well, *The Monkees*! Bloody hell!'

'I have a lot going on...' I try to explain. 'In my mind and everything... Look I don't normally speak to people much and when I do... It gets muddled...sort of...'

I trail off. Because this is hopeless. How can I tell her what goes on inside my head; about God and the need for prayer and how I am keeping it all together for everyone because if I cease to pray everyone will die and there will be CHAOS and RETRIBUTION because *'Vengeance is mine; I will repay, saith the Lord!'* When all is said and done, I am all that stands between HIS vengeance and us.

So I say, 'Sorry.' In a sort of plaintive voice and she smiles back at me.

'It's all right. Nutcase!' She is laughing at me and the moment is over and the embarrassment is past. BUT I know now that I should not have let the moment pass. I should have prayed there and then and I should have prayed harder than ever. If I am all that stands between us and the vengeance of the Lord our God, then I should definitely have prayed right there and then for her – for the girl who was laughing at me – because now it is too late and I was responsible for her... But for now we are still in the Wimpy, in Leeford High Street... *and... nothing... has... happened... to... her.*

'Right. Cinema,' she says in sort of brusque, 'come-along-let's-get-on-with-life', kind of way.

We are standing-up when I hear a voice cut through the noise of the people chomping through their greasy Wimpies.

'Oy!.. Bog Brush!'

I freeze.

'Bog Brush...'

A few of the Wimpy eaters look around, first at the owner of the voice and then across at me. It is obviously me who is being addressed because everyone else in the Wimpy has fashionably long hair and does not look like a prisoner from a Second World War concentration camp.

'Bog Brush... Bring your sister over here and show her what's she's been missing.'

The other boys in Edwards' gang fall about laughing. They have pulled two tables together to fit them all in and they are occupying most of the corner on the far side of the restaurant. I am amazed that we hadn't seen them earlier or that they hadn't seen us but I suppose that they have only just sat down as some of their Wimpies are still uneaten and most of them have piles of untouched chips in front of them.

Edwards sits at the head of the table, his slicked back hair shiny under the neon lights, there is some acne on his forehead and there is a little whisk of beard on his chin and jaw. I do not have any hair on my face yet, but Edwards seems to be determinedly growing what my father would call 'bum fluff!' all over his.

He is wearing fashionably wide flared trousers today and not his Teddy boy stiff. He has on a floral shirt with a big collar and he wears a gold chain round his neck and another one dangles form his wrist as he raises his hand and points at me.

'I said, bring her here, Bog Brush. You deaf or summat?'

I think to myself that it is odd that even though our school is full of rich boys from wealthy Home Counties homes Edwards and his gang all speak like Diana/Emma/Katherine and her mother. This is probably snobbery on my part. In fact I am certain that it is, as it is the kind of thing that my mother would say and I know she is a snob because she once said to Mrs Carlton from 'The Oast House' at the bottom of our Lane, 'Call me a snob if you will, but if it comes to building council houses in a village like ours, then I am just that and proud of it.'

The girl looks at me. 'Who's your friend?' She asks.

'They go to my school,' I say. Then I add, probably unnecessarily, 'they don't like me, much.'

'Oh, and I thought Bog Brush was a term of endearment.'

This time it is quite definitely sarcasm!

'Come on,' I say. 'We'll miss the film.'

We turn towards the door.

'Where you goin' Boggy. I told you to come over 'ere!' Shouts Edwards.

I am going to turn and say something but she is quicker than me. 'We can't hear you, arsehole!' She says loudly. 'Your mouth's full of shit!'

Then she puts her hand through my arm *(again! Oh, forgive me!)* and she steers me towards the door and out into the street. Over my shoulder as we sweep past the window, I can see a few mums and dads at the little tables with their kids looking shocked and I can see Edwards with his mouth open and a red flame on his cheeks.

We march triumphantly along the High Street. A little part of me wonders what punishment will be in store for me on Monday, when Edwards gets hold of me. I desperately do not want to be beaten up or milked and while I am really IMPRESSED at the way the girl has snapped at EDWARDS, though not at her language which is in my book disgusting, 'the language of the gutter,' my father would say, while I am, as I say, impressed, I am also pretty sure that she has condemned me to a terrible fate.

So there I am, arm in arm, with my nemesis and my mind is whirling away in prayer and the next thing I know, she is saying. 'Two one and nines, please.'

I look up and we are in the cinema at the box office and she is handing over a ten shilling note to the lady behind the glass who doubts if we're old enough to see an 'X' certificate but can't be bothered to make a fuss.

She leads the way to our seats. I have a little prickle of anticipation as we mount the steps that take us into the auditorium and I find that I quite like the look of the faded velvet curtains that hang over the entrance and of the worn red and gold flock wall paper. Everything in the foyer is red or gold, even the carpet is red with golden swirls in it and everything smells old and of another time.

I think that my father and mother probably came here when they were my age and that they climbed these steps in the forties and now they still look the same (the steps, not my F & M who like quite faded really). I am pleased about that. I like continuity. I like to reach back into the past and feel that I have roots and that my world isn't changing. This makes me feel secure.

Although I have always believed that I don't like going to see films, as we walk into the auditorium I find that I am quite excited. A bored girl with bad acne in a black and white uniform bearing a torch, holds out what they would call in a novel a 'limp' hand for our tickets and she tears them in half with a fed-up look and she chews gum with her mouth open, making little chewing noises. This is DIS-GUSTING and DEAD COMMON – but what can you do? It's probably only her Saturday job, but if you ask me, she will end up working here full time when she leaves school or she will work in a fishmonger's shop (which must be the worse job on earth), as I doubt if she is going to get any qual-ifications. She definitely looks like she couldn't take O-Levels, unless they have one in gum chewing or in being bored. I reckon she could get A's in those.

She stares at me as she hands back the tickets.

'What you lookin' at?' She says.

I feel myself go red again and the picture of her in my mind in a white, blood stained apron with fish scales on her hands vanishes.

'Nothing,' I say.

'Down the aisle, third row from the front, on the left,' she says and jerks her head in a sort of dismissive way.

It is nearly dark. The curtains are drawn over the screen and the lights are up and some of the lights shine on the cur-tains from below and make a sort of halo of colour over them but despite this it is nearly dark and my eyes do not adjust in time and I stumble a little as I step forward.

Maybe it is also because of the dark that Emma or who-ever she is, suddenly grabs my arm again and this time she presses her whole body quite close to mine and she lays her hand on top of my hand so that she is sort of leaning on me as we walk down the aisle to our seats. I feel sweat begin to prick-le on my forehead and some of it trickles down my back from the nape of my neck. I have never, before today, touched a girl in my life and yet in the last few hours I have virtually had one glued to me for a good percentage of the time. I am really not sure that this is good for either my moral well-being or my health as I reckon that living where she does, she probably has quite a large number of germs or dubious viruses about her person and besides which, I don't approve of too much con-tact between the sexes as you will probably have gathered. This is a result of my education and my firmly held beliefs.

We sit in our seats, which are near the middle of the row. The cinema is nearly empty and there is nobody near us. The few people who are there whisper to each other as if they were in Church and you cannot hear them over the sound of the really corny music that is being played over the loudspeakers. It is Mantovani. I know that because my father plays quite a lot of Mantovani on Sunday mornings on his 'radiogram'. 'You can't beat a good tune,' he says. 'And that Mantovani, knows a good tune when he plays one.'

Most of the time my Dad talks rubbish, I suddenly think to myself. Then I also think, and realising that is part of growing-up.

This thought is just about to overwhelm me as I realise that I am on the verge of something major, when she squeez-es my arm a bit harder.

'So tell us about the bully boy in the Wimpy,' she says. 'I thought only posh boys went to your school.'

'There's not much to tell,' I say reluctantly. 'He's just that – a bully.'

I stare at the curtained screen. I am not one for making conversation and I can't see the point in telling her much about Edwards – he will not affect her life when all is said and done. He will not bully her or grab her private parts and try to wrench them off her body. He will not call her names and push her as she goes downstairs, or trip her up in the playground so that she falls on her knees and little pieces of sharp grey tarmac covered stone weep blood when you stand up again. He will not sneer at her, mock her and embarrass her – nor will he make jokes about her parents and tell people that she is a mutant, cripple, spaz, sub or wanker..

No. He won't do that to Emma, to the girl who sits beside me confident and relaxed, smiling and happy. He won't haunt her dreams at night and put a cloud over most of her mornings.

Then I see from the corner of my eye that she is looking at me. I turn away from the curtained screen, back to her and her eyes are staring through me, into me, which makes me uncomfortable. I'm not one for direct eye contact if I can help it – too much staring at each other is bad for your peace of mind, in my book.

Suddenly she has put her hand back on mine. Just resting it there, gently on the back of my hand. Normally I would pull away from such intimacy but as she has touched me so much today already, there doesn't seem much point. I look up from her hand into her eyes, which I realise are very nice eyes. Quite gentle and a kind of deep, sea blue.

'I'm sorry,' she says.

And then she says quite slowly and carefully, like she is talking to a child, 'You ought to fight back, you know. You should really.'

I have another uncomfortable feeling that I have spoken my thoughts out loud yet again but surely I haven't, have I? So all I do is nod and look back at the screen. Then she starts to talk about the film we are going to be watching, and about all the other films she has seen in the past and she is all bright and jolly and I even offer to go and buy some ice lollies from the stall by the ticket booth, which is dead cool of me and v. nice of me as I have only got seventeen shillings and thruppence left from my pound and that has to last me, until my father gives me some more pocket money at the end of the month. Fortunately, she turns down the offer, saying that she is completely 'stuffed' after her Wimpy and ice – which is a relief but a horrible way of putting it, if you ask me. I was taught that nice people say 'full'.

Then, just as I am starting to feel more comfortable about things and I am beginning to get used to being in a cinema with a girl who talks a lot and touches me at regular intervals, the lights go dark and there is a fanfare, the curtains swish apart and flickering, scratched images announce the adverts from *Pearl and Dean*.

I sit in the flickering light and *Martini* and chocolates, tonic water and cigarettes wash over me and round me and into me, through my eyes and my ears, and I am conscious too of smells everywhere – the cigarette smoke in the cinema – old and stale; the faint and not v. nice odour of bodies; the perfume that was on the hanky she gave me in the stream; the greasy smell of the wimpy bar and another smell – something I can't place, something I have not experienced before. It must be her – her particular scent – her special smell – and it is quite pleasant and warm, almost friendly and somehow it reminds me of home and of being much smaller and of being hugged by my mother when I had fallen over and cut my knees.

I turn away from the man looking down his nose at the camera because a parrot has died from drinking the wrong tonic water, and I steal what is called, in the romantic novels my mother sometimes reads, a furtive look at her, at the girl who sits beside me. She is concentrating on the screen as if it really matters to her that *Martini* is the right one, the bright one, and she does not notice me looking at her. I glance more closely at her, my eyes wander over her, as it were.

She is relaxed and sits back in her seat; she is, if anything, leaning slightly to one side towards me and her hands are in her lap now, which makes a pleasant change from pawing all over my body, I can tell you. She is breathing quite heavily, like she is sleeping but the adverts are reflecting off her eyes and the lights in them dance back at me. Her chest rises and falls, then, slowly, 'languorously' is a word that springs to mind (and I think to myself that I must look it up in my Chambers 20th Century Dic. to see if it is the right word in these circumstances) she raises a hand to her face and rubs the tip of her nose with the tip of her forefinger really slowly and lazily and I don't know why, but I find this fascinating.

She drops her hand back into her lap and I wish she would touch her face once more. But she doesn't. Then I watch her breathing again. I find myself thinking that her chest is not so rounded, not so well formed as her mother's and I cannot see the nipples poking through her top – I think this is because she is only a teenager and also it is probably something to do with her underwear. As I believe I may have mentioned before, I have a passing acquaintance with the *Gossard Cross Your Heart Bra* as seen on Southern Television and I assume that she, Diana or whoever she is, has not discovered the mysteries and benefits of *'the lift and separation'* offered by this garment.

I sigh. I don't know why, I just do. I hadn't intended to, but I do. It is a long and rather tragic sigh and it must be quite loud because she suddenly looks at me. I look away hastily, back at the screen. But it is too late, out of the corner of my eye I can see that there is a little smile on her lips, just a slight up-turn at the corners of her mouth but definitely a smile. I don't know why but it makes feel unhappy, that smile. It is mysterious and grown-up. It is a smile from the OTHER world and I am a little shocked to discover that she lives in that world too. I had not realised that she was there when I am not and I feel curiously disappointed – like I did when Father Rogers told me in front of the whole class, that my Latin exercises that I had written out so carefully, were all completely wrong.

I was very hurt by that.

I was VERY LET DOWN by Father Rogers because I had made an especial effort, especially for him because I admire Father Rogers and it would not be beyond the bounds of possibility to think that we have a quite a lot in COMMON and I had thought, up until that point, that he shared a similar feeling.

I sit numbly looking at the screen and then, as the man tells us to *'go well, go Shell,'* I think that perhaps it doesn't matter if I don't have anything in common with Father Rogers after all, nor does it matter either if she is of that other world. Nearly everyone I have ever met is already there or ends up there and they all leave me behind eventually, in my world – my little lonely, completely-on-my-own world.

So it doesn't matter. I cannot touch Diana/Emma or whoever she is, or reach her or make her understand anything about me. In the end, when all is said and done, we are worlds apart and rather oddly that makes me feel quite content, if not happy. I can sit with her here in the cinema and I can buy her ices and eat Wimpies with her – but I do not have to be with her not REALLY BE WITH HER. I will stay here, alone and on my own.

So I smile at her in the dark cinema and she smiles back at me...

...And a man tells me, *'You're never alone, with a Strand...'*

They are showing the trailer for the next James Bond film and there is too much what you might call 'love interest' in it for my taste. Although I don't go to the cinema much, I have seen all the Bond films and I have to say that I prefer *The Man From UNCLE* on the telly – not just because you don't have to go out to see it but because it has all the advantages of guns and spying and the high-tech gadgets of Bond films but without the unnecessary relationships with women. Let's face it, you hardly ever see *Napoleon Solo* becoming involved with a 'sex siren!' And *Ilya Kuryakin* to my certain knowledge (and I am a big fan) has hardly ever looked twice at a woman – which is a good thing in my book for a man of silent but decisive action, such as the ice-cool Russian – as played by the angelic Mr McC.

On the other hand, you do get to see quite INTEREST-ING things *about* women in Bond films – like underwear and stockings and bikinis.

I like that. I don't like the sloppy love stuff but I do like that. I like what you might call the paraphernalia of women, if you follow me.

However, mainly I like the action in Bond films and I like the gadgets – like cars with rocket launchers and machine guns and jet packs. So, let's forget the romantic stuff and get on with the shooting and bombing etc. That, with a bit of underwear and some brief swimming costumes thrown in, would be my ideal Bond film.

I am thinking all of this just as James Bond is kissing a girl on a beach in a v. nice bikini and then shooting a man in a rubber suit through the stomach with a spear gun but I am suddenly distracted by a noise from behind me. There is a lot of giggling and a bit of muffled laughter, then seats in the row behind us creak as they are folded down and then some of them snap back shut with a thump and there is more giggling.

I know what has happened, even before he speaks, I know what has happened.

He whispers very loudly in my ear and he is so close to me that I can smell the hamburger on his breath and the stale cigarette smoke.

"ello Bog Brush!' He says. 'Fancy you bein' here.'

They have followed us. They are going to ruin the day and the film and they will get their revenge on us for what she said to them in the *Wimpy Bar*. I slide down into my seat and wish that it would fall through the floor and take me to another place far away.

His hamburger breath envelopes me and I feel him lean forward and push his sweaty head between me and the girl. I don't want to but I sort of look at him out of the corner of my eye, half turning my head to him and half trying to look away. He is grinning – first at me and then at her. He is like some mad monkey, hanging from a tree branch and grinning at both of us. I half expect him to start chattering at us with his lips pulled back to reveal his hideous teeth, like I have seen Orang-utans doing on *Zoo Time* with Desmond Morris. But he doesn't chatter, he grins and then he says.

'Well, Bog Brush, you didn't introduce me to your sister – which was very rude of you...' And he puts a kind of condescending sneer on the word 'very' and then he goes on: 'And your sister was *very* rude to me back there in the Wimpy, which was not *very* nice of your sister. Not *very* nice at all!' Then he grins at us again and without turning round he speaks to one of his gang by raising his voice.

''ere Steve...' He is talking to Steve Morris, who is in my class and who is, in my opinion a very unsavoury person whose school uniform is always dirty and who does not seem to be aware of or care about, the v.v. dubious white stains that he always has around his trouser flies.

''ere Steve,' repeats Edwards, 'Wouldn't you say that Boggy's sister was a bit rude to me, just now, in front of all those people in the Wimpy?'

Steve Morris inserts his dirty face into the conversation, leaning over the seat backs on the other side of Diana/Emma. He leans too close to her and he breathes into her face as he speaks so that she pulls back, looking disgusted.

'Definite..' He says. 'Definite, Teddy. She was dead rude. Disgustin' you might call it.'

From behind him, the others in Edwards gang, about five of them I reckon, make Neolithic grunting sounds which are about all they are capable of when it comes to conversation, in my opinion.

'You see,' says Edwards and he is speaking much too loudly for a public place. 'You see girl, I'm what you might call a friend of your little brother and I look after him and things at school and I reckon when a friend of your bro. asks to be introduced, you should be bleedin' nice about it and make the effort to come over and say hello – not call 'im a fuckin' arse'ole!'

'With his mouth full of shit.' Adds Steve Morris.

'Shurrup, pratt!' Snaps Edwards, who obviously does not want to be reminded of exactly what Diana/Emma said – not in front of everyone anyway.

I can't help but notice that Edwards is more common than ever and he is speaking even more badly than usual. Any trace of his middle class Surrey upbringing has now gone completely and I think to myself even through my total misery, that it is a sort of competition with her, with Diana/Emma, to show that he is just as rough and as dangerous as she is. I think this is totally stupid. I mean she *can't help* being common, whereas he does not have to be at all!

She just looks at him. For a second, when he had first sat down behind us, she had looked terrified but now her features are relaxed, although I notice that there is a dangerous glow in her eyes.

'Look...' She says, 'I just want to watch the film, so be quiet and stop bothering everyone. And also, pratt face, for your information, I am not his sister. All right?!'

Edwards seems genuinely taken aback at this news and both he and Steve Morris stare at her and then at me. I am not sure what this means. Either A) they will be impressed at me going out with a girl and I will be lifted into some higher opinion than they have of me now or B) they will be jealous and jeer at me every time they meet me and 'milk' me a lot.

I wish she hadn't said anything.

'You, 'is girlfriend?' Edwards says, slowly and incredulously, as if the idea was just too difficult to grasp.

'Just a friend,' she snaps back.

'Fuck me!' He says, which I think just about sums him up – bad language being the last vestige of the moron, as my father would say.

'I'd rather not,' she says, quick as a flash. 'I prefer my men to be human.'

I am suddenly aware of the fact that the cinema is going quiet and that the people in the seats near us are all beginning to look in our direction. The place isn't very full and there is no one actually in the rows we are in, nor indeed within the next few rows but nevertheless people are staring at us and this is quite APPALLING. I think several people have heard Edwards use the 'F' word and probably a few have heard her reply, judging from the way we are being looked at.

As you will have gathered I do not like being the centre of attention in public and the incident in the Wimpy is about all I could be expected to cope with in one day, in fact about all I could cope with in one lifetime! So this is now much too much for me. I am not meant for this sort of thing. I like the quiet life. So now, I desperately want to run away. I am starting to breath heavily and to sweat even more than usual and I am aware that a panic attack may be coming on.

Edwards's voice begins to drone on again and I realise he is telling her that she shouldn't be wasting her time with 'mongols' and 'spaz's' like me and he is saying again that she should apologize and if she does he will, '..show her a good time, as he and the boys know a place or two to go on a Saturday night...'

I can hear the other boys grunting and mumbling but suddenly, I am not listening to them. I am instead clinging to what I know best in such a dangerous and embarrassing situation. I am praying to the Lord our GOD, I am begging HIM to spare me all this and to save my soul and in this case my body, from the danger I am now in.

'*Our Father who art in Heaven hallowed be thy name, thy kingdom come, thy will be done on Earth as it is in Heaven, give us this day our daily bread and forgive us our trespasses as we forgive those that trespass against us...*'

Forgive? But do I forgive them? Do I forgive these gibbering, sneering, vicious boys who are determined to make me the centre of attention, in this faded cinema where my parents did their courting..? Forgive these boys who will beat me up and mock me and crown me with the thorns of their derision...as HE was crowned by the sneering, laughing crowds..?

Then I remember the chapel and how I thought Christ was bleeding on me, and I feel a sudden trickle of wetness and I lean forward and place a hand on my crotch to stem the flow, before it becomes too much. Thank you Lord, for letting me be wearing black jeans which will not show the damp patch...

I can feel the girl go tense next to me as Edwards chunters on about taking her out and showing her things that the cripple (me I assume) doesn't even know about! But she doesn't look round. Instead, she leans close to me and she says quite loudly, so that she can be heard in the row behind even over the giggling and the talking: 'They get a lot of rubbish in this cinema, don't they, on the floor like ice cream wrappers and fag ends and such..?' Then she pauses before saying in an icy voice, '..and there's quite a lot of it on the seats behind us too.'

The boys behind me go quiet. The people in the cinema who have been watching us seem to sit-up and take even more interest in what they probably thought was nothing but a rowdy group of teenage 'yobbos,' as my father would call us, but who are now sounding much more interesting.

Now I can sense that it is Edwards who has gone tense. I steal a glance at him and he is sitting very upright, his eyes are cold and he bristles with irritation. The corner of his left eye is twitching slightly but for once he seems to have run out of things to say. Then she turns round and she stares straight at him and she doesn't even blink. He stares back at her, surprised at the directness of her gaze.

'Listen mate,' she says in a sort of matter of fact and 'for your information' kind of way. 'We just want to watch the film, so why not just sit there quietly with your bum chums or just fuck off, like the little wanker you probably are!'

I cannot believe it. She has a filthy mouth. She says things that even Edwards does not say and she says them in really public places, like cinemas and burger bars and she doesn't seem to care who hears her. Not far away there is a middle-aged man and his wife and they look totally horrified and a boy and a girl, who have been kissing each other for at least five minutes, actually stop what they are doing (which is dead unhygienic by the way) and look up.

The usherette in black and white who has been watching us from half-way along the aisle, suddenly pulls herself straight and starts to bustle towards us, flashing her torch angrily and clucking in annoyance.

''Ere...' She says. 'You lot shut-up and stop all that filthy language... I'll call the manager, if you don't bloody shut up.'

But we all ignore her.

The gang and I are staring fixedly at Edwards and the girl, who are staring fixedly in their turn at each other. We are lost now in this conflict, this battle of two wills and I cannot believe that Diana/Emma or whoever she is can be doing this, that she is actually confronting Edwards and speaking to him like that – in public – or anywhere else for that matter.

I feel I should warn her and try to tell her that he will kill her, that he is really dangerous and that she is walking a 'precarious path' as they say, but I cannot warn her because A) she wouldn't listen to me B) she wouldn't care and C)if I say anything – either he, or she, will probably tell me to shut-up as well and I may put myself at risk from Edwards' violence or from her vengeance – both of which would, I suspect, be quite awful!

I feel hopeless and inadequate, watching the two of them staring at each other. Why, I think, am I always put in these situations? I just want to live my own quiet life but there is always someone who wants to take you out and put you on a bus or a train or a tube and drag you through a town and into a cinema and other places of similar EXTREME danger and then there is always some conflict or problem or difficulty just like this and you just cannot lead a peaceful life. 'Not for love nor money!' As my father would say.

I don't want to be here risking everything while she squares up to Edwards and spits revolting words in his face and he stares back at her trying not to blink and trying to think of something to say to her in return.

I know what will happen. He will stop staring at her and he will begin to swear at her. He may very well lash out, even though she is a girl. His gang will join in too and worse than all this, they will have a go at me and probably hurt me quite badly and also they will rip-up the seats, these old velvet seats that are part of my past, part of my family and they will cause a dreadful scene and we will all be thrown out of the cinema and the police will come and we will all get in trouble and I will be lumped in with them as a trouble-maker, and I will be expelled and disgraced by my school. So I slip further down in my seat and I try not to look round so that I will not antagonise Edwards and his gang even more than she already has.

Inside my head I start to pray, 'Dear Lord our God – let this trouble stop and let Edwards and his gang go away and do not let me be hurt and do not let Diana/Emma or whoever she is (and you know who she really is, better than any of us) be hurt either... Hail Mary, full of grace...'

I am trying very hard to climb inside my prayers and to reach a Holy State but it is hard to concentrate because beside me the small, blonde, freckled spitfire quivers with anger and indignation and I can feel the heat come off her body as she stares rigidly at my enemy, and I am aware of everyone in the cinema staring at us and I am aware of the usherette, who has become sort of frozen in time, staring at us too and pointing her torch in our direction. It is as if we are all there in a still frame in a film and we are waiting for something to happen. And then something does happen that I cannot believe.

Edwards lets out a sort of sigh and I sneak another quick glance at him. His head sort of slumps and he turns his eyes away from the girl and he looks half at the floor and half at the other side of the cinema.

'Sorry,' he croaks. And he is speaking to the usherette, who has come closer with her torch, but I know that actually he is speaking to Diana/Emma. 'Sorry,' he goes on. 'We just want to watch the film too... Sorry...'

Then he turns to his mates and some of his bluster comes back, although they are looking at him, dead astonished. 'And you lot can shut up too,' he says. 'I want to watch the film... Alright?' Then he falls back into his seat and focuses on the screen. The Usherette takes one last long look at us all and then turns on her heel, relieved that a fight hasn't broken out.

The gang sit back in their seats, strangely deflated and muted and the people who have been staring at us look away and back to their wives and lovers – disappointed probably, that something worse hadn't happened to spice-up their afternoon. She turns back and settles down beside me. She suddenly takes my arm in hers and leans close to me. 'Thanks for the help,' she says...

The curtains in front of the screen begin to swoosh wide apart and the lights go low. The certificate says that *The Graduate* is an 'X'...

So the film begins and I am a little surprised to find that *Simon and Garfunkle* (one of my top rated groups) are singing the title song. I had not known this. I've heard the song and got the record but am I the only person in the world who did not know it was from a film? Probably I think miserably to myself. I'm usually the last to know so many things.

Then I think about what she has just said, 'thanks for the help.' What did she mean? She hasn't put any particular stress on the words and she hasn't said it like 'dead' cynically, as in 'thanks for the help – you loser!' but equally she hasn't said it in a 'Thanks for the help, your silence definitely prevented him from lashing out..' kind of way either.

I suspect that she thinks I am a 'loser' but I am puzzled because she is clutching my arm and she is doing her very best to make it plain to Edwards and his gang, that this is what she is doing, by pushing herself very close to me and occasionally sort of 'scrunching' up still closer to me, with a little wriggle. I am v.v. confused, because at the same time that she is pushing herself close to me, somehow I know that she is not actually very close to me at all – not in every sense of 'close' anyway.

In fact in some ways I think she is moving away from me – but I cannot quite put my finger on how.

* * *

They are dead quiet through the film. They hardly move and when one of them farts so loudly that you can actually hear it, they hardly giggle at all – which in my experience is a miracle because when that happens in class they roll around and shriek like madmen. Personally I cannot understand why they cannot control themselves. Bodily functions can be controlled and should be kept for the toilet, in my b.

For me the film has been ruined because:

A) I am worried that the damp patch in my pants will soak through to my jeans and she will either feel it, because she seems to be placing her hands all over my body and she might easily stray into a wet area, or she will smell it as the temperature in both the cinema and in my personal areas begins to rise.

It is also ruined because...

B) I am very uncomfortable about all this touching and clutching that she keeps doing – especially as it now seems to be as much a show for Edwards and his gang as anything else.

And finally the film is ruined because...

C) I just cannot be comfortable with Edwards and his mates behind me. I find their very presence intimidating, even though they are sitting quietly and have apparently been subdued by the wild girl next to me.

The music, though, is dead brilliant and I already know all the songs from my record collection but to see them over pictures is amazing and I wish that if I could be anything in the world it would be Art Garfunkle's voice so that I could soar like it does high above the world and look down on the earth, like it seems to do when I listen to it.

I perk-up briefly when we catch a glimpse of Mrs Robinson's stockings and suspenders, which is something I really quite enjoy but apart from that I can hardly tell you what the film is about, except that at the end it all gets v. v. silly and Dustin Hoffman ruins someone's wedding and runs off with a much younger girl. Which is mad in my opinion, as he would definitely have been better off with good old Mrs R and her interesting black underwear.

The film ends and I am sort of relieved and terrified at the same time. In the dark, with the film playing I was safe but now I do not know what might happen. Edwards and his gang might decide that they have had enough of good behaviour and they might take their revenge on us – either here or perhaps outside in some alley behind the cinema. The answer is to stay here or avoid alleys I suppose, but of course neither of these solutions is very practical.

People are leaving the cinema. I notice that one or two of them glance in our direction – so that they can get a good look at the trouble makers I suppose, now the lights are up to full.

Diana/Emma doesn't seem to want to move. I think it must be because she too is aware of our very AWKWARD situation. The gang behind us seem quite reluctant to move as well. But finally there is a clunking of seats snapping up-right and they begin to drift away. They do not look at us and they don't seem to look at Teddy Edwards either, who stays seated. In fact they seem dead subdued and they only mutter to each other in low voices, which is not like they usually are at all.

I look at the girl, she is still staring at the screen even though the lights are up and everyone is leaving. The credits for all the people who made the film are still showing and she is watching them, like they are really interesting or something. White on black, obscure names that we have never heard of doing weird jobs that I don't care about, crawl across the screen.

...*Mick Aston, Best Boy; George Ardinni, Car Wrangler; Dick Thoroughgood, Stand By Prop...*

So what? I think.

But I am pleased to see that all the songs by *Simon and Garfunkle* are listed at the end, and just watching the names going by is good and makes me hear the music again in my head. Then it really is over and there is not even the screen to see because the curtains have been pulled closed. So I slowly stand-up looking down at the top of her head. She looks up at me and her eyes are kind of misty and a bit wet – strain from watching those flickering white names I suppose.

'That was brilliant,' she says. 'Don't you think that was brilliant?'

I try to look enthusiastic but my mind is on the brooding, hunched figure of Teddy Edwards who I can see out of the corner of my eye. 'Yes,' I say. 'I liked the music best. I've got all the songs in my record collection.' I do not tell her that I liked the black suspenders and stockings too, for obvious reasons.

She stands up and we edge our way along the row to the aisle. Edwards has stood up and he is level with us, making his way along his row. We sort of meet him, awkwardly in the aisle and he seems to be blocking our way as he steps right out in front of the girl. She stops and looks defiantly at him. She has a sort of grin on her face.

'And what did you think of it, wanker?' She says.

But she says it in a kind of jokey way, like when she has called me 'wanker' in the past and I am a bit taken aback at this. He takes a breath and I think he is going to swear at her.

'Please God, help us…' I pray inside my head.

'I think…' Edwards begins. '…I think it was brilliant. I really liked the bit where he goes to her house for the first time and at the start when he's just lying there in the swimming pool and his family are all around him dead annoying him… It's like dead real. I know how it feels. I feel like that at home, you know… sometimes…'

And he tails off and I am really surprised. At school when they give Edwards a really good book like a classic such as *Charles Dickens* or *William Golding*, he is just plain rude about it and he has nothing to say when he is asked to comment on it but here he is sounding like *Jack Tinker* in my mother's *Daily Mail*.

I stare at him. She stares at him too and then she says,

'Yeah, I know. I guess we all feel like that. My Mum bugs me sometimes and my brother. He can wind you up.'

Edwards looks at me.

She laughs. 'Not him. I told you. He's *really* not my brother. He's just a friend.' I feel v. hurt at this. Suddenly I don't want to be JUST a friend. Something has happened here I realise, and I am getting confused. I feel like something is taking place in front of me and I may already have missed a bit of it. This happens a lot in my life, as you know, but this time it is really unexpected and v.v. sudden.

Then she starts to walk towards the exit and I find that I am behind them, behind her and Edwards and they are side by side and this is pretty bad and makes me feel very silly and even more so when I hear her say, 'So what you doing now then? Thought you knew somewhere good for Saturday evenings? That's what you said.'

Now we are in the foyer and I notice the woman in the ticket booth is looking at us and she has got her arms crossed in a defensive way, so she has obviously heard about what went on before the film began but Diana/Emma doesn't notice – she is looking at Edwards and they are laughing together at something he has said that I haven't heard, which she obviously thinks is dead funny. Then I hear her say. 'All right then. I'll have to give my mum a call first 'cos I said we'd be back after the film.'

And Edwards says. 'Is Boggy comin' then?'

She gives him a sharp look and says, 'His name's Billy.' Then she turns to me. 'You coming with us then, Billy or what?'

I am completely confused. What is it that was said as they walked through the foyer that I haven't heard? Where are they going? How come, I think, that I was with her and now I feel like I am hanging *around* her instead? 'I don't know...' I say. 'Where are you going?'

And I am panicking because it has all gone wrong and I have lost control and also because her invitation to me seems a bit half-hearted and if she doesn't let me go with her then I will be stuck here in this town outside of the cinema without the faintest idea how to get home as I have never caught a bus on my own before and I have no idea which bus I need or where it goes from.

They are both looking at me.

'We just said!' She says, and I think she sounds a bit annoyed. '...To the fair!' She snaps at me.

I look at her blankly.

'There's a funfair,' she says. 'On the other side of town, by Parker's Park.'

'I don't know,' I say.

But I do know. I know that I have to go. I have no choice – but what is worse I can see in her eyes that she knows I have to go, and she doesn't want me to.

I can't work any of this out. She hardly knows me, that's true, she has only met me twice but she has thrown water at me in a stream, she has helped me when I have been sick and she has taken me home and introduced me to her mother *and* she has brought me into town and to the cinema and a Wimpy bar. I mean, I know that hardly makes us what the Sunday Papers would call 'a couple' but it must mean something; more at least than making friends with your worst enemy in just under five seconds flat and deciding to go off to a funfair without consulting you or considering the dangers and difficulties such a situation can cause. Yes... I am confused... And yes, I am even more confused to find myself in the midst of Edwards' laughing, sneering, farting, belching gang marching through town and barging into people who are in our way, hustling them off the pavement and making too much noise. At least that's what they do, the gang. Me? I just trail along with them, being largely ignored by them as they roll their shoulders and strut through the streets in their denim jackets and their flares as we all march along behind the figures of Edwards and the girl with the blonde hair – who have become our leaders.

I do not wish to be here.

I am praying so hard in my head that I might somehow get home. I do NOT want to be here! I REALLY do not. But dusk is falling and in the distance I can see the flashing lights of the funfair and the eerie electronic blue glow that it throws into the sky above Parker's Park and I can hear the sound of pop music and the noise of the dodgems and that funny shrieking sound that you always get with fairs...

And the prayers aren't working...

In between the prayers as we walk along, my head is full of the big q. Which is: 'Why are we doing this?' Why does she want to be with Edwards, who she hates, when we could be on the bus on our way home?

I don't understand.

I don't understand what they can see in a funfair that is better than going home or being out in the fields and looking up at the moon and being with God in your head. Which is why I am different, I suppose. Just a little bit different.

* * *

As you know, I am a bit of an expert on modern popular music – and there is nothing wrong with that in my book. Every boy needs a hobby and that, together with my love of dissection, gives me a fairly wide range of interests and as my parents often say, '...An active mind is a happy mind.' But the music at the fair is terrible and would not make anyone happy!

For a start it is too loud and there is more than one piece of music being played at once; the dodgems have got some old *Billy Fury* going, the waltzers are playing *Bill Hayley* and there is a sort of terrible sound track from an old horror film, complete with screams and moans, coming from the House of Horrors. The Tunnel of Love is playing some really cheesy thing, which I think is by *Matt Monro* – but as I have never listened to him as he is simply oily and revolting and should have stayed a bus conductor in my opinion, I am not sure if I am right. BUT it is *so* bad that I probably am!

So, there is all this music and it is all clashing with other bits of music and it is all too loud and it is all terribly distorted – as it is being played over really bad amplifiers, not like the excellent *Marshall* amps, as favoured by Rock gods such as *The Who* and *The Rolling Stones*. The sound is so terrible that it is making me feel sick as I stand by the dodgems and watch the little cars go hurtling round and smacking into each other.

All of Edwards's gang are on the dodgems and they are screaming and swearing and deliberately driving full tilt into one another and into complete strangers who are only there to enjoy themselves, not be barged around and jolted into and sworn at. They are behaving so badly that at one point the man who runs the dodgems has to turn off the electricity and go over and talk to them. I cannot hear what he says but

I guess he has tells them that he will throw them off if they don't behave better. I just hope no one recognises that they are from our school as this will undoubtedly bring the school and the Catholic Church into disrepute locally – and that would be a v. v. bad thing.

Of course, Diana/E is on the dodgems too and she is sharing a car with Edwards who is doing the driving and showing off by trying to hit everyone and everything as hard as he can. She asked me if I was going to go on the dodgems and I said 'yes,' because I thought she had meant with her but she smiled and said, 'Good. See, you can enjoy yourself, if you try hard enough!'

Whatever that meant!

And then she got into a car with Edwards, which made me feel really small and silly, so I made some excuse about just popping over for some candy floss and I turned away and sort of ran towards the candy floss stall knowing that the dodgem ride would have started before I could get back. I could feel her watching me go, so of course I really did have to buy some candy floss (which means I now have only seventeen shillings left of my money) and I have to stand here with this big, pink fluffy thing on a stick, looking like a complete wazzack, watching them while they roar around.

And I hate candy floss.

In fact I hate most sweets. I have what the Supplements call a 'sophisticated palette' and I enjoy such things as prawn cocktail and cheese fondue – as my mother makes for her visitors on Saturday evenings when she and my dad have what they call their 'soirées'.

The music is awful. The dodgems are silly. Edwards and his gang are appalling and I am having a really lousy time because I still cannot work out what has happened. How come I go to town with D/E and she goes on the dodgems with Edwards? It is of course I realise, as I discreetly chuck my candy floss into a rubbish bin, to do with that Other World thing again. Somehow in the Other World which I do not understand, something has happened between her and Edwards that has turned two mortal enemies into friends in less than five seconds.

I will never understand this and if I did I would probably not be the person I am and I suspect that it is better to be the person I am than something different. After all God made us all and he chose to make me this way and not another way – so that must make it all right, whatever I do, or whatever other people think of me. This should be a comforting thought, especially *in view of what is going to happen to me over the next few weeks...*

But for now, I am standing by the rubbish bin and I am staring at the girl who brought me to this place as she thumps and bumps and jostles her way round the dodgems. I have sort of focused in on her while I have been thinking and it is like you see sometimes on telly programmes where everything goes out of focus in the picture, apart from the one thing you should be looking at. In this case all the other dodgem cars and Edwards' gang and Edwards himself have disappeared from my view and all I can see is Diana/Emma, with her hair streaming out behind her, her freckles, her smiley face and her white teeth because she is open mouthed and laughing... laughing... laughing...

She is laughing because she is having fun. Because she is at a fun fair and she has had a brilliant day eating Wimpies and seeing a brilliant film and walking through the streets and riding on a bus and because she has done all this with me and I am different from anyone she has ever met before and I make her laugh and I puzzle her and I fascinate her. I am all those sexy movie stars we were talking about: I am Dustin Hoffman, and Paul Newman and Donald Sutherland... and... and Oliver Reed and anyone she wants me to be... all rolled into one. I am her idea of sexiness – sexiness on a stick like fluffy, pink candy floss. She turns to look at me and I realise that she is looking at me in the same way that she was watching the credits at the end of the film, with damp eyes and a kind of misty, faraway look.

And somehow, even though I am over by the rubbish bin I can lean in towards her, I can put my face very, very, close to hers and I can almost smell her perfume and touch her lips. But then I realise that Diana has gone. As I lean into her, her face is changing. It is older. It is more freckly and it isn't Diana in the dodgem car at all. It is her mother and she has her head thrown-back and she is laughing and shrieking as she jolts and bumps into other cars. And when she does hit the other cars they sort of evaporate away, like little puffs of steam. Anything she drives into just blows away and vanishes and she is laughing at this incredible power she has to destroy all the dodgem cars filled with Edwards' horrible gang.

She is pursuing them, chasing them – she is avenging all the people they have hurt and made to look stupid.

Poof! Poof! She touches some more cars and they vanish in little puffs of steam. Poof! Poof! Two more gone and lost forever. Poof! Goodbye Steve Morris! Poof! You deserved it Will Larkin! Poof! Take that Jim Milligan.

Emma's Mum – my avenging angel. Diana's Mum in a chariot of fire! And it is a chariot that is going faster and faster.

Round and round the Dodgems it goes, faster and faster.

Now I can see something else, quite clearly, even here by the rubbish bin, I see that the speed of the dodgem has pushed the flimsy cloth of her blouse close to her chest, so close that her nipples are showing through it, really clearly. I can easily see her firm, protruding nipples and they are getting larger and firmer as the cold night air whips against them, they are protruding through her shirt, hard, perfectly curved, her stiff, thrusting nipples, that I want to reach out and touch...

'Wassup with you, Wanker?'

It could only be the girl. No one else can call you 'wanker' without really insulting you. It can only be her. She is standing close to me and looking at me, with a puzzled look in her face. I try to focus and understand what has happened. It is like everything has been in black and white and it is now gradually returning to colour. It is like I have been somewhere else, asleep or in a dream and I am having to wake up again and sort out what is real and what was a dream. I suppose I stare at her for a second because she says, 'Shut your mouth, idiot, you look like a goldfish!'

I shake my head a little to clear it and to be honest I am a little shaken-up by what has happened. I know that the odd things I see (of which this is only the latest) are some kind of visions or revelations but I have always rather thought that being such a religious person and seeing as how I spend q. a lot of time in prayer and a HOLY STATE, that one day these visions would become more like St. Bernadette's or even St Paul's on the road to Damascus. I am therefore, a bit disappointed to find that this latest revelation is a bit like the others in its triviality and involves yet again, a strong emphasis on Diana's mum's nipples! I suppose this one has been brought about because of:

A) my extremely stressful and unusual day..
And..
B) Excess of blood sugar from eating Candy Floss. (Only two mouthfuls but you never know). I have recently read an article in the *Femail* pages of the *Daily Mail* about what too much sugar in our children's diet can do to their health and well-being and *Femail* is seldom wrong in the opinion of my mother and myself.

I swallow hard. I breathe deeply and so I get a grip on myself and speak to the girl.

'Sorry,' I say. 'I was daydreaming...' And I add, 'I think.' Which I had to do, to make sure that what I had said wasn't inadvertently a lie.

She give me a long curious look. 'The once over' they'd call it in a gangster film.

'The boys have gone to the House of Horrors but I don't want to go,' she says.

I can't think who the 'boys' are and then I realise that she means Edwards and his gang.

The Boys??!

I cannot believe that she is calling this tawdry mob 'the boys'. It makes them sound like *The Beatles* or something.

'So,' she is going on. 'What shall we do? You haven't been on anything yet. Do you want to try the Waltzer..? or the Flying Teacups or have a go on the coconut shy and see if you can win me one?' Suddenly she takes my arm, just like she has been all day, and she is pushing herself close to me again. It is all too confusing. Why does she keep grappling me and smiling at me and making me feel so… so… well, so belonged to, and then going off on the dodgems with Edwards? How can she do that with such an awful creature and what does she want of me? I stare at her and I cannot think what to say as she tugs at my arm and grins at me.

'The Dodgems,' I suddenly say. 'Yes. Let's go on The Dodgems – 'cos I missed the last ride, 'cos I wanted some candy floss.'

'OK,' she says. 'You may take me on the dodgems, young sir.'

She is doing her funny voice and being a lady from the Edwardian era or something, like has she done before. But as we walk off towards the Dodgems I can't help but notice that she glances back at the rubbish bin and at my uneaten candy floss that perches on top of the overflowing litter… And I feel a bit of a fool.

We sit in a manky old Dodgem car that has definitely seen better days if you ask me. It is very battered and most of the yellow paint has been chipped off it. Also there is quite an unpleasant odour and although I don't say anything in order not to upset her, I suspect that someone has been sick inside it at some point.

The bell rings and the terrible music starts but we just sit there and we don't move. She looks at me as if I am mad. 'Well press the accelerator, you loon!' She says.

I look at my feet and see the little metal pedal and I realise that the car won't start unless I put my foot on it – well, I am not a qualified driver when all is said and done.

Suddenly I jolt forward and I nearly crack my head on the steering wheel. I look around furiously at the grinning idiot who has cannoned into the back of us.

'Pratt!' I say.

Immediately I feel awful, like I did when I called the girl a 'b--ch.' It is definitely not a Christian thing to do, to swear – and I do not know what has come over me.

The man who has driven into us has a leather jacket with studs in it and a girlfriend with lots of make-up and blonde hair piled on top of her head.

'Fuck off!' he says to me as he reverses away.

'Little tosser!' His girlfriend says.

I am appalled.

Diana/Emma is giggling and takes no notice at all of the terrible insults that have been hurled at me.

'Press the accelerator harder,' she says. 'And drive into someone for Gawd's sake or just drive anywhere.'

I decide to ignore her blasphemy as it is essential that I move the screeching little vehicle out of the way of another yobbo who seems determined to smash into us head first.

We start to make some progress round the track and I realise the safest bet is to head right for the outside of the arena and hug the barricade and go as slowly as I can. Diana/Emma keeps glancing at me as we make our way round in our slow but safe circle.

'This is exciting,' she says.

'Some of the driving in here,' I say firmly to her, 'Is not of a standard you would expect.'

For some reason she starts to giggle again. Then she puts her hand over one of mine, which is clutching the steering wheel. 'Oh, Billy,' she says. 'You are a one off.'

Again, as so often happens with her, I am not sure what she means, but she is smiling and seems happy, so I let it go and instead I say what is bothering me. 'Look...' I begin. 'Look, have you had a good day, today?'

'Yeah,' she says. 'But I think we could risk going out into the middle, don't you?'

I carry on round the outside edge as I am driving and I reckon the choice, therefore, is mine.

'And it was alright... the film I mean..?'

'Yeah,' she says again. 'It was great. Couldn't you go a bit faster.'

'And the ice cream..?'

'What?'

'The ice cream in the Wimpy, that I bought you, for two and ninepence... was that OK?'

She suddenly seems a bit annoyed and says, 'Yeah, fine. And how was the burger and shake that I bought you for nearly a quid?'

'It was OK,' I say. 'But you can't get the greasy taste out of your mouth for ages afterwards. And it was a bit cold and the chips were soggy, but it was OK.'

'Oh, good!' She says and there is a certain 'tone' in her voice that makes me think she may be a little upset about something.

'So I was wondering,' I continue carefully. 'I was wondering you know, about you and Edwards... '

I trail off because I can't think what to say next.

'Teddy?' she says. 'What about him?'

So it's '*Teddy*' now, is it? I think to myself.

'Edwards is a bit 'formal' don't you think?' She says 'formal' in one of her 'la di da posh-lady voices' and I get that horrible feeling that I may have spoken out loud again.

'He's alright,' she carries on. 'You want to stop winding

him up at school and he'd probably leave you alone. Look at it this way, he's only like my brother – you know always showing off and trying to be bigger than he is. Once you slap him down he's alright.'

I look at her and I can't believe what she is saying. *Me*? Winding *him* up? I immediately regret looking at her as I crash the Dodgem into the wall and have to try some tricky manoeuvring to get back onto my nice safe circuit. While I am doing this she carries on talking.

'You frighten him I expect, 'cos you're more clever than him with your long words and posh voice but he's all right really... In fact he's a bit of a gas!'

A gas! A gas! I do not know what she can mean but I can't help thinking of *The Rolling Stones* and *Jumping Jack Flash*.

'He's just a posh as I am,' I say. 'He goes to the same school and his Dad owns that big garage on the Leeford road and he has a flooring firm in Winchester.'

'I know,' she says and then she says something very mysterious. 'Being posh isn't just about how much money, you have Billy.'

I am thinking about what to say next and about what she means when the yob in the leather jacket with the blonde girlfriend crashes into us again, really hard and sends us spinning back into the barrier. He must know these rides because as soon as he has done this the bell rings and the power is cut off for the end of our turn – so I can't possibly get revenge. We get out of the car and she takes my arm again, which is nice but spoilt because I can see Leather Jacket flicking two fingers at me as he leads his girlfriend towards the burger stall.

I am dragged by Diana/E to the Coconut Shy, to the Lucky Dip and to the hot dog van for my second greasy meal of the day and because of that my stomach is too upset to go on the Big Dipper. So I watch the others go instead and once again she shares the ride with Edwards but I am quite pleased to see that Steve Morris is totally green when the ride finishes and he disappears for quite some time into the bushes on the other side of the park.

I think we are never going to go home but at nearly ten o'clock she announces that she has to get back and asks me if I am going too? Which is a silly q. if you ask me. As if I would stay!

She knows where the bus stop is, which I think is very impressive as we are on a completely different side of town from where we arrived and soon enough we are on the bus and on our way home. She is sitting next to me and I am squashed up against the glass window. But we don't speak to each other for ages. We are tired I reckon. I know I am.

It is completely dark outside in the country lanes but it has begun to rain and I can see trickles of water running down the glass and when the bus goes quicker they are swept back and break into little dark drops. I watch them until my breath mists-up the glass on my side and I can't see them anymore.

I keep thinking about *Simon and Garfunkle* and boarding a Greyhound bus with a girl called Kathy in Pittsburgh...

Dina/Emma looks at me. I have done it again and obviously I have sung the lyric out loud.

'It's Leeford,' she says. 'And we've got a long way to go to look for America.'

And I keep thinking of what Edwards said to her when we left for our bus.

'See you then,' he said

And she had said, 'Yeah, I'll see you around'.

* * *

Twenty minutes later we get off the bus at the stop near the theatre. It is v. v. dark where we are but down the lane the floodlights are still on all over the theatre and it sits there glowing in the dark night like some sort of weird spaceship that has landed in the middle of the fields. There are lights on too in the windows of the Brewers' Cottages and further along the lane you can see the first lights of the village.

One or two cars are driving away from the theatre car park, and they splash past us as we walk towards the lights and I guess they must be the people who work there as the play would have finished ages ago – which shows how v. late it is. I am suddenly a bit worried about the time, as I have not told my parents to expect me so late.

'What's the time?' I ask the girl.

'Oh, you speak then!' She says.

I glance at her.

'Only you haven't said a word since we got on the bus.'

Fair enough I think. I haven't because I haven't had anything to say. I'm not one to waste words and the breath required for them if I haven't got anything much to say.

'Sorry,' I mutter. 'I was tired and I was thinking... You didn't say anything either.'

'I was thinking too,' she says.

'What about?'

And then I realise that may be a bit personal and rather rude, so I add, 'If you don't mind me asking.'

'I don't,' she says. 'I was thinking that the film was good and the fair was good and Teddy was a laugh and that you are pretty odd but I quite like you and that if it has been a nice day, which it has, then why do I feel a bit... well, a bit miserable... You know, deep down, inside... It's just so diffi-cult isn't it, to be completely happy, even when you should be... Sometimes I think all we can ever do is hope to be hap-py and that's what keeps us going and if we knew the truth we'd just all of us give up bothering... If you follow me?'

I don't, to be honest and I'm a bit taken aback by all this:

A) Because it is a very long answer and a lot to think about when I am tired and it is still drizzling and v. dark and I have v. long way still to walk home through the lanes unless I am going to cut across the fields, which I do not really want to do in the pitch black.

B) I am completely gobsmacked that anyone could find Ed-wards (I *cannot* call him *Teddy)* 'a laugh!'

C) I am not good with people's emotions and feelings. And finally...

D) I do not understand what she means when she says the thing about not being completely happy...

I suspect that this may be something that is quite, what they call 'esoteric' but as I don't know what 'esoteric' is I am not sure. And I make a mental note to look the word up in my good old Chambers 20th C Dic.

We carry on trudging up the lane with our heads bowed against the rain and I think I really ought to say something but nothing will come to me that is worth saying or is appropriate to the mood she has now created. Then suddenly, all the lights in the theatre go out. Just like that – in one swift 'click' and we are plunged into even deeper darkness. It is like a black velvet cloth being thrown over my head.

'It's eleven thirty,' she says. 'They're on a timer, because we all complained, in the cottages, you know, that we couldn't sleep if they stayed on all night.'

I suppose it is the shock of the darkness but we have stopped walking and we are standing together staring into the blackness at where the theatre used to be. Then I feel her move in the black velvet even though I can't see her, but she is not moving away from me as I expect instead I can smell her perfume very close to me and then I can feel her breath, hot against my face – it smells a little of the hotdogs she ate earlier but mostly it is warm and damp against my face. Then I feel her hand on my arm and her other hand drops onto my shoulder.

'Billy...' She whispers in the dark.

And her lips, a little dry and cracked, brush against mine. I freeze. My whole body goes tense. She presses her lips against mine and they linger there for a moment and I do not know what to do about it. My hands hang by my sides, I feel a knot in my stomach and I can hear blood rushing in my ears. To be honest I am terrified. Then she lets go of my shoulder and slips her arm through mine.

'Come on,' she says, as if nothing has happened. 'I want to get home.'

She almost drags me along the lane, past the theatre towards her house.

I don't speak. I can't.

She has nothing to say either.

* * *

We are outside her front door in less than a minute, the broken gate swinging behind us. There is a light on in the hallway but the rest of the house looks dark. She pushes the door open and I am pretty amazed at this. I have to take my Yale Key with me everywhere I go; my mother is horrified at the idea of a front door being unlocked after nine p.m.

'Shh!' She says to me, although I haven't said anything.

I step into the hallway with her, which on reflection, I think, is a dumb thing to do as I really ought to just say good night and make my way home. But somehow I want to be there. There is a sinking feeling in my stomach though, and I am terrified by what has just happened and even more so by what may now happen – but somehow I do really want to be there, with her in this sleeping house. She closes the door v. v. quietly behind us but even so as soon as it clicks closed, a sleepy voice calls from upstairs.

'Di..? Diana? Is that you?'

'Yes, Mum... I'll be up in a tick.'

'Lock the door, will you.'

Diana/Emma replies that she will, but in fact she just stands there with her finger to her lips and we both stay v. still like a couple of statues, with our backs to the door looking-up at the empty staircase. I am waiting for her to do something; I sense that she is in charge – though come to think of it I guess she has been in charge since the moment I met her.

A long time seems to go by without either of us moving and I start listening to the ticking of the clock that I can hear through the kitchen door. Then suddenly, and I am not at all ready for this, she spins round and pushes me back against the front door. The impact of her body against me almost knocks the air out of me and I make a sort of 'puffing' sound.

The next thing I know I can feel her wet duffle coat pressed up against my nylon wind-cheater and yet again I feel her hot breath on me. As she is a fair bit taller than me I have to look up at her. She has a funny far away look in her eyes and one of her hands has snaked round to the back of my neck and she is sort of tugging at my hair. Then she starts pressing hard against me – her whole body pushing me back into the door and she starts to move up and down on me rubbing her body, as it were, against mine.

It is quite a shock, I can tell you!

And it is even more of a shock to feel her breasts pushed against me, right through her duffle jacket. I can feel them really distinctly, quite firm against my own chest...and her thighs – she is pressing her thighs hard against mine and massaging them up and down, up and down...

She doesn't say anything at all while this is going on but she is breathing v.v. heavily and staring at me dead intently... she has what you might call a manic look.

Then she bends her head down to me and presses her mouth against mine. Her lips aren't dry any more... in fact, they are q. wet. She kind of moves them over mine, rubs them over me and then she starts to suck at my lips, opening hers a little to nuzzle at me – it reminds me of when I saw our old dog Bessie (now dead) suckling her pups. Then to my utter horror she starts to try and prize my lips apart – and she is doing so *with her tongue!!!!*

It is a really hard, pointy, wet little tongue and she is trying to push it into my mouth. My legs are going weak and

I push my hands flat behind me against the front door to gain some kind of support. She must feel me move them, because without pausing in her tongue manoeuvres she reaches her hand round and grabs one of mine and pulls it away from the door. I cannot resist her because I would if I could, I can assure you. She raises my hand and twisting her body slightly, she pulls her duffel coat aside and she places my hand firmly over her left breast.

I do not squeeze. I would like to make that quite clear. I do not feel, press or squeeze. I have been praying repeatedly since all this happened and one of the things I have made clear in my confessions and requests for forgiveness is that I took no active part.

Forgive me Lord. Forgive me. The spirit is willing but the flesh...

The flesh is round and firm and milky white, that's what I keep thinking and that's what I am thinking right now, as she pushes my hand firmly over her breast.

But at that moment (and I thank you God, as we cannot imagine what all this might have led to) at that moment there is a sound from above and it is definitely creaking floorboards and then I hear a door open in the landing.

A light comes on at the top of the stairs. Diana/Emma/whatever, leaps away from me and instantly assumes a casual attitude about three feet to my left. I am not sure if I look quite so casual. I am feeling somewhat stunned and I think my mouth is hanging open and I feel hot and uncomfortable, as well as damp and wet from the night air.

I look up and I see Emma's Mum leaning over the banister at the top of the stairs and she is looking straight down at us.

She blinks as she tries to focus on us.

'Oh,' she says and her voice is quite sleepy. 'I didn't know you were here Billy.'

And she gives me the sort of look that says I shouldn't actually be there at all.

'Diana hurry up and say goodnight..'

Then she looks at me again.

'Goodness knows what your folks'll say, young man!'

'It's alright,' I croak. 'I'm off now.'

'Goodnight then,' she says pointedly, and even more pointedly she adds, 'And be quick Diana!'

She disappears into the shadows of the landing.

Diana/Emma grins at me and tilts her head to one side. 'Phew!' She whispers with a little laugh. 'Right then. Off you go.'

Just like that. 'Right. Off you go!'

She swiftly opens the door and she pushes me out into the wet, dark night and leaning against the half closed door she says to me, 'You take care in the dark.' And then she says, 'See you then.'

And I say, 'Yeah, I'll see you around.'

And she closes the door on me and leaves me in the dark. She doesn't even give me a second look.

But it is not the kiss that has given me the enormous erection that presses against the inside of my Jockey Y's, nor the feel of her breast and her body rubbing over me; it is not even the fact that she has said to me this time, and not to Edwards, that 'she will see me...' No, what has given me this slight impairment to the way I walk down the garden path – what has given me this hot throbbing embarrassment in the top of the leg region was the sight, through the banisters, of Diana's mum's legs, which I had not realised were so v. v. long.

Also I am v. excited by having seen them through the gap in her dressing gown which fell open as she talked to us and which, most tantalisingly of all, revealed something black and lacy in the way of undergarments; something with suspenders attached to black silky stockings, that cling to shapely thighs: undergarments just like the ones Mrs Robinson wore, I realise.

So, I am *The Graduate* then, I think.

And then the guilt begins. How will I ever make amends with my MAKER?

I walk through the dark roads and in front of my eyes burns the cross of Jesus. He has suffered for me and this is how I repay him, ogling women in black suspenders and fondling their daughters. I see the flames lick around HIS feet, I see the blood drip from his crown of thorns but sometimes the image of my Lord fades away and I see a pair of long legs and black underwear instead...

...And they too burn deep in my soul.

I am going out with a boy!!

I might even be going out with two boys!!!

Bllooodddddyyy!!!! Heeeellll!!!!!

Yes. It's dead bloody true – I am!!

What is more I got a snog last night. My first proper, real, dead groovy, dead sloppy, tongue on tongue, lips pressed together snogerooney!!!

I can't wait to tell Vicky and Karen – who have only ever had a quick squeeze in the back of the village hall with that Mong Charlie Hooper (Not together at the same time, that would be *revolting* but nevertheless on the same night!) They didn't speak to each other for weeks after that. I wouldn't touch Charlie Hooper with a bleedin' barge pole, as he is not only unfaithful but has black heads and his breath smells of fish paste!

I have at last met THE boy in the woods (when I say *met* I mean I have at last tracked him down and got him cornered – it's taken ages but is dead worth the effort). The whole thing is like a nineteenth century novel like what we do in Eng. Lit and might be by Bronte or another romantic writer like Barbara Kartland! Or is it Cartland? (Who cares, she's fucking awful anyway).

He (THE boy) is a wild child and a creature of the woods and fields just as I suspected from seeing him on the bus and he is very close to nature. His face is brown from the sun and dirt and he has scratches (various) over his arms and hands and knees, and I know all this 'cos our whole first conversation took place with him in his keks. Yes!!! Only in his keks!

I think he was worshipping the sun as I found him on his knees praying. He told me he was doing a school-play but I know he was praying! I think he took his clothes off to worship the sun and the trees.

I imagine it is something Catholics do. He is one.

I started by teasing him and I definitely thought he was a bit of a pratt but when you come down to it he is a BLOKE who can string three words together and that body..! WOW!!! THAT BODYYYYYY!!! And there aren't many of them around in these here parts, let's face it!

Turns out he's quite nice and quite interesting as well as handsome. And he does have dead gorge brown eyes – which look almost black sometimes – and quite big shoulders, though he does have a loser's haircut, like it was done in borstal or the army or something! But SO WHAT – anything is better than the useless twat boys like we have in Wilmot Lane Secondary Modern, with their bad manners and acne and small brain cells lodged in their low browed stone-age heads!

Billy, that's his name, (Note – what's his other name??? – Find out!) says daft things – he said 'amen' on the bus – which is bleeding Weirdsville Arizona!! and he is generally quite odd.

I found him the other day by a stream and he had been drinking – because he threw-up. BUT I thinks that's OK. You can't tame his wild soul. He is an independent spirit and his head is spiritual and in the clouds – in that sense he is a bit like the Dalai Lama or even Cat Stevens!

He called me a bitch, (Billy not the Dalai Lama) – admittedly I had thrown cold water over him but it was bloody rude. I have forgiven him for it but it was touch and go. I told him never, NEVER to say that again. If he does I will punch him in the balls. I suppose in a way it shows his ~~mavorik mavarik~~ wild nature.

Having said that, you have to admire his passion. We went for a wimpy in grotty old Leeford, and he said bloody interesting things about The Monkees and other stuff – and he really came alive – eyes flashed, and fists clenched – and that's when I decided we would have to snog.

BUT…

BUTTERY… BUT..

That's also where we met TEDDY.

Oooh! Teddy. Teddy. Teddy.

Boy number two in this week of BOYS, BOYS, BOYS and more BOYS!!!

Teddy is a real REBEL (like Mick Jagger or that actor that drove over the cliff in that old American film from the

1950s). He is bloody good looking – sort of rough and muscular and he has a bloody sexy gold wrist chain and another round his neck – which could have made him look a pratt but in fact suits his RUGGED deem demean demeanour good looks.

He doesn't give a fuck about anything and he is dead rude and he will probably get expelled, Billy says. His hair is bloody gorge. And he has it greased up into a kind of quiff and his jeans are so tight you can see everything – I mean *everything* inside them!!

He is a *dangerous* boy...

He came with us to the cinema and tried to be a bit arsy. I reckoned he was total pratt at first (though a bleeding good looking one!!) and I told him to shut his fucking bollocking head – or something like that and he was dead bloody shocked, I can tell you!

They should come to Wandsworth on a Friday evening after school, if they want to hear some real bad language!

Anyway, he and his mates are bleeding good fun and we went to the fair with them and had a right laugh. He kind of grew on me – he likes having a good time and you don't have to think too hard and he can be really, REALLY funny.

Billy is bloody serious – but ARTISTIC. Teddy isn't what you'd call bright but he is a LAUGH!

I'm confused!

I've got two boys...

...and I can choose!!

Is this really happening to me?? I mean a week ago I thought I'd just never, ever get a boyfriend. EVER.

Maybe I don't have to choose. Maybe I can go out with both.

(Greeedddddyyyyy!!!!)

Anyway, will have to see what Teddy's like at kissing as so far have only snogged Billy. I think he was a bit surprised but it was late and I wanted to get on with it. He didn't do much kissing back – even when I let him feel my boob.

I hope he isn't queer! Like the bloke at the bottom of our road in Putney who got arrested for wearing a basque and high heels at the bus stop.

This is all so exciting. I probably won't sleep a wink to-night. Can't wait to phone Vicky!!!! (Gloat! Gloat!!!)

Wish I could tell Mum – she is definitely my real best friend but there's some things you just don't say, do you, to your Mum.

* * *

It's been nearly a whole week and I haven't seen Billy or Teddy. Their school is too far away from mine and they don't go in the same direction home, also I have been busy in the evenings because we have a lot of homework especially from the awful Miss Armstrong – (who wants to learn Boyle's Law anyway? It's no use to me, I'm going to be a film star when I leave school or a film director, I haven't decided) and the other reason I have been busy is because Mum has needed a hand at home to get the tea and stuff. Now she's got a job in Leeford she can't be home as early as she used to be and Paul's so bloody useless we'd all starve or live on baked beans if it was down to him.

He really ought to be doing more round the house to help out but he never does. Teenage boys Mum says, are all the same – their minds are on other things. In Paul's case on the pages of the mucky mags that he keeps under his bed. I know 'cos he left the corner of one sticking out the other day and I saw it when I went into his room to borrow a pencil. He's got about ten of them and they're called '*Parade*' and '*Fiesta*' and '*Men Only*' – revoltings-ville Arizona! Why would girls do that, take off their clothes and everything? I didn't tell mum – I am waiting until Paul pisses me off again and it'll be like in a court – evidence I can use against him if he doesn't stop or apologize for whatever it is that has pissed me off.

I cannot bear to think of my brother doing things like he probably does when he looks at those pictures. It's not NATURAL. He used to like Noddy.

* * *

My diary continued…

Saturday. This is gear. Went to the woods this morning to what I call Billy's clearing.

Whacky! Whacky! Wha Whoo! He was there. Chatted about this and that. Asked him if he had plans for the summer hols. Unbelievable. His Hols started Friday and we've still got another week to go! Soooo not fair! Must be to do with it being Catholic or maybe it's because his parents pay for him to go there. Either way, bloody not fair.

We had a bloody weird conversation about Catholics. The priests do not have sex with women and I upset him a bit by pretending not to understand and saying 'fuck'. You should have seen his face! Anyway it ended OK because I gave him a peck on the lips. He looked even more shocked at that!!

It was like dead warm and I had deliberately put on my red mini-skirt and I could see him looking at my legs when I sat down again and pulled him down beside me. He sat next to me in a kind of awkward way like he was embarrassed or something and I gave him a lemon sherbet.

Then we snogged. Not like the peck I'd given him after the Priest conversation but really, really properly

Yahhooo! Snoggy, snog, snog! It was amazing! Really good cos it lasted longer than the other week after the fun-fair. He doesn't open his mouth though and my tongue got tired trying. It may be my fault – I've not snogged much before – apart from Peter Entwhistle and we were in the se-cond form so that does NOT count, no way – so I may be doing something wrong.

It (the snoggy-rooney) ended when he started to splutter and blew all this sticky spit over me. Seems he still had the lemon sherbet in his mouth and it started to fizz and got stuck in his throat. Fortunately I had a bottle of squash in my bag and he had some of it. But like he was dead embar-rassed and went red – which was quite nice really – he is a gentleman.

I said I was going to Leeford this afternoon, did he want to come and he said no he couldn't because his father needed him to hold some wood in his workshop which he was cut-ting-up to make a cupboard. Seems his father is into DIY and likes to do things to their house. Wish he'd come round to ours – our is a dump.

I said, don't bother with your dad, come with me. He said he couldn't because it was his filial duty. I said, what the fuck's that? And he went pink again and said it's what a son does for his father. I said my father used to say he got a pain in the neck from Paul, which is dead witty, if you think about it. I said, 'come on. He won't mind.'

He said, dead seriously, 'You don't know my father...' And there was a look in his eye. I hope his dad doesn't beat him up or anything. 'I'd like to,' he said. 'But the consequences wouldn't be worth it.' So I reckon his dad does beat him up.

He does talk in a funny way. Like a book.

* * *

What a day! (Oh Vicky, you will eat your heart out when I tell you!)

So Billy went off to his dad – bit awkward, I went to give him a goodbye peck and he didn't see me coming and he turned as I puckered-up and so I sort of kissed his ear hole – well, licked it really and he had to wipe his ear with a tissue when he thought I wasn't looking. After that perhaps we should have just said goodbye but for some reason Billy shook my hand – he is dead weirds-ville or maybe he is eccentric.

Then I went to the bus stop and Wooo! Wacky Woo! Who should be there but the mad, bad and dangerous Teddy.

Ooh! Teddy! Teddy! Teddy!

He said, 'Hi Girl, how's you!' Not 'Hello Diana. How are you?' Like some square – he is so right-on! And his hair is dead gorgeous. His shirt was nearly unbuttoned all the way and he has a HAIRY chest, real proper hair, like a man. FAB!

I asked him if he was going into Leeford and he said. 'Actually, I was going into Ewhurst, but now I'm going into Leeford – if *you are!*'

Which was so cool, like a film and we got on the bus together and sat in the back.

As we were leaving I looked back and Billy was running down the road, chasing the bus, waving his hands. And I thought, 'Oh, God he's changed his mind and wants to come.' And then I suddenly thought, 'I hope the bus doesn't stop for him...' which I know is really not nice of me, especially with all the snogging and everything but that's how I felt and I might as well be honest.

Anyway, the bus didn't stop and I glanced back again and he was standing with his hands on his hips and he was looking straight at me and he must have realised it was Teddy next to me and I did feel a bit bad for a minute but then Teddy said, 'We could walk in the park if you like and then go to the chippy... And I'll buy the chips!' Which was dead romantic, like an issue of *Jackie* mag.

And that's what we did and he's not at all like I thought he might be when I first met him and he was so dead rude. When you get him alone he's actually dead nice and quite gentle and caring – though he's always got that, what do you call it? (Billy would know 'cos he's good with words) *Edge* – I think that's it. Teddy has got 'edge' – like he doesn't mind what he says or who he says it too. Like in the chippy when the bloke serving, who was about thirty and had really bad acne (I shall never work in a chippy as you'd always have greasy skin) got a bit arsy when I asked for more chips than the three he'd put in the bag – Teddy just said 'give the lady what she wants, mate' and the bloke did and Teddy must be years younger than him but he has this 'way' and the bloke gave me a double portion for the same money. You have to admire that in a man – being strong and firm, and he has big shoulders, I like a man who looks like a man, if you know what I mean.

In the park we ate the fish and chips and talked about school and everything and he says he's not going to get good O-levels 'cos he can't be bothered and anyway his dad's going to give him a job laying floors next summer, so he doesn't much care.

'They're only any use if you want to go to university or work in an office,' he said.

I told him I was planning on being a film director or an actress and he said, 'Fair enough, you'll probably need them then and A-levels too.' Which shows he has thought it all out and he has an open mind. Can't help but think Billy would have been shocked and would have said it was a duty or something to do your O-Levels well. I didn't say that to Teddy though, as I didn't want to mention Billy to him and spoil a dead fab day.

The he took me to this coffee bar. I didn't even know there was a coffee bar in Leeford and this was not the boring old Wimpy but a place with a juke box.

Apparently, according to Teddy, it was big in the fifties and the sixties and all the local kids hung out there but now it's nearly always empty because everyone stays at home and watches the telly. Which is an interesting point. Teddy goes there because he likes rock and roll and they have it on the J Box. I cannot believe it – Rock 'n Roll, like Elvis and things that our parents listened to. I wasn't expecting that!!! This is a whole new side of Teddy but it explains how he dresses and now I know why he has his hair in a quiff... Teddy has hidden depths as well as broad shoulders.

Oooooh! Whacky! Wooo!

We had coffee in glass cups (which was only Nescaff like at home but looked cool in the glass cups) and he put some coins in the J B and played a song called '*Hound Dog*' and another one called '*Rock Around the Clock*' or something which he said were classics. I didn't say anything but I thought they were rubbish and dead old fashioned and I wondered what Billy would think of them who knows all about pop.

Apparently, Teddy gets all this fifties thing from his dad who has his own Juke B and a huge collection of fifties records. He said his dad used to be a 'Teddy Boy' and I said, 'Is that why you're called Teddy, then?' And he looked at me and said, 'No. It's 'cos my name is Edwards.' Which is obvious and I felt a bit stupid. Then he said, 'I'm really called Frank.'

'Oh,' I said. 'Frank Edwards.' Then I said, 'I prefer Teddy.' Which I hope wasn't rude but he shrugged and said, 'Whatever…' So I think it was OK.

Then we walked up the road to the bus stop 'cos I really had to go as I'd told Mum I'd be home by six. There was a bus shelter and we sat in it and there was no one else there and the bus wasn't due for ages and then he put his arm round me….

Wooooo~~~~~!! WoooeeWoo!

Oh, boy! Can he snog or what! Wow. Tongues and everything – I reckon our first kiss lasted for ever and I could feel his stubble on my face and everything and then he sort of nuzzled my neck and sucked on it and he touched my boob, well held it really and his breath was all hot all over my face and he kept saying, 'Oh, baby…baby…' and it was really sexy. He even put his hand on my thigh…

When I tell Vicky she will die, she will just die…

And then this old geyser came into the bus shelter and

sat down and said, 'Do you mind!' All pompous like and then, 'This is a public place.' And I thought Teddy would say something but he didn't and he stopped kissing me – he was probably right and he was probably embarrassed – so I sort of looked at the geyser and said, 'Well, you don't have to look...' Which was a bit arsy of me and Teddy said, 'Leave it Di.' He is so masterful. I like a strong man. So I didn't say anything else and then the bus came anyway.

I thought we would snog on the bus but he didn't seem keen, but he put his arm round me and I kind of snuggled up beside him – which was nice. My stop's before his and I did wonder if he'd get off with me and maybe we'd have another snog but he said his Mum would have his tea ready so he gave me a kind of little peck on my cheek and I got off and just stood and watched the bus go and I stood there for ages like in a kind of trance or something but then the pavement got a bit busy with people going to the theatre so I crossed the road and walked home.

Good job we have a mirror in the hall. Fortunately I looked at it before I went into the kitchen – I have a great big love bite on my neck. Wow – can't wait to show the girls, even more heart eating for V. I'll be the first in our year. I ran up stairs and got my long Laura Ashley scarf and tied it round my neck before I went down for tea.

Over tea Mum suddenly said, 'That boy came round this afternoon.'

'What boy?' I said.

'Your friend... Billy, is it?'

'Oh,' I said, being dead cas', 'What did he want?'

'Wanted to know if you were back from Leeford.'

'Oh,' I said again.

'I told him no…' She picked up her knife and fork again and ate some bacon. 'Mmmm… she said with her mouth full, '…and he said to tell you that he hoped you had a nice time.'

I could feel the blush creeping up under my Laura Ash and going up my neck.

'Funny boy isn't he,' she went on. 'He wouldn't look me in the eye, kept staring at my blouse…very odd!'

Paul looked up from dipping his bread and butter in his fried egg. 'Perhaps you had something spilt down it,' he said.

As I said before – what a day!

* * *

Friends!! – I give up on them. You could see that Karen and Vicky were dead jealous of the L bite and then V got all arsy and said she'd had one years ago but hadn't bothered to show everyone as she didn't need to prove anything 'in that department!' I said, 'When you say years ago you must mean in kindergarten and having poster paint on your neck doesn't count!' And she told me to fuck off, which shows how well developed her mind is.

Then K said – who gave it to you? Which was great, 'cos I was able to say, 'I'm not sure,' in a dead meaningful way and you could see both of their jaws drop – literally.

V said, 'And what does that mean?'

And I said, 'Well I'm snogging two blokes right now and it might have been either of them.' It was great! I could almost see V go green.

K said, 'You never…'

And then V said, 'Well if you are, you're a slut.'

Which was the most disgusting thing to say, especially coming from her, who's absolutely gagging for it and wears such low cut jumpers you can nearly see her belly button.

They were desperate to know who they were but I thought 'sod you both – you can gag away,' and I just said they weren't any of the mongs from our school, that was for sure and that I preferred a classier kind of boy. Then I sagged off to the toilets and left them to brood on it.

Ha! Ha!

* * *

It's ages since I wrote anything in here. So much has been going on since we broke up from school. My mind's all a whirl.

Where shall I begin?

I am now officially Teddy's Girlfriend. Every one knows now – so that makes it official. Mind you, it's not been easy but that's what they say about the course of true love, isn't it? It's never easy.

After the day in Leeford with Teddy I had a good old think about things – about my life in general, about friends and about boys etc.

I made a list of things as they occurred to me. Here it is:

Di's List Of Important Things–

1. Love Life:
 – Decide Teddy/Billy

2. School Life:
 – Hols. Great. BUT Report due, probably bad apart

from Art and Eng Lit. Be nice to Mum until it arrives (Tea in bed at wk end???)

— Can now forget school until Sept. Good.

3. Home life:

— see 2 above

— Also PAINT bedroom. Pink poss, with big flowers painted on walls and thin scarves thrown casually over lights and joss sticks everywhere — also yellow sun with a face stuck on ceiling (NB check with Mum first!!!)

— Buy some dye & tie-dye cheap T-shirts from Woolies.

— Should I talk to Mum about 1) above? She's cool but just how cool. *'Hey Mum, I'm seeing two boys…'* She might say — *'Oh, Di are you some kind of tart??'* And be narky or she might say, *'Oh, Di what fun — but do be careful, if you know what I mean!'* That's the trouble with mum you never know if she's going to be the young hippy mum who was an actress and went to drama school with Tom Courtenay and Albert Finney before she met Dad or the boring vicar's daughter that she once was when young.

4. Discuss all of above with Paul? No because he is being a boring spassy mong right now who is dating some girl but he won't tell me who it is. Pathetic. I must remember to follow him and find out.

I decided the list was useless. When you come down to it sometimes you just have to go with the flow.

Then things happened.

On the second day of the hols Teddy phoned me up and said would I like to go into Leeford again, which of course I did as I was already dead bored at home.

The thing about living in the countryside is that there is not much to do when you reach a certain age – like my age, in fact. I mean if you want to go out there's Leeford and then that's it unless you want to go about another zillion miles and end up in Winchester which has a got a cathedral and a C&A but nothing else of interest (actually C&A is a lot more interesting than the Cathedral but that's probably 'cos I'm more of a rock chick than a historian and I am not religious as I am thinking of becoming a follower of the Maharishi.)

So we went into Leeford, went to the Wimpy, saw a film and had a walk in the park. Yeah, like what else can you do? We've done it all before I know, but that's it. We sat on a park bench by a statue of a little cherub with bird pooh on it and it was really sweet because the pond was in front of us and there were all these ducks and their ducklings came out of the water and started quacking all round us looking for food. I wanted to feed them but we didn't have any bread and that's when I realised that for all his gruff exterior Teddy was a real gentlemen. He went over to a waste bin and found this newspaper with some soggy chips in it and gave them to me to feed to the ducks.

They were horrible, cold greasy things but I didn't say anything even though it made me feel sick to touch them because it was such a kind act. When I'd fed the ducks he took the newspaper back to the bin and gave me a tissue from his pocket to wipe my fingers. Actually the tissue was a bit snotty but it was another kind gesture.

It was then I realised that he was a real man. I mean he was all tough and strong on the outside, like a knight of old, and inside he is really soft and kind and I suddenly understood what it means on the tins of Lyle's Golden Syrup I use when I'm helping Mum make flapjack. You know, there's this picture of a lion with bees all round it and underneath it says, 'Out of the strong came forth sweetness...' which must be a quote from some old book but it's dead right and it's dead like Teddy is.

So I kissed him. Really hard. Right on his lips and then I gave him my tongue and squeezed him tight and he grabbed me and kissed me hard back and then he held my boob and when he'd done that he rubbed his hand up the inside of my leg, right over the top of my black patent leather knee high boots and right up under my Biba Zig Zag mini dress that Mum got me for my birthday.

It was good job some kids and their mum and dad came along to sail a model boat or anything might have happened, right there on the park bench by the cherub with the pooh on it. We sort of pulled ourselves apart and smiled at the kids but their mum and dad looked dead disapproving like we'd actually bonked or something right there and then in front of them, and Teddy said loud enough for them to hear, 'Come on let's go to the coffee bar before we get the bus home.' Which sounded dead grown-up and I wondered if the mum and dad might think we were a young married couple and if they did I hoped that made them feel less prim and proper about us.

In the coffee bar Teddy put on some really noisy record called '*Shake, Rattle and Roll*' that went right through me. How do I tell him that I'll never like that old stuff? When it finished he said do you want to hear '*Dizzy Miss Lizzy*'? but I asked for another coffee and said I'd rather chat before we got the bus and it was better to chat without music. He grinned and said, 'You're weird!' and I suddenly felt a bit like

Billy because I am always telling him he was weird. And thinking about Billy made me go a bit hot and I felt a bit, you know, flustered. I suddenly felt like I was letting him down, which I suppose in a way I was – not that I'd ever said anything to him, you know, like 'I'm your girlfriend'. I mean I'd just pecked him a bit in the woods and on our doorstep.

And as I was thinking all this I looked out of the window and suddenly right opposite, on the pavement on the other side of the road, I saw him… Billy!!

Wow! I mean that's…what's the word? Existential? Anyway it was dead spooky. I mean, thinking about him and there he is. He was with his Mum and Dad (at least I suppose that's who they were) and he was sort of trailing along behind them carrying a couple of shopping bags and looking really miserable. And then he turned and looked across the road straight into the coffee bar and straight at me.

Oh, God! I nearly died! I don't think he spotted me at first and then suddenly he stopped walking and just stared at me a bit vacantly and then he put down one of the bags and started to wave at me with this silly cheesy grin on his face. I didn't know what to do and just then Teddy came back with the coffees and sat down next to me.

I could see Billy kind of freeze, with his hand in the air and then he dropped it to his side and looked at me with like a real look of shock on his face and then he grabbed the bag and just walked quickly away and all the time I'd just stared at him and didn't do a thing.

'What's up girl?' Teddy said.

I said it was nothing. I'd just seen someone walking by that I knew and he said, 'Who was that then?' And said, 'No one. No one you know.' And I felt really shitty.

* * *

I felt so bad about Billy that I decided I'd go and see him. I didn't know what I was going to say. I mean, like I said, it's not like he was my boyfriend or anything. But I sort of thought I ought to see him, if you know what I mean.

I've had long chats with Vicky and Karen about it all and they're dead jealous that I've got two BFs (well one proper one and one who is sort of a semi-BF) but they were also really helpful abut my dilemma i.e. that I may inadvertently have given Billy the impression that I fancied him or something. Vicky said, 'Come off it Di, you led him up the garden path and no mistake.' Which was harsh but probably a bit true.

They've never met him but I've told them all about him and Karen said, 'You need to tell him that you've got a proper boyfriend and you hope he understands that all the snogging was just one of those things.'

'Yeah,' Vicky said. 'But you'd better let him down gently 'cos he sounds like one of those boys who might go mad and top himself when the full hurt of being jilted kicks in.'

Which is a stupid thing to say as all I did was let him feel my boob a couple of times and throw water over him. And I'm sure he wouldn't do anything silly just because we had a quick snog. I mean that happens every night in London at the bus stop on the Lower Richmond Road when school finishes for the day. Mind you this is the countryside and the people are a bit strange around here.

But in a way V and K right. I owe it to Billy to be honest I guess and to put him out of his misery, after all I reckon he must fancy me rotten judging from his face outside of the Coffee Bar. I expect it is because in many ways I am an older woman than him. (I don't mean he's a woman, of course, or that I'm really older than him – not in years anyway. I'm just more mature than he is – because in many ways Billy is dead immature...Actually in nearly *every* way Billy is dead immature, come to think about it!)

'You're right,' I said to V & K. 'I'll have to go and talk to him.'

And Karen put her arm round me and said, 'How brave!' And Vicky said, 'And then come and tell us all about it – *straight away!*'

'I expect it will be a private conversation,' I said a bit icily.

'Well, tell us anyway,' Karen said, 'and I'll lend you that Mary Quant Powder Compact you've always wanted.'

Vivky said, 'Don't bother, she'll tell us anyway.' Then she looked at me and sighed, 'I mean you couldn't keep a secret if you tried.' There are days you can go off Vicky.

But somehow I didn't do anything about it for days because Teddy kept calling me on the phone or popping in to see me. My mum didn't like him much at first but she got better with him, and he and Paul got on great – especially when P discovered that Teddy was going to get a motorbike when he left school. Paul has always wanted a motorbike but Mum has told him 'over her dead body' as they were a good way to kill yourself, she reckoned.

So Teddy and I have spent the last week or so just mooching up in my room playing records (I am trying to get him to understand the good stuff like The Beatles and The Kinks and the Small Faces (ooh! Sexxxxy!) but he still likes all that old rock and roll stuff better – YUCH!) and we've been out to the flicks a few times and also we went to see *Othello* at the theatre, which Teddy said was dead boring but

I loved it. I think I might spend some time as a stage actress before I go into films.

Anyway, last weekend Teddy went away with his mum and dad for their holiday. They've gone to the Costa Brava 'cos Teddy's dad earns sack loads of money doing floors and the garage and everything and Teddy says they always go abroad every summer on a 'package' whatever that is. I am dead jealous. I have never been abroad. Usually we go camping in Norfolk or sometimes to Devon but we're not going this year 'cos mum says money's too tight and she needs to work every hour she can at her new job. Which is OK and I really admire Mum for coping in the circumstances. Dad didn't leave her much and Mum had never really had to work when he was alive apart for a few summers in the theatre in a place called Southwold – so you have to admire her now as work is not her strong point. Anyway, I hate camping, especially as it always rains and I have to share a tent with Paul who makes disgusting smells all night!

I was, what's the word, bereft (??) after Teddy left. Well dead mis anyway. But come last Monday I thought I'd better go and find Billy. This was a bit of a prob as I don't actually know where he lives and I never got his phone number, so I decided to mooch down to the stream and then across the fields up into the woods. I reckoned I'd find him somewhere out and about as it was a nice day.

Well, talk about a shock!!

I went to the water meadows and he wasn't under what he calls his tree (though I'd renamed it 'vomit willow', which had pissed him off when I told him) – and he wasn't up in what he likes to call his clearing in the woods – it's funny how Billy likes to make nature all his own. So I set off towards his school. I walked through the woods, down the slope and then out onto the meadow. His school is on the other side of the meadow and there's this low, old brick wall running all the way round it.

I didn't think he'd necessarily be there but I walked over to the wall 'cos I was curious to see what a posh school looked like. I could just about see over the top and there was a big grassy area with a raised bank and at the top of it and in front of the bank there were actually tennis courts – two of them, with wire fences and proper tarmac. How posh can that be. The school, what I guessed to be the school anyway, was at the top of another bank and it was gi-genormous, this really huge old mansion, like a real stately home, like my mum and dad had taken me to in Norfolk one holidays. There were hundreds of windows and a huge pair of French doors in the middle on the ground floor which led onto a big paved terrace.

I just peered over the wall and stared. I mean, imagine calling a pad like that school! As I was watching some people appeared on the inside of the big glass doors, three women. They opened the doors and stepped outside. I ducked down so I couldn't really be seen but I kept on looking 'cos I wondered if they were going to do something, you know, some sort of Catholic thing, whatever they do, like when Billy was kneeling in the woods that day. Perhaps they were going to have an outdoor mass or communion or a ritual sacrifice because of the sunshine and everything.

I didn't really think they were going to do something like that, of course, it was just fun pretending and anyway I reckoned they'd need a priest for that sort of thing and there wasn't a man among them. So I was a bit shocked when I saw that the woman in black had a short back and sides and was carrying some sort of club on the end of some poles and that the woman who was in a short dress was holding a sword and the other woman was in a really long dress and a tiara. It looked really mad. Crazy.

The one in black was talking all the time and kept wiping his nose with a hanky and as they got closer to where I was, I could hear that she had a surprisingly deep voice and then I got a big shock. I suddenly realised that the one in black was actually a bloke and he was wearing a black dress thing, like our vicar used to in Putney. What's it called? A hassock?? So this wasn't a woman, it was actually a real live catholic priest. Wow. My first.

Then I realised that the girl with the sword was actually a boy and I thought now that is weird, a boy in a short skirt with a sword. What is going on here? But that wasn't my biggest shock. They stopped a few yards away from me and I had to scuttle along my side of the wall with my head bent low to where a tree was growing and hide behind that before I could peek out again. You will not believe this and Vicky and K. will be gobsmacked, that's for sure. The other boy, the one with the tiara and long skirt was only Billy. YES!! Billy. MY Billy. BILLY the WEIRDO in a skirt and a tiara.

I think I forgot to breathe for a whole minute and my eyes were definitely out on stalks, I can tell you. I almost stood up and said something or laughed, I'm not sure what I wanted to do most, but fortunately I stayed behind the tree and out of sight.

It turned out that the priest man was carrying a little cine camera thing on a tripod and he set it up and then he started to tell the boys what he wanted them to do. He had a little thin voice that drawled a lot and he kept sniffing and stuffing something up his nose and wiping it with the big hanky. Then it dawned on me that they were making a film. I reckoned Billy must be dead keen on acting to give up his holidays for it and I wondered why he'd never told me about it, I guess it was because of the skirt wearing thing. I mean you wouldn't exactly want to boast about that, now would you.

I settled back against my tree as I was interested to see what would happen next. The priest wanted the boy with the sword to jump out from behind this bush while Billy lay on the ground pretending to be asleep. So the other boy hid behind the bush and Billy lay down and I could tell even from where I was that he was just hating it. The Priest said he was lying down all wrong, which sounded a bit odd to me, I mean how many ways are there to lie on the ground and he kept prodding Billy and grabbing his legs and twisting him into different positions. And then he'd skip over to the camera and look through it and move it a bit ('lining up his shot,' he kept saying) and then running back to Billy and twisting him a bit more and pulling his skirt up round his legs in what looked like a dead disgusting way to me and I was gobsmacked that Billy let him. I mean, what a freak!

Finally he was happy and he said the shot was 'going to be very dramatic!' But from where I was standing, which was dead behind the camera, it looked more like a picture out of one of my brother's mucky mags, only with a boy instead of a bird 'cos you could see right up the skirt to Billy's pants and I reckoned if Billy had realised he'd be really pissed off, but as he had to tip his head back and gaze 'longily' at the sky he had no idea.

It all seemed a bit bloody strange. Anyway, I stayed and watched them do all these different shots and I could hear the priest telling them what to do. He was always grabbing the two boys and moving them where he wanted them or acting their parts out for them to show them how he wanted it to done and to be honest, it began to dawn on me that the only person enjoying it was the priest because Billy and the other one looked totally pissed off about it all.

It was getting really hot because the sun was now right on me, and I soon lost interest in the whole thing. I needed a sit-down 'cos my legs were aching from all the crouching down, so after about half an hour I crept away and cut across the fields, over the style at the footpath and walked along the edge of the stream to Billy's tree and I flopped down in the shade and had a big swig of squash from my bag.

I didn't make the decision to go there deliberately. I mean I just went there because it was hot and this place was cool but I suppose it was in the back of my mind that when Billy finished he'd come over there. I dozed a bit and watched some ducks swim by and a tractor doing some ploughing in a field way over on the other side of the stream. It was dead peaceful and the whole thing looked like an old oil painting, you know that *Hay Way In* – or whatever it's called, it was really nice and tranquil and then I thought, 'Blimey, I am becoming a country girl!' Which made my heart sink and I was suddenly dead homesick for Putney High Street and my little park by the Thames.

I must have fallen asleep 'cos when I woke up Billy was standing there, just in front of me, with his legs astride and staring down at me. He looked hot and bothered and as I opened my eyes I could see right up the leg of his shorts to his pants. Seems like we were all everyone was getting an eyeful of his pants today.

'What you doing here?' He said and he didn't sound too keen to see me, if you know what I mean.

'I can see up your shorts,' I replied, which was a bit mean and he went red like he does.

I patted the grass next to me and pulled out my bottle of squash and held it out to him.

'You look hot,' I waved the bottle at him and he sat down next to me and took it.

I didn't like to say that I'd seen him dressed up as a girl, making a film. I thought he'd probably want to keep that sort of thing to himself. But I did say, 'What you been doing then?' In case he wanted to tell me about it.

'Nothing,' he mumbled and looked away, staring at the stream.

'Shall we paddle, you know, to cool off,' I suggested.

'No,' he said firmly. 'I find paddling with you leads to unnecessary wetness in the shirt area.'

Which was like dead rude and rather pompous all at the same time.

'Oooh,' I went, dead sarky like. 'Who's a little ray of sunshine today!'

Which was what my Dad used to say to me when I got into a bad temper. Then we both sat still, without speaking and all you could hear was the birds and the tractor in the distance. At last he lifted the bottle to his mouth and had a drink and then handed it back to me.

'Thanks,' he said. 'For the squash… though frankly, I thought you preferred coffee…'

And I knew he was thinking of the coffee bar with Teddy but I decided to ignore him and I just said, 'Not when it's so hot!' And then, because I thought we'd end up sitting in silence again I added, 'So what have you been up to? I haven't seen you for ages.'

'No,' he said and then he paused as if he was thinking about something. 'I had other fish to fry,' he added, which sounded a bit weird but then Billy is a bit weird.

'Oh, have you been seeing you're friends from school?' I asked.

He looked at me. 'No. I don't have many friends – not ones you can rely on, anyway.'

So he wasn't going to talk about the filming then and in fact all he was really talking about, between the lines you might say, was me and Teddy. So I took a big gulp of air and swallowed hard. For some reason my mouth went dry.

'Look Billy,' I said. 'I hope you're not upset about me and Teddy. I mean about seeing us in the coffee bar the other day…'

'And on the bus…' he interrupted.

'Yes and on the bus. I mean a girl can like lots of people. You know, have lots of friends. I mean you and me… We only went to the cinema and to the Wimpy… I mean it's not a big deal…'

None of it was what I really wanted to say or at least not how I wanted to say it and I sort of trailed off. He looked at me with his brown eyes and he seemed to be looking right into me and when he spoke it was like he had sandpaper in his throat or something.

'What about my secret clearing? What about the funfair and in the cinema when you held on to me and at your house when you… When we… You know when you…' And he tailed off, looking really lost.

'When we snogged,' I said, to help him out. 'That's all!'

'That's all?' He said and his face had gone a funny colour. 'You pressed up against me, you made me touch... I touched... *bits* of you.'

'Oh, God,' I thought and I suddenly realised how young he was, only a kid. What had I done?

He stopped speaking and stared into the water. I thought I saw his lips move but he seemed all far away, just staring.

'Look, we're friends,' I said. 'Just 'cos I'm seeing Teddy doesn't mean we're not friends. Of course we are. I like you. Really I do. I'm not marrying him or anything... Blimey in a year or two I'll be at college or RADA or something and I won't even see him...'

He was beginning to cry now and I was getting desperate. I hate seeing people cry, especially if it's my fault.

'Look,' I went on. 'There's a big summer disco at the St Mark's youth club the week after next, in the village hall. Why don't you come. We'll have a bop.'

WHY did I say that? I'd already arranged to go with Teddy as it was the day he got back from Spain

'I don't bop,' he said. 'I can't.'

I should have left it there but instead I said, 'They'll have good records – The Stones, The Who, The Beatles.'

He looked at me and said quite firmly through his tears, 'As I said, I don't dance.'

I laughed.

'Blimey, Billy. You only have to jig up and down and wave your arms a bit. It's not fucking Fred Astaire.'

He looked at me again and this time he looked really hurt, like I was taking the piss out of him or something.

'Go on,' I said desperately. 'Please come... I'd like you to.'

No! No! I really wouldn't like him to come! So why did I say all that? Because I feel so flaming guilty and he looked so sad, I suppose. Oh Di, you should have shut-up. When will you learn to shut-up?

He sighed, like he had all kinds of problems on his mind, a real deep sigh and he muttered something I couldn't hear and then he said, 'Alright... Maybe...'

'Good,' I said. 'See, we're still friends, aren't we?'

And I realised I was talking to him like he was a baby or a retard or something. And then I did something dead stupid, even more stupid than I already had, like completely the action of a total mong. I leant over and kissed him on his wet, teary cheek. Actually *kissed* him! I mean, here I was and I was supposed to be telling him that I was going out on an exclusive basis with Teddy and we shouldn't see each other any more and instead I had just invited him to a disco, said I'd bop with him and even given him a kiss! Sometimes Diana you are thicker than a short plank.

'Well,' he said. 'If it's like that...' And there was a kind of hopeful glint in his eye behind the tears that made me feel a bit awkward and a bit like I'd been caught cheating in an exam.

He didn't finish the sentence, just kept staring at me. I couldn't think what to say next, so I stood up and looked down at him, which was a bit odd as he was now looking up at me like a dog expecting a walk. We sort of stayed like that and neither of us knew what to do next and all I could think was, 'I want to get out of here!'

I found a Kleenex in my bag and leant down to give it to him. He took it and wiped his face dry.

I finally managed to say, 'Well, I'd better be going,' and I turned away and started to walk along the bank. When I looked back, he was still staring at me but as I turned he gave me this big cheesy grin.

'Thank you,' he called. 'Thank you.' And he waved the Kleenex in the air but I knew he wasn't thanking me for that – and my heart sank.

'Oh Gawd,' I thought, 'he hasn't got the foggiest idea what I was I trying to say!'

* * *

A POEM BY DIANA DI WATSON:

FAR AWAY WITHOUT ME

Far away on the sunny shores of another country
is the boy I love.
He is wild and rugged, like the sea in which he
swims.
His body will be tanned, his muscles bronzed and
strong,
Far away without me.
And I wonder does he think of me or is there some
sweet senorita on his arm?
I wonder has she won him with her Spanish charm
And seduced him with her long black hair and Spanish
eyes which are foxy brown?
But I will get him home and caress him and we will
dance into the night, walk England's sad lanes
And he will tell tales of Spanish nights and warm my
cold, rural heart with exotic spice.
And he will never be far away again without me.

ANOTHER POEM BY DI W

BILLY THE KID

Billy the kid what shall we do
You're too young for me
And I'm too old for you
Oh Billy the kid, run to the woods
Before it's too late and while you're still good
The dark lonely woods will take your soul and
make you old
And the river you splash in will make you wise
So swim Billy, swim and don't look round
I'm not on the bank, I've gone for good
But swim Billy swim
Before you drown.

Not bad. I reckon I'll be a modern poet as well as acting. My Eng Lit teacher, Mr Tracy (whose nick name is Tina – 'cos he's obviously queer) says poetry is all about 'style and the individual voice'. Queers are good at all that sort of thing, so he's probably right. I reckon I've got my own style and my own voice, though some of it's a bit like William Blake not that it matters 'cos he's dead. I will definitely give these to the ed of the school mag. (Anonymously???)

Well, the shit has hit the fan, as they say in the movies.

What a Saturday evening!

It's like this. Teddy came home this morning and he is

just sooooo sweet. He came straight round to see me. Apparently he didn't even unpack or take his bag upstairs – which pissed his dad off, he just came straight round to the Maltings. He was all hot and sweaty when I answered the door and he'd said he'd run all the way – which is amazing as it is at least a hundred miles or maybe three and it was still only eight in the morning.

He grabbed me and gave me this great big kiss and squeezed me tight so I could feel the hot sweat on his chest right through my nightie and pink baby doll dressing gown.

'Wow,' he said after we'd snogged for ages and ages, 'I missed you, babes.'

He often calls me 'babes' which is dead cool. Sometimes he calls me 'doll' which is even cooler.

'So you haven't hitched up with some dark eyed, Senorita then?' I said.

He laughed. 'Don't be daft, there aren't any senoritas in the Costa Brava – just spotty girls from the Midlands with mums and dads like mine. It's just like Bognor only with sun.'

I was a bit disappointed. I quite fancied fighting for his affections with some sun kissed, dusky maiden with castanets and a fan.

Mum was still in bed and so was Paul, so I took Teddy into the kitchen and made him some tea and we had another good snog, tongues and everything (Well nearly everything – and it wasn't even breakfast time and we weren't in the bus shelter at the back of the Hurstwood Village green, if you know what I mean!!!)

Anyway, I could hear mum moving about upstairs, so I made him stop (not that I wanted him too – ooh, noooo!!).

So he finished his tea and said he'd better get back and un-pack or his mum and dad would go ape. I wanted to see him again during the day but he said his family had to go over to Winchester to see his granny and he wouldn't be back until tea time.

'Don't forget the disco tonight, then,' I reminded him.

'It's engraved on my heart,' he said and he was dead serious and not sarky at all, though it was a dead soggy thing to say.

We had another ace-a-rooney snog and then he had to go. I went back to the kitchen and made myself some more toast and I kept thinking how amazingly handsome he looked with his tan and how jealous V and K were going to be tonight at the disco and then Paul came downstairs in his vest and pants, scratched his belly button and farted – which took a lot of the gloss off it all.

The Village Hall is actually just outside Hurstwood, along a little lane off the High Street. I got there a bit early because it was really hot and close and I wanted to walk slowly so I wouldn't be limp and sweaty when I got there and also I wanted to be there when he turned up. As it was, I had to hang around outside waiting as he was a bit late.

I reckoned I looked alright. I was wearing my best Mary Q, tartan mini (well, it was C&A but you'd never have known) and some drop dead fab black boots and I had like a sort of flower power hair-band on, which was covered in lit-tle silver stars and I wore some beads on my wrist and round my neck (I am gradually becoming a hippy as I think I men-tioned before) and I'd put LOADS of kohl on my eyes – on reflection – and though I do say it myself, I was gorgeous.

Then Vicki and Karen turned up and well, frankly, K hasn't got the legs for that skirt and if V's blouse was any tighter she might just as well have taken it off and let her boobs flop around in the breeze. (And I mean FLOP!! I reckon it's 'cause she did all those exercises to try and make them bigger in the third form – she's paid the price for that all right).

I could see they were dead impressed and dead jealous of what I was in. But V had to be catty and she said, 'Have you got a black eye? What happened, did he hit you?'

'It's kohl!' I replied icily.

And K said, 'Really? Have you left any for your mum to put on the fire?'

Cow!!

And then because she'd been rude and she knew it, she tried to make up by saying, 'I like your skirt. I've not seen it before. It's very you.'

Which was nice but V spoilt it by saying, 'And so short we can see your knickers, that's very you too.'

And she smiled that syrup sweet smile she does that makes you want to punch her in the gob.

I was just going to say something like, 'You shouldn't have bothered to dress up yourself... Oh, I see you haven't...' when fortunately Teddy turned up, which was a good thing as it might have been about to get nasty.

He looked fabulosa!

His hair was slicked back, his skin was so brown that his teeth looked like they were painted white and he had on this black shirt open to his waist and this really chunky gold chain with a kind of medallion on the end of it. He was wearing amazingly tight black jeans which were tucked into a pair of black cowboy boots, with stack heels. Mmmmmm! Lick me! Lick me all over!

I could see that V & K were sooooo jealous. V sort of ogled him with her mouth open and you could almost see her dribbling and K started patting her hair and straightening her dress.

'Evenin' gals,' Teddy said, dead smooth. 'Fab evening for a bop.'

He is so smooth and so cool in ANY situation. Then he gave me a great big smackeroony right on the lips and when he pulled away he ran his hands over his hair to straighten it.

'Hi ya Sugar Pops,' he said. 'I've missed you all day, and that's for sure.'

I could almost feel V and K seething with envy.

He held out his arm for me to take.

'Let me escort madam, to the ball, if you will be so kind,' he purred and I latched onto his arm and he swept me through the hall doors.

And, although I didn't look back, I reckon K and V were standing there with their mouths open.

Serves 'em right.

Inside, the hall was hot and dark and I had to blink to get used to the light after the evening sunshine outside. Teddy insisted on buying the entrance tickets which the vicar was selling from a trestle table in the entrance hall. I decided to keep my ticket forever as a keepsake. I thought I would stick it into this diary and even though it's just an old raffle ticket I would treasure it for years and one day I would give it to my children and say this was my first token of true love and I'd look back on a long and happy life and say it started here.

Anyway, that was before what happened.

There were only a couple of other people in there when we arrived, so Teddy and I went straight to another trestle table where Mrs Cundy the Vicar's wife and another old bird were selling pop and crisps and things and we got a couple of plastic cups of coke and found a table near the stage where the disco equipment was set-up. Teddy was muttering about the coke being a rip-off because we only got a plastic cup of it for thruppence which was, he said, 'a dead liberty,' when you could buy a bottle for a bob in Jutsoms, the grocers shop round the corner.

By now the place was filling up. I reckon nearly all the kids in the area from my school, from Billy's school and even some from the grammar school in Leeford must have been there. Well, there isn't much else to do around here, let's face it.

The Disco was put on by Tim Hitchcock and his twin sister Alison. They go to my school and they are in the second year sixth. Tim is like this real science wizard and he built the disco gear himself. Alison is more of freak and into music so she chooses the songs they play and gets the records. It wasn't bad. They had a couple of record players and some big loud-speakers and there were loads of lights, they even had that one that makes your teeth go white or shows your bra up under your top and he had this oil wheel that put really cosmic shapes all over the back of the stage, real flower-power stuff – melting globs of light and all weird colours and everything. I was glad I'd worn my head band.

They were playing Tom Jones, *The Green, Green Grass of Home* when we went in, which is really naff but as more people arrived they started to put on the louder stuff.

'I don't think there's going to be any of your fifties music,' I said to Teddy.

'I don't mind,' he said and then they started playing *My Generation*. 'I like that,' he said. 'Let's dance,' and he kind of grabbed my wrist and dragged me to the middle of the hall where there were a few other kids were bopping along to the gorgeous Roger Daltry.

He may have liked fifties rock and roll but he could really dance. He was so coooool! He like stood quite still and just swayed his hips to the beat and held his hands out in front of him, so that they sort of waggled in time to the beat, and the oil wheels reflected off his medallion and all the time he fixed his eyes on me and looked right into me, like he was challenging me to do something or to dance like he did, instead of jigging around like I was. It was like having sex (I imagine..!). I soon got really hot and bothered, but in a nice way, a dead exciting way, if you know what I mean.

And then...

And then I saw him over Teddy's shoulder – he must have been watching us for a while. He was in front of the table where they were selling drinks, standing there staring at us and he wouldn't move out of the way so people were having to go round him to get their cokes and things. The queue was quite long now, so it had a kind of loop in it and at the centre of the loop was Billy.

I kept on dancing and tried to focus on Teddy but I couldn't help notice that some of the blokes and the girls were staring at Billy not just because he was in their way but they were nudging each other and laughing behind their hands at how he looked.

And if I'm honest he did look weird, totally out of place. I mean, all the boys were in T-shirts and jeans or open necked Ben Sherman shirts and flares but Billy was standing there in his school blazer, a white shirt and tie and grey flannel trousers, with black brogues. He looked like he was at a wedding not a youth club disco. I was beginning to feel hot and uncomfortable for him and I must have stopped dancing because suddenly Teddy said, 'You all right, girl?'

I told him I was OK and I tried to sway along to the beat but I just couldn't get back into the dancing, even though some boy had told Billy to move and I couldn't actually see him anymore. The sight of him in his silly shirt and tie staring at me, kept flickering into my mind and I just couldn't focus.

They started playing '*Sugar Sugar*' which is a shit song and also they played it on *Top Of The Pops* the night before my dad died, so I've always hated it. I told Teddy I didn't want to bop to bubble-gum music and he said, 'Too right, girl,' so we went and sat down again at our table.

Teddy pulled a packet of ciggies out of his pocket, Players Number Six, and lit one, which was about the coolest thing he'd ever done and he was always cool, I mean fridge-like but this was iceberg. I mean, he'd obviously done it before because he wasn't just showing off – he pulled the top open dead casually, pulled the ciggie out with his teeth and lit it with a gold zippo like he'd done it a hundred times before... And when he lit it he sucked the smoke right down.

He must have seen me staring because he said, 'Sorry Babe, do you want one?' And as he spoke the smoke puffed out of his mouth with every word and he looked up at the ceiling and blew the last bit out when he finished. I went all red and said, 'No, no thank you,' and then because I didn't want to look like a twerp who hadn't ever had a ciggie, I added, 'I think I might be getting a cold, actually.' And then something occurred to me. 'You'd better not let Mr Cundy see you...'

'Who?'

'The vicar. He doesn't allow smoking in the youth club... In case of fire.'

Teddy laughed. 'Well if old Cundy wants a word about it he can, but until then...' And he took another big drag and when he said Cundy it sounded suspiciously like another word but I don't know if he could really have said that and I couldn't hear because they were playing *'Sugar Sugar'* too loud! I hope he didn't say it 'cos although I am dead liberal and into the alternative society even I don't like that!

I watched him finish his fag and I began to wish I'd said that I would have one as it seemed so cool and apparently can help you lose weight. I bet Twiggy smokes.

Then Teddy said, 'Want another coke?' And I said, 'yeah, but I'll pay.'

'No need, Babe. I can afford all the cokes you want My Dad told me today that I can start doing floors with him from now on – you know, at weekends and in the holidays until I start full time next year. And I'm goin' to get paid – ten bob an hour!'

Wow. He is the richest man I ever met.

I watched him go to the drinks table and I started to dream about how we might stay together and maybe get married and he'd take over the family firm from his dad and I'd just got to thinking what sort of wedding dress I'd like, when I saw Billy again.

It was really odd. He was on the other side of the hall and he was staring at me, like he had been when Teddy and me were dancing, staring, not even blinking. Creepy.

When Teddy came back I popped to the loo while he kept our seats. V was in there 'touching up' her face as she put it. (Actually the amount of make-up she had on she'd have been better off calling in a plasterer).

'Oh,' she said. 'So that's your bloke, then.' And I knew she was eaten up with envy.

'Yeah,' I said. 'Hunky, eh?'

'I wouldn't say that, Di. I mean let's be honest he's a bit of a square.'

What??? Was she mad???

'You're kidding me,' I said. 'Look at his clobber.'

'Like I said, Square or what! In fact he's a bit of a spaz if you ask me?'

I could hardly keep my hands off her. I so desperately wanted to chin her, but somehow I took a deep breath and clutched the side of the manky old chipped wash-hand basin for support.

'He's got a gorgeous tan and his shirt is ace and... and what about the chain and everything...' I said angrily.

Vicky was walking towards the door but she turned back to me and pretended to be surprised.

'Oh,' she said like butter wouldn't melt in her knickers. 'Is *that* your bloke? Sorry, I thought it was the mong in the blazer and tie.'

And she smiled sweetly at me and went through the door. I was so angry that I had to cool down by running cold water over the back of my wrists.

Five minutes later I felt better; I had a pee and went back into the hall. I couldn't believe it, Billy had manoeuvred himself round the room and was leaning on the opposite wall staring at the door of the loo waiting for me to come out. I ignored him but his eyes followed me all the way back to the table. And then I had another shock. Teddy wasn't there. I looked round and he was only on the flaming dance floor with Karen bopping away to '*Roll Over Beethoven.*' They were doing proper jiving, or he was anyway – he was spinning her round and pulling her by the arms towards him and then pushing her back or twirling round her arm and he even did that thing when you lift the girl up and throw her between your legs. It was a disgusting display actually, because they were both showing off and she was screaming and shrieking and giggling hysterically – just so everyone would look at her.

I was furious and I felt stupid. I mean everyone must have known he was my boyfriend. I was sitting there wondering if I should go over and say something or whether it was cooler just to wait until he came back when a shadow fell over the table. I looked up and it was Billy. I gave a little jump because he had crept up on me and because he was standing right in the rays of the UV light from the disco and his shirt was glowing in the dim lights of the hall and his teeth and eyes had a sort of ghost-like blue mist to them.

'Blimey,' I said. 'You gave me a shock.'

He stared at me like he had done all evening and then he said very slowly, 'Now you know what it feels like then – to be left on your own when you were supposed to be with *someone.*'

Oh, Gawd, that was all I needed just then.

'Billy...' I began.

But he interrupted me. 'No. We were supposed to be here together.'

'No we weren't,' I said.

'But you said, down by the stream, under my tree...'

'No,' I said, trying to be gentle. 'I just said, you should come along. I didn't mean with me...'

He rocked back on his heels and it was like I'd hit him.

'You said we'd dance!'

'I just meant, you know, one dance… for fun… just for fun…'

He went white and his face seemed to crumple and I could see his lips moving and I couldn't hear what he said, but it must have been pretty intense because he had his eyes all screwed up. And then '*Roll Over Beethoven*' stopped and a slow smoochy song came on and Teddy came strolling over without K, thank God. I mean if he'd done the slow song with her I'd have killed him or something.

'Alright?' he said breezily, looking at Billy in surprise.

'Yes,' I said.

Teddy looked Billy over and I could see him thinking what a wazzack he looked in his tie and blazer. Then he said, 'You OK then Boggy?'

Suddenly Billy's eyes flashed or it may have been the oil wheel but either way he looked very angry.

'You shouldn't be here,' he said.

'What?' Teddy said and he laughed. 'Why not?'

'At this disco,' Billy said. 'It wasn't what I wanted…'

Teddy looked at him as if he was mad, which I was beginning to think he might be.

'Free world, Boggy. I paid for my ticket,' and he nodded at me, 'And for hers come to that.'

Billy clenched his fists and pressed them into the pit of stomach.

'Not here… I mean you shouldn't be here with her. It wasn't what she said. She said I'd be with her.'

Teddy didn't seem to notice how upset he was and he just kept smiling at him.

'Go and get yourself a coke, mate and cool off,' he said, then he sat down opposite me, reached across the table and grabbed my hand and squeezed it.

'No,' Billy said. And now he was speaking quite loudly and one or two people turned to look at us and I wished they'd play something noisy again. 'No,' he repeated. 'You go away. She promised…'

And he sounded like a little boy who wasn't getting his own way, which just made him look silly and Teddy laughed even louder at him.

'Oh, Bog Off, Boggy!' he said. 'Just Bog Off, will you, you're spoiling our fun.'

And then Billy did something really silly. He picked up the half drunk cup of coke in front of Teddy and threw it in his face.

By now everyone nearby was looking at us and if they weren't, they certainly did when Teddy jumped to his feet and sent his chair crashing to the ground. He wiped the coke from his eyes and clenched his fist.

'NO!' I said loudly and I grabbed Teddy's arm and held on to it. 'Just stop it, both of you.' I looked into Teddy's eyes and then I could feel him relax and he unclenched his fist.

'Yeah,' he said. 'I'll sort it later…' he looked at Billy. 'We'll wait until next term mate.'

He sat down and got out his hanky and wiped the coke form his face while I turned to Billy who was pale and shaking.

'Billy,' I said. 'You're being a fucking twat. Now go home…'

'But…' he began and I suddenly realised that this had to stop and I had to be firm. 'Billy,' I said, 'Just go. I want to be with Teddy.'

And I could see the hurt in his eyes.

'Do you understand?' I repeated and I said it slowly. 'I... want...to... be...with... Teddy.'

'But...' and he looked at me hopelessly.

'Look,' I said. 'It's like I said, we'll meet up sometimes. We'll stay friends. I'll...I'll come and see you in the clearing...in the woods... your clearing...soon. I promise.'

He looked at me and shook his head as if he was trying to clear it of something.

'But I made the sacrifice...' he said quietly. 'Your supposed to be with me...'

And I didn't understand what the fuck he was talking about and it occurred to me that he really was going crackers.

'Just go,' I said again. 'Please.'

'Now?' He said.

'Yes,' I said. 'Now.'

But he shook his head again and looked up at the ceiling. 'Now...' he repeated.

'Christ! I just said,' I almost screamed at him.

'Now...Now...Now...' he said again, like some sort of crazy chant. 'Now...Now...Now...' and he was shaking, clenching his fists and there were tears in his eyes.

'Now...Now...Now...' He went again.

'Yes, Now... And now get out!' I said getting really pissed off with him and Teddy was looking up at us as if to say, 'What the fuck is going on?'

'Now...' Billy said again and this time he was looking at me. 'Now...now...now...'

'Why don't you bloody shut-up and go,' Teddy snapped.

Billy looked at him and he had this really funny expression

on his face. 'Now…now…now…' He said again.

All around us at the other tables, people had started to look over at us. It seemed to me the only ones who weren't looking were the kids on the dance floor because they couldn't hear us over the music.

Suddenly I lost my temper. Billy was taking the piss. He was behaving like a silly kid who'd thrown his rattle out of his pram and he was trying to embarrass me. How could I have ever liked him, let alone snogged him!

'Shut-up I,' I said. Then I went close and whispered in his ear, 'Bloody shut-up, you stupid kid or I'll tell them about you wearing a dress, you little perv.!'

This was definitely the meanest thing I have ever said to anyone but I was getting desperate. Everyone was looking at us and I was really embarrassed and even Teddy was looking at me as if to say, how come you encouraged that twat to come here! Looking back on it (it's midnight now and a few hours have gone by) I can't believe that I actually said that to him nor what happened next. Yes. I am definitely ashamed of it all now, but you have to realise that he was ruining my night, my special night with Teddy and I had just about had enough of it.

He stopped chanting 'now' as soon as I hissed my threat in is ear and his eyes grew really wide and he looked at me. 'H…How…?' he stammered and then he hesitated. 'It had to be done,' he said. 'He's a priest – and when all is said and done you have to do what a priest asks of you.' There were tears in his eyes and he was shaking now.

I swallowed and then I spoke really slowly, like he was simple or something, 'Billy just fucking go, please.'

I was getting desperate to see the back of him but I was sure that was it and he'd leave now. But instead he looked straight at me and he didn't even blink and when he spoke he sounded sort of far away and lost, 'I can't go,' he said. 'It's not allowed until I have asked.'

I didn't know what he meant but now, thinking about it, I guess he was truly batty and he was having a break-down or something like that. It was horrible but at the time I was just so angry and frustrated that I don't think I really took all that on board.

'Get out,' I hissed. 'I mean it – I really do.' And then I raised my voice, 'I promise you Billy, I will tell them about how you like to wear dresses and what you were doing with that other boy.'

And it was just my luck that as I said that the music stopped and because I'd been speaking dead loud to get over the sound of it, my voice kind of rang around the hall. Suddenly everyone was looking at us and this time I mean really from all over the hall, not just a few tables next to us. You could have heard a pin drop and everyone was kind of like in a cartoon where they all turn and look at you and their mouths hang open.

Teddy looked up and his eyes were actually, literally jumping out of his head and then he began to laugh. It was a quiet laugh at first, like a giggle and then he started to roar really loudly and then so did everyone else. They were all laughing and guffawing and pointing at Billy... and someone shouted out, 'Eh, darling do you wear suspenders and stockings as well!' and they all laughed some more.

Some of them probably saw Billy's shoulders hunch and how he put his hands over his ears to block out the sound, or they may have seen him blush bright red or they may have seen the pain in his eyes but I didn't – when he looked at me, I saw something else – I saw the exact moment when his heart broke.

And then he turned on his heel and ran out of the church hall.

* * *

I should of course go straight home. I am tired and my head is aching and there is a pain inside me like I have never felt before. I can't even think properly. Everything is spinning around me and I feel sick… I can still hear the laughter, and the noise and it is going round in my head and I can see her face – mocking me and tormenting me. She is the devil, she is Peter denying me three times, she is my Judas, betraying me with a kiss.

I am in PAIN. I HURT SO BADLY.

I walk away from the village hall as quickly as I can and eventually, when I am so far from it that I can't even see its lights, I stop under a tree and take a deep breath and then another and the noise and the blood singing in my head begins to quieten down.

It's very hot and the air is steamy (muggy, my mother would say. 'There'll be a storm soon, you can feel it in the air,' my father would say) But it is not raining yet, not exactly – though the air is heavy with damp.

It is a really dark evening, the moon hasn't come out at all, so I feel a little afraid as I begin to walk again, further away from the place where I have been made to look a fool and where my private life has been exposed like something in *The News of The W* for people to laugh at.

I will have to go through the village, then past my

school and all the way along Longdown Road to reach my house – which is miles from anywhere. I tramp through the village High Street and then out into the darkness on the other side.

I still have a mile to walk in the dark and there will be no more street lights. The more I walk, the more I slip into what I call silent contemplation and quiet prayer. Prayer is a v. potent thing. I am v. sorry for those who do not believe in God – such as agnostics and some of the followers of the more exotic religions being foisted upon us by otherwise amazing people, such as George Harrison. My prayer is a comfort to me in this troubled time, in this night of horror.

Then, as I leave the village behind me, stepping out into the thick, wrapped-around darkness of the night, the heavy storm clouds suddenly move apart and from between them comes the light of a v. v. full and summery moon. Immediately, the whole world is flooded in silver grey light and it is a sign from God that He has heard my prayers and He is watching over me, even now at the time of my betrayal.

I have been tortured and humiliated, but He is well pleased with me. It is enough.

My mood changes at once. I can forget the embarrassment and the deep, deep hurt caused by the girl, my Judas Iscariot at the disco. Even the hot dampness of the air seems to have cleared a little and suddenly I feel dead excited, like when you get up on a summer morning really early and the day is spread out full of excitement in front of you.

I can see towards the first bend in the road, I can see across the fields towards the water meadows and I can see across the valley and up the hill, all the way to my woods, where my clearing is. It is beautiful and wonderful and mysterious.

I think the moon is God's light even more than the sun is. The sun is so hard and hot and harsh and burns at you and startles you; whereas the moon is gentle like a spirit and makes you look soft and attractive – even when you have acne, such as I do, and bad hair.

I have stopped walking and I am looking around at all this moonlit beauty and my eyes keep going back to the woods at the top of the hill.

My woods.

I suppose it is because I am confused by the terrible events of the night and everything that has happened today with the girl and Edwards and.. and ...well... just confused by pretty well everything that has made up the last few weeks of my life. I suppose also, that I realise that I owe a lot to GOD in the way of prayer and penance... I suppose it is because of all this that I decide that I must go to the clearing – even though it is so late.

You are probably wondering why. Why not just go home? Why not pray in bed or on my bedroom floor, as I do every night? I don't know. I just know that this seems right and is what I must do. I am DRAWN, as it were, by some inexplicable power.

I suppose it is GOD'S WILL and HIS will be done!

So I must go.

I cut off down Miller's Lane, which runs along the side of my school's cricket pitch and which peters out after a few hundred yards and becomes a farm track. I trudge along the track in the moonlight, towards the edge of the field that slopes up towards my woods, and although the moon is still bright I stumble occasionally on pot-holes and I discover that something happens to sound in the night that I had not noticed before: the track is damp and gravely and my feet crunch over it and yet, oddly, the sound of them seems to be echoing behind me.

It is almost as if someone is following me and I have a sudden strange feeling that the sound has been with me for a while, in the background as it were, at the back of my head where I haven't paid it much attention. Perhaps it is an echo, because it stops when I stop, and once or twice I pause and spin round to see if I can catch anyone behind me and there is nothing there, nothing at least, that I can see.

When I slip into the darkness of my woods, the trees above my head stir in a gentle breeze, dropping globs of night dampness onto my head and a thought occurs to me; if I am being followed it doesn't matter, because now that I am in the woods I am with my angel, because this is where my angel lives and becomes present to me. Now I am here I will be protected...

...From all things.

* * *

I must be mad! It's well past midnight and I am going to go out and find him. I can't believe that I really intend to do this. He's probably at home and I don't even know where that is but I just have this feeling he won't be. He is a child of the wild, child of the night, child of the woods... And I know that's where he'll be – in his clearing.

It's a bright night outside, the moon is out and I am really not afraid. I guess I should be, but I am not. I need to see him. I need to explain. I have never seen anyone who looked in so much pain, and I did it! I made him like that and I need to put it right.

And there is something else… I think I still fancy him. I can't believe it, even with Teddy and everything that has gone on… When I saw his face, how miserable I'd made him, I like felt dead sorry and I also felt, well, you know… Like… Like I wanted to… Shit! Di, sometimes you're weird… How could I?

Tomorrow I'll write in this dairy again and I wonder what I will be saying. That he accepted my apology I hope, or that he hates me and he always will… or…

Well, we shall see… Tomorrow is another day.

* * *

I could get to my clearing even with a blindfold on, let alone at night. I could do it, let me tell you, from any point, anywhere in these woods, even if you just took me there with a hood on my head and let me go and said 'OK find the clearing!' I would. Guarantee it!

And that's what I am doing now, pushing through the undergrowth and the ferns that grow everywhere and bumping into trees, stepping from patches of silver moonlight into dark shadows and wading through blobs of darkness and all the time climbing up to the top of the hill on which these woods grow, which is where my secret clearing is – far away from my parents, from my school, from Teddy Edwards and the youth club and the people in it and from… *HER!*

When I get to my clearing I push my way in through the little opening by the Sycamore tree and I have to stop for a second: I have never seen the clearing look like this. Never. I am here most days; I have been here in fog and I have been here in wind, rain, hot summer sun and even in the snow –

but I have never seen it like this. The moon shines down on it and it now looks like I have always known it to be, inside my soul.

Yes. Now, even more than usual, my clearing is a mystical place, a spiritual place. The place where I can pray and reach my God and where my angel visits me. It is glittering and strange and there are ghostly shadows and shimmering shapes; there is a stillness and strangeness and it is beautiful – not beautiful like the girl's beauty or her mum's beauty, or the inside of the cat, nor beauty like when I look at the countryside in the sunshine and ache for the water meadows and the hay which the farmer cuts and stacks in his fields. It is not even beauty like I have seen when we went on a trip to the National Gallery and looked at lots of dark and cracked old masters that could have done with a bit of a scrub-up in my opinion, and which, although everyone said they were beautiful, were not as good I reckon as the Rowney & Co. paint by numbers oil – *'View Of A Spanish Village'* that my Dad did when I was nine and hangs on our living room wall.

No, this beauty is like the beauty of classical music, of which I only know Beethoven, but which deeply moves me at times. It is even like the most beautiful of all earthly things – the work of the pop music legends Lennon and McCartney, when at their absolute best in producing such landmark works as *'Eleanor Rigby'* and *'Yesterday'*.

It is this kind of beauty that I look at now in my clearing: spiritual, mysterious and deeply moving, touching something in my soul.

I stand there looking around and I am filled with awe at HIS mysterious works. That HE could create something so extraordinary, spin a kind of magic from trees and brambles and scruffy grass that I have seen so often, every day for years. This is why GOD is great in my O.

So, I fall to my knees and the wet grass soaks uncomfortably through my trousers and I don't care. I have to join my hands together in prayer because there is much to pray about.

First, I must thank God for creating this awesome sight, my clearing by moonlight – next, I must beg forgiveness for touching a girl and for allowing her to press her busty substances against my wind-cheater as she did in her house; I must beg even more forgiveness for lusting after an older woman and becoming, what they call in certain novels 'aroused' at the sight of her legs and her black, enticingly gorgeous underwear, that I want to run my hands over and press my 'arousal' into... and I must beg forgiveness for tonight, for being a fool and allowing lust to rule my mind, for wanting to be with a girl instead of being true to myself and to my God.

OH, GOD…

OH, GOD…

Forgive me! But even as I pray to YOU, I think things I should not and I have a picture in my head of my erect penis encased in the black fabric of her mum's underwear. I am so ashamed. I am mortified.

I must be punished.

I...

Must...

Be...

...PUNISHED!

I press my hands to my head and I squeeze my eyes more tightly closed to keep the pictures away and I bend my head low towards the ground. I press my fists so hard into my temples that I can feel stabs of pain behind my eyes and I make myself feel dizzy and faint.

I start to say my confession:

'*Confiteor Deo Omnipotenti...*' I pray to Almighty God. '*Quia peccavi nimis cogitatione, verbo, et opera; mea culpa, mea culpa, mea maxima culpa...*'

I beat my breast as is appropriate every time I utter the word 'culpa'.

But I can't concentrate. I feel sick. Nauseous. And then through the pain and the prayer I *hear something*.

There it is again...

There is a sound. Somewhere on the other side of the clearing I have heard a small rustle of branches and leaves; surreptitious, insignificant you might think it – but to me it is different from the other sounds of the woods which I know so well.

I freeze, my right fist raised over my left breast and I listen intently, though I am pretty sure I know what it is that I can hear. It will be my angel again, made flesh and come to follow me, to watch over me, as he invariably does, here in the woods.

I seem to stay like this, fist suspended over my chest, my head in whirl of confession and prayer and my soul in torment for ages, listening for another sound, waiting for HIM to appear.

I look up at the place where I think the sound has come from and my head spins as the blood rushes from my brain. I can't see clearly, it's hard to focus in the silvery light, and the more I stare, the more the trees and the bushes become blurred and distorted..

And then...

Dear Lord Our GOD, and then...

The trees start to move and they fall apart, literally (and I mean literally as in reality, not like when you normally say literally and don't mean literally at all). The trees swish apart like curtains being swept aside, like on the stage in a theatre – like when I have been to the Leeford Civic Halls for the panto and the lights go down and the curtains whoosh apart in the middle.

I can see a deep, black void on the other side of this split in the trees and for a second nothing else happens. Then, all at once, the darkness is shattered as a bright light, such as the spotlight they use when the fairy godmother appears, cuts into the night.

It wheels around the clearing for a second or two before it settles on the gap in the trees and pierces the shadowy void. I am amazed to see that it has picked out a small figure, clad in a white robe, who has moved into centre stage in the moonlit night.

The figure stands for a moment, looking out at me, blinking in the bright light. Then it raises its arms, holding its hands out to me, appealing to me, turning its palms as if to show me something.

And at first I think it is JESUS CHRIST, the word made flesh, HIMSELF – and that he is showing me his stigmata. I start to tremble in dreadful awe and fear at this.

But it is not. It is not HIM.

I realise that it is the figure of a girl that I am looking at. She is small – slight, you might say, and very, very beautiful. I have never seen anyone so attractive. Even watching her from this side of the clearing I am astonished at her beauty, she seems to radiate it from deep inside herself.

Oddly, even though I am so far away, I can see straight into her eyes and they are stunning too, like her face, and they are even more beautiful because they are softened by a rim of smudgy freckles and framed by her long, fair hair.

We seem to be here frozen in time, in this moonlit clearing; silent, without moving, just looking at each other for ages and ages. Then, quite slowly, she starts to walk towards me. I have to bow my head. I have to bow it low because I am not worthy to look into her eyes – into the eyes of the Mother Of God.

For this is she.

This is the BVM. The Blessed Virgin Mary, herself and I am NOT worthy.

As I have told you, I have had my visions before and I have always expected something like this to happen. It is my reward I think, for being in a Holy state and for being in a state of grace and prayer but I am astonished that tonight, on this night, when I am so unclean, when I have been sullied and mocked, that tonight of all nights, I should have my ultimate vision. 0ow could it be that tomnHow could it be that tonight I am to become one of that illustrious company that includes Bernadette and the three children of Fatima?

How can I have been chosen?

I notice that she is carrying something – a rosary perhaps and she has another round her neck, and on her head there is a crown made out of silver stars... And her robe..? Why, it is so bright, that you might almost think the sun was shining down on her – not the moon in the night sky above our heads.

She is very close now. I could reach out and touch her if I wanted to but I am too respectful to do such a thing to

HER, to the VIRGIN mother, the MATER DEI, the STELLA MARIS...

I say quietly, under my breath, 'Ave... Ave Maria!'

She lowers her head when she hears me speak and she seems to lean forward to hear what I have said and she looks puzzled. We stand like this, awkwardly facing each other until I begin to shuffle uncomfortably. But she is still staring at me from under a fringe of golden hair and through those long eye lashes.

She is, I think, like a young girl, shy in front of a stranger. Her eyes are so soft and tender, a little frightened perhaps, yet deep within them there is a real spark, a flame of brightness that you would have to be blind not to see. There is something dead attractive about this, the way that she is looking at me from under her fringe.

My mouth has gone dry and I swallow uncomfortably, but I can't take my eyes off her and her gaze never leaves mine; she is staring at me intently and there is a little quiver of amusement at the corners of her mouth, as if she knows something about this situation that I do not. Which is, of course, more than likely as she has been involved in several visions and visitations and this is my v. first experience. In a way, you might say, when it comes to visions she is definitely a bit of an expert, compared to what you might call my amateur status.

At last she opens her beautiful red lips and I think she is going to say something but I am dead surprised to see that she traces the outline of her lips with the tip of her tongue, whilst she continues to gaze at me. I realise with a shock she is being, well, *sexy,* and that she is flirting with me.

With *me!!*

I cannot take this in at all. I mean this is the B.V.M!!

Then I realise that my imagination is running away with me and I feel a hot flush of embarrassment and shame. I don't know what to say or do. I am dead uncomfortable, as she must know what I have been thinking because after all, she is both flesh *and* spirit, when all is s. and done. So she will definitely be into mind-reading and looking deep into my soul!

I want to die of humiliation...

And yet, she is still looking at me in *that* way. And she is still licking her lips and staring up at me in what you might call a 'coy' fashion.

I am not proud of what happened next. I really am not...

She walks forward, all of a sudden. There isn't much of a distance between us at this point in time and what there is she covers remarkably quickly, I mean I can't even draw my breath to say 'No!'

So, I don't.

She flings her arms around me, which is a bit of shock I can tell you, and she presses her body very close against mine. Once again I feel busty substances pushing into my chest. And to think that up until recently I have hardly got near a breast – even my mother bottle fed me.

Then, that hard little red tongue that I have been looking at starts tease my lips. I try to pull away but it is hopeless. Perhaps I don't really want to, because tiny kisses are now showering my eyes and cheeks. They are gentle kisses, like being touched by a feather.

I am too stunned to know what to do, so I do nothing. I stand there with my hands by my side as the B.V.M. grasps at me and runs her hands over my body and presses her lips against mine. I am immobile. She kisses me more eagerly, with more urgency but I am a statue, rigid in immobility and this only seems to make her more eager and she clings more hopefully to me, pressing herself to me.

I feel her reach for my crotch as she rubs herself up and down over me, pushing her breasts provocatively against me. But she barely touches me there before she slides her hands from the front of my body round to the back and she begins to manipulate, to knead, you might say, my buttocks, clasping them and rubbing them, tracing the shape of them with her fingers and then her hands creep round again to my zip area.

I draw in a sharp little breath – I suppose I should not be surprised that she has found my penis so easily, for I suddenly realise that it is huge and swollen and pressing against the front of my trousers like a cricket bat or, as is more appropriate in the circs, like a baseball bat.

Then I hear the zip go. She is pulling it down hastily, she has my belt buckle now and pulls it undone too, flicking the tips of the belt back so hard as they fly open that I can feel them snap against my thighs; she tears at my gaping trousers and the little steel catch flies apart, probably breaking it for all I know, and the black button pings off and sails off somewhere into the distance. She rips my trousers open and pulls them roughly down.

Men never look dignified without their trousers, my father once said, and I am no exception I think, as I look down at my white legs which reflect the moonlight. And then, with a lurch that makes my heart race, I suddenly know what she is going to do and I brace myself for the shock.

I should be embarrassed, I should push her away, I should pull her hand away and hide my nakedness or I should run screaming for my angel. But I do nothing. I can only stare down at the top of her head, at the golden hair.

Yes, I do nothing because as she presses herself against me I know that for the first time I am properly alive, that I am John Lennon, Paul McCartney and Superman rolled into one; that I am perfectly complete with body and spirit; that I am the music of '*Abbey Road*', the '*9th Symphony*' and the cold water of the stream and glow of the moonlight and heat of the sun and the rustle of the leaves and the rain in the night.

And I am powerful and strong – I could break Teddy Edwards in one hand if I wanted or pick-up a dodgem car and hurl it through the night with the other if I preferred. I could stamp on the youth club and crush those who laugh at me. I can give life. I can take life. I am perfect. I am all powerful. All good and all bad.

I watch myself as if I am in another body and I look down as if I am high on a hill and I see the spurts of white semen as they pump from my penis and arc into the air and splash onto the wet ground beneath and trickle over the fallen leaves and drip from the blades of grass and I don't care that my angel is watching me from the bushes and I don't care that I have broken all the rules I set for myself and that I have completely lost the total CONTROL over myself which I value so highly.

I sink back to my knees. I close my eyes as the waves of power fade away and my muscles unclench themselves and my mind lets itself slide back from the brink of infinite happiness where it has just been.

I rock back on my haunches and look up at the moon through the branches of the trees and I see the dark clouds scurry across its face and I sigh and let my body shudder and it is the most COMPLETE sigh I have ever made.

I feel myself slump, my head tips back and dozily I let my eyes readjust and focus and it does not of course surprise me that she is looking at me and grinning.

And I think, OK. This is just another of MY visions. Not a Holy one. Not at all! Just my imagination again, playing tricks on me as it did in Emma's Mum's kitchen and at the fairground – and it is all so clear to me for a moment. It is all my imagination. Everything is my imagination.

All the things that I do and believe in, all my fears and hopes and little routines and suffering and penance. They are none of them real. I look around with newly opened eyes – *'nothing is real, nothing to get hung about'* as John L., would say.

Except one thing is real. The bushes are moving over on the other side of the clearing. They are real and they are moving because my angel is there; shocked no doubt at the sight he has seen – despairing no doubt at the hopelessness into which I have sunk and the pit of despondency into which I slink. Knowing, as he does, that he will probably not be able to rescue me from such perdition he is still coming for me, intent on my rescue, and the BVM turns to face him with a sudden look of surprise on her face.

I lower my forehead to the ground and the salt tears mingle with the seed that I have left there on the dry grass.

And just before I pass out I think, I wonder what will grow here – dreams or nightmares?

* * *

I don't like lying in bed in the morning. It's not my way. 'Slovenly start to the day, slovenly all of the day,' my father says and I must say he has a point. Some of the boys I know who don't get out of bed at the weekends until gone ten or even later, are what you might call the worse kind of person. They are also the ones who cause trouble in class and distract the better pupils. Naming no names but they are all like Edwards who I bet doesn't get out of bed until at least twelve.

So, as I say, I am normally up by seven, even at the weekends and when it's summer and the weather is fine I like to think that I can rise with the sun. I reckon if God gives us nice days it is our duty to make the most of them. I like to be out and about and if you haven't seen the sunrise from my little clearing in the woods, then you haven't lived in my H opinion.

So it is unusual for me to be here in bed dozing on a Saturday morning. However, for the last week I haven't been sleeping well. It is because of the terrible and horrific events of the previous weekend. For the last week I've been going to bed later than usual because I don't feel like sleeping and when I have got into bed I've hardly slept at all, so that I am still tired in the mornings. I have suffered terribly reliving the events of what occurred last Saturday: the humiliation, the embarrassment of the disco and worse, the experience in the woods...

As I have tossed and turned all night I have repeatedly told myself that I never asked her to come into my life, that none of it is my fault; I never asked her to take over my clearing, to sit next to my stream and drag me through the crowded streets of Leeford like a... like a dog on a leash – but she did all this and more... She invaded me... she made what I can only call intimate advances – some with her tongue; she put her hands where no one except my mother has ever put their hands – and even she hasn't put them there recently, not since I was a baby in fact.

It wasn't my fault I started to *like* her attentions – I was sucked into her web as if she was a black widow (I do not mean a mother of one of the little African babies we collect for in class but the deadly spider) and through no fault of my own, I started to enjoy being with her.

So I have been lying in bed with a muddle in my head of words and memories and the things she said to me that keep whizzing around and colliding with each other. I don't know what I feel about her or what she feels about me or why it has all changed as quickly as it started. But I do know above everything, that I feel hatred for Teddy Edwards. One of the romantic novels that my mother likes to read would have put it like this – '...*his smooth but dangerous charms have destroyed everything that Diana/Emma and I might have been.*'

And realising this I suddenly feel very grown-up. We – she and I – might have been *on the verge of something* – This thought shocks me and with a start, I realise I am beginning to be mature at last.

I must get a grip.

I take a deep breath and at last I open my eyes and look around my room, at the open window and the sun coming through the gaps in my *Treasure Island* curtains that my mother says she will replace only when they wear out (though frankly, I have moved on from Mr Stephenson's stories). I look at my book cases, at my crucifix above the door, at my collection of useful reference books on the shelves and these things make me feel good, safe. They are mine, unsullied by the world outside.

Lying here in bed, hearing the familiar sounds of the birds singing nearby, the sound of a tractor further off in Butler's farm, the bell ringers practising for tomorrow, I begin to feel happy again, content you might say. And then I am surprised to look at my watch and see that it is now nearly ten o'clock.

I must get up, although I don't want to, but if I don't my mother will think I am ill. I pull on my summer holiday khaki shorts with the snake belt and my second favourite Aertex T-Shirt. My favourite hasn't been quite the same since the wetting it received in the stream – I think not drying it properly may have shrunk it a little, and I put on my white socks and a pair of leather sandals.

In the kitchen I find my parents but they look odd – unwell it seems to me and they don't smile at my cheery greeting. You could say they look ashen.

This is strange. They both seemed full of beans last night at their bridge evening and my mother's *Angels on Horseback* had been very well received by her friends, which had made her very jolly – and I expect the gin helped too, of which she had quite a lot.

My father looks at me.

'Billy,' he says. And there is something in his voice which makes me feel cold and my mouth goes dry.

'Billy,' he says again and then he swallows and carries on in a funny, croaky voice. 'I don't want to alarm you and I'm sorry to have to tell you this but I have some bad news. Those woods where you like to play…'

'Yes,' I say. 'Play!' I think. 'I am not seven!'

'They've found something Billy. Something terrible and you mustn't go there today or for a very long time.'

I look at him. I am confused.

'Found?' I say.

'Yes,' the police have been round asking everyone in the area to keep away while they carry out some investigations.'

'What have they found?' I say.

My father looks at my mother and she puts her hand to her mouth and sits heavily on a kitchen chair.

My father clear his throat.

'They found...' he looks at my mother but she is staring at one of the floor tiles beneath her feet.

'They found,' he says, 'A... A body...'

I look from one to the other of them but I can't say much. Not in the circumstances.

My mother looks up suddenly and her voice is oddly shrill.

'Or to be more precise,' she says. 'They found *part* of a body... They're looking for the rest.'

I don't know what to say. So I say, 'Oh.' Which isn't much but the best I can do.

'Oh, that poor girl!' My mother says and she begins to cry.

* * *

Tell me everything, that's what you said.

Apparently I have gone mad. Depression, you said. The affect of grief you said, I've been plunged into a dark tunnel, you said. This happens to everyone apparently, after a sudden and unexpected death.

Actually, and I know you're the expert so do forgive me, but it happens after any kind of death in my experience, expected or not. After James died I went into a very dark place, a dark and very lonely place and that was not an unexpected death, that one we'd seen coming for months. Anyway, you tell me I will get through the darkness and out the other side. Soon I will catch a glimpse of the light at the end of the tunnel... One day the sun will shine again and I will want to live my life again. That's what you said. And in my head I thought, if he's going to talk in bloody clichés I will go even more mad than I already am. You know so much don't you, you psychiatrists, but you don't know that it's the little things that irritate the most.

I wonder how long it takes you to qualify? I'm hopeless about education and things. Do you have to become a doctor first and then learn to be a trick cyclist or do you just start off as one at university? Is there a degree in trick cyclery? I suppose there must be. How complicated it must be – learning all that Jung and Freud and... and... is it Adler? Or maybe Adler plays the harmonica – I get confused – whoever, it doesn't really matter. I don't know anything about psychiatrists whereas you must know loads of them, I mean the famous ones. What a lot of work, what a lot of reading you must have done, what a lot of studying. What a drag!

My higher education was three years of voice coaching, learning to breathe right and walking round a stage projecting like mad and trying not to bump into the furniture and smoking quite a lot of marijuana, hugging each other and showing-off. So, unlike you I've never read much, apart from plays.

How glamorous I felt in those days, how important. After all, we were the new generation of actress: hip, real, sexy and liberated – Julie Christies and Susannah Yorks – we were to become birds in a Michael Caine movie – dollies on the pill, sassy girls on the box. Not me though. I got up the duff, instead.

This isn't what you wanted is it, when you said record it all on this little tape machine I'm going to give you? It's a kind of therapy you said. Tell the tape machine just how you feel, say what you want, whenever you want – even in the middle of the night when you can't sleep. Imagine you're sending me a letter from inside yourself. Record how you feel about everything, you said

Shit! That's how I feel, Doctor. Totally fucking shit.

Are you shocked? Does your generation not approve of women (even women from a 'theatrical' background) swearing like a docker? Probably not – but then as a psychiatrist you must have heard a lot worse. I remember once in my third year at RADA they sent us to Caine Hill, which is a nut house in Surrey (but you probably know that) and we had to perform for the loonies. It was supposed to be good for them and to teach us to perfect our art, to teach us to 'involve' even the most difficult audience. We did extracts from *The Three Sisters* – which was a fucking stupid idea and pretentious to say the least. I was Irena: *Tell me, why am I so happy today...?* I began and this voice in the audience said, '*Cos you're a cunt!*'

And next thing we knew they were all shouting '*Cunt...Cunt...Cunt...*' Some of them were on the floor, rocking back and forwards on their arses, one woman was hitting her head with the back of her hand and another one started to run round in circles – and they were all shouting '*Cunt...*' absolutely together – perfect timing... and then they went crazy – jigging around, throwing themselves against the walls, crawling on the ground, one of them even shat himself. It was like the *Marat/Sade* only better or maybe worse. We stood and watched because they weren't taking a blind bit of notice of us – their own performance was far more entertaining. Performance art at its best by a bunch of loonies. Eat your heart out Bertolt Brecht!

Why did I think of that? Ah well, happy days!

I'm not doing what you want am I? I'm not coming to terms with the reality of what's happened. Well fuck it! Life's a bitch. Who did it? Why? That's all I really want to know... Who killed her? Who killed Diana? Who killed my daughter?! There's nothing else say, is there?

THE GRADUATE

Yesterday I went back to the woods. To my clearing. I haven't been there for a long time, in fact for a moment I couldn't remember just how long it was. I tried to work it out as I climbed the hill: the 'thing' happened to the girl the year before I did my O-levels; then there were the two years in the sixth form, the ill fated trip to France, the year with the rock group and then three years at Cambridge. So that's what? I work it out on my fingers because I still can't – how did he put it? – add, subtract, multiply or divide and I realize I must have been fifteen maybe sixteen. A teenager! And so confused – a muddled-up teenager if ever there was one. But I think I have moved on. I've cleared my mind of a lot of things. It's for the best, I think...

I should have come to the clearing before. I mean, I've been around in the vacations, well, not every vacation because of work – summer jobs in recording studios, anywhere I could get a bit of work in the music business. But I have been home quite a lot really, against my better judgement truth to tell, but a good feed and a washing machine aren't to be sneezed at when you're a broke student. But I don't know, every trip home it just hits me more and more how bloody, what's the word, 'provincial' it all is. And let's face it my parents are not exactly 'right on' when it comes to the things I like – rock music, theatre, cinema, new writers – anything really.

Let's face it, down at the Golf Club they don't often discuss prog rock and I suppose the merits of '*King Crimson*' over '*Genesis*' barely figure at a Bridge Evening. Mind you, there's not much to discuss on that one – '*Crimson*' every time rather than the dreadful Mr Gabriel.

So, I don't know why, but yesterday I went there at last, to the clearing.

I climbed the hill, just like in the old days, with the school and Butler's farm behind me and the water meadows and the stream off to my right, and all the way I was saying to myself that I was just going for a stroll as it was a nice afternoon and my head was still buzzing from doing finals – well, buzzing from the May Ball to be more honest – I just needed a bit of a walk to clear my head and then there I was, pushing through the scrubby bushes, being stung by the nettles and scraped by the brambles and stepping into the clearing.

I looked around quite slowly – as John Lennon might have said, and I was a bit frightened and shocked at what I'd done. Fortunately though, there are no ghosts, not in my book anyway, and there was no girl with kaleidoscope eyes to haunt me.

The trees seemed heavier, their branches a little more over-hanging and the scrubby bushes that surrounded the place and kept it private and away from prying eyes were even thicker than I remembered. But that's nature for you –

always on the move. Otherwise it was still the same. The grass grew thickly, the old fallen tree trunk still lay on its side, rotting slowly and the branches of the sycamore tree, though a little faxed in the hot sun, were still casting their shadow on the ground. In the centre of the clearing where I stood, out of the shadows, the sun beat down as hot as it always seemed to in my memories and looking up I couldn't see a cloud in the deep blue sky above my head. Suddenly, I was fifteen again.

Over there was the place I used to lie down and do my homework and behind me was the sacred area, the bushes where my angel hid and kept guard over me. I glanced around quickly but there was no sign of him today. He was gone – at least for now – and who could blame him after what happened, after what he witnessed. I wondered if he had gone for good. Perhaps he had waited there in the shade of summer days and the cool of autumn ones and in the rain and snow of winter wondering what had become of me, waiting for me to come back, until wet and bedraggled, his wings sodden and dripping, he had given up and gone away.

Over there, under the sycamore tree, was where I kept my bag with the tools of what I liked to call my 'trade' – though really it was just a hobby. I could have dug them up there and then but on reflection I decided to let them lie. And there, there was where *she* had found me, pushing through the bushes in a flash of blue and gold and memories of blonde hair, freckles and dangerously short skirts crashed into my mind, so that I had to close my eyes and shake my head to clear it.

Yesterday I went back to the woods. To my clearing – but I didn't stay there very long because...

...Because of what happened there, seven years ago.

Before I left, I stood in the centre of the place and I looked up and then I turned slowly round, looking at the whole place, spinning slowly through three hundred and sixty degrees, like a camera shot in an *Antonioni* film, surveying what used to be mine and when I'd taken it all in I started to walk away. I was going home... But then I stopped because I'd trodden on something.

I looked down and there was a little posy of dead flowers under my foot. I bent down to look more closely. I'm not great at flora – fauna are more my thing – but I recognised thyme and violets and the little roses. A poem crept into my mind but I couldn't remember all the words, yet somehow I knew that the other unknown flowers must be woodbine and oxlips.

There was a little card and someone had written something on it – I could just make out some shapes of letters in red ink but the weather had washed the words away and the card was crumbling.

Although the flowers were all dead I felt guilty about standing on them, so I tried to brush them up a bit and restore the shape of the posy but the dried flowers fell apart and the leaves scattered on the afternoon breeze and that made me feel even worse, like I'd violated something or trodden on someone's memories.

Angry with myself I picked up what was left of the arrangement and I threw it into the bushes. But I couldn't help wondering who had left it there.

'Ah, well,' I thought, 'It's not really my problem.'

And so I left.

I was half-way down the hill on the way back to my parents' house before I remembered:

'*I know a bank where the wild thyme blows; where oxlips and the nodding violet grows, quite over-canopied with luscious woodbine, with sweet musk-roses and with eglantine.*'

And I said to myself, 'It's Shakespeare, stupid.'

* * *

'You'll love it,' my mother says.

'It'll be a nice crowd old son,' my father says. 'And apart from the family…' (by which he means my grandparents, aunts, uncles cousins and various distant in-breds from the countryside and even the North of England who I barely know and don't particularly want to) '…They'll be some of the of crowd from your school days,' he goes on, 'And quite a lot of my chums from the Golf Club too.'

Inwardly I shudder. I'd rather spend time with the in-mates of a mental asylum.

'And some of the ladies from the Amateur Dramatic Club and their hubbies,' my mother says.

'Hubbies!' I think. Why do I have to have a mother who uses a word like '*hubbies*.

The World has gone mad I think. Stark staring bonkers. Why on earth do my parents think it is worth their while to throw a party just because I am about to be twenty one. As if she has read my mind my mother says, 'Of course, it's not just your twenty-first, it's a chance to celebrate your degree and your future…' And then she hesitates. 'I expect you'll want to invite your friends from Cambridge won't you?'

Oh, God! She's going to spend the entire party telling her friends about Cambridge and trying to introduce them to what she has taken to calling 'the glitterati' of my generation.

She's bored them to death for three years while I've been there with her showing-off about me and now she wants to rub my friends in their faces as well. And she'll say to Mrs Barry, 'Oh, do bring your Edward with you if he's back home – oh, no I forgot he'll still be at Sussex. One forgets how short the Oxbridge terms are.'

And she'll invite Mrs Tunny's Sarah, who is desperate for a husband (and probably more besides) and say what a chance it is for a nice young girl to meet a few well educated undergrads. And no doubt my father will make some ridiculous and deeply embarrassing speech about my academic success and glow in the after-light of my education, revelling in it as he always does and wondering if he might have had the chance to go to university if it hadn't been for the war.

'We had to do our bit,' he'll say, 'And that was my higher education in its way – fighting Adolf.' Apparently the Ratings office was considered a reserved occupation. I am not too sure how close he would actually have come to Adolf or any German come to that, in County Hall, Park Lane, Croydon.

Then my mother says, and I should have seen this one coming, 'I don't know if there's anyone special you'd like to invite..?'

She means a girl. More precisely she means a girlfriend..

'No there isn't,' I say sharply.

'Oh, Billy,' my mother sighs. 'Hasn't there been anyone since... Well, you know?' and she stares at me like a hopeful dog expecting a walk.

I sigh.

'Do we have to do this?' I ask, ignoring Lassie and turning to face my father.

'Yes.' My father says coldly, glancing at my mother. 'Yes we do. And it's all fixed. Kindly don't upset your mother by complaining about it. It's a very nice gesture.'

I realise he is about to go on about how much it has cost to send me to university and how it isn't asking much to ask me to attend my own party, so I nod and say, 'Fine. Fine... But I'm not wearing a suit.'

* * *

It's a beautiful sunny Saturday afternoon a few weeks later and my parents have gone to a lot of trouble. The French windows are open onto the back garden and they have put up a whole variety of little camping tables (borrowed from friends) and covered them in paper tablecloths which they have weighted down with bowls of Cheeselets and cheese and onion crisps to stop them blowing away in the gentle breeze. They have pulled the kitchen table out into the centre of the lawn and my mother's writing table too and these are also covered in paper cloths.

Everywhere there are various chairs for the guests: dining chairs, kitchen chairs, little folding camping chairs, I even spot the piano stool over by the fish pond. Under the kitchen window there is a long trestle table that my father refers to as the 'bar' and it is covered in various glasses – everything from our kitchen tumblers through to his favourite crystal whisky glasses and bottles of wine, scotch and gin. There is a bucket for ice and the kitchen window is hooked open so that additional supplies of cold beer and cans of coke can be passed through from the fridge. He has even splashed out on a couple of *Watney's Pipkins* that he has placed at each end of the table and through the window you can smell the vol-au-vents and sausage rolls cooking in the oven.

To my horror they have made a banner that hangs from their bedroom window. It says, 'PY BIRTHDAY BI' because they have had to fix it by folding each end and trapping them in the window jams – but you can tell what it is meant to say and as my father explains to his guests, 'The execution went a little awry but the message is heart-felt.'

The garden is filling up with people and I am trying to hide in the far corner between the shed and the fence. I am near the bolt-hole I used to use as a kid when I wanted to slip away and go up to the woods and I must admit that right now I am very tempted to scrabble onto the ground, push the broken fence paling to one side and run away.

Although I am in the shade, I am sweating inside my suit. It is very hot, even for August and my collar is too tight and my tie is strangling me and I think about the granddad shirt and the shorts I have left on my bed, because in the end I didn't have the courage to be a rebel. I am clutching a tin of *Harp*. My father had offered me a pint glass to put it in but I thought, 'No. If I can't rebel in my clothes, I will drink out of the can instead.'

'A disgusting habit,' my father says – which rather pleases me.

I slump against the side of the shed and hope that I won't be spotted as I watch the influx of guests. I take a slurp of the beer, which is already warm and I make a note to write to the brewers to point out that it has not stayed '*sharp right to the bottom of the glass*' as promised in the TV advert. Of course this may be because I am drinking it from a tin and I am just thinking that I'll put the next one in a glass after all and see if there is a discernible difference when I see a familiar figure stepping through the French windows.

I'm pretty speechless I don't mind saying, well actually I am not talking to anyone but if I was I would definitely be speechless. Already swathed in a cloud of cigarette smoke, his hands nervously shaking as he clutches his glass of scotch and his left eye twitching erratically, his red moustache glowing in the afternoon sun, Mr Terry looks around, blinking in the light. I don't think I have ever seen him outdoors before, so this is probably something of a shock to him.

'Why on earth have they invited him?' I think. I drop back further into the shadows. Suppose he spots me? What on earth are we going to say to each other – him a teacher and me just a school kid. It's a bit of a shock for me to remember that I am not a kid anymore and he is not my teacher, but you know what I mean.

Shit! He's seen me and he's coming over, carving his way through the Bridge Club ladies and the Golf Club committee like a small tug-boat or, judging from the way people are backing away from him, a trawler loaded with yesterday's rotting fish.

'Ah,' he says, arriving at my side and blowing smoke in my face and I think he'll say something else but he doesn't and so we both stare awkwardly at each other and then we both take a drink at the same time, which is deeply embarrassing, like we're some kind of terrible double act.

Finally I swallow hard and say, 'Hello, Sir.'

He grunts. 'Not Sir. No need now...'

And there is another silence during which I am careful not to take a drink. Finally he says, 'So, graduated, eh?'

I nod.

'Kind of your parents to ask me along...' He looks around at the steadily filling garden and he doesn't look like he's that happy about it really or maybe he's trying to remember which ones my parents are – some people, especially in this village, all look the same. 'So, you're going into music I gather?' He says at last.

'Yes,' I grunt. 'Well, at least I hope so. You know if I can find a job...'

'I didn't know you were musical. You weren't at school – in fact you had fockin' awful voice as I recall.'

I'm a bit shocked at that to put it mildly, both at the obscenity in my parents' garden of all places and also at his rudeness.

'Actually,' I say with some dignity, 'I always played the guitar and I played a little piano but I never brought my instrument into school...' This sounds a bit odd so I add, '...for personal reasons.' Which sounds even odder. The truth was that I was terrified of being mocked. I had seen a school band playing at a talent contest in my third year and even though they were quite good the 1st XV had thrown jelly and jammy dodgers at them and the lead guitarist had been hit quite painfully in the left eye by a wayward garibaldi.

'But you read English at Oxford, didn't you?'

'Cambridge,' I say icily. 'Yes I did, but I wrote a music review column for *Broadsheet* and the band I played in gained quite a following and was voted the best in Cambridge two years running.'

He grunts. 'Handy,' he says. 'Writing your own reviews.'

He slurps some more whisky. 'Your parents said they

had me to thank for getting your English up to standard. Wanted me to be here as I helped get you into university.'

I don't know what to say, so I just say, 'Thank you.' Which is a bit lame really.

'No. Credit where credit is due. You did well. I mean considering...'

And suddenly he looks uncomfortable. At first I'm not sure what he means but then he goes on. 'You know, seeing as how there was all that trouble, when that.. when your friend... Well, it must have been very distracting. I'm surprised you came through it.'

We both shuffle awkwardly and I suppose we're both wishing he hadn't said anything. He takes another sip of whisky and blinks at me.

'What with the police and everything...'

I take a sip from my can.

'I did my bit to help. That's all...' I say.

'Still... You know... her being a friend of yours...'

'Yes... It was very upsetting.' I pause and add. 'At the time.' Hoping that he will realise that I mean what's in the past should be left there.

I look away from him and we both look out across the garden, staring at the guests, both feeling awkward in each others' company but neither of us wanting to leave the safety of the shed and mingle with people we don't know and probably wouldn't like.

'I suppose I must have helped you with the music,' he says suddenly. And he turns bright eyes on me, actually they're kind of glinting behind the bent gold frames of his glasses which gives him a rather manic look, well more manic than usual. 'Christ we did some singing didn't we, in class?'

he says and to my horror he begins to hum '*Danny Boy.*'

'I'm more in the rock line really,' I say quickly. 'Prog rock. Though I've got time for the classics like *The Beatles* and *The Stones.* Have you heard *Exile On Main Street?*'

He looks blankly at me.

'Sounds black to me.' He says. 'Did I ever sing you *Jump Down Turn Around?*'

My heart sinks. Last time I heard him sing that it had got unpleasantly loud and raucous. I have visions of the guests staring at us as he gets carried away picking a bail of cotton, picking a bail a day.

'Yes,' I say. 'You did sing us that. A classic in its way. Would you like some more whisky? I'm just going to get another beer...I'll bring you one.'

I snatch the glass from his hand before he can say anything and beetle rapidly across the lawn towards 'the bar.'

I am almost there when a short, incredibly fat woman with bright red hair that looks as though it may have been cut with a pair of garden shears, steps in front of me. She grabs hold of my arm and virtually spins me round to face her. I stare at her skew-whiff glasses, her crooked eye-liner and the spot on the end of her nose. She is beaming at me, pleased with her catch.

'Bet you don't remember me?' She says.

I always find this sort of introduction difficult. The truth is I haven't got the foggiest notion who she is but if I say so she may be offended, on the other hand if I say, 'Of course, I do,' implying that once met you could never forget her charm, wit and vivacious personality, she will be delighted but I will end up having a long and complicated conversation trying not give the game away.

I end-up saying, 'Erm...' Which is useless and I might just as well have said, 'No. No, you're dead right I've no idea at all. Who are you?'

Her face falls. 'I'm Sandy,' she says. 'Carla's daughter...'

Now, this opens up a whole load of other complications as I have no idea who Carla is either. She sees my blank look and sighs and I know I've ruined her day.

'Your mother's friend, Carla Simpson. We lived in the same road as you in Croydon, before you moved out here.'

The woman's mad. We left Croydon when I was six. How am I meant to remember that? No one can remember that far back.

'We used to play together...'

We did!?

'And you had that red trike you would never allow me on although you used to ride my scooter all the time...'

Trike? Scooter? I don't even remember the house we lived in as kids let alone the transport we used. This woman has the memory of an elephant and looks a bit like one, come to that.

'And we had parties for our teddies in a tent in my garden, until it got burned down one day.' She looks thoughtful. 'I think you got hold of some matches from somewhere,' and there is a slightly puzzled look on her face as she tries to recall something that should be long forgotten, but then she goes on cheerfully, 'And you used to call me Thandy – because you'd lost your front teeth. This is Jensi, by the way.'

For a second I am confused but she gestures towards a tall, thin man in khaki shorts with fair hair, an angular face and an intense stare who has been standing silently beside her.

'Hello,' he says, in a depressingly enthusiastic voice that

reminds me of a scout master and he takes my hand and shakes it heartily. 'You're looking good, the garden is looking good. It's a good day.' He says and beams around him.

'He's Danish,' Sandy says. 'He's still not very good at English.'

'I am in design,' he says – though I haven't asked him what he does he seems keen that I should know. 'Yes. I am travelling all over England bringing good Danish design to the British car manufacturers. Windscreen wipers I specialise in. I have drawings for some in my car, if you're interested.'

I'm beginning to lose my grip on reality.

'Not really,' I say.

'So you graduate,' he says. 'Have you thought design for the future? Automotive parts design? It's a booming business. I could show you some sales figures. I have accounts also in the car. You might be excited.'

'I'm not very technical – well, not like that,' I manage to say but he carries on regardless.

'You could join my firm. I could be speaking to the marketing guys. We need bright young men.'

And because he looks so hurt I add, 'Music is more my thing, actually.'

He nods, intensely.

'Ah… I see. Beatles, Stones, Monkees…'

'Well a few years ago, maybe but I'm more into Prog Rock now.'

'Yes,' he says, nodding enthusiastically. 'Like Abba. Good band.'

Abba!! The world is beginning to spin and I think maybe I have woken up in the middle of an episode of *Star Trek* and I am surrounded by aliens. Then just as I am about to say something I will regret like, 'Can I get you a drink?' Or possibly, 'You're boring me rigid, I must go and put my head in the oven,' a woman in a very big hat with even bigger sunglasses calls across the garden, 'Cooeeee! Sandy, you must come and meet Mrs Gardener.'

Sandy looks at me apologetically.

'You remember my mother… When she calls, we must obey. But we'll catch up with you later.'

I remind myself to hide under a table.

'Well,' Jensi says. 'We must talk the music more later but I will still be trying to make you consider the automotive design business, just you wait and see.' He pulls himself up to his full height and for one awful moment I think he is going to click his heels together and salute and then to my relief they both push their way through the guests towards the lady in the hat.

I suddenly realise that I am still clutching my Harp can and Mr Terry's empty scotch glass, so I turn towards 'the bar' and I am almost there when she comes through the French windows.

My first reaction is to think, 'Bloody hell, she still looks gorgeous.' My second is to wonder what on earth could have possessed my parents to invite her. Her of all people! But it is only a fleeting thought because I find myself swept away on (and I know this is mushy) a tide of emotion.

I've forgotten how tall she is and how very slim, but I haven't forgotten her breasts, which are still rounded and voluptuous – just as I remembered them in my many fantasies over the last few years. Her dark hair falls in long curls onto her shoulders and she wears a dark red summer dress; under her arm she holds a little bag – a clutch bag I believe

they call it – and her face is perfectly made-up, her lips luscious, deep red and, well, at the risk of being repetitive they
too are voluptuous – voluptuous and full (actually this might
be tautology as well as repetition but we'll let it pass for
now). Her whole being radiates class and style and she moves
across the lawn with the grace and elegance of a movie star
on the red carpet at the Oscars or a panther in the jungle (if
panthers live in jungles – must check that one). She is, in my
humble opinion, a… a… what's the word? A siren, a Venus?
No, she is quite simply a sex goddess!

I am amazed that the men in my parents' garden aren't
all falling to their knees on the lawn dazed by her beauty;
that they aren't swooning at her elegance or that the women
aren't seething with jealousy and riven with the inadequacy
of their own appearance. Am I the only one who can see that
the most beautiful woman in the world, the most mysterious,
the sexiest lady on the planet is walking across the lawn of
'Wrinkles End', Two, St Margaret's Drive, Leehurst Village?

It appears that I am, as apart from the odd smile or
hand wave from one or two guests, Diana/Emma's Mum is
largely ignored, even by the Golf Club Committee.

She looks over in my direction but she doesn't even smile
at me. Perhaps she doesn't notice me or maybe she doesn't
recognise me – after all I have changed considerably in the last
few years. I no longer have short hair, it is now fashionably
long ('Looks like a girl,' my father said, inevitably) and I think
I have developed something of a fashion sense in the clothing
department – my suit has twelve inch flares and I wear a floral
shirt with wide collars (Man at C&A, you can't beat the price)
and I have developed a little more muscle since taking up
squash (not that I was ever under-endowed in that department

– thanks to the magic of the Bullworker); I believe I may even have grown an inch or two taller – possibly three in my Chelsea boots. But even so, to be passed by without a glance hurts and makes me feel foolish, especially as I have waved at her from the bar and my father is watching.

'A friend of your Mother's, I suppose,' he says following the direction of my look. I turn back to him, surprised that he doesn't know who she is.

'That's Emma's... er... Diana's mother,' I say quietly. He looks puzzled for a second and then draws in a breath.

'Oh,' he says, in that voice that people use when they are speaking of the dead. 'You mean *the* girl...'

He tails off as he stares at her. 'How awful for her,' he says. 'How awful...'

Then he looks at me.

'I'm sorry old son. I don't know why your mother... Shouldn't have, raking it all up...'

There is a gentleness in his voice despite the awkwardness that I have never heard before and I am lost for words.

'It's OK,' I mumble and I am afraid to say anymore – we have never been like that, *emotional.* He turns away in a hurry to pour the vicar's wife another 'Gin and It' and I can feel his embarrassment too.

So I take another can of Harp and drift off towards the rose-bed and I pretend to admire the floribunda, though actually I am watching Diana's mum as she moves through the guests making small talk here and there, smiling at some, nodding in earnest conversation with others. Her face is so animated I can tell just by looking at her what she is saying and when she throws her head back to laugh at something someone has said, or when she turns to face another and I see her in profile, I am drawn in by her beauty, the line of her sculpted neck, the elegant way she gestures, the expressive hands, the luscious curves of her body, her long legs, the black stockings, the vivid red of her dress and even the little ruckles of cloth where it rides up over her bum, until she lowers a discreet hand to smooth the fabric, straightening the creases and recovering her poise.

I am entranced just as I was when I was fifteen, only now I am more knowing, more – what's the word – carnal? Yes. Carnal.

'Have you said hello to Mrs Watson, yet?' A voice says in my ear, and I nearly jump into the middle of the *floribunda Rob Roy* (delicately scented, a profusion of blooms all season) that I have been pretending to examine for the last five minutes. My mother has crept up behind me. I wilt with the fear of discovery.

'Sorry… err… Mrs Watson?' I reply, pathetically trying to adopt an innocent expression.

'Yes… The mother of… you know… *the girl.*' My mother says in hushed tones.

'Diana,' I say, and suddenly I'm a bit angry that my mother and my father can't use her name. 'Her name was Diana,' I say indignantly and then confusingly I add, 'Or sometimes Emma.'

My mother looks at me blankly. 'Whatever,' she says. 'You must have met her in the past before… you know… You should go over and say hello.'

'I haven't seen her since the funeral. Why's she here?'

My mother looks surprised, 'Because of the Hurstwood Players, of course…'

She sees my blank look.

'The new amateur dramatic club. We're all members…' She waves her hand airily round the garden. 'Well, most of the ladies in the bridge circle are. We're doing *Rebecca* in September. I'm doing costumes by the way. Anyway, Sydney… Mr Pontefract, he's directing it, and he was having terrible trouble finding a second Mrs De Winter and then along comes Mrs Watson and well, my darling, she's too old and far too glamorous but it turns out she used to be a professional as Mr Ponterfact was, and they actually knew each other in rep, years ago…'

I nod.

'Yes. I remember Diana saying she was an actress,' I say.

'She's been living like a hermit of course, since well… what happened… and this is a real chance for her to get out again and meet a few people. I mean it's good for The Players and it's good for her.' She sighs. 'A community like ours can do so much good…My God – what is that man doing?'

And she has left me as abruptly as she arrived. This is because she has heard what appears to be an animal in excruciating pain but is in fact Mr Terry, who has mysteriously found another large glass of whisky even though I'd forgotten to get him one, and who is leaning against the shed, shrouded in smoke and singing *Dunlavin Green.* He has only just got to the part where the blood is running in streams down the dykes, when my mother gets to him and leads him off to the kitchen for a vol-au-vent.

'Saved from the agonies of another Irish revolt, thank God,' a low, husky voice says in my ear and my skin tingles and a shiver travels from the base of my spine to the back of my head.

I turn to look at her. She is perfectly relaxed. She is cool in the hot afternoon sun, unblinking in its glare and anyway I think, the sun is pale next to her.

'Hello, Billy. Happy Birthday. Well, how are you?' Diana/Emma's mum says smiling at me.

And I can't think what to say. Which is really stupid because 'Hello, Mrs Watson,' is all that is required. We look at each other in silence or at least I look a her in silence and she looks at me wondering why I don't say anything. Finally she says, 'Billy..?' and I say, 'Mrs Watson.' Then she says, 'Billy...' again and because I am still hopelessly tongue-tied I say, 'Mrs Watson,' again, which makes her laugh, a gentle low and dead sexy laugh and she says. 'Well, I think we've established who we are, don't you?'

'Sorry,' I say, pulling myself together. 'It's been a long time and... and...' I know what I want to say but I can't find the words so finally I end up mumbling, 'I've been meaning to come and see you... and... and...' I suddenly realise that I can't remember Diana's brother's name, so I say, '...and your son. You know since...' I tail off, aware that I sound like my parents – and hopelessly, pathetically I want to crawl away behind the shed or batter my head on my father's crazy paving patio.

Instead I say, 'I'm sorry I never visited.'

She still smiles at me and when she speaks her words are like warm honey poured over me, not that I've ever had warm honey poured over me but I'm sure that's what it would feel like.

'Billy... It's all right. It's very nice to see you again.'

And then the honey turns to vinegar.

'You're young,' she carries on, 'You have a life to lead and really we hardly knew each other...'

Hardly knew each other? The vinegar has become sulphuric acid. My world spins. How could she say this after the nights of passion we have spent together over the last few years, after the intimacy, the fervour, the animal sex, after the things she has done to my body and me to hers in the dark of her bedroom or under the skies in the fields and woods or in my room in Cambridge, through cold Fenland wet and windy nights. And then I remember with a terrible feeling of loss that these were only fantasies – it was just my imagination running away with me, as the singer says. Of course, as far as she is concerned I was merely a schoolboy friend of her daughter's seven years ago and now I am a student who has graduated, is about to be twenty-one and whose parents are throwing a rather naff party for him. She has no idea what we have been through together in my imagination and now she is here not to see me, not to be with me, but as a guest of my mother because she is in the Hurstwood Players. Something inside me crumples and fades.

But she is still smiling at me, unaware of the turmoil going through my head.

'How was university?' she says

'Not bad,' I say reluctantly dragging myself back to reality.

'Your mother says you want to get into the music business. I don't know why, but I always thought you wanted to be an actor – it must have been something Diana said.'

Her name. She has said Diana's name and she hasn't cried or looked sad when she did so, which puzzles me – especially as so far, since I've been back home, no one mentions her name. If they talk about her she is just 'that poor girl.'

'Well,' I say. 'I did used to act at school but I always loved music and I started writing about it at university and I played in a band too...'

'Ah,' she says and I suddenly realise that she is not actually interested in what I did or wrote about at university and I feel really hurt about that, I can tell you.

'Paul, you know, Di's brother,' she says. So that's his name I think, Paul. 'He's into music too. In fact he's got a job in London in EMI, in what's it called, Abbey Lane…'

'Road,' I correct her and I loathe Paul for being where I would like to be, at the holy shrine of the sixties musical revolution.

'Yes,' she goes on, 'He's only a runner or whatever you call it in the record business, gopher or whatever, but you should come round one day, when he's next home. He might be able to give you a few tips.'

'I'd love to,' I say. And I mean it.

'I'm sure he'd love to see you again.'

I don't like to point out that I never met Paul, that Diana only ever told me about him and most of what she said wasn't very nice – but I'm not going to miss the chance to get an insider's view of the holiest of holies, and who knows, he might even be able to introduce me to one or two people if I butter him up enough – but mostly I'm thinking that if I go round to see Paul I will have the chance to see her again, Emma/Diana's mother and who knows… when I am not here in the garden with my parents and with their terrible friends hanging around, perhaps if I turn-up with some flowers and a bottle of something posh, like say, Mateus Rosé and Paul happens to be out, anything might happen.

I nod, happily. 'That'd be great,' I say. 'Really good.'

'Tell me,' she says. 'Do you ever see that other boy? Diana's boyfriend. Teddy. The one who got in such awful trouble.'

I stare at her. How could she say that? Diana's boy-friend!

'I feel so sorry for him.' She says. 'I believe after the police realised they'd made a mistake, he became rather ill. A breakdown of some sort. Poor lad to lose your first love and to be blamed for it like that...'

She tails off. How can she talk about him like that? Love? Boyfriend? I feel the anger welling up inside me but fortunately, nowadays I have learnt to control things better than in the past, so I bite my tongue (metaphorically of course, not literally) and turn innocent eyes on her.

'Oh,' I say. 'I didn't know she and him were that close.'

'I was terribly angry with him. If I could have got hold of him... well, you know, and then when they told me it was a mistake, that someone had given them the wrong information, well, I felt dreadful for him. I should really have gone to see him I suppose but at the time... you know, I wasn't in a fit state.'

I am feeling very uncomfortable now – for many different reasons.

'I expect he's pulled himself together now,' I say. And she gives me a funny look.

'Pulled himself...? Yes... well, maybe.'

'Actually, I never thought they were as close as he liked to make out.'

'Really? But the police...' and she gives me what I feel is a bit of an odd look. 'Anyway,' she goes on without finishing the sentence and looking away from me towards a group of giggling women surrounding a tall man on the other side of the rose bed, 'If you ever come across him, now you're home, do tell him I'd like to see him. I think it's important. That's all.'

Her eyes flicker round the garden and I suddenly think that she wants to end the conversation and I can't bear the idea of that. I mean, I've waited so long… But she is already drifting away and although I say, 'I'll look out for him…' She doesn't hear as she is already on the other side of the rose bed homing in on the group and a tall man who is wearing a paisley cravat and a pink shirt. I hear her say, 'Sydney, darling. There you are. If you're in the mood, I'll have another gin…' He smiles at her and holds out his hand to take hers – and I guess that this is Mr Pontefract, the director of *Rebecca* and I make a note to keep a careful eye on him as my immediate reaction is to wonder if he is much too friendly with Diana's mum by half, if you catch my drift.

I look down at *Rob Roy*. There is a caterpillar crawling along one of his leaves. I pinch it between my thumb and finger and the creamy juice of it spurts over the pale pink rose blossom and drips onto the ground below. It might have been a butterfly one day or perhaps a moth, but now we'll never know.

* * *

Here's an odd thing. I was invited to a party by one of the am drams. We haven't even started rehearsing yet but they're all terribly chummy and we've had about three 'committee' meetings to discuss things, even before we've opened a script! God how awful! Anyway, Sydney said we had to go. It showed good form and all that.

There was another reason for asking me apparently. The party was to celebrate a young man's twentieth. I'm afraid the name meant nothing, and the mother, a ghastly pushy woman who is the epitome of everything appalling about the British middle classes, kept banging on at me before we went about how her 'Billy' would love to see me again. I didn't have the faintest idea what she was talking about or why her Billy should want to meet me or that I'd met him before but I reluctantly agreed to go.

It wasn't until I was actually there in their awful little garden at the end of a new cul-de-sac of terrible modern houses in an otherwise idyllic part of the world that I spotted the 'Billy' in question and the penny dropped. He was the rather awkward child Diana befriended who came round to our cottage a couple of times and kept staring at me. Only of course now he was much older and he had actually grown into rather a good looking and quite pleasant lad, which was good, as frankly I always thought he was a bit retarded or something else unpleasant like that.

I dutifully said hello and I'm pleased to say that he was oddly well mannered for his generation. I was quite surprised though, when he said something about Diana and Paul, and it made me think that perhaps he was still carrying a lot of the pain he felt for her after what happened. I felt a little guilty and I'm rather kicking myself that I have never made an effort to see him or some of her other friends over the years since she died.

I think maybe Diana and this odd young man may have been closer than I had guessed – it would be typical of her to take pity on someone like him. To be honest, I suppose that when I do think about her friends I always think more about those two girls she was so close to and her boyfriend – the rather dangerous and slightly bad Teddy, who as you know I rather took to. I can't blame Diana for falling for Teddy. I mean, I may be long in the tooth but sex appeal is sex appeal. That poor lad. What he went through… That someone could do that to him. Make accusations, send those terrible letters to the police. No wonder, when they released him, he had to go away. Apparently he went abroad – but I think we all know what that meant. Something more in your line I think Doctor, than to do with a travel agent.

Anyway, I think I was perfectly pleasant to young Billy at the ghastly party, and I even suggested he might want to pop round some time and chat about the past.

God! I hope he doesn't. That would be awkward. Surely he'll know I was only being polite. Mind you, he is still a little, well, you know, a *little* odd, I think.

I can't find a bottle of Mateus Rosé in the village shop so I settle on a bottle of Blue Nun, which Mr Tidyman (who owns the shop) assures me is very sophisticated and quite fashionable in London circles – though how he'd know living in Hurstwood all his life I have no idea and I rather suspect that as the only alternative he offers is Watney's Pale Ale he may be spinning me a bit of a line. Anyway, I reckon it's the gesture that counts and I splash out on a box of Dairy Milk as well (a half pound one, what's more).

Mr Tidyman gives me a funny look as he drops the chocs into a brown paper bag.

'Courting?' He says.

Mr Tidyman has a reputation as something of a gossip to put it mildly and I certainly don't want this getting back to my parents who will nag me incessantly for weeks to come about who I am buying wine and chocs for.

'No,' I say quickly and my brain goes into overdrive. 'My mum wants them for a relation... an aunt...'

This doesn't seem quite enough, so I say, '...who lives in Croydon...' and then to give the lie a little polish I add, '...she's ill in hospital.'

Mr Tidyman looks puzzled. 'Wine and Dairy Milk?' he says. 'Must be a funny illness... Come to think of it, must be a funny hospital.'

I panic and grab the brown paper bags. 'It's a mental home,' I say quickly. 'She's had a breakdown...' I begin to back out of the shop but for some reason I cannot shut-up. 'Yes... depression...' I say. '...Nervous breakdown... still, these'll cheer her up.' And I turn and sprint out of the door, leaving it to bang behind me and setting the little bell jingling wildly and I know that Mr Tidyman is standing there underneath his jars of boiled sweets and aniseed balls, grinning at me. No doubt Mr Tidyman will be entertaining his customers with this for weeks to come. But oh well... '*C'est la vie*,' as they say on the continent.

It's two days since I saw her at the party and I judge this to be about right. If I'd gone yesterday I might appear too eager, whereas forty-eight hours seems to suggest that I am keen to renew her acquaintance without actually spelling out the fact that I want to make passionate love to her all night until she is worn out and screaming for mercy.

I haven't been to the Brewers' cottages for a long time and when I arrive there late in the afternoon, I am surprised to find that nothing much seems to have changed. I don't want to be seen until I am sure that the coast is clear i.e. that her son, Paul, or whatever his name is, is not at home, so I hang around on the corner, peering round the side of the Maltings Theatre at the little row of cottages on the other side of the road.

The gate of number three has now broken off completely and someone has propped it up against the faded and peeling little fence but they haven't bothered to re-hang it. The garden is still overgrown and the front door is still appallingly shabby, the window frames on each side of it look rotten and one sill has crumbled away. A little part of me that is my father, shudders at the state of dis-repair. If he was here, I think, he'd have his Black and Decker out in no time and he'd be hard at it with some two-by-two before you could say DIY.

I may have mentioned this before, but for many years in my childhood Barry Bucknell of the BBC's '*Bucknell's House*' was a saint like figure in our household, almost on a par with St Joseph himself and it would be fair to say that there isn't a door in our house that hasn't been panelled over with ply-wood or a fireplace that hasn't been boxed-in to his strict directions.

Anyway, the wonders of Mr Bucknell aside, I feel a bit of an idiot hanging around on the street corner, trying to look inconspicuous while clutching two brown paper bags, one with chocs in it and one with a bottle of wine. So I pretend to be looking at the theatre posters (*Hedda Gabler* with Diana Rigg – which seems like odd casting to me for the goddess of the Avengers, and Ibsen's *Enemy Of The People* with Patrick Macnee – I guess that Diana and Patrick come as a package when not filming together) and then when I have looked at the posters so many times I can even tell you the name of the printer which is in very small letters on the bottom left hand corner, I walk down the street a couple of times and then back up it. I even stand by the bus stop as if waiting for the number forty three to Leeford but I end-up looking a complete mong when it arrives and I turn away and don't get on it. As no one else is waiting or getting off the bus and so he has stopped for nothing, the conductor calls me some very unsavoury names and 'bings' the bell angrily – and as the bus pulls away, he waves two fingers at me. Honestly the working man today has little or no respect. I blame Harold Wilson.

I am beginning to think that maybe I am being an idiot and that I should just go over to the cottage and knock on the door and that perhaps Paul will be out anyway, or perhaps they are both out, when the front door opens at last and Paul steps into the garden. He is a big lad I think. Very big. Diana never mentioned that.

I sigh with relief. Had I gone over, it would have been very awkward as I realise on seeing him that if he had answered the door I would definitely have made a fool of myself. I have this terrible vision of him standing in his doorway, filling the space with his massive shoulders, while I stumble over my words and end-up saying something to the effect of, 'Good afternoon, I've come to seduce your mother. Is that all right with you?' And I rather suspect it wouldn't be.

Fortunately, I won't have to end-up committing such a *faux pas* as he is now half-way down the street on his pushbike and doubtless off to meet his somewhat dubious mates in the pub. (Actually I am making quite a lot of assumptions here about Paul and indeed about his friends, which is a bit unfair really, as I haven't even met him).

So, all I have to do is cross the road and knock on the door and she will be there and let me in. That's all.

I swallow drily...

...Walk across the road...

...Knock...

...That's all I have to do...

So, I don't. My nerve fails me and I turn away and wander off in the direction of Hurstwood, clutching my two brown paper bags.

About a mile away there is a dusty lay-by with a bus stop. I'm too tired to walk home so I decide to take the bus and I sit on the grubby bench with its broken back and look at the message written in black marker pen on the seat next to me that tells anyone who's interested that '*Shirl shags like a ryno*'. I don't have a pen to correct the spelling, which is a shame as I think we could all benefit from spelling the language of Shakespeare as it was intended, even yobs and delinquents who write on bus stop benches.

I sit waiting and stare across the fields towards the hills and the woods where my clearing is. It's been another beautiful day and the sun will soon be setting in a blaze of colour and I expect tomorrow will be another nice day and I will make my way back to The Maltings and pluck-up my courage again, only this time, as soon as the coast is clear, I will knock on the door... I really will.

A bus arrives and pulls up at the stop, throwing out a waft of dust and crunching on the gravel of the lay-by. Wearily I climb on board and flop down on the rear seat. The conductor eyes me angrily. It's the same bus, the same conductor – they have been into Leeford, turned round and now they're making the return trip.

He stomps over to me.

'Staying on this time are you?' He grumbles.

'Hurstwood,' I say and hold out my ten pence piece.

'One and six,' he says.

And I think, it's five years since decimalisation but some of us still cling to the past.

He pushes two and a half pence and a ticket into my hand.

'There you are,' he grunts. 'Tanner change.'

I want to tell him that he'll never turn back the clock so he might as well learn the new system but I can see he won't listen.

* * *

I am back the following afternoon. There's a mid-week matinee at the theatre, so it is easy to mingle with the crowds and stare across at the cottage but I still can't summon up the courage to cross the road and knock on the door. I pace around. I stare moodily at the posters and photographs in the foyer windows of the theatre and I am still there when the last of the audience has gone into the building and taken their seats.

And then I go home, again. I am ashamed of my weakness. Embarrassed by my lack of courage. Annoyed at my inadequacies. I can't help wondering if Romeo or Abelard had similar problems getting their love lives off the ground but somehow I doubt it.

When I return the next day I am determined to get on top of my nerves and go for it. I square my shoulders, I grasp my brown paper bags tightly in both hands and I stride across the road. I am now a man on a mission. Nothing can stop me. And I am nearly at the gate – the gate to the temple within, as it were, when I see the front door open. I brace myself to face the man-monster that is Paul: 'Hi I'm just visiting your mother. Try to stay out for as long as you can, there's a good chap, as we'll probably be romping in her bed and possibly all over the house in various positions of sexual ecstasy for the next few hours and I wouldn't want to embarrass you.'

Of course, I won't actually say that. It's the sort of dialogue you keep in your head but never actually use when the crunch comes. I'll probably just say, 'Hello. How are you? I was just passing.' Mild, inoffensive and relatively safe from getting you beaten to a pulp.

It isn't Paul and stupidly I'm quite surprised at that. It's his mother – her – the goddess of The Maltings – the graceful beauty, the Cleopatra of Leeford and looking at her locking the shabby front door, I stop in mid-stride and stare at her and just seeing her there makes me feel different, feel better, feel confident and my head reels and old words I'd half forgotten from my A-level English come into my mind; '*I am fire and air…*' And I really feel that I am, I could float above the ground and something inside me is ablaze.

She turns and is almost at her gate before she sees me on the pavement. She looks a bit puzzled, possibly because it's not every day you leave your house and find a former boyfriend of your daughter's frozen to the spot and staring at you with his mouth hanging open, but you have to hand it to her, she has grace, poise and charm and she can handle any situation with ease.

Her puzzled frown turns instantly to a smile, 'Well, hello…' And a fly buzzes round her head and she waves a hand at it, '...Billy. Fancy seeing you here.'

I suppose this is my cue to say something, anything will do like, 'Hello' or 'Good afternoon, Mrs Watson.' Instead I... well, I suppose you might call it *gurgle*. I'm not really sure what the noise I make is, but gurgle will do. My mouth has gone very dry and I can't remember simple things like how to form words, so I gurgle and stare.

Now you'd think she'd probably decide I had gone completely mad and that she'd rush indoors and call the police or something but instead she walks towards me, still smiling. She's a cool one this goddess, this siren...

'Oh,' she purrs, 'Have you come to see Paul?'

Of course I haven't come to see Paul. Why on earth would I want to see Paul? Then I remember what she said about the job he has at Abbey Road.

'Um, is he in?' I say.

'No. I'm afraid he went back to London this morning. He was only here for a few days. But he'll be back at the end of the month for a long weekend, I think. You could see him then, if you're still planning to be around.'

Oh, I'll be around all right. She can count on that. But I'm not waiting until the end of the month and I'm actually hugely relieved that the dreadful muscle-bound boy wonder is not here for a while – 'long enough to get my feet under the table,' I think ungenerously and perhaps a little unpleasantly.

'Oh,' I say. And then trying to be casual, I add. 'Are you off out then?'

She smiles at me or perhaps she laughs at me – I suppose it was rather a blunt question.

'Yes,' she says. 'Was there something you wanted?'

Sex, passion, a wild affair for the rest of our lives, torrid lust, erotic activities on the bedroom floor, explorations into sexuality and sex acts that no one has ever experienced before – all of these things are what I actually want.

I swallow as well as I can with a dry mouth.

'Actually, I was wondering if I could see you sometime... There's things I'd... I'd like to talk to you about.'

For a second she looks puzzled and then she reaches her own conclusion.

'Oh, of course. About Diana. Oh you poor dear...'

And she reaches over and touches my hand, yes she actually touches the back of my hand with her beautiful, long, lustrous fingers.

'Of course,' she says. 'How awful for you. You were friends and you went away without... without ever really letting it all end. How silly of me. You need to talk about her, of course you do.'

She squeezes my hand and looks at me with deep, sad dark eyes that float down into my soul. I feel electric shocks run from her fingers to my heart and my head. She is holding my hand and I think to myself, 'Who's Diana?' And then I remember, and I don't care because her mother is holding my hand and that puts everything right... Everything.

'I really do have to go,' she is saying. 'I am sorry but I have to be at rehearsals and someone's picking me up in the theatre car park...' She glances at her watch, '...at any minute. Look why not come round tomorrow? About six would be good for me. I have to go into Leeford but I'll be back by then.'

'Yes,' I say. 'I'd really like that.' And I know that I sound like a child trying not to get over excited about

Christmas. She lets go of me and I look down at my hand and I remind myself never to wash it again.

'I'll see you then,' she says, moving off. 'Sorry, about this but well, you know how it is, you can never be late for rehearsals if you're an old pro.'

I stare at her back as she crosses the road and suddenly a thought occurs to me.

'I could buy you dinner,' I call out.

She stops in the middle of the road and looks over her shoulder at me, giving me a quick smile.

'Oh…' she seems a little puzzled and turns to face me. 'You don't need to do that.'

I guess she must see my face because then she says, 'Ah… well… Look I'll… I'll get something in… OK?'

I nod dumbly and she starts to walk away again and then she adds, 'Just a light supper, you know. Nothing elaborate… while we talk.'

Then she turns down the alley by the side of the theatre and the words, 'light supper,' never sounded so sexy I reckon.

I start to drift back towards the bus stop but my head is whirling round, and for some reason my legs have gone wobbly and I keep losing touch with the ground and floating upwards. How did that cheesy musical go..? *'All at once am I several stories high…'* Normally I hate musical theatre but right now I know exactly what the bloke means.

I am standing at the bus stop when the car whizzes by me. It is horribly expensive, open topped and very cool and she looks great sitting in it with her long black hair streaming behind her in the wind, her dark glasses reflecting the evening sun.

I don't think they even notice me but I see them – well, I see her anyway – I'd never miss her if she was travelling at a thousand miles an hour on the Star Ship Enterprise – but I also see the driver and I think to myself, 'That bloody Mr Pontefract. He's going to be a pain. I can feel it!'

* * *

I've had the most peculiar visit. Well it wasn't actually a visit, more of a coincidence really.

Sydney had a meeting at the Maltings Theatre. He'd called them to try to persuade them to support their local drama group by loaning us the costumes for *Rebecca* – they'd done a production a few years before and they keep all their old costumes in an old hop store they'd refurbished at the back of the theatre. They'd offered to show him what they had and I was going to meet him in the theatre car park afterwards for a lift into rehearsals.

Well, you're not going to believe who was standing outside my front door when I went to meet him. Only that boy Billy, Diana's old friend – the one whose party I got dragged to.

He was standing there staring at me as I walked up to the gate (well, where the gate should be – I must get someone in to fix it one day). There was something about him that reminded me of a small puppy waiting for a walk. He had a sort of soppy look on his face and he was clutching two large brown paper bags. My dear, he looked awful, unkempt and rather grubby. It didn't look as if he'd slept for a week or indeed taken a bath. Really the young today. I mean dear Albert may have been a working class lad from the North but he'd been introduced to the idea of carbolic from quite a young age and as for Tom – well, he was always scrubbing at 'the pits and the parts,' as he put it.

I tried to be pleasant but I hoped he hadn't come to see me as I was already late for Sydney.

'Hello,' I said and then I couldn't remember his name – which rather threw me. I pretended a fly was buzzing round my head and waved at it frantically while I tried to think. It came to me suddenly, 'Billy,' I added. Hoping he wouldn't notice my hesitation.

Such an odd boy. He sort of spluttered at me and I rather think he may have caught a cold or something equally unpleasant. I tried to back away as surreptitiously as I could, I really don't need a cold at the moment, not with a performance looming.

'Have you come to see me?' I asked, desperately hoping he hadn't and then I remembered what I'd said about Paul and how he'd been interested in the music business – so I told him Paul was away for a few weeks. I hoped he'd go then but, oh Lord, it turned out that he wanted to see me or at least he wanted to talk to me about Diana.

What on earth put that idea into his head?

Every time I think I'm beginning to get over things and that I can put that awful night away and move on, something or someone pops up to drag it all out again.

For a second I was almost angry. I wanted to say to him, 'Leave me alone, leave her alone. You haven't talked about her for seven years, so don't start now – lets move on.' And I was thinking of Sydney sitting round the back of the theatre in his gorgeous car waiting for me.

But of course I didn't say anything; the boy looked so forlorn, so miserable. I've always been a pretty good judge of people's emotions and right then I could feel that he was rather a troubled young man. I realised that he needed to talk and who was I to say no, though not now, dear God – not with Sydney waiting for me.

I told him that I was on my way out but (and I will probably live to regret this) I suggested he come round to-morrow evening and then feeling much better for what I must admit was a pretty selfless act of charity, I started to cross the road.

Well, my dear doctor. I nearly fell flat on my face. He suddenly called out that he'd like to take me out to dinner. How odd! I was about to tell him that it would probably not be a good idea or indeed very enjoyable, when I realised that he was just being polite, of course. He probably thought he was being terribly grown-up. I also realised that it was bit churlish of me not to have offered him a meal and I also thought a bite and a bottle of wine might make things a little less awkward and I could always invite Sydney along too, which would definitely be better than spending the evening alone with an intense young man remembering my daughter and all the pain of her loss.

All of this flashed through my mind in a split second. I quickly told him not to bother about dinner and that I'd get in a light supper – though for some reason I didn't mention inviting Sydney.

I almost ran across the road then and as we drove to-wards Leeford in Sydney's car I saw him shuffling along to-wards the bus stop. He stared at us and actually waved but I pretended not to notice. I was very glad we were in a two-seater and we couldn't offer him a lift.

'Who's that,' Sydney asked noticing my glance at him.

'That rather odd boy. You know the daughter of that ghastly woman in The Players. He was a friend of Di's and

I've been compelled to invite him for dinner tomorrow. I rather think he needs to talk about her. Will you come?'

'I'm awfully sorry,' he said. 'But I've got a meeting in town tomorrow with my accountant. I'll be staying overnight.'

'Oh,' I said and I tried to sound breezy but I was a bit annoyed that he hadn't mentioned this before – annoyed that I wouldn't see him for two days or annoyed that I would have to spend an evening alone with a strange boy? I really don't know.

Mischievously and quite deliberately, I said, 'Well, I'll entertain the young man alone then. Thank goodness he's rather dishy.'

Sydney gave me a sidelong glance.

'Is he...?'

'Oh, yes,' I grinned.'

'Can I trust you?'

'Of course not darling.' And I reached over and gave him a peck on the cheek.

It was only a joke of course, but I had to admit to myself as we raced through the country lanes at some ridiculous speed, that young Billy may have been rather odd and scruffy but under the stubble he was a bit of a looker.

She had good taste, my daughter.

* * *

I didn't sleep much last night. It's pathetic I know but I am terribly excited about tonight. I spend most of the morning in a daydream up in my bedroom reading Dostoevsky (I did the Russian novel in translation as one of my papers at Cambridge and I pride myself on being quite at home with a Russian Count or even a revolutionary peasant, should the need arise).

I eat a simple lunch so as not to spoil my appetite for this evening and also because I am too nervous to eat properly – just a few Heinz beans on toast and then I take a short walk through the village to calm my nerves. Finally I can begin my preparations for this evening and at about three thirty I start what I believe are best described as my ablutions.

I have allowed myself to become a little scruffy recently due to my slight depression at being back home and my preoccupation with the events planned for today and I am shocked when I look in the mirror. My hair is getting longer and it is Q definitely rather greasy and I have several days stubble on my chin. Now, I've always been a little fastidious about personal hygiene, as you may know. Let's face it, apparently we have several thousand receptors (whatever they are) in our nose and although that's not as many as a dog it's plenty enough to get a whiff of a dodgy armpit or an unfortunate staleness from the various appendages, so I usually spend a reasonable amount of time in the bath and I have a pretty comprehensive collection of useful roll-on deodorants that have been recommended on ITV's commercial breaks; so my current disarray comes as something of a shock and I wonder what she must have thought of me when we spoke in the road outside of her house. I realise with a deep feeling of disappointment that I may not have cut the fine figure I had hoped for.

Therefore I set about making myself presentable with vigour. I'm not ashamed to admit that I have from a very early age, encouraged my mother to buy household soaps a cut above the average offering in the Leeford branch of Sainsbury's where she does our weekly grocery shop.

Thanks to me you'll find a pretty good selection in our bathroom cabinet from *Pears* to *Camay* and not a hint of *Lifebuoy* let alone the dreadful *Coal Tar* in sight.

Today I choose the 'piéce de resistance', as our French cousins would say, and I have a long lingering bath during which I wield a bar of the luxurious *Roger and Gallet* to pretty good effect. I intend to follow this up by carefully shaving using the latest in Wilkinson Sword technology with a proper badger hair brush and soap, before splashing on a considerable amount of *Brut*.

However, when I look in the mirror, holding my soapy brush in one hand and the razor in the other, it occurs to me that the bearded look, or in this case the stubbly look, has a certain, how shall I put this, *macho* charm about it. In a moment of reckless abandon I decide to rinse the brush out and put away the razor. I reckon my new facial appearance gives me a hint of danger with just a soupcon of artistic suffering thrown in for good measure.

'Wow,' I think, putting a good coating of *Right Guard* under each armpit and slipping into a new Ben Sherman, 'She'll be pouncing on me before I make it through the front door.'

I set off for the Maltings far too early and I could easily have walked there in the time I allowed, but because it is so hot I decide to take the bus. By the time the it arrives I've been standing beside the dusty road sweating in the heat for some considerable time and I might as well have walked after all. My shirt is sticking to my back and I am regretting wearing a tie as I can feel my collar has become sodden and the sweat has even trickled into the tie knot. As for my armpits – I am thinking of writing to the manufacturers of Right Guard and making a few strong points about the efficacy of their product.

It's the same bus conductor as before and he grunts at me as I take a seat.

'You look hot son, it must be the weather.' And he grins at his own humour. I've got the change for the fare in my pocket but instead I pull my wallet out and give him a five pound note just to shut him up.

He stares at the note.

'You are fucking joking,' he says which is absolutely disgusting language and he wouldn't have said that if there had been any other passengers on board.

'The Maltings,' I say.

'I'm not changing that.'

'I haven't got anything else, so you'll have to.' I snap angrily at him.

'Right, you'll have to get off.'

'Why?'

'Cos you haven't paid your fare. Next stop and you're off.'

He is turning to go when I say, 'If a fare has been offered then it's deemed to have been paid and the bus company cannot refuse to accept said fare.'

'You what?" he says spinning on his heel.

'It's the transport bye-laws. Surely you know them. I think you'll find that's section one, sub-section D. I could report you to the police if you make me get off.'

'Bollocks!' He says.

'I read law at Cambridge – so I know,' I say arrogantly. 'I'm a lawyer, do you want to take me on… in court!'

He looks at me and I can tell that he would like to pick me up and throw me off the bus right now, even though we are bowling along at thirty miles per hour. For a moment we stare at each other, two warriors locked in battle and then I see him look away and I know I have won. I thrust the fiver towards him again and he turns the handle on his machine and hands me the flimsy ticket. He looks at the fiver.

'Forget the money,' he says. 'I can't be bothered.'

And he stomps off to the back of the bus where he stands in surly silence apart from hissing rudely at the odd passenger when they get on, until we arrive at The Maltings and I walk past him, my head held high.

I can't believe what I have done. I have won a huge victory for the small man against the faceless bureaucrats who run the country. I am sure that Dr Ellerman, who was my English supervisor at Cambridge and who is a Marxist, would be proud of my small battle against the repressive forces of our dictators – it was after all Dr Ellerman who pointed out to us in a seminar on Jane Austen that all new police stations built in England in the last twenty years are designed along the lines of protected fortresses in order to repel the revolution when it happens – and he has a point. To be honest my sympathies are usually with the police and of course Dr Ellermnan's are with the red rebels, but on certain occasions such as this one, I can see what he means about our slide into faceless bureaucracy.

OK, so I know I've had to bend the rules of morality somewhat in order to fight my battle on the bus – after all, I am not a lawyer and I know nothing about transport bye-laws, but I think Dr Ellerman would argue that the end can on some occasions justify the means, and this is one of those times.

It is, therefore, with a certain feeling of smug self-righteousness that I find myself standing in front of the grubby little front door of number three The Maltings a few minutes later.

I can't help but think of Diana as I look at the fading paintwork and my hand hesitates as I reach out to press the bell. I remember the day she first brought me here, I remember the night we kissed passionately on the other side of this door and I also remember that it was that night that I saw Mrs Watson in her underwear – and a vision of impossibly long, nylon clad legs swims into my mind and this is closely followed by memories of some of the more vivid fantasies I have had about those legs and the rest of the body they are attached to during long lonely nights in my college room.

I haven't pressed the bell but suddenly the door swings open and the central figure in these fantasies is standing in front of me.

'Hello Billy,' she says. 'I thought I heard you on the path. The bell doesn't work I'm afraid. I really must get someone in. There are so many things I need a man to do for me.'

The world spins at the thought and I catch my breath but of course I know she only means DIY.

I should say, 'Hello Mrs Watson' or 'How are you Mrs Watson' but instead I say, 'My dad's pretty handy with a screwdriver.' Which on the face of it, is a very odd thing to say and to be honest she does give me a funny look.

'Really,' she says. 'Well, we should have asked him along... Do come in.'

And she stands to one side in the narrow hallway to let me past and it is very hard in what you might call such a confined space, not to brush against her and the lightest touch of her body against my arm makes me suck in my breath and my legs feel shaky.

We go into the kitchen at the back of the house.

'Do you mind being in here?' she says. 'Only I've got some food for us and we can chat while I cook. Do sit down.'

I sink onto a wooden kitchen chair that wobbles slightly and survey the clutter on the table: there are some mugs that need washing up, a pile of old newspapers and copies of *The Stage*, a saucer filled with one and two pence pieces, a dog-eared notepad, a broken stub of pencil, a paperback, a script for *Rebecca* with notes scribbled all over it, a half empty bottle of OK sauce, a plastic salt and pepper pot that don't match and a disgusting over-flowing ash tray, filled with lipstick stained cigarette butts.

Before I went up to Cambridge I might have found all this just a filthy and slovenly mess but having mixed with a few 'arty' students and knowing that Mrs Watson was once a professional actress and remembering what Diana had said about her being at RADA with some of the iconic figures of the British stage and screen, I know now that this is simply what we might call the evidence of a bohemian and artistic life style and it is not a mess at all.

'She was beautiful, wasn't she. We all miss her you know.'

I snap out of my reverie. What is she talking about?

'It's not a bad photo is it. They took it at her school you know.'

She reaches past me and picks up the framed photo that is in the centre of the table. It's quite large and I don't know why I haven't even noticed it. It's in black and white but I know that the dress is blue, and so are the eyes and that the complexion is slightly pink and of course her hair is more yellow blonde than the white it appears to be in the photo.

'Yes,' I say. 'It's a good photo.' And I add, 'Better than the ones they took at our school,' which is a bit lame really and Mrs W gives me a look. So I say, 'I bet you wish it was in colour.' Which is also a completely stupid thing to say and she looks at me again and I think she is thinking something and I wonder if she will tell me. But instead she puts the photo back on the table and says, 'Don't you want to put your bags down?'

I can't think what she is talking about and then I realise that I am still clutching the two brown paper bags from the village shop that I have carried around now for so many days that they are almost glued to me and I have becomes so used to them that I forget that they are there.

'Oh,' I say. 'Yes... No, these are for you.'

I plomp the now very grubby and rather creased bags on to the table and from one of them I pull out the bottle of *Blue Nun* and I hand it to her.

'Oh, how kind,' she says and I can see she is impressed. '*Blue Nun*. Well we'll just pop that in the fridge for later.'

'And there's these,' I say. And I pull out the box of Dairy Milk. Unfortunately they don't look too good after their travels. The corners of the box have got rather creased from where they have been jolted around in the bag, the cellophane wrapper is beginning to peel off and the whole box isn't... well, it isn't quite as box-shaped as it used to be.

'Sorry,' I say, handing them over. 'They seem to have got a bit knocked around.'

For a second there is a look of surprise on her face but she quickly says, 'Well, never mind, I'm sure they'll still be delicious. We'll have one later, shall we?'

And I get the feeling that I am being talked to as if I was a disappointed child, which is not what I wanted to happen at all.

'Right. We'll get the supper on,' she says suddenly.

I assume that although she's spoken in the plural she didn't necessarily expect me to join in so I sit tight and watch her opening packets and putting things on trays into the oven.

When she's finished she says. 'Good. There we are. Drink?'

'Yes please,' I stammer and I realise I desperately need one as so far things are not going quite as I'd planned. In fact in the scenario I'd been imagining over the last few days by now she should have been down to her underwear and we should have been upstairs romping on her bed, which for some reason I always imagined would be an old fashioned four poster affair in a moodily lit room with heavy velvet curtains.

She says she's got to find her cigarettes if she's going to have a drink and she leaves me alone for a minute or two while she looks for them in the front room. It's long enough for me to... well... stare at the picture of Diana apart from anything else. But I can't really focus on it and I should be ashamed of the mad ideas that run through my head...

When she comes back with her fags she pours us a glass of some French red wine that she gets from the dresser on the other side of the kitchen. I am a bit disappointed that she hasn't gone for the Blue N but I suppose it isn't cold enough yet for the discerning palette. Frankly, I find the red stuff a bit on the vinegary side and it reminds me of the college sherry that all the dons used to pour down us at their little drinks parties in Cambridge. I've always preferred something a bit sweeter myself. In that respect I am rather like my mother who always says you can't beat a nice sweet Martini and lemonade and I must say I agree with her on that one.

'So,' she says (Mrs W, not my mother) putting down her wine glass and lighting a cigarette, 'You wanted to chat about Diana.'

Did I?

'Well,' I say. 'Umm...' And I can't think what to say next. She stares at me and I stare back at her...

The she reaches out her hand and lays it over mine.

'Let's not pretend Billy,' and now she is talking in a very quiet voice. 'I know why you're here and you know why I invited you...'

She puffs on her cigarette and lets the smoke exhale in a slow trickle from her pursed lips. Her eyes are narrowed against the curl of smoke as it rises over her face but they are focused on me, burning, searing their way into my heart.

We stay like this – looking at each other through the smoke and then she leans her head a little closer to mine and raises her hand. She cups my cheek and strokes my face very gently. I can smell the perfume on her wrist, I can feel the softness of her skin and I know that she will lean even closer and kiss me, and she does so – a gentle, soft kiss that sends electric sparks through my body. After a while, in which our tongues explore each other and gently mimic the actions our bodies would like to repeat, she reluctantly pulls her mouth away from me but she is still so close that I can smell the red wine on her breath, taste the cigarette in the air.

'I want you,' she says in a low, husky voice. 'God, I want you...'

...I blink and she is saying, '...and this is Diana when she was nine and we all went to Bangor for a holiday. Not much of a holiday but we never had a lot of money I'm afraid. Here she is having donkey ride on the beach.'

I shake my head. She has got an album of photos in front of her and we are looking through them apparently, and I wonder how long we have been doing this. It's a long time since I had one of my visions. Sometimes I want them to go away but I had wanted this one to last forever and I am heart-broken that it has ended.

We look at the photos and drink wine and eventually she says that dinner is cooked.

Well, I have to say that cooking is clearly not her strongest point. Still you can't be a sex goddess and be a great chef, now can you? But my mother would have shuddered in horror at the hard potatoes and as for the chicken breasts in white wine sauce that she produces from the oven, I can almost hear my mother groan at the sight – both at the fact that it is 'new fangled continental food' and that it has a rather *odd* smell. Odour aside, I'm no *Galloping Gourmet* but even I know enough to suspect that the chicken should not have pink bits in the centre and that white wine sauce does not usually have chewy bits. I am also a little put-out by the accompanying vegetables – in my house the *Findus* peas are usually defrosted before they are served – in this case a couple of canon balls definitely got in the pack – Mr Orson Wells, who recommends this product on TV, would have been shocked.

However, I'm not going to complain. Mrs W may not be a great cook but very few of us can be perfect at everything and anyway we are now on our second bottle of wine and frankly I don't care about my food – what it looks like, how it smells or what it tastes like – and judging by the fact that she pushes her portion around her plate and barely touches it before she clears away, I guess she doesn't care much either.

Never mind the chicken, I think, *I have other fish to fry* and at last I think I'm beginning to understand what Mark meant all those years ago on our Spanish holiday.

'Would you like some coffee?' she says as she clears the plates.

'Yes please.'

'Help yourself to a cigarette if you want. The pack's on the table.'

Now this is an awkward one. I have never smoked. I hate smoking. It is a disgusting habit and only yesterday I heard doctors on the excellent *World At One* programme on *Radio Four* (still called the *Home Service* in my house, by the way, where we are not happy to throw away tradition) saying that smoking is probably related to things like lung cancer and other unpleasant diseases. In fact they are now bringing out a new cigarette that is made from something called New Smoking Material instead of tobacco because it will be better for you.

Looking at Mrs Watson's packet of Peter Stuyvesant, I suspect there may not be very much NSM in there and judging from the lingering fug that fills the room I suspect they may be rather high in the *Old* SM instead. So now I am faced with a dilemma – I don't want to look un-cool; I do not want her to think that I am NOT a man of the world. I have a feeling that in Mrs Watson's sophisticated arty circles her theatrical friends may consider smoking *de rigeur* – as the French would say.

Nevertheless, I say 'I won't actually,'.

She doesn't even turn round from where she is filling the kettle but for some reason I feel compelled to say more.

'Dicky ticker,' I say, tapping my chest over my left breast. And immediately I feel a complete fool. Why on earth did I say that, for crying-out loud? I could weep.

She turns to look at me, the tap still running, the kettle in her hand, her eyes open wide in surprise.

'At your age?' She says. 'You poor boy.'

I should shut up of course and change the subject but it's hopeless – I have diarrhoea of the mouth.

'Yes,' I say. 'It's congenital.'

And once again I want to fall through the floor.

She puts the kettle on the gas and comes over to sit beside me. She looks genuinely concerned.

'How awful. I had no idea.'

I need to get out of this and change the conversation.

'Oh well,' I say. 'These things happen.'

'But a weak heart. It must have ruined your life. Have you been very ill?'

'Oh, no. Not at all really...'

'You're very brave.' And as she says this she lays her hand over mine, just as she had done in my vision.

'Well,' I say, looking at her hand and feeling the little squeeze she is giving mine and remembering the fantasy wine-tasting kiss, and I suddenly think that maybe I'm onto a good thing. 'Well, it's not always been easy, of course, but I don't like to talk about it too much. It… it mainly affected me as a child…' And then I remember something I saw on Panorama years ago. 'I was what you might call an early pioneer of hole in the heart surgery…'

'Really?' she says, genuinely impressed. 'A blue baby.'

'Oh, yes… dead blue. I mean, I don't mean, you know *dead* not like that, I mean very blue. Blue as a summer sky my mother used to say.'

'Oh,' she seems surprised. 'I didn't know it meant blue like that?'

'Anyway,' I say hastily. 'I'm OK now. I just don't smoke. That's all.'

'Oh, God!' she says, flapping her hand around in the fuggy air, 'I'm so sorry…'

'No, that's OK… I like the smell actually. I'm sure I'd smoke loads if I was allowed to.'

'Hell, should you have had..?' and she nods at the empty wine bottles.

'Oh yes. Definitely,' I say. 'The Doctor says it's very good for me, especially red. It's the iron in it.'

And then I add:

'And German wine too, like *Blue Nun*. It's something to do with the grape apparently. Very good for the heart, German grapes are.'

She gives me an odd look.

'I don't think we should open anymore, Billy. We'll both get squiffy.'

And I think, what a lovely old fashioned expression, like *Brideshead Revisited* or something, which is one of my favourite books.

She stands-up again because the kettle has started to boil

and I feel cheated that she has taken her hand away from mine. I watch her beautiful figure as she crosses the kitchen. She is wearing a light floral summer dress. It's Laura Ashley I think and although it's all loose and floaty you can see the shape of her bum through the thin material. The dress stops about half way down her shins and I can see how beautiful her legs are, encased in black nylon and I wonder if she is wearing tights or stockings – somehow I know it's stockings but the dress has got so many folds that I can't see the outline of suspenders beneath it – which is a shame as this is one of my absolute best fantasies. She's got on black shoes with a raised heel and I reckon they make her ankles look great and for a second I can hardly catch my breath as I have a picture in my mind of her wrapping her heels around my head, complete with those shoes and stockings, the dress ruckled-up over her hips as we lie in her bed having the wildest sex imaginable.

She turns round holding up the kettle.

'Coffee?'

I nod, my mouth too dry to speak.

'Did Diana know?' she says with her back to me as she makes the coffee.

For a second I am confused. How could Diana know that I fancied her mother, how does her mother know, come to that?

'Sorry?' I squeak.

'About your illness,' she says. 'Did Diana know?'

'Oh…um… I'm not sure… maybe.'

'She was always so caring, wasn't she? I should think she was very concerned about you.'

I think of her daughter's first words to me in my clearing; 'Hello wanker' and of the ice cold water she threw over me.

'Yes,' I said. 'Very caring.'

'That was Diana,' she said.

I suddenly realise that the evening is getting late and I need to get things to move on, towards the ultimate goal, as it were. It is time to take the bull by the horns, if you'll pardon the expression.

'Mrs Watson,' I say firmly as she puts a mug of coffee down in front of me. 'Mrs Watson,' I repeat and then I'm not sure what to say next.

'Yes, Billy,' she says.

I want to say that I am madly in love with her and that I have known this since the day I met her all those years ago with Diana.

'Mrs Watson...' and she gives me a funny look as so far all I have done is repeat her name.

I swallow. 'Mrs... erm... Look, I just wanted to say do you remember all those years ago when we first met? You know, here in the kitchen...'

And I look at her with what I hope are appealing eyes.

'No,' she shakes her head. 'No, I don't really...'

I am stunned and it must show on my face because she says, 'To be honest I have a vague memory of you being here a couple of times but I don't really remember you that well. I know more about you from what Di said than anything else...'

She must see my expression because she adds; 'And now I can see for myself what a nice young man you are. It's been very kind of you to visit. Very kind. I'm just sorry that I didn't see more of you and the rest of Di's friends after she died. But it was very difficult. It was a bad time... I... I wasn't sure I could cope with all of you. You would have kept reminding me of her.'

Please, I am thinking, can we stop talking about her daughter and start talking about us.

'But...' I say and then I don't know what to say next.

'Yes?' she says mildly.

'Well, do you remember me coming here in the evening and you were leaning over the banister?'

She looks at me very oddly.

'Um... No... well, vaguely, I suppose. It was late I think and I told Di to go to bed, didn't I? Err, why?'

'Because... because...'

And I am going to say, 'Because I fell in love with you and you wore the sexiest clothes I have ever seen and you were more glamorous than Anne Bancroft in *The Graduate* and I am a lot taller and in my own way more sexy than Dustin Hoffman any day...' But I don't say any of that – instead I look at her and I say feebly.

'Oh, nothing. I just wondered – that's all. Shall we have some more wine. There's *The Blue Nun*.'

'Perhaps, Billy,' she says gently. 'Perhaps it's time to go. We have had two bottles already, and actually I think maybe we've both had enough. Oh, God, are you driving? You really shouldn't. Your parents would think I was terribly irresponsible.'

'No,' I say. 'I don't drive. I did learn but I failed my test. I don't think the examiner was up to the job really. Actually, I've lodged an official complaint but I haven't had a reply to my letter yet.' I realise that I am rambling on a bit, so I finish by saying, 'I took the bus.'

'Oh good.' She glances at the kitchen clock. 'You'll just be in time for the nine thirty then, if you get your skates on.'

I suddenly feel that I am being dismissed and it reminds

me of being sent out of class by a teacher.

'It's been lovely, having a chat,' she says standing up.

'I haven't drunk my coffee,' I say, a bit put out.

'Oh, dear but I'm afraid the there isn't another until midnight...'

I decide to be blunt.

'I could stay,' I say. 'With you.'

She stops in mid-stride towards the door which she was going to open for me.

'What?'

'I could stay,' I say less certainly.

She looks a bit surprised at this.

'I'm afraid I haven't got a spare room for you. You know, Paul's is a terrible mess and.. well, we don't go into Diana's.'

'I don't need a room... Not one of *those* rooms anyway...'

And I hope this last bit sounds dead suggestive in a sort of sexy, James Bond way and then I think, did I really say that? I have astonished myself and as soon as I have spoken I regret it and I pray silently that she didn't hear what I said, or didn't understand what I meant at least.

She stares at me and shakes her head very slightly as if a thought has crossed her mind that she was trying to get rid of.

'Err – No. I'm afraid the sofa is terribly uncomfortable... That's what you meant, isn't it?'

And I nod stupidly.

And then she laughs, throwing her head back. 'And besides which, what would the neighbours say? Me having a good looking young man to stay for the night...'

She is still laughing but I can't hear a thing because those words are echoing round and round in my head and repeating themselves over and over, '... a good looking young man... a good looking young man...'

So it's true she does fancy me then! I hardly notice that I have followed her down the hallway to the little front door. It is only the feel of the cool night air as she opens the door that brings me to my senses.

'You'll just make it,' she is saying.

I stand there gawping at her like a complete idiot. Oh, Lord. She is so beautiful and so sexy I want to throw myself on her. She pulls her dress tight to her body against the cool air and gives a little involuntary shudder and I want to wrap my arms around her to keep her warm.

'It's been really nice,' she says. 'It's always nice to chat about Di and from now on I will try to see more of her friends. I don't know. It sort of keeps her alive doesn't it. I'd forgotten that, how important it is to speak about her.'

But I'm not listening because I know what I must do – when I leave, I mean. I don't want to leave but I figure if I must, then I have to leave properly.

She pulls the door further open and squeezes herself against it to let me by and as I slip through she says.

'Well, goodbye Billy.'

I turn quickly on the door step and take a half pace towards her and I lean forward suddenly and kiss her. I don't give her some silly, French type brush on the cheek but I pucker up and plomp a great big kiss right on her lips. She is totally taken aback and I can feel her rock backwards against the door and brace her back against me. I keep my lips pressed against hers for a good few seconds and I even try to work my

tongue into her mouth but her lips stay tightly closed although she makes a sort of 'Mmmmmm' sound and wriggles a
little which I take to be a mix of surprise and delight.

Then I pull away.

'Goodnight,' I say. 'Adieu, ma cherie.'

If I know anything about women that piece of French
will bowl her over and I reckon we'll be able to start where
we left off the next time we meet and move forward along
what you might call more physical lines.

I decide it is better to go immediately and to leave her
while she is still surprised and hopefully thrilled and delighted – therefore, I don't look back as I stride down the garden
path and turn left into the dark night...

* * *

Somehow I managed to shut the front door, though I was so
bloody shocked my hands were shaking as I pushed it closed.
Once it was shut – and bolted I might add – I leant back
against the wall and let out a breath.

'There's a turn-up!' I thought. 'Good God!'

It takes quite a lot to get me flustered but that young
man had come very close to it.

'So, where did that come from?' I thought.

I went back into the kitchen and lit a ciggy. The air really was filthy with stale smoke by now so I walked over to the
kitchen window and threw it open, puffing on my fag and
breathing in the damp night air by turns – and then a sudden thought occurred to me; I leant forward and pulled the
window shut with a bang and quickly pulled down the roller
blind, which usually I never close.

We back on to fields, there is a foot path... Supposing he was out there, watching me?

I don't know why I thought that. He was just a silly young man who'd drunk too much and made a clumsy pass at an older woman. It was nothing threatening. He'd be mortified in the morning and probably – hopefully – highly embarrassed.

I dropped the cigarette butt into the bowl of washing-up, it hissed and steamed and I stared at the little grey puddle of ash floating in the greasy water – and then I shuddered and a little spasm of fear shot through me. Ridiculous, I know, but I went through to the hall and checked the bolts on the front door, even though I'd only just closed them and then I checked the latches on the living room windows and drew the curtains.

I felt better then and I got myself a glass of water and took a couple of aspirin. I didn't have a headache but it occurred to me that I probably would later, what with the wine and everything – so better safe than sorry. Then I went upstairs to bed, but I left the downstairs lights switched on. I have no idea why. I suppose I wanted to make the house look alive, occupied.

At the top of the stairs I hesitated outside of Diana's bedroom door. Now you ought to know that every night for the last seven years I have gone into her room on the way to my bedroom and I've whispered goodnight to her.

I know you won't understand this doctor... Or come to think of it, maybe you will – yes, of course you will, silly of me. That's your job, after all. But, I have to tell you something, something I haven't mentioned to anyone, not even to you in what you call our 'sessions' together (which by the way, I like to think of as our little 'chats'). Paul has an idea of course, but as I do not allow him into her room he doesn't fully understand.

Doctor, I know it's foolish. It's like visiting her grave – I know she isn't there, but it brings us closer and although it's overwhelmingly sad, it is at least some form of comfort – a kind of reaching out, a touching of spirits. Oh, dear… I feel so awkward sitting here, talking about this, into this little tape recorder. But perhaps it's the only way; I'm certain I couldn't tell you if you were here with me, if I was looking into those steely eyes – did you know you have steely eyes, doctor? Little, sharp, steely blue eyes. Like a weasel.

The fact is Doctor… The fact is, I have left Di's room as it was; as it was on the day she died. Nothing has been moved, nothing has been changed. It is as it was when she left the house to go to the disco at the village hall with her friends on a summer's night seven years ago.

Does that make me mad – or madder than you thought I was, at any rate? I bet you have a name for this. You psychiatrists have names for everything, don't you? Let me guess, the 'Mrs Haversham, syndrome' perhaps? Or maybe you just call it just plain sad and pathetic.

I don't care really. It's what I've done and it felt, feels right to me – has done for all these years. It's not maudlin. I hope not, and I hate self-pity. It's simply… well, it's how I cope. And that's the only justification I need. It's where she is, where I can find her.

Though Diana was everywhere tonight – in the photos we'd been looking at, in our conversation, in my mind. And she was in the house. I could feel her all around me… My darling girl.

So I stood there on the half-lit landing, hesitating by her door. What was I frightened off – that she was waiting for me, in the shrine I've made to her, a shadow among her discarded clothes, her records and her home-work books?

Do ghosts walk?

I hope so...

I pushed the door open and stepped inside her room. I didn't switch on the light and even though the landing was dark, there was enough light reflected from the hall below for me to see the shadowy outline of her things; even if there hadn't have been it wouldn't have mattered, I knew her room so well I could move around it in the pitch black.

I went over to her bed, stepping past the little table with the record player, it's lid still open as she had left it that last night and although I couldn't see it in the dark I knew that The Beatles' *Rubber Soul* LP was on the turntable. I had never put it away and the sleeve lay on the floor where she had dropped it.

Instinctively, I lifted my foot to step over the discarded jeans and underwear that she had thrown on the floor when she put on her disco clothes and just as easily I side-stepped the plate which still had crusts of bread on it left over from the snack I'd made her while she had got ready to go out. They hadn't rotted as you'd think. They once had mildew on them, then they had curled and shrunk but now they were hard, bone like, fossilised souvenirs of her life.

At her bedside I let my hand fall gently on the indentation in the pillow, where her head had rested for her last night's sleep and then I ran my fingers lightly, so lightly it couldn't cause a disturbance, over the crumpled under sheet. Did I still hope to feel her warmth there, to touch the outline of her sleeping figure?

Once again I resisted, as I had done for many years, the temptation to pull the sheets up and straighten the bed that she hadn't bothered to make that morning. I have this terror of doing that one day, of making the bed – half asleep, not concentrating perhaps and then I will have destroyed one of the last real, tangible things about her. Oh, I have my memories but I need to touch, to feel, to cling to something real.

'Goodnight, Darling,' I whispered into the night. 'Don't let the bed-bugs bite.'

If I stayed there beside her bed I would start to cry because even after all these years, I do often cry for her. So I took a deep breath and closed my eyes for a moment, in a sort of... well, the only way I can explain it Doctor, is to say it was in some sort of prayer. Sorry, I bet you're an atheist, aren't you? Scientific people tend to be that way.

Then I went over to the window to draw the curtains. I did this every night and I would open them again in the morning on my way down for breakfast.

It was all a kind of ritual, I suppose. A ritual I performed nearly every night if I could. It was to keep my fears at bay, to bring her to life perhaps, to give me hope, maybe to take me back to another world. A world I'd lost and that time wouldn't give back to me. I could just about get a glimpse of it here in her room at night, I could just about conjure up our old world, the world I shared with her.

All this doctor, it's a secret thing. A special thing. You will keep my secret won't you? You won't destroy it with your probing will you? I don't want you to analyse her into oblivion. I hope you understand that. I really must insist, after all, I'm paying the bills.

Does all this surprise you doctor? Were you ready for

this? Had you guessed that my obsessions ran so deep? Do you care? Are you thinking I must talk to her, this poor mad woman, I must get her out of this habit? What does she think she is, Christ having a Lazarus moment?

I do so hope you won't take this away from me – please don't try to change me – because I don't want to change. I will never change. I might be bright and breezy on the outside. I might play *la grande actrice* at the Am. Dram. Society but I am actually pathetically weak and my ritual, my one means of keeping her alive and present and close – well, I won't, I can't give that up.

I am very happy for you to try and repair the damage, to patch up my battered inner-self but this is one part of the battered me that I need. It is me. She is me. I am me and I am Diana and she is here in this room. So there!

I went over to the window and started to pull the curtains. It was a pitch black night. There must have been heavy cloud because I couldn't see any stars or even the moon through the window and I was glad of that. I still felt rather uncomfortable about that boy Billy. I mean I knew the kiss had just been an awkward, incredibly gauche *faux pas* made by a young man who had hot blood in his veins and not enough sense in his head – but even so I was glad of the thick darkness that wrapped itself around the house. It was like a curtain covering my secrets, keeping me safe.

And then, as I began to close the curtains the moon did suddenly appear, just fleetingly and the clouds briefly parted. The dead flat darkness was wiped away and the garden below and the fields and trees beyond leapt into a silvery, silhouetted relief for a brief, tiny moment of time. I gasped. And then the clouds closed again as quickly as they had opened and the flat blackness folded itself back against the window.

Catching my breath I quickly pulled the drapes, then I pivoted on my heel and pushed myself flat against the wall beside the window.

It could only have been for a split second but I had no doubt. He was leaning over the fence at the end of the garden, staring up at my house, at the window where I stood.

Billy was out there. Watching me.

* * *

I stayed pressed against the wall, trying to control my breathing, trying to calm down. Quite frankly, I was frightened. I mean no woman wants to think there is someone outside her house in the night, watching her.

Then it gradually dawned on me that I was being ridiculous. I'd spent the whole evening with Billy. He was a perfectly pleasant young man – a little awkward perhaps and lacking in any social skills but after all, he was youthful, inexperienced. OK, he'd behaved stupidly when he was leaving but he'd obviously had too much to drink.

And then it hit me and I laughed – leaning against the wall, still clutching a corner of the curtain – I laughed, because it was only then that it occurred to me: 'Oh, my God,' I thought, 'He's got a crush on me!'

It was blindingly obvious – the wine, the chocolates, the moody looks, the silly, clumsy attempt to kiss me.

'Oh, the silly boy,' I thought. 'He wasn't only drunk, he's in love.'

Well Doc, I suppose you'd have a field day with that one. I mean a young man loses a friend and falls for her mother, an 'older' woman.

I suppose there's another technical psychological term for it and you could give me a long explanation, but in my book it was a crush, plain and simple – and having a crush was harmless, he'd get over it.

And now I felt very silly, standing against the wall like a medieval maiden protecting her virtue. He probably wasn't even out there. It was just me, letting my imagination run away with itself because I was thinking about him when I drew the curtains, thinking about him and Diana, and I'd probably seen nothing more sinister than a shadow, or a stump of a tree or even some bales of hay – or whatever it is farmers stack-up in their fields at this time of year. The night was very dark, the brief flash of moonlight would play tricks on anyone's eyes especially on someone who'd had a bottle or so of red wine and a socially rather exhausting evening.

How stupid of me to behave like this, about a silly boy. So I took a deep breath, went to the window and deliberately threw back the curtains.

I couldn't see anything of course, even though I waited for a while in the hope that the clouds would part again, but they didn't, and anyway I knew that he wasn't there... in fact, I was pretty certain he hadn't ever been there.

'Go to bed,' I said to myself. 'You need a good night's sleep and you need to sober up.'

So then I went to my own room, still telling myself off for being so stupid.

'You idiot,' I thought. 'You're imagination is out of control. There's no one out there.'

Then I pulled the curtains very tightly shut and undressed in the dark.

* * *

I'm in bed now and it's late. Much later than I intended – I had unexpected delays getting home.

It occurs to me that I should be ashamed, that I should be begging forgiveness. In the old days I would definitely have been on my knees but tonight I'm not.

I have lusted after an older woman. I have made advances to her and done other unspeakable things.

And…

…And it was great!

* * *

Daylight brings an end to most fears. Ghosts only walk at night and strange young men only peer up at windows after the sun sets, and usually only in our imagination – so the next morning by the time I'd dressed, had coffee and soaked in a long hot bath I was asking myself what on earth I'd been frightened about. However, quite ridiculously, I felt a small shock of fear run through me when someone knocked on the door at about half past ten.

'It's broad daylight,' I told myself. 'People are out and about.'

I put down the magazine I'd been reading and went to the front door.

'Hello, stranger.'

Sydney stood in the doorway, larger than life and grinning from ear to ear. He raised his horrible little pork pie hat and smiled cheesily at me.

I stared at him a little blankly before I remembered that

we'd arranged to go to lunch.

'That's a horrible hat,' I said.

'Oh,' he said looking like a little boy who'd had his train-set taken away. 'I thought it was quite trendy.'

'In nineteen fifty five, Sydney, it very possibly was.'

He led the way to his car and we drove off towards Leeford. I knew that I should be telling him about last night but I knew what he'd say. He'd be furious, want to call the police and get all hot under his collar. I was tired, I wanted to forget the whole thing so I said nothing and we drove in silence.

We had lunch in the little pub at the end of Sydney's road – *The Wattle and Daub* – because he likes to think of himself as a 'regular' and he's stupidly proud of having his own tankard hanging behind the bar.

Between ourselves, I hate the place. The landlord, Derek, leers at me behind Sydney's back and the food is lousy – never anything other than what Derek calls a 'ploughman's lunch' which seems to be all the rage in pubs nowadays and which at the *Wattle and Daub* isn't much more than a bit of dry French bread, some mouldy cheddar and a couple of pickles. As usual there was no wine, so I had to have a sherry. Apparently, Derek doesn't think there will ever be a demand for wine in pubs, so he never orders any in. It's too continental, he says.

Then we went to *Rebecca* rehearsals in the Methodist Church Hall. Billy's mother wasn't there, thank God. We weren't doing anything that involved her, which isn't hard as she only has one small scene as Mrs Lacy – and even that she murders with too much enthusiasm and less talent. Of course, she's on the committee (she would be) and usually, even when she isn't needed on stage, she rushes around all the time noisily organising things – generally while other people are trying to rehearse.

The fact that there was no sign of her today was a relief. I'm not sure if I could have looked her in the eye: 'Oh, hello – your son stuck his tongue in my mouth last night... No completely uninvited... but then boys will be boys, eh..? Of course I can be available for photos – tomorrow at twelve?'

* * *

I haven't made any recordings for a few days. There has been nothing much to say. We've been rehearsing *Rebecca*, Sydney has wined and dined me, (I should feel guilty about how much he spends on me – But I don't!), Paul phoned a couple of times to say London was 'groovy,' and life at Abbey Road was, 'cool,' and that's about it.

Oh, and I pushed the whole incident with Billy to the back of my mind. I didn't hear from him, which was good as actually I'd half suspected that he would call round again. But there hasn't been a trace of him. I did wonder if maybe he'd send me a letter, you know, apologising for leaping on me by the front door – but I have I heard nothing.

I suppose I shouldn't surprised. I imagine he was squirming with embarrassment when he woke-up with a hang-over the next day and remembered what happened. I think that in later years that will be one kiss he'll want to forget when he looks back on his love life.

In an odd way, I almost felt sorry for him. Of course, he may have been so drunk he didn't even remember the night before, but I doubt it. Anyway, I heard nothing from him and that suited me just fine.

So by Wednesday afternoon I had almost forgotten the whole thing. It was another wonderful day but not quite so hot as it had been and I wanted to get out, I needed to be away from my little home and clear my head of *Rebecca* and housework. So I figured that an extravagant shopping trip and buying a few clothes for Autumn was as good a way as any to pass the afternoon.

* * *

I didn't buy much but window shopping is just as therapeutic and a lot cheaper and after I'd met Sydney for lunch (in a different pub, thank God) and feeling much better about life, I went home to study my lines again.

The bus, of course, was delayed so when I got home I went straight into the living room and started work. I had the whole of act four to learn, which I was ashamed to say I had barely looked at. I used to be so good at learning lines. I fear *anno dominie* is catching up with me.

After an hour or so I began to lose concentration. It was a hot afternoon, the room was stuffy and I felt sleepy. I decided I needed a cup of tea to wake me up (Yes, Doctor – a cold drink would have been more sensible but I'm English and I have tea in the afternoon – Oh, God did I really say that!? I am getting old!)

I wandered into the kitchen to put the kettle on, and I found myself staring out of the window while it boiled, looking at the view on the other side of the garden. The countryside as always looked wonderful, but it was tired at the edges – there was a heat haze on the hills and a dust cloud was being blown into the air from a tractor making its way across the fields and even the leaves on the apple tree in the garden looked a little exhausted.

I made my tea and decided to finish studying the script in the garden, even though it was now early evening it was too stuffy to stay indoors.

I went to unlock the back door but the top bolt was already shot back. I bent down to the bottom bolt – it too was shot back.

'That's odd,' I thought.

We always leave the key in the lock and I turned it now but that too was already undone, and when I pushed down on the handle, the door swung open, letting in a rush of warm air.

I stared at the door and touched the key as if by doing so I would know why the door was unlocked. I was really quite surprised. I always locked the back door. In fact I was very strict about it. I used to nag the kids when they came in from the garden – 'always lock-up,' I'd say. 'We may not be in Wandsworth now but there's a footpath at the bottom of the garden and you never know…' And they'd pull faces: 'Fussy, Mummy.' But we always did it. All of us. We always locked the back door. But now it wasn't locked and the bolts hadn't been shot across and anyone could have wandered in.

I kicked myself. How had I done that? Although the weather had been glorious I'd been so busy with the play and with shopping, and with Sydney, come to that, that I hadn't been into the garden for ages.

And then I thought, had the door had been open all that evening, when Billy was here? Had it had been open when I was upstairs in Di's room, when I thought I saw…

And despite the evening's heat, I shivered.

'Idiot,' I said out loud.

And then I realised it had been open not only then but for the last three days – at night while I'd been asleep, and during the day when I was out of the house – like I had been today. All day…

I looked around and ridiculously I felt my stomach churning and suddenly I was convinced that someone was watching me, someone was behind me, perhaps looking through the gap in the door from the hallway… or… perhaps they were upstairs…

'Nonsense,' I said annoyed at my own stupid fantasies and surprising myself at my own voice. 'Don't be stupid, you've been in for an hour and nobody's leapt on you while you read *Rebecca*, have they? You've been in and out all week and no one popped up from under the floorboards, did they?'

I turned on my heel and marched into the hall. I've no idea what I thought I'd do – face my demons, I suppose. Of course, there was no one there. I went into the living room, which I knew was empty – I'd just been in there reading the script after all, but nevertheless I still looked behind the sofa and even in the corner cupboard, though what I expected to find there I have no idea – a dangerous midget perhaps.

I went back into the hall and started to climb the stairs and then half-way up I hesitated. Someone *could* be up there, I suppose. Someone could have slipped in while I was out shopping and be waiting… I held the banister a little tighter.

'Nonsense,' I thought. 'This is ridiculous.'

There was no one on the landing. Well of course, there wouldn't have been, but I opened Paul's bedroom door and went in.

Nothing.

I strode across to his wardrobe and threw the doors open.

...God!

I rocked back on my heels, recoiling and putting my hand to my face...

The odour of sour clothes was disgusting and I winced at the smell and at the sight of the old sports kit he'd left piled up in the bottom of his wardrobe, suppurating in its own dirt and stale sweat. It was green with mould.

'Dirty pig,' I thought. 'You'd think at his age he could learn to use the washing machine!'

Although I was appalled at his disgusting habits the sight of something as normal as dirty sports kit was a relief and I found myself giggling out loud as I made a mental note to wear some rubber gloves when I carried it down to the machine.

I breathed a small sigh of relief before crossing the landing to my own room. Everything was as I had left it. The bathroom too, was just as it had been this morning after I'd taken my long soak.

And that only left Di's room.

I pushed the door open and stepped into a bright, cheerful room. The afternoon sun was streaming through the windows, I could hear the pigeons cooing on the roof above my head and everything seemed disconcertingly normal.

Relieved, I stepped inside and looked around at the familiar surroundings. Everything was I had left it, as it had been for the last seven years. Everything appeared to be in its place, untouched, unsullied.

And then it hit me – a great tidal wave of misery and pain, it washed over me, sucking me down, sucking me into a bleak darkness of fear and anger. The sun seemed dimmer, the light seemed to fade, the pigeons clattered away above my head in a great whirl of feathers and fluster.

Someone had been in here. Someone had come into this room, into her place. Into this special place. I could feel it. There was no obvious evidence of anyone having been there but I could definitely feel it. The room wasn't the same. It simply wasn't! I had been in here every day, once or twice a day, sometimes more, for seven years and I knew every inch, every fraction of it but more than that, I knew its *feel*, I knew its atmosphere – the dreams, the memories, the spirit of the room were like second nature to me. And now, it felt different.

I looked around. I wasn't frightened anymore but I was angry. Very angry.

I walked further into the room, stepping instinctively over the cover of *Rubber Soul* where it had lain on the floor for so long – and then I stopped dead, my foot hovering in the air. The cover wasn't there! It had gone...

...And then I saw it.

It had been placed neatly on the table next to the record player, and the record was no longer on the turntable – it was in the sleeve.

* * *

I panicked. I turned on my heel and ran down the stairs, I have no idea why but the walls seemed to be closing in and I couldn't breathe – not up there, not in her room.

I stood at the bottom of the stairs and clutched the newel post, my legs seemed to have abruptly gone from under me and I couldn't take another step, all I could do was cling on, gasping for breath. And I was thinking, someone was here, someone has been in Di's bedroom and then I thought, 'And they might still be here…'.

But oddly, in another part of my mind a calmer, cooler part, I was thinking how ridiculous, how stupid I must look standing there, clasping the banisters, panting as if I'd run a race, my hands trembling. But I couldn't get rid of that thought: '…Someone had been in her room – in my dead daughter's bedroom…'

And then the doorbell rang – a long, loud shrill ring, that cut through the house. I stood gaping at the front door, at the silhouette of a man's figure behind the glass.

I didn't move. Stupidly I stared at the shape of the man and I didn't even call out.

And then he rang again and I still didn't move.

At last the figure raised a hand and brought it down against the glass and when he did so I shrank back, perhaps I expected to be showered in broken pieces of window. But he only knocked – quite gently in fact – and then a voice called out:

'Hello. Are you there?'

I didn't want to go to the door. I didn't want to see another human being just now.

So he knocked again.

'Hello…' he called

My heart hammered in my chest – it was so loud I thought he'd hear it, even through the door.

'I've got a delivery. Hello.'

I've no idea how long it took to pull myself together but eventually I let go of the stair post and, shaking a little, I went over to the door.

But I didn't open it. Instead I reached out and leant my weight against it.

'Yes...' I said and I was surprised at how strong my voice sounded. 'Who is it?'

'I've got a delivery for a Mrs Watson. Is this the right address?'

'What is it?'

'Some flowers madam. It's Jones the Florists from Leeford. We've got some flowers for you.'

I pressed harder against the door.

'Just leave them.' I said. 'Put them on the step.'

'Really? Don't you want to take them in?'

'I've just got out the bath. I'm not properly dressed – just leave them. I'll take them in later.'

'Alright. If you're sure...'

'Yes. I'm sure. Leave them please... Thank you.'

I heard the sound of rustling tissue paper and footsteps retreating down the garden path. I sighed – a kind of relief swept over me – but then the footsteps stopped. There was a pause and I heard him turn back and trudge towards me. I could hear blood pounding in my ears.

'Hello,' the voice said. 'You still there?'

'Yes,' I said and my voice sounded dry and cracked. 'What is it?'

'Well, don't leave them out here in this heat for too long. They'll go limp.'

'Thank you.' I whispered. 'Goodbye.'

'What did you say?

'I said goodbye.'

'Right... well then, bye for now.'

And this time I heard the footsteps fade away as he walked to the road; then I heard a door open and close and the sound of an engine starting. I stayed there, leaning against the door until I heard a noisy crunching of gears and the sound of a van driving away.

I let my breath out in a long slow sigh as the sound of the engine faded into the distance.

'Pull yourself together – get on the phone to Sydney and get him over here.'

And I did so. I dialled his number praying that he'd be in. He was, and by the time I'd told him what had happened and heard that he was on his way and that I was to lock everything up tighter than a drum and let no one in apart from him, I was beginning to feel a little better.

I went to the sink and poured myself a glass of water and while I did so I found myself looking out surveying the view through the kitchen window – perhaps I was looking to see that there was no one on the footpath or in the fields. There wasn't, and I was aware that I was behaving stupidly.

Although I try never to drink in the evenings before seven, water wasn't enough so I went to the dresser and my hand hesitated over a bottle of Gordon's, but I didn't pick it up. 'Nothing's happened, you don't need a drink,' I said to myself.

And then I thought, 'Sod it. Yes I do.'

I ignored the Gordon's, instead I found a bottle of Scotch and poured myself a large slug of that. I tipped a little water in it from the other glass and I knocked it back in one and then I had a refill. Usually Scotch affects me pretty quickly and the taste blows my head off but I didn't even notice it this evening.

Then I went right round the house and locked every door and window.

* * *

I heard Sydney's car about twenty minutes later. I was behind the closed front door waiting for him by the time he came up the path.

He didn't knock at first and through the frosted glass I could see him stooping to pick up the large bouquet that the delivery man had left there.

'Just flowers,' he called through the door. 'No surprises.'

I held the door open and he stepped inside.

'You OK?' He said.

I nodded. He looked at the flowers he was holding.

'I'll put them in the kitchen,' he said, and I followed him along the corridor.

'Better lock the front door,' he said over his shoulder.

I was already doing so and I slid the bolts across and joined him in the kitchen.

'So what's been happening?'

I let out my breath. I felt as if I hadn't actually breathed properly for the last hour or so and then I flopped onto a chair. I told him about the back door being open and about searching the house and how I knew someone had been there. But I didn't tell him how I knew, because that would have meant telling him about Diana's room and I never speak about that and I have certainly never told him about it. So when he said:

'But how do you know someone came in? I mean OK you may have forgotten to lock the door but it doesn't mean anyone actually came in.'

I just said that I could tell. I could sense it.

'Is there something missing? Has anything been stolen?' he asked.

'I don't think so. But someone was definitely here.'

For a second I thought I saw a look of uncertainty flicker across his face but then he said:

'What's going on? I feel like I'm missing something here.'

I swallowed.

'Well there is something else,' I said. 'And you won't be very happy about it.'

So I told him about Billy the other night and the stupid, silly, childish attempt to kiss me and about thinking there was someone outside in the field.

Predictably he was furious but to my astonishment he didn't suggest calling the police as I'd thought he would though I did have to dissuade him from driving round to Billy's house to 'poke him in the nose,' as he put it.

Finally he calmed down.

'I need a drink,' he said at last and he glanced at my empty glass. 'Shall I get you another?'

'Please.' I handed him my glass and he went to the dresser where I'd left the Scotch. As he poured the drinks I picked up the enormous bouquet the florist had delivered and started to peel away the layers of tissue paper.

Roses.

They were lovely. A deep, deep shade of red and such a wonderful scent. They must have cost a fortune. I mean there are roses and there are roses and these were the best – a dozen of them too and beautifully wrapped in tissue.

'Who are they from?' Sydney asked from the dresser.

I raised an eyebrow.

'Not me,' he said. 'Though I wish I'd thought of it.'

'Then I've no idea,' I said. 'Unless they're from Paul.'

Then I saw the envelope that I had nearly thrown away

with the tissue paper. I tore it open. There was a card and written on it in small, neat handwriting there was a message:

In our life I'll love you more.

I have no idea what it meant. I suppose it's a quote but I couldn't tell you from what. But I knew, of course, who'd written it on the card.

* * *

Sydney didn't want me to stay in the cottage that night, he absolutely insisted on it – and I didn't need a lot of persuading.

I quickly got changed and threw a few things in an overnight bag and we locked the place up and climbed into his car. It was a relief to get outside into the now slightly cooler evening air.

The top was down and the breeze was in my face as we drove through the countryside. My head began to clear and I felt a lot better the further we got from The Maltings.

'You OK?' he said after a while.

'Better for getting away,' I said. 'I love my little cottage but the last few hours have put rather a damper on it.'

'Of course,' he said.

We drove on in silence when a thought struck me.

'Sydney,' I said. 'The bell. The front door bell…'

'What?' he glanced over at me; he probably thought I'd gone mad.

'It doesn't work,' I said. 'It never has but this evening the delivery man rang the bell and it worked.'

He looked at me again and then the penny dropped.

'Christ! Well, your young friend is a little fixer isn't he?'

'Yes. So he must have been inside the house. You can't fix a bell from outside.'

'Quite.'

'That's it then,' I said. 'I'll have to go to the police. I mean that's breaking and entering.'

'Well entering, at least,' he said slowing the car down, so we could hear each other better. 'I don't think he actually broke in.'

'He must have unlocked the door when he came round for dinner. Come to think of it I had to find my cigarettes – he was alone in the kitchen while I looked for them. He must have done it then.'

Sydney grunted and stared at the road ahead.

'Look…' he said and then he went quiet.

'What?'

'I don't know… '

I thought he seemed troubled about something but eventually he said: 'It's all a bit of a mess, that's all.'

That was an odd way to put it but I didn't say anything – though I did think that sometimes Sydney didn't quite, well how shall I put it, grasp the nettle.

When we arrived in Leeford he insisted we go for dinner. I wasn't sure if I felt like it, but he wanted to take my mind off things and I think he was right about that.

It was a kind of unsaid but mutual thing that while we ate, we both resolutely avoided talking about what had happened. I'm sure he wanted to but I made it plain that I didn't. I'd had enough of the whole thing just then, so instead we talked about well, nonsense really – trivia – things like plays and about Sydney's travels over the last few years – he was very funny about cockroaches and turds in India –

and how he was not a born traveller: 'It's the sewerage, you know,' he said. 'I think the mark of any country is how good its drains are and I've yet to find any system of drainage better than the British.'

Ah, Sydney. He is so English. So provincial. Stiff upper-lipped restraint for the most part and truly passionate when it comes to the bowels. It's amazing how Sydney – so public school, so formal – ever became so rich and to think he made all his money as an agent in Las Vegas. It must have been purgatory for him – all that chutzpah and glitter – still American plumbing is quite good of course, but I bet he was glad to come home.

I feel very comfortable with Sydney. I don't know if I love him but I am very fond of him. Of course, I know he loves me, but I keep him to some extent at arms length. I don't think I am really ready for a full blown love affair again. As you know Doc, James casts a long shadow – even now.

It was wonderful when we bumped into each other a few months ago after so many years; we'd been best friends in Southwold in our salad days and he'd always had a crush on me, but I didn't know if I really wanted to go much beyond being good friends. He made me laugh, he was very easy going, he was very wealthy – but I don't know if I had a burning desire to spend my life with him.

Oh and we hadn't slept together, even though I knew how much he wanted to, I'd been avoiding it. I felt it would make things more complicated than I wanted. Which was silly really – after all we were both grown-up, both people of the world, both married before and this is 1976.

But then, right there in the restaurant over peach melbas, it occurred to me that tonight, I wanted to make love to him: I wanted to have something intense and physical, some-thing that would completely absorb me and take my mind off what had happened that afternoon – I wanted an escape from thinking about Billy and deciding whether I should go to the police and above all I wanted to forget the fear I'd felt on the stairs and the other night when I thought someone was outside the house.

Oh, forget all that – getting down to brass tacks, to put it bluntly Doc, I wanted a good shag!

When he eventually asked for the bill (I know it's not very liberated but he always pays and quite frankly I'm broke and he isn't), he said, 'Well I'd have liked a brandy but I think we should get back. You need to get to bed and get some sleep I expect.'

I took the cue: 'Well, I need to get to bed…' I raised an eyebrow. 'And afterwards we could have a brandy, if you like.'

He looked disappointingly blank.

'Well, let me order you one now.'

'I meant …you know…' I simpered.

Again he looked at me blankly.

'Um…' he said.

Sydney is a bit slow on the up-take sometimes and he didn't seem to be catching on very fast. Short of putting up an advertising hoarding, I didn't know how else to spell it out.

I suddenly had to hold back a fit of the giggles, so I took a sip of my coffee instead and I whispered, 'Brandy can wait, can't it. I need something else, Sydney.'

He looked disappointingly confused.

'Well, I could get you a liqueur, I suppose.'

I put down my coffee cup. 'Oh for God's sake Sydney

don't be so obtuse. I don't want a drink…'

'Oh,' he said. 'Don't you? Well, if you're sure…'

I frowned at him.

'Sydney. We're both adults. We can go back to your place and do adult things all night if we like.'

There was a polite cough and the waiter who I hadn't seen creep-up behind me placed the bill on the table. He had the good grace to look a little embarrassed. Poor Sydney looked mortified and I could see he thought he'd never be able to eat there again and I'm afraid this time I really did get a fit of the giggles.

'Oh Lord, Sydney just pay the bill will you and then let's go to your flat.'

We did and once he'd poured the brandies and the lights were low he put a Miles Davies record on his stupidly expensive HI-Fi (that was actually slightly bigger than my cottage) and we cuddled up together on the sofa. I felt fabulously young again and I could feel my skin glowing with anticipation or it may have been the brandy hitting the wine I'd had with dinner… or of course, it may simply have been good old-fashioned lust.

I pushed myself close to him and ran my fingers through his hair and over his face. He had a little stubble round his chin and I enjoyed the feel of it against my fingers. I hadn't felt a man's beard for ages and there's something so intimate and masculine about feeling the bristles on a man's face.

I leant a little closer to him and brushed my lips over his but instead of responding, he pulled slightly away. I was surprised.

'Darling,' I whispered to put him at his ease. 'This is so lovely…' and I pecked at his lips once again. And although he let me kiss him he didn't respond... well, you know, how shall I put this, as I expected.

I suddenly realised that he was nervous. Which seemed ridiculous. I mean we were neither of us spring chickens and I assumed neither of us were virgins, come to that.

'Are you all right, Darling?' I whispered in his ear.

'Yes...' he said but there was a little crack in is voice.

I decided to slip off my dress. I mean one of us had to get the ball rolling – absolutely no pun intended. So I slid off the sofa and reached behind me to ease down the zip. Making sure that he couldn't miss the show, I let the frock fall slowly down over my breasts and over my hips. I had on my black silk slip underneath (I may live in poverty in a slum but I have never seen why that should mean one has to dress like a tramp) and I eased the little shoulder straps down my arms and with just a little wriggle of my hips I let it slide to the floor.

I may be getting on, and I'll admit the low lighting helped but if I say so myself my figure has lost none of its shape over the years and I could give most girls half my age a run for their money. I could see his eyes widen with lust as he drank in my black bra, the lacy French knickers and the suspenders. This fad for tights is all very convenient but they never have the same effect as stockings and suspenders when it comes to the bedroom – not that we were strictly speaking in the bedroom we were actually in Sydney's beautifully furnished living room on his huge, comfortable and no doubt very expensive sofa.

'Wow!' he said, sounding a little breathless.

'Wow, indeed, darling,' I replied lowering myself back beside him. 'Now, where were we... Oh, yes...'

He started gamely enough and he was certainly a good kisser and he could do wonderful things with his tongue. I don't know how he knew but I have a little 'thing' about my earlobes and he had little thrills of electricity running down my spine in next to no time and to feel his hands slide over me, exploring the curves of my body, and to feel his hot breath on my neck and his little groans of pleasure was really rather delicious.

But, and how can I put this delicately for the ears of a young psychiatrist listening to this rather adult tape, he was perhaps not as experienced in the ways of the world as some of us. Ah well, doctor – let's put it this way – we never got past first base. Actually, I suppose we got to second or third but a home run was out of the question, apparently. Things that should have happened didn't happen. Poor old Sydney – he couldn't achieve what we both wanted him to achieve.

Now it wasn't for want of trying on either of our sides, let me make that plain. We both of us are creative people and I'm not known for my shy retiring nature or for my want of imagination. I did everything a woman could do. I played the lover, the sensitive and demur woman, the worldly-wise and pitiable lady in need of succour and finally the whore with every trick in the book, from verbal encouragement to making downright physical pornography but by two in the morning we were both exhausted, frustrated and frankly, unsatisfied – and worse, I was beginning to wonder what was the point – which I know sounds harsh – but let's be realistic there's only so much a lady can take or in this case *not* take in the course of one night.

By mutual consent we both lay back on the pillows – by now we had moved to his bedroom and we were on his large king sized bed – a trail of my underwear marked our route – and I stared up at the ceiling. The curtains were open and the windows were open because it was such a humid and warm night. I could hear the occasional car making it's way along Leeford High Street at the end of the road and I could smell the air of the hot town outside and by turning my head a little I could see the clear night sky and through the window, the brilliant full moon that lit the room with its silvery glow.

'Sorry,' he said after a while, in a very quiet voice.

I said as gently as I could. 'There's no need, honestly.'

But actually I was quite disappointed. I was too old and wise to be hurt but I decided there and then that when it came to the bed department, Sydney was going to be a dead loss. That sounds a bit harsh I suppose but it was obviously true and that got me thinking. I mean I am… well, of a certain age – but I didn't want to slide into my declining years gracefully, I want to go into my dotage absolutely *disgracefully,* if I could.

The last few years have been pretty barren ones on the sex front, but now I wanted to spread my wings again, and my legs come to that – sorry I know that was crude doctor, but I do love to shock you when I can. Anyway, the last few hours, albeit that they'd ended a little flat (to put it bluntly!), had reminded me of what I was missing. I had denied myself the pleasure of a physical relationship for too long.

Suddenly I wanted to be a young woman again, I wanted fun and laughter, I wanted to go out and dance and go to parties and drink too much and, well, let's face it, I wanted sex and lots of it.

'I don't know what happened.' Sydney's voice crept into my thoughts and I had to drag myself back to the here and now. 'I… I've things on my mind – you know,' he was saying and he sounded like a little boy who'd not done his homework. 'All this… You know, what's happening to you with that boy… I am sorry.'

'Oh, but you mustn't worry about me,' I replied and I probably sounded far too breezy. 'I'll be fine. We'll sort the kid out. I'm sure we will.'

I hadn't turned-over to face him when we spoke rather I lay there with my head turned away from him, staring out of the window.

'I am sorry,' he said again.

'Never mind,' I said as gently as I could. 'It must be the full moon… It can do funny things to a man.'

'Really?' he said and there was an almost childish note of hope in his voice.

'Oh, yes. It's an old Irish fairy tale apparently.'

There was a long silence and I began to feel tired.

'I didn't know you were Irish,' he said eventually and his voice sounded as sleepy as I felt.

'I'm not,' I said. 'But let's hope you are.'

And we both giggled very quietly before we fell asleep.

* * *

I don't know what woke me. The moonlight was as bright as ever so maybe it was that, maybe it was because it was so airless, so close, and I could feel sweat running down my face and arms. I felt hot and uncomfortable even lying on top of the sheets. I turned my head to look Sydney. He was sound asleep, dead to the world. I lay there for a minute or two listening to his steady breathing. I found the sound strangely irritating, there was an intimacy and a closeness about it I disliked and it's perfect rhythm was more irritating than if he'd been snoring hideously. I couldn't go on lying there – I felt stifled by the warmth of the night and by his being next to me.

This summer has been so strange. It didn't feel like an English summer at all. The heat made me think of being abroad – Spain, Italy or the South of France, maybe places even more exotic that I read about but never go to and probably never will.

I puffed out my cheeks and slid off the bed and wandered over to the big bay window. Not only were the windows open but we had left the curtains wide open too. I stood in front of them breathing in the night air, trying to find a little coolness, tasting the night in my mouth, smelling the warm dampness in my nostrils.

I stared down at the street below.

Leeford doesn't boast many street lights in its side roads; there was one a little further along from where I stood but none outside of the window. By its light I could vaguely make out the shape of Sydney's sleek car parked below, the outline of a post box on the opposite pavement and the slinking walk of a cat that picked its way along the top of a neighbour's wall. I watched it for a while, fascinated by its deftness, the suppleness of its stride, before it jumped down into the garden below.

And then, on the other side of the road, a shadow moved under one of the plain trees. It might have been the shadow of a branch moving in the breeze, except there was no breeze. It seemed to separate itself from the dark outline of the tree trunk and then fade back into it and that was all. Nothing much. Just that slight movement but I stepped quickly back into the darkness of the room, away from the window. I was suddenly terribly conscious of being naked…

…and of being watched.

…and the idea of that, sent little electric charges along my spine.

* * *

Dear Mrs Watson,

Would you like to come to the theatre with me?

I really enjoyed our meal together at your house the other night, more than I can ever tell you. Just to sit and talk meant so much to me and I feel that we have so much in common, such as Diana of course – but also our passion – I mean for things like the arts and theatre, though I may not have said too much about them at the time but knowing you were/are an actress is a bit like me being a musician. We are both creative spirits in a material world, looking for like-minded people to share our passions, don't you think?

I am here – wanting to share with you whenever you feel like sharing with me, as it were.

Somehow I think we really 'met' the other night, I mean on what Blake – or another visionary, perhaps even someone like Mahatma Ghandi – might call on another spiritual plain. (Though, let's face it Hindus don't have the monopoly on spiritual plains, I mean lots of religions are essentially looking at a higher level of existence, like Catholics for instance, if you know what I mean).

Basically, I reckon our creative life forces could be pretty intertwined.

It was wonderful having dinner with you and I hope you realise how I feel about you. I tried to show you as I left – it was the most wonderful moment of my life, by the way.

I have got two tickets for Hedda Gabler on Monday – apparently, according to the Daily Telegraph review, Diana Rigg is 'superb' and I quote. I would love to take you to see it. I could collect you at say seven O'clock and we could go over to the theatre bar for a drink first. I could book a table for dinner afterwards in the theatre restaurant too.

I do hope you will say yes.

Billy

* * *

Dear Billy

How extraordinary you are.

We've got a lot to talk about and I am not at all sure if going to the theatre is appropriate in the circumstances.

I think it is better if we go somewhere for a chat. I'm probably insane. I should really be calling the police not meeting you for a talk but I have always been one for sorting things myself when I can.

We'll meet on Monday as you suggest but earlier in the day. Shall we say at two pm? Please don't call at my house; I will meet you in front of the theatre.

Yours

* * *

Billy was already waiting. He smiled broadly when he saw me and he came trotting over to meet me. He reminded me of a dog I had when I was child: she was a long haired German Shepherd called Beth and when I came home from school she'd come rolling towards me, her tail waving like a banner and her head held low, looking up at me through black, excited eyes, almost shaking with pleasure at the sight of me, desperate for a hug and some fuss.

And that's how he was. Fussing around me and trying to escort me across the road, holding out an arm like a policeman trying to stop some imaginary traffic.

'Gosh,' he said.

I didn't think his generation used the word 'gosh' anymore.

'This is great.' He added.

I tried to take a firm line from the off.

'Don't get too excited, Billy,' I said. 'I've got a bone or two to pick with you, to put it mildly.'

He didn't seem put-out at all. In fact, he as good as ignored me.

'Are you sure you don't want a drink. The bar's still open for theatre lunches. I checked. Perhaps you would like lunch… Let's have lunch.'

It was like being with a highly strung child.

'Billy,' I said perhaps a little harshly. 'We are not having lunch. I really don't want lunch with you. After all that you've done I'm not even sure I really want to see you at all. This is not easy and I wish I wasn't here but there are things that have to be said.'

He had the grace at last to look a little crestfallen.

'Oh,' he said. 'Is something wrong?'

'You are more obtuse than I thought you were. Come on lets walk. This way.'

I'd already decided that we would walk a half a mile towards Leeford where there was a little sports ground set back off the road. The local cricket club played here in the summer and the local football teams in the winter. There were some benches to sit on and I knew that during the week it was pretty well empty apart from a few dog walkers so we could be private there, but equally I would not be completely alone if he did anything silly. Although, looking at him now as he trotted along beside me – reminding me still more of the departed Beth – I couldn't believe that anything sinister was going to happen.

He was a very handsome boy, I had to admit. He looked different from the other night. At first I couldn't see why and then I realised that he hadn't shaved – he had several days stubble on his chin, perhaps he was growing a beard. He was wearing jeans and a rather tight T-shirt and I noticed for the first time that he was very muscular, very tanned.

In other circumstances, I thought, I might have been quite flattered to find myself being escorted by such a good looking young man and I have to admit I felt a little pang of something, a stirring deep inside that I faintly recognised as lust. Dear God, Doc – what will you think of me!

We hardly spoke as we walked, at least I didn't. Billy seemed capable of keeping up a pretty consistent stream of babble with no help from me. I tuned out of it, thinking ahead to what I wanted to say.

We entered the playing field.

The grass on the pitch had turned almost completely brown in the weeks since I was last here. Last time I'd been here, back in the spring, the place was lush and green but now the hot summer had done its damage and the grass was dead and the place was dusty and even the usually neat brightly painted pavilion looked tired and unkempt in the heat. I wondered if they could still play cricket on a pitch like this? Paul had briefly been a member of the local team and he'd played for them a couple of weeks ago when he'd been home, so I assumed they could, the thought reminded me that I needed to put his kit in the wash.

We sat on a bench near the pavilion and I tried to compose myself, to find the right words.

'Would you like a lemon sherbet?'

Billy was thrusting a rather sticky, crumpled looking bag at me.

'No thank you.' I said.

'They're supposed to be refreshing on a hot day apparently, but I find they make my lips stick together and make me more thirsty,' he said, screwing the bag up and thrusting it back into his pocket. 'Anyway, that's according to Mr Tidyman in the village shop. But knowing Mr Tidyman it's just a con to sell more sweets, wouldn't you say? I seldom buy sweets nowadays but he still thinks I'm a kid and he's always trying it on, to get me to buy as many as I used to.' He smiled at me and added: 'Actually, I did have a bit of a sweet tooth as a kid – but not so much now.'

I shook my head and tried to cling on to why I was here and forget about Mr Tidyman and his lemon sherbets but Billy seemed to have verbal diarrhoea.

'It's funny,' he went on. 'As you get older you lose your palette for sweet stuff. I'm much more sophisticated now on the taste front.'

I remembered the bottle of *Blue Nun* and lit a cigarette.

'Billy, as fascinating as this may be I want to talk to you about something rather more serious.'

He looked at me.

'Oh?' he said and you might almost have thought he had no idea what I was talking about.

I turned away and blew a lungful smoke into the afternoon air. Looking back at him, I went on:

'What on earth do you think you're up to?'

He stared at me blankly.

'I'm sorry,' he said. 'I don't understand.'

'Do you realise just how close you've come to being in serious trouble?'

He seemed puzzled.

'Why..? What have I done?' He opened his eyes wide and stared at me. 'You've got me lost, I'm afraid.'

I puffed on my cigarette and this time I let the smoke blow into his face. He waved the smoke away and pretended to cough, which really annoyed me – there was something priggish in his manner, and for some reason I thought of Sydney. I deliberately took another drag and let it blow over him as I spoke.

'If you'd behaved like this with anyone else,' I said, 'I think they'd have had you arrested by now; so thank your lucky stars that you decided to play your silly tricks on someone who's been around long enough to give you the benefit of the doubt.'

He shook his head.

'But... I really don't know what I've done?'

'Do I have to spell it out?'

'I don't understand... really.'

He looked genuinely surprised and then he gasped.

'Oh,' he said.

And he put his hands to his face.

'Oh, no,' he said. 'Is this about the other night? Outside of Mr Potefract's flat? Oh, no. Oh, hell! – You saw me, didn't you?'

'I most certainly did.'

'Oh no…'

He'd gone quite pale.

'I am so sorry,' he was saying. 'Look, it's not what you think. It's really not.'

'What do I think Billy?' I said. 'You tell me what I think.'

'I… I didn't… I wasn't trying to look or anything. I… I don't know what came over me. I… I was in Leeford because I'd gone to the pictures, to see *Annie Hall*. I don't know if you've seen it yet, by the way. Frankly, I think it's quite over-rated. Rather self indulgent, in my opinion. There's quite a funny bit outside of a cinema but the basic premise…'

'Billy!' I said and I was getting annoyed now. 'I am not interested in Annie bloody Hall. Why were you following me?'

'I wasn't. Not really. I don't know. I came out of the cinema and I went to wait for the bus and I was standing there for ages – it's supposed to be the five past ten but it's always late, once it didn't turn up until ten thirty three…'

'Billy..!' I snapped again.

'Sorry. I was standing there and I saw you and… and Mr Pontefract coming along the road in that posh car of his and you turned into the road opposite the bus stop… I could see the lights of the car as you drove along and then I saw you pull up. Or at least I saw the lights stop moving and then they went out and… and… I don't know why… I don't know… I really don't know but I… I just crossed the road and walked after you…'

He stopped speaking and pressed his hand to his forehead, looking down at the ground. There was something terribly dramatic about the gesture and it made me annoyed. I know a perf. when I see one.

He was breathing heavily and when he looked up his face was pale and bathed in sweat.

'So why, Billy?' I said. 'Tell me why did you do that? Why follow us?'

'I… I really don't know. I… I… wanted to see you. To be near you, I suppose, and…' He took deep breath. '…And I was jealous of Mr Pontefract. Really jealous.' He swallowed drily. 'I'm… I'm really sorry. I didn't mean any harm.'

'Jealous?'

'Yes, you know…'

'I don't. Actually Billy, I don't understand what you're talking about at all.'

'You must know. You must…'

His voice was hoarse and low and he couldn't look me in the eye. For a while he stared at the dusty ground and then he looked up at me. There was an odd look in his eye.

'I think I love you…' he said.

Well, that was a surprise, Doctor, I must say. I'm not unusually at a loss for words but I certainly found myself pretty speechless just then.

He suddenly leant towards me and I moved away from him, wincing at the tang of sour breath and lemon sherbet.

'I... I've loved you for years, I think. Ever since I first met you and I can't help it.'

For an instant we both looked at each other, rigid in the moment, two statues on a park bench not moving, while his words seemed to hang in the air around us – and then, and I couldn't help it, I threw back my head and laughed.

'Oh, Billy... Oh, Billy...' I giggled. 'You are an idiot. That's not love you're feeling. That's lust. It's just lust.'

I reached out my hand and laid it on the back of his, but as I touched him he jumped to his feet, his eyes were shining as stared down at me.

'No.' he said. 'I do love you. Really. In fact, I'm mad about you. That's why I followed you the other night. Because you're always with him in his silly flash car and you can't love him because he's old and fat and going bald. And you shouldn't be with him... You should be with me.'

'Billy...' I said. And I noticed that my hands were shaking a little. 'Billy. This is silly. Of course you don't love me. I'm old enough to be your mother...'

He started to speak again but I cut him off, raising a hand to quieten him.

'Billy, is that why you've been doing all those silly things? – Because you think you love me?'

'I do love you.'

'Oh, Billy I think you may have got a little crush, that's all.'

'No. It's not that... It's not a crush.'

'But Billy even if that was true, you can't do the things you've been doing. You really can't. It's... well, it's not very grown-up – or very attractive. It's not how to 'woo' someone, is it?'

He was staring at me, still leaning over me but now he looked puzzled.

'What things?' He said. And there was something in his voice that made me look at him.

'You know perfectly well,' I said. 'Frightening me, watching me – *coming into my house, uninvited* – is that your idea of love?'

He looked genuinely puzzled.

'I… I would never frighten you and anyway, you asked me in… for supper.'

I laughed. 'For supper, not to come and go as you please. And you have frightened me. What did you expect? do you think that someone coming into your home and being watched in the night isn't frightening?'

He looked confused and took a step back.

'I couldn't see.. I couldn't see anything, you know, through the windows. I just saw the lights and then when they went out I just stood there. I didn't do anything. I wasn't looking, not deliberately. I just wanted to be there. You know, to be near you.'

'Do you mean the other night outside of Sydney's flat or do you mean watching me from the field at the back of my house?'

Now he really looked even more surprised.

'I don't know what you mean,' he said. 'I've never been in any field, well not at the back of your house. I mean I've been in lots of fields obviously… Look, I've been stupid. I know that. But I only followed you once, the other night. I… I really don't know what came over me. I am sorry. Honestly.'

'Please,' I said. 'Don't lie to me Billy. I'm not stupid.'

* * *

'Please don't lie to me Billy. I'm not stupid,' she says and I feel like I've been punched in the face. I don't understand. I am completely confused. Obviously she has every right to be a bit annoyed. I mean I stood outside of that man's flat looking up at them in the middle of the night. It was a really dim thing to do. I pride myself on being of above average intelligence (after all I went to Oxbridge and officially that makes me in the top 2% of intelligence in the country and you can't top that, lets face it – unless of course you happen to be in the top 1%, I suppose).

Anyway, that night outside of his flat was not my finest hour, if I am perfectly honest – or to be more perfectly honest, not my finest four hours thirty minutes, which is how long I stood there.

It was as if some awful urge had over-taken me when I saw them drive by and I couldn't control it at all. I had to be with her, to see her and to see what he was up to. I have had my suspicions ever since the terrible birthday party that they may be more than Director and Artiste if you follow me – more even than, what you might call, Platonic friends (presumably Plato had a lot of friends – I must look this up later).

I know I was mad to follow them, not least because if you miss the ten-o-five then the chances of the eleven O'clock arriving are pretty slim and after that you won't get another bus until midnight if they can be bothered to run at all.

As I say, it was an urge and I couldn't control it. Which is dreadful to admit but obviously symbolic of my strong feelings for her – but what does she mean about the field and other things? What is she talking about?

I've just told her the most important thing in the world; my BIG secret. I love her. I love her. I love her. I have done for years and now she's banging on about fields and things.

Oh, this is all going terribly wrong. This is not how I planned the afternoon at all. Obviously following her the other night was big mistake, I knew it was. I was mad. I was mad with love. And now she calls my love 'lust'. She calls it lust, which is so... so belittling.

Lust?

I am not the sort of person to feel lust. I have higher emotions than that. Personally I consider, and I think my father would back me up here, that lust is something for the coarser personality. Viewers of *Coronation Street*, and *Crossroads*, *Sun* readers and factory workers feel lust. But not people like me.

She doesn't seem to have taken much notice of my apology, she is still going on about being watched and then she says:

'I could have had you arrested, you know Billy. Breaking and entering is a serious criminal offence.'

I feel a bit faint now, as well as confused. The world seems to be going mad. She seems to be going mad. What is she talking about? I can't work it out, so I ask her.

* * *

'What am I talking about?' I repeated, and I had to make real effort to control my rising anger. Either the boy was a much better actor than I had given him credit for or he was cretinous.

'Well,' I said, and even I was surprised at how angry I

now sounded. 'Where shall we begin Billy? Let's start with you coming into my house and unlocking the back-door so you could come back later – uninvited.'

He gaped at me.

'What?' he said.

'I've been thinking about that,' I went on. 'I had to go into the front room for my cigarettes, didn't I? Was that when you did it? When I went out of the room? You slipped the bolts and turned the key, didn't you? And then you sat back down again and never blinked when I came back? My, you are a sly one. Were you planning to come back that night? I think you were weren't you? What happened Billy, did you lose your nerve? Or was it that I looked out of the window and you thought I might have seen you skulking in the field so you ran away? Christ! What had you got planned? What were you gong to do if you'd got in?'

And the thought of that made me shudder. It was ridiculous, but I'd never actually thought of that before, what he'd got planned – what he was going to do to me.

He looked as white as a sheet and he opened his mouth to speak but no sound came out and I carried on anyway.

'Then there's the bell. What was the point of that – of your ghostly DIY efforts? Was it to frighten me or to flatter me? That's what I keep wondering. And going into the room, into… into… into that room.' I finished with an effort.

The thought of him in Diana's room…

…I had to take a deep breath before I continued but now I could feel tears welling up inside me, which was silly but I couldn't help it.

'How could you?' I managed to say, trying not to cry. 'And those fucking roses. *In our life I'll love you more!* Will

you indeed? More than what Billy? More than you loved
Diana? I don't think so, because you never loved her and she
didn't love you because you were just kids. You were silly
kids – only she was more grown-up than you, wiser and
more sensible and more down to earth than you'll ever be…
Do you hear me? More than you will ever be!'

* * *

She's crying now. She's screaming at me and she's crying at
the same time and I don't know what to say or what to do. I
don't understand. I don't understand any of this. I just
don't.

'I never…' I say and I think I might start to cry as well.
'I never,' I repeat. 'I never did any of those things. I don't
know what you mean and I don't know what you're talking
about. I didn't unlock your door. I didn't – and I only ever
watched you once and that was in Leeford and even then I
couldn't see you – just your shadows once or twice. I just
stood there in the street, looking up, so I could be near you.
That's all. Honestly.'

'Liar.' She screams at me and on the other side of the
cricket field a little old woman with a poodle looks up to see
where the noise has come from, but her dog pulls at the lead
and she turns away again.

'I didn't do anything,' I say again. 'Honestly, I didn't.
After… after I said goodbye…'

'Grabbed me and kissed me,' she says. 'Which was terri-
fying enough.'

I ignored that. It was only because she was angry. She
knew the truth.

'Afterwards, ' I said. 'I... I went and got the bus and I went home. That's all. I went home.'

And I don't tell her that I was in a fever of excitement for the whole bus ride and that I went to bed dreaming of holding her in my arms and making love to her. I don't tell her how she moaned in my imagination and told me she wanted me and begged me for more, even when I... even when I was 'spent' as it were. I don't tell her that.

She looks at me and doesn't speak this time. Instead she seems to be gazing deep into me, right into my soul and I remember how once before, a long time ago, eyes like that had made me feel that that their owner saw too much, knew too much. Those eyes. The same eyes, in fact, when all is said and done.

She is standing now but she turns to face me, takes a pace towards me, she gets uncomfortably close, and then she speaks very slowly. She is more controlled now and her voice is quieter but it is cold and harsh. The sound of it makes a little part of me die.

'Did you come into my house when I wasn't there?' she says in what I believe are called slow and measured terms. 'Did you fix the bell, did you go into the bedrooms?'

This is ridiculous. We are talking abut serious things and she's worried about her fixtures and fittings.

'No,' I say and I am pleased to say that I sound as measured and controlled as she does. 'I am not a handyman. My father is completely at home in his shed with a power tool in hand but I didn't inherit the same proclivities, I'm afraid.'

I make a mental note to use the word 'proclivities' more often as it sounds quite erudite and shows that I have been educated to the highest standards, I reckon.

'Did you go into my house and… and find a record on the floor and put it back into its sleeve.'

So that's it. She's had a burglary or worse and thinks I am responsible. Mind you I reckon they must be pretty neat burglars to be clearing up record sleeves.

'Absolutely not,' I say with some dignity. 'I've only ever entered your house by invitation – both recently and in the past with… When I was much younger.'

She stares at me and it seems that for a very long time neither of us speak and neither of say anything.

'And the roses?'

'What roses?' I say.

'Beautiful red roses that were sent to my house?'

'I bought you chocolates,' I say and I try to sound haughty as I am getting a bit fed-up with these accusations. 'And wine. I'm not sure my budget runs to roses as well. I am unemployed as it happens.'

I can see that my words have struck home.

I was thrown by this. I had to admit that they were very expensive flowers. Ridiculously so. For the first time I felt a little nagging doubt in my mind. He did seem so sincere. He seemed so offended and put-out by my questions and he had a point – he'd have needed a lot of money to buy those flowers – they were quite beautiful blooms. Would a boy who'd brought me a broken box of *Milk Tray* and a bottle of *Blue Nun*…?

I didn't finish my own question. I didn't need to.

I looked at him again, wanting to see some trace of fear or doubt or… or duplicity in his eyes…

* * *

She stares at me and I stare back. I am filled I might say, with rightful indignation, but there is just one drawback.

I am worried.

I mean I do not think I could have done what she says, obviously, and I have no actual recollection of any of these things but strange things do occasionally happen to me.

And then I guess I must blackout for a second or two, because when I open my eyes I am back on the bench, onto which I have slumped and she, Diana's mother, my Cleopatra, is looking down at me and for all her anger there is a look of worry in her eyes.

'Are you all right,' she says and her tone is different now.

'Yes,' I manage to say. 'I'm sorry. I...'

What am I sorry for? For being in love with her? For the things she is accusing me of? For something too awful to think about to do with her daughter, something so awful that I cannot think about it without feeling ill, without becoming faint.

I don't now what I am sorry about. And that's the truth

...and that's my Gethsemane, I suppose. My own personal garden of agonies. And I can feel the sweat pouring from me and a dull pain behind my eyes. A tightness around my head – and that's my crown of thorns.

* * *

I didn't stay. I made sure he was OK and that he was breathing normally and I went over to the little pavilion where there was an outside drinking tap and I brought him a tissue that I'd wetted from it.

And then I left him sitting, hunched over on the bench and made my way back to the lane and turned towards home.

I had those roses on my mind. I kept thinking, were roses like that, really a young man's style?

I'm feeling a little better. I had felt really quite awful but now I struggle to my feet and I start walking towards the Maltings not that I'm going to see her if I can avoid it. I'll get a bus on the outskirts and wiz past her house sunk low in my seat and I won't look out of the window, that's for sure.

As I walk I begin to feel better and soon enough I begin to sing. That may sound weird to you in the circs in which I found myself, but in fact I often do this when I am worried or unsure about something – quite often the song reflects my innermost thoughts. It's what I think is called a psychological trait. I sing the infinitely beautiful *In My Life* on the Beatles' *Rubber Soul* album.

It's a beautiful lyric in my H opinion and one that can be used on any number of occasions and for any number of reasons. I know, I've often done so.

I wasn't sure if I really felt up to dinner with Sydney after my traumatic afternoon, but he insisted.

I was a little concerned when he picked me up that he seemed to have been drinking already and it was only just seven. I could smell the booze on his breath when he leant over to kiss me. I'd noticed that Sydney (always a fairly heavy drinker) seemed to be drinking a lot more than usual in the last few days and when I asked him if he'd been to the pub he did admit to dropping into the dreadful *Wattle and Daub* for a couple of pints on his way to meet me.

I suspect these were followed by a couple of chasers judging by his breath but that's up to him of course. It was hardly my place to say that I thought recently he'd been hitting the sauce rather hard.

We drove very quickly and rather exhilaratingly through the country lanes to Leeford. Sydney is one of those fortunate men who drive a little better with a few drinks inside him.

We go to the flat and he hurried into the little kitchenette to open us a bottle of wine and start cooking. Sydney rather fancies himself as a bit of a galloping gourmet and he wanted to try a new recipe on me – fillet of Beef Meurice – which turned out to be steak smothered in mushrooms, butter, brandy and cream – not great for the figure but delicious and he assured me it was very good for us – apparently we don't eat nearly enough dairy produce and red meat is full of iron.

Sydney can be rather a bore when he gets onto a hobby horse and home cooking was a new found passion – I'm not completely convinced it's a very manly thing but apparently more and more men are taking it up. I believe bread making is becoming a very popular past time on a Saturday morning in the winter when lawns can't be cut.

Frankly, I much preferred the nights when Sydney took me to a restaurant or a little bistro – but I wasn't going to dampen his enthusiasm. Though I think the Roux family won't have much to fear in the way of competition.

Again, I noticed that he seemed to be drinking a lot of Burgundy while we ate – and I did think that perhaps I should say something. Bluntly, it worried me that the other night's, how shall I put this delicately, the other night's *let down* in the bed department might be related to his over-indulgence. But I wasn't going to spoil his evening just then and besides I had other things on my mind.

Over our desert (Pavlova – presumably to use up the left over cream from the steak recipe) he asked me if there had been any more upsets at home and if I'd decided what to do about 'the boy' as he liked to call Billy.

I'd rather been dreading this moment.

'Ah,' I said. 'Well, I don't want you to be upset but I went to see him.'

He stared at me, a spoonful of raspberry dotted Pavlova half-way to his mouth.

'What?' He eventually managed to say.

* * *

Doctor, I don't want you thinking that I hide things from you and I think it's pretty reasonable to say that I have been more than frank and very, very honest in these little record-ings we've shared but I am going to pass swiftly over the next half an hour or so. Suffice it to say that Sydney became very bad tempered and rather silly about my 'going behind his back' as he called it, and foolishly he began to drink rather a lot of brandy as his indignation rose by the minute at what he called my 'bare faced lunacy!'

Eventually I told him firmly that I was bored with the whole bloody thing and that I never wanted to hear the name 'Billy' again. As far as I was concerned I said, the whole thing is over. Billy had denied he'd had anything to do with the door and the flowers and the bell and it would just have to stay like that – an unsolved mystery – and that was that.

'But you don't believe him, do you?' Sydney asked and the question was a good one – one that I'd been racking my brains over all afternoon since I'd left Billy in the cricket field.

'I don't know,' I said, quite honestly. 'I really don't. He seemed to be telling the truth but then if he didn't fix the bell and if he wasn't watching me, then who was? I think I may go to the police after all.'

Sydney hiccupped and looked blearily at me over the top of his brandy balloon.

'Oh… Oh, I don't know,' he said. 'I don't know if that would solve anything really.'

* * *

I'm lying here in bed and I should be happy – I should be looking forward to the rest of the weekend. I bet Niall Mahoney is looking forward to tomorrow and Patrick Flynn and Ian Shane. I haven't seen them for ages of course, but I gather Patrick Flynn has gone back to Ireland to help on his father's pig farm, and Niall Mahoney is in a seminary learning to be a priest, and Ian Shane is studying in a London art college – apparently he designs women's clothes and there is rumour that he has a very promising future in the boulevards of Paris, not to mention Milan.

I should be happy – I am a Cambridge graduate but the truth is I don't have much more than that to show for my life so far and actually I only just managed to get my degree, scraped a bad third, in fact.

And I have been accused of dreadful things today. Things I don't know if I did or not. I should be happy but my soul is dark with the terrible guilt of some awful thing I may or may not have done seven years ago, almost to the day.

There are two worlds. In one of these worlds everyone is happy and safe in the other they are not.

Sometimes I think I belong to one world and all the other boys who were at my school and some of the teachers and Mrs Watson and Mr Pontefract – they all belong to the other. I get glimpses of their world but I cannot really understand it, let alone explain it. But the trick is to know which world you belong in.

And I do not.

* * *

I was getting bored. Sydney was being boring. Drunk and boring. We'd changed the subject (my idea) and instead we were talking about the old days and suddenly he'd held up his hand to stop me speaking, in a very pompous manner I might add.

'We should sweep away the past. Forget it. As I get older, more and more I want to relive the old days but in fact we should make the most of the present and live it to the full, don't you think?'

'Maybe,' I said annoyed at the hand gesture. 'Yes. I suppose you're right.'

'But we don't do it, do we? Either of us?'

He walked over to the sideboard and poured himself another brandy; he waved the bottle at me but I shook my head.

'Look at us,' he said. 'We talk about Southwold all the time as if it was some, I don't know, golden paradise visited in our youth. But actually it was a grotty seaside town and we were silly teenagers with more ambition than talent.'

'No.' I said. 'I don't like that. It was important. Maybe not in any grand way – I mean we didn't change the world or produce great new drama or shape the face of modern of theatre – we weren't John Osbornes or Harold Pinters perhaps – but it was important because it was fun. It was fun to us and we stretched our wings. It was where I learnt to be a grown-up. And, well, I loved it. Is that so bad? Is growing-up and finding a new world to fly in, so bad?'

'You're clinging on, you see. There you go. OK it was nice at the time but what really matters is what we did afterwards. You talk about a new world and yes, you're right about that. What we do *now*. What we are *now* – That's the new world, that's the important thing. The past is that – the past. It's finished.'

'Getting older is what we are now,' I said.

He swayed slightly and raised his glass, shook it at me.

'That's only your body getting older. It doesn't have to happen to your soul, to your mind. We've still got lots we could be doing – should be doing. I refuse any longer to become old and I'm going to stop thinking back. I'm going to forget the past. We've got to stop it – all this nostalgia...'

He slurred the word and looked surprised, then carried on. 'We've got to go forward – tomorrow is what counts. If you think about tomorrow you stay young. You can still achieve something.'

I'd never seen him so drunk, nor so passionate, his voice trembled with booze – an alcoholic fervour.

'Well,' I began but he turned blazing eyes on me.

'Clear out the room,' he said suddenly. 'She's gone, not forgotten, never should be of course, but gone. Clear out the room and move on.'

He stood looking down at me, glass half raised, eyes bleary, rocking back and forth on his feet.

'Move on…' he repeated and belched.

The world lurched. I felt sick. And for a moment there was a terrible silence as we both looked at one another.

Then I saw him turn pale. He pressed his hand to his forehead as if he had only then realised what he'd said.

Sorry…' he muttered. 'Shouldn't have… Don't know what came over me…'

In an instant it seemed to me that he sobered up and as he focused on me he drew in a deep breath.

'I… I didn't mean…' he said.

I sat stunned. My head still reeling.

'What did you mean?' I said slowly and then I raised my voice. 'What did you mean?' I repeated and I could hear the anger in my own voice.

He opened his mouth as if to speak but said nothing, he merely stood there gaping, like a drowning animal.

Then it hit me – exactly what he'd said and what it meant.

'How..?' I managed to say, and then I jumped to my feet, angrily slamming my glass down onto his precious an-tique table. 'What the fuck! How did you know about the room. How did you know? How did you fucking know?' I shouted.

I was seething now and I was also terribly shocked.

He took a step back in surprise.

'What have you been up to?'

'N...nothing.' He stammered. 'Forget it. I don't know what I'm talking about.'

'How did you know about the room?' I hissed. 'How did you know about *her* room?'

'I... It was just a turn of phrase that's all. I meant... I meant, clear out the room in your head, empty your mind of the past, you know.'

'Cobblers! Don't give me all that pseudo hippy shit. You always were a crap actor.'

He winced at that. Then I had to spell it out for myself as much as for him.

'You've been in there, haven't you? You've been in her room...'

'Oh, Christ!'

He seemed to deflate – a rather pompous balloon with a pin-prick in it. He scrabbled at the back of one of the dining chairs, pulled it out, scraping it over the floor and slumped down onto it.

He sat there head bowed and neither of us spoke or moved for a few seconds and then he looked up at me.

'Yes,' he said at last. 'Yes, I went into her room.'

He looked down at the table again and I looked down at him and for the first time I noticed that his hair was thinning around the crown of his scalp and that his roots were gray. I'd never realised before that he dyed his hair.

'How could you?' I said

He wouldn't, couldn't look me in the eyes – so I grabbed him by the shoulders and pulled him round to face me, making him look up at me.

'How could you?' I said again. 'Why?'

Then a thought struck me.

'When did you do it? When did you open the back-door?'

'I didn't,' he said at last. 'You're always leaving it open. How often have I reminded you to shut it?'

I couldn't think what to say but I felt my hands digging into his shoulders and he squirmed a little under my grip.

'Go easy,' he said.

'When did you get in? After Billy had gone home that night?'

'No. Absolutely not. I did not come into the house that night. I wouldn't do something like that – not with you there – frightening you half to death. But I did come and see you. I just wanted to make sure you were all right. To check up on you.'

'But you were in London.'

'I was meant to be… but I finished with my accountant earlier than planned and I thought I'd come and see you, so I drove back. I knew you were seeing the boy. I was worried about you being with him so I drove from London straight to your cottage but I hit a traffic jam and by the time I arrived it was late. There were lights on but I suddenly thought… well, I was embarrassed, turning up like that, like I was checking-up on you. So I waited for him leave and then I walked round the back just to check everything was OK. I leant over the fence for a while, just looking really and then all of a sudden the moon came out. That's when you must have seen me.'

I snorted angrily.

'You could have knocked on the door. It's what people normally do.'

'I really didn't want to appear a fool, fussing over you. You're always so damned independent. I thought you'd laugh at me.'

'Then why not tell me about it the next day, when I told you that someone had been watching me?'

He shrugged.

'Embarrassed,' I suppose. 'Silly isn't it?'

He grinned sheepishly at me, his boyish, 'oops I made a silly mistake,' look – 'but you'll forgive me won't you?' he said

And I thought: 'I've seen it all before. Men. They're all the bloody same. Liars and unreliable bastards.'

I leant closer to his face.

'And then a couple of days later you just happened to turn up again.' I snapped at him. 'And you thought, "Oh, well while I'm here I'll fix the bell?" Is that what you thought?'

'Yes… Yes. Look, I won't deny it. When I said was going to the bank the other day, I didn't. I drove here instead. I went round to the back and sure enough, you'd left the door unlocked. I just thought as it was open I'd take a look at the bell and see what else needed doing while I was there. The bell was easy by the way, it was just a loose connection.'

'What did you think you were doing, coming into my house like that?! Trespassing.'

'I didn't see it like that. Really. I thought I was doing you a favour. Look, there's so much I want to do for you – but you never let me. I thought I'd just do things for you and then tell you later when it was too late for you to say no.'

'Unbelievable!'

'Well frankly, you are skint and you've had a rough time of it for the last few years and that terrible… terrible loss… I simply wanted to help but whenever I offered, you turned me down. And that's crazy. I'm loaded and you must know how I feel about you. So I decided that I'd just get a few things done for you anyway. Regardless.'

'Regardless of my feelings.'

'I wasn't trying to insult you. But I knew you'd never take my money, you'd look on anything I did as charity, and you'd be offended. So I got on with it anyway.'

'And you wandered around sticking your nose in here and there, opening doors, looking in cupboards. What did you do? Go through my laundry basket? Did my dirty knickers give you a thrill?'

He shuddered and looked away.

'And then you went into her room. You... went... in-to... her... room.' I repeated slowly.

'I'm sorry. I am really sorry. I only looked in – out of curiosity. I didn't take it in at first, I thought maybe it was your room, and then I realised...'

He stopped and stared at me.

I couldn't speak.

'I realised,' he said slowly. 'I realised what it was... What you'd done... How you'd kept it... you know, as it was...'

Suddenly he took a breath and shook my hands off his shoulders.

'It's not good,' he said and there was a flash of anger in his voice.. 'It's really not good. It won't help and you should stop it. You really should clear it out.'

'No.' I said. 'Not that it's any of your business, but no. Never.'

'Then,' he said. 'You'll never move on. You'll be in that other world, the old world. The dead world, for ever.'

I looked at him. He shook his head and spoke slowly as if spelling it out to a truculent child. 'I *was* going to tell you I'd been there. But I didn't know how, and now I do. I went in there and I saw what I saw and it was sad and terrible and destructive and self-indulgent and if you ever, ever want to share another life or to be part of someone else's life... Christ, if you want to be part of my life, you're going to have to move on. You are going to have empty that bloody room.'

I looked back at him, into his dark eyes and I was frightened at how very much I hated him...

...And at how very much I loved him.

...And suddenly I felt there was a choice. For the first time for seven years, I thought there was a choice.

'I am sorry,' he said.

'But you didn't tell me, did you. You didn't say anything. You let me blame everything on Billy and you didn't tell me,' I said.

He looked at me and his eyes were steady. Eyes that looked at me not from the past any longer but from this moment.

'That was bad of me,' he said. 'But I don't know if I regret it.'

I swallowed.

'I said some terrible things to Billy. I made some awful allegations,' I mumbled.

'He'll be fine. I really wouldn't worry about Billy,' he said. 'If he didn't do anything, he hasn't got anything to feel bad about and being young, I don't suppose he took any notice of you anyway.'

* * *

I keep it in my wallet, a faded, yellowing newspaper cutting.
I don't know why. I hardly ever read it.

I get out of bed and cross the room to my chest of
drawers. My wallet is on top of it and even though it is dark
I feel for it and find it. Then I go back to bed and switch on
my bedside light. I haven't taken the cutting out of my wallet
for a long time. It is more frail than it was and the dry paper
begins to tear along its folds as I open it out.

Leeford Echo – September 196
Murder Victim's Last Goodbye

*The funeral took place yesterday of Diana, Emma Watson the
local schoolgirl found murdered in woods near Hurstwood Village.*

*The funeral was attended by staff and pupils of her school,
Leeford Secondary Modern, as well as by family and friends.
The girl's mother, who is a widow, was supported throughout by
her son and by Diana's friend Frank Edwards, a pupil at St
Joseph's Catholic School.*

*The Service was conducted by the Reverend Peter Jones who
spoke of Diana's vivacity, appetite for life and good nature.*

*After the service Mr James Arbuthnot, headmaster of
Leeford Secondary Modern, spoke of Diana's bubbly personality
and how her presence would be missed throughout the school. He
said pupils at the school had been shocked at Diana's death but
they would 'soldier on' as they were resilient young people.*

*Later in the day Detective Sergeant Jim Hoyle of Leeford
Police read a short statement to the press in which he offered his
deepest sympathy to the family and friends of the deceased. He
added that enquiries were ongoing and he appealed for any help
the public might be able to offer.*

Local Postman celebrates Ruby Wedding
Jack Billups and his wife Peggy…

Frankly, it isn't very much – not the thing about the postman, that just got left on the end when I tore it out of the paper – I mean about Diana/Emma, you'd have thought they'd have written a bit more about her, but on reflection the national newspapers had written an awful lot at the time so I suppose the *Leeford Echo* thought there wasn't much point in their wasting space when everyone was reading the more 'salient' details in the terrible *News Of The World* and even more moronic papers like *The Sun*.

I do not have any cuttings from those papers. I refuse to lower myself. I have my standards you know and I think despite its brevity, the *Leeford Echo* hit a restrained and appropriate note in its coverage. There is after all, a certain dignity in death.

I read the cutting again and then fold it up and put it back in my wallet.

I turn out the light…

And then I begin to cry.

It really has been a very stressful day, when all is said and done.

'Now my charms are all o'erthrown, and what strength I have's mine own, which is most faint...'

Shakespeare, The Tempest

Dear Billy

We should talk again. It appears I have been rather hasty and I owe you at least an explanation and almost certainly an apology. I'm embarrassed about some of the things I said to you and would like a chance to tell you so in person.

You probably never want to see me again but if you can bear it, lets go for another walk – we might as well, the weather is so perfect and you can show me the beautiful countryside. I've lived here for ten years and never really got to know it at all.

I was thinking of Tuesday, if that suits you? At twelve-ish? Let me know if that's all right. And we'll meet at my house this time.

Yours

Dear Mrs Watson

Absolutely. Yes. Wow! Great idea. Of course I want to see you again.

I know just the place we can walk to.

See you then.

Billy

I am knocking on her door and it is exactly 2 pm. It is best I reckon in these sort of circumstances, to be absolutely punctual.

She opens the door and I catch my breath. She is wearing a beautiful summery skirt, it has white, blue and yellow patterns, sort of squiggles and circles and things all over it, and she also wears a white top that shows off her firm and voluptuous (if I might use that word) bust to perfection. On her head she wears a straw hat and her dark hair falls from beneath it.

'Hello, Billy,' she says. 'How lovely to see you.' And then incongruously she adds. 'You can ring the bell now, it's fixed.'

'Thank you,' I say, which is probably a daft reply and then I don't know what to say next so I sort of stare at her.

For some reason she is carrying a wicker shopping basket. I offer to take it from her but she says no, she never thinks a man looks very masculine carrying a shopping basket. I completely agree. She is all woman and she obviously knows what she wants in a man. In my humble O men were not made to go shopping.

I smile at her and her face is beautiful. The smile she gives me in return is… well, radiant. (I must stop reading my mother's romantic fiction. I am falling into *the style*.)

'Well,' she says. 'Where shall we go?'

And she pulls the door shut behind her and looks expectantly at me.

I swallow. This is all so different from how it had been the other day. I am a little confused and for a minute I forget what I had planned. In my mind I had two ideas: if she was still, how shall put it, grumpy and making terrible and unfounded accusations vis-à-vis my honesty, then I had planned to tell her so early on and march off on my own. In which case we would have started by heading across country, along the footpath at the back of her house, because I could easily have dodged away from it and gone over the hill towards home, and she could have jolly well made her own way back. If on the other hand she was in a friendly mood, I planned that we would catch a bus and get off near Butler's farm and from there we could walk to one or two of my special places.

It is obvious that plan B is now a 'must' – as they say in American television programmes.

'Let's get the bus,' I say. 'There's somewhere I want to take you.'

We are just in time for the two ten. I shudder when I see my old adversary the grumpy bus conductor and he glowers at me as I sidle past him. He glowers at Mrs Watson too.

We sit in the front and she turns to me and says, 'Did you see the look the conductor gave us? Does he know you?'

'He's like that,' I say. 'Every time I see him, he's rude. I try not to engage him in conversation as I'm sure the outcome would be boorish in the extreme.'

For some reason she giggles and presses her hand to her mouth.

'Oh, Billy,' she says. 'Where on earth do you get your turn of phrase from? Jane Austen?'

I have no idea what she means by that so I say, 'I'm more of a Dickens man myself, though when it comes to modern literature it takes an awful lot to beat William Golding. Don't you think?'

She stops smiling and looks serious but I can see she's only pretending, actually she is still shaking with what you might call 'suppressed laughter' which is a bit rude, frankly.

'Yes,' she says. 'William Golding is quite a favourite of mine but on the whole I'm more of a Jackie Collins kind of girl.'

I have no idea who Jackie thingy is, so it is almost a relief when the grumpy bus conductor appears next to us.

'Yes?' he says.

'Two returns, Butler's Lane, please,' I say.

'Three bob,' he says. 'And I suppose you're going to pay with a fifty pound note you little squirt.'

'Good heavens,' Mrs W says and she looks quite shocked.

'It's all right,' I assure her and I look up at him with my eyes narrowed and what I hope is a menacing glare.

'Something in your eye?' He says and giggles.

I hand him three five pence pieces and he grunts and prints off our tickets.

'Well,' she says when he's gone. 'Is he trying to be funny?'

'I think he may have a screw lose, so I try to humour him,' I say.

'I think you might be a little too kind there Billy. I rather suspect he's just a nasty, ill tempered old sod.'

And I am quite surprised at her turn of phrase. I have never heard swearing in such a posh voice before.

We sit quietly then and it is just a bit awkward as to who should speak next and what we should say. So to break the silence I point out the hay stacks that are being built in the fields.

'It's that time of year,' I say. 'Hay making. Well, to be strictly honest the hay was harvested some time ago, it's the haystacks they're building now.'

'Ah,' she says and looks out of the window. 'Fascinating.'

And we don't say much else until we get to Butler's Lane.

As we are getting off the bus the conductor suddenly leans forward just as Mrs W walks by him.

'You want to keep that son of yours under control,' he says to her pointing in my direction and he kind of leers in her face.

'He can be a smart arse,' he adds.

I am already standing on the road but I am about to leap back on and give him what my father would call, 'a piece of my mind.' But I don't have to.

'Oh,' says Mrs Watson as smoothly as can be. 'I do hope he is smart. He's training to be a zoologist, you know like that Desmond Morris on Television. And it's so kind of you to help him out.'

'Help him out?' The conductor says.

'Yes. He needs to get all the experience he can with dumb animals, especially baboons.'

With that she steps neatly onto the road. There is something about the put-down and the way she delivers it that takes me back to a Wimpy bar in Leeford.

'Gosh,' I think. 'Like mother, like daughter – and somehow that makes me feel good.

* * *

We walk through the fields and along the footpaths and we say very little but I think we are both reasonably happy to look at the beautiful scenery. Eventually I lead her to a place where there is some scrubby looking woodland. I lead her through the trees and she gasps when we step out of them into my special place by the stream.

'How beautiful,' she says looking around.

And it is beautiful, the branches from the willow dip into the clear water and the sun sparkles off its surface and the soft mossy grass below our feet is even greener and cooler for all the dryness everywhere else. Except for here, it seems to me, the countryside has crumpled in the hot summer heat.

'It's beautiful,' she says again, 'and so cool. I'm pooped.'

She flops down under the tree and for a while she looks into the water and stares at the reflections of the trees and the sky and of us that dart around in the ripples of the stream where the current breaks against the roots of the willow.

'Oh, Billy. It's very lovely here,' she says at last, looking up at me.

'Yes,' I say and I am about to say that her daughter loved it here too but I figure that might spoil what you might call the mood, so I don't but I suddenly feel a shock of freezing water and remember bright eyes giggling in a freckled faced, water dripping form cupped hands...

'Won't you sit down, Billy?' She says. And she pats the soft grass beside her and I am reminded of crinolines and mop caps and tea in a Georgian vicarage and I think perhaps I do like Jane Austen – maybe too much.

I flop beside her and there is silence again and we both look awkwardly at the water. Perhaps we are aware of things unsaid about what happened the other day on a bench by a cricket pitch, or perhaps we are aware of how close we are to each other, under a willow tree, by a stream. I don't know.

Finally though, she looks up.

'Billy,' she says and I know we are about to move onto delicate territory.

'I want you to know that the things I accused you of the other day. Well... Well I now know that they were nothing to do with you and I am very sorry for what was said. I was mistaken.'

'Oh,' I say. Which seems a bit inadequate, so I add. 'Think nothing off it.' Which seems a bit lame.

'Somebody else, someone who thought they were doing me a favour, who wanted to be kind to me did the things I mentioned but stupidly they didn't tell me.'

'Wanted to be an anonymous benefactor, I expect,' I say

– which sounds not only lame but rather weird.

She hesitates and again I see a little hint of a smile on he face but it is gone in a flash.

'Indeed,' she says. 'He meant well but he got it wrong in… In… Oh, I don't know how to put it…'

'In the execution of it,' I say to help her out.

And she looks at me quickly.

'Yes,' she says. 'As you say, in the execution of it.'

'It happens,' I say. 'I've often found good deeds can be misunderstood. Or sometimes we misunderstand why other people are kind to us and we make too much of it…'

And for a second I am in a village hall with a noisy disco and a broken heart. But only for a second.

Suddenly she takes my hand. Well, OK that's not totally true, she rests her hand on the back of mine but then she does actually give it a gentle squeeze. This sends all kinds of electric shocks through me and my heart starts to thump rather awkwardly against my rib cage. There is a singing sound in my ears and I cannot look at her. She is holding my hand and if the world ended now it would be OK with me as I have seen a glimpse of paradise.

'I'm sorry,' she says, very quietly almost under her breath.

I don't know what else to say so I nod and look at the water and she squeezes my hand harder and suddenly I want to push her back against the tree and kiss her. But I don't. Of course I don't. It'll never happen, I guess. And that thought makes me more sad than thinking of the disco all those years ago and of being made to look a fool, of having love thrown back in my face.

'Food,' she suddenly says and I am dragged back into today. She speaks brightly and loudly, and a rook perched high on a branch of a Scots Pine on the other side of stream breaks cover at the sound of her voice and flaps away with a squawk.

'We could go into town I suppose,' I say. 'Or walk to the lane and then go *The Farmer's Arms* in Bidderford.'

'No,' She says, 'No need. I came prepared.'

She pulls the basket towards her that she has placed on the ground next to her and begins to pull packages and Tupperware boxes out of it and even a bottle of red wine and a corkscrew. There are tomatoes, bread rolls, some ham and some pâté in a plastic packet and a couple of apples.

'There you are,' she says. 'Let's have a picnic.'

* * *

We eat and food has never tasted so good to me. I am with a beautiful woman, we are beside a cool stream in the countryside on a hot summer's day and I guess that heaven must be similar to this.

We both lie back when we finish eating and close our eyes against the sun that flickers through the branches of the willow tree. The red wine has gone a little bit to my head and I feel comfortably numb in my face and lips. I am very close to her. We are beside each other and we are lying down together. She is so close that I could reach out and take her hand or caress her breast without having to move. I could roll over gently and kiss her beautiful mouth, lick the red wine from her lips, press my body against hers. We could make love here in the sun, by a stream in the English countryside...

'Let's walk some more,' she says, sitting up. 'We've eaten and drunk too much and I need to walk it off.'

My heart misses a beat. I feel suddenly very sad. The moment, as they say, has gone.

* * *

I know where we will go of course. I'm not sure if I think about it and I haven't planned it but the moment we start walking again I turn towards the hill and the little wooded are on its crest.

We trudge along the footpath, gradually climbing higher and she says:

'Billy, are we going mountain climbing? I only wanted a stroll.'

I stop and look at her over my shoulder. I've obviously been setting too quick a pace, so I wait for her to catch up.

'I want to take you somewhere special, well special to me at any rate,' I say.

'Right,' she replies. 'I knew I wasn't as fit as I should be. When I was younger I'd have trotted up here, but it's not so easy.'

'You look young to me,' I say. 'And beautiful,' I add and then I feel a complete idiot and remember how she had been at the cricket pitch when we moved into these kind of, what you might call, *dangerous waters*. So I turn away before she can say anything and start walking again.

I stride away for a few yards and then I look back. She is standing watching me and her head is tilted to one side as if she is thinking about something, there is a puzzled look on her face.

I look away and start to walk again and then I hear her footsteps following me.

It doesn't take long before we leave the footpath and strike off across country. Soon we are at the woods, my little woods. I stop and turn round just before we enter them and look down at the valley below – at the fields spread out, the little farm house, a tractor moving like a snail cutting lines into the brown dusty earth as it ploughs, the stream – a blue streak cutting through the countryside – and nearby the old manor house that is my school – or *was* my school I should say.

She is next to me, panting a little from her exertions and she looks down at my world.

'It's fabulous,' she says. 'What a view.'

Then she looks at me. 'I wondered where you were bringing me but it was worth the climb.'

I point and say, 'That's my school. St Joseph's.'

'I know,' she says. 'You were very lucky. I gather it's a wonderful school. Sydney was telling me all about it.'

I'm shocked and I feel a little stab of pain run through me.

'Sydney?' I say.

'Yes. My friend. He's directing the play I'm in, the one your mother works on. He went to that school too. A long time before you, but he speaks very highly of it.'

I'm shocked, Appalled actually. That terrible, pompous man with the cravat and his loud voice and louder car went to my old school.

'Yes,' she says, 'You've got that in common.'

I don't know what to say. I have nothing in common with that man. He is vulgar. Garish. Flash, you might say and he is far too close to her for comfort.

'Really,' I say and even I can hear that my voice is quite cold. 'Well over the years the school has had its ups and downs, I suppose.'

Which is really rather rude and once again I feel very embarrassed. I must learn to control what I say. – when I am with her I tend to speak before I think. Fortunately, she doesn't seem to take any notice of me, perhaps she didn't hear.

We stand there looking at the countryside for a few minutes and neither of us speak until at last she says, 'So this is your special place. I can understand that. It's beautiful.'

'No,' I say. 'Not here. Come on. This way.'

And to my amazement I actually take her hand and lead her towards the little grassy path in the trees that leads into my clearing.

The path has become rather overgrown since I was last there and I have to trample down brambles, and break off some wayward tree branches to get us through but eventually we step into the magical place and immediately I am hit by the same sense of serene peace that I always find here. The silence – the only sound being the gentle rustling of leaves moving in the early evening breeze – the canopy of green branches over head that opens onto the disc of blue sky, the soft moss and grass under our feet which, like the ground by the stream, has survived the heat of the summer and is still damp and soft.

I step reverently into the middle of the place and I suddenly think that it seems much smaller than it was. My eyes turn instinctively to where my angel used to hide but I know he's not there. My angel has gone and I haven't felt him nearby for a long time. There is something else too, buried under the sycamore tree, but I shut my mind to that. I haven't used the contents of that old satchel for years and I don't suppose I will again.

The thought of them sends an odd chill through my spine and suddenly I panic. What did I bring her here for? Why? It's crazy! Here of all places where... where... things happened that I have forgotten but I still dream about or think I dream about.

I turn to look at her, hoping she won't see the panic in my eyes.

'Is this it?' she says, looking round.

'Yes,' I say.

'It's not much is it?'

'W... what?' I can't believe she has said this.

She laughs. 'I was expecting... I don't know... More, I suppose, you know after the stream and the willow tree. Still it's a nice cool spot.'

Spot!? And a straw boater, a blue skirt, white socks and a school satchel canon into my head – all unwanted but I cannot control what I see in my mind.

'Oh... I don't know what I was expecting,' she says. 'The way you spoke I thought...'

Then she looks at me and she must see something in my face. She takes a step towards me and holds out a hand.

'No... of course, I'm being stupid. It's... it's a wonderful place Billy, and I can see it's a precious place to you. It has your memories in here and you've been happy here...'

She looks around and then back at me.

'There's a place that's precious to me too you know. Oh, it's not like this, not tranquil and private but a town near the seaside where I was once very, very happy. It's my magical place. It's where I was young and where I grew-up and where I fell in love and all kinds of things. So I understand – about this. I'm sorry I didn't at first, but I do now.

This is your place. This is where your heart is.'

And when she says this, I think my heart will break and I can't speak, so I nod and then she says in a different kind of voice.

'My feet are killing me. Permission to sit down?'

I smile back at her, catching the new mood.

'Of course,' I say. 'This place is your place.'

And as she drops to the ground I catch a glimpse of her long thighs under her skirt and even a glimpse of her underwear and I feel things stirring in me and I have to fight back my thoughts – thoughts of lust, if I'm honest – but instead of falling on her and covering her in kisses, which is what I want to do, I sit down slowly in front of her, my legs folded under me.

* * *

Everything has changed. I want you to try to understand that Doctor. In just a week or so my whole world has become a different place.

And my feelings towards Sydney have become completely different too. He had betrayed me, true – but in a very confusing way, I think I was attracted to him more than I ever had been before. I was so angry with him but I had to admit that he had acted with the best of intentions.

I suppose I could have forgiven him going into my home in order to do me good deeds – though I think he was an idiot not ask me first. What I thought I couldn't forgive was going into Diana's room. Violating it was how I saw it. Her room was my place – mine and hers.

Do you know, her bedclothes and some of her clothes smelt of her perfume. I don't know what it was. Some cheap teenage stuff, *Charlie*, or whatever it's called and for months and months afterwards when I opened the door, the scent of it was as if she was still there, as if she would look up from her homework books and smile at me or ask me for a cup of tea. But what's so sad is, that if you leave it long enough, even if you don't open the windows, the smell of cheap perfume begins to fade and then it goes.

Although I hated him at first for what he had done I slowly began to realise that Sydney had done me a favour. I couldn't go on. I couldn't live like this, secretly haunting her room, stepping over things left scattered on the floor, not even wanting to dust it in case I took something of her away – I couldn't go on like that. The scent had faded you see, long before Sydney let fresh air into the place.

He was right. I had to move on. But I couldn't do it. You see the truth is that I felt dead inside. I clung to her room like I clung to Southwold, like I clung to being a one time nearly famous actress, like I clung to my bright and breezy self – the aloof, rather mannered theatrical grande-dame, the character I adopted for the benefit of the Leeford Players. I clung to her like I clung to Sydney and his pub lunches and his fast car and his money. All these things I thought gave me purpose, gave me life – but really I was dead, because she was dead.

And then I made love to a young man.

And everything changed.

Are you shocked, Doctor? I was.

Billy and I sat together after that long climb up the hill, in his clearing, in what he calls his special place and the sun was setting and the evening was warm and he was good looking and muscular and vibrant with life. The life I didn't have, the youth I had lost, and at some point he reached out his hand and touched mine and I leant forward and I kissed him – on his mouth, just as he'd try to kiss me a few days before, only this time I kissed him with passion and... and lust. And he responded with all the vigour and passion of his young blood...

...And so we made love. We had sex, there in a clearing, in the woods at the top of the hill, under the stars.

I must be mad.

Or maybe I am now the sanest I have ever been.

* * *

I'm lying here in bed and I am happy – I am looking forward to tomorrow and to the rest of my life.

For now I can push the shadows to the back of my mind, I can ignore the worries that haunt me, I can feel alive and free from guilt – from both the guilt of original sin and my more recent crimes.

I am happy at last.

I wonder if Niall Mahoney is looking forward to tomorrow and Patrick Flynn and Ian Shane.

Actually, I don't care any more if they are or if they're not.

I really don't care.

* * *

Dear Doctor

I am just scribbling this quick note to accompany this bundle of cassette tapes that I am sending you. You will understand this better when you have listened through them — though I warn you there are rather a lot of them and I should have a stiff drink at your side when you play them.

I think the enclosed represents a phase of my life which I hope is now over. However, you asked me to keep this audio diary and I have done so. I don't think I will need to see you again, as I say, I have moved on, into a better world I think, but you may want to keep these for your records or as a reference just in case I ever pop back to see you in the future. (I don't mean this unpleasantly but you'll appreciate that I pray to God I won't need to do that).

Should you listen to the tapes, then you'll find the entries aren't quite complete. However all I need to add is the following.

I have decided to make a life with Sydney after all, in view of the incident I reported in my last tape with a certain person in a certain place.

That may surprise you but in fact my brief liaison has served to bring me to my senses and I realise that Sydney and I are in so many ways, made for each other.

The other thing I should add is that tonight I intend to clear out my daughter's bedroom. In fact I have booked a decorator to come in next week to give it a fresh coat of paint. It is something I should have done before. As I say, the enclosed tapes will explain.

For now I am grateful for all your help over the past seven years.

With many thanks

Your sincerely.

'...This thing of darkness I acknowledge mine...'

Shakespeare, The Tempest

I don't use the little grassy path. I push my way through the brambles around the perimeter instead. Over the summer these have grown thicker than I ever saw them and some of the thorns are now spitefully long and leave vicious looking scratches that trickle little dots of blood down my arms. Even the bushes, unknown things that look like privet but probably aren't, have become much thicker and are harder to crawl through.

Why don't I enter the clearing in the way I normally do, the way I did with her, through the little trodden-down grass path by the sycamore tree? I can't explain, not even to myself. There was something in her message, some tone in her note that has made me uncomfortable and uncertain, more uncertain than I have been about anything for... for years. Somehow, ever since I received her note I have felt an odd sensation, a prickling, you might say, behind my eyes, a dull aching in forehead – a sense of foreboding.

It's ridiculous, of course. Like she said, I have spent some of my happiest days here, here in my clearing and the last time, a few days ago, with my goddess, with my Cleopatra was the happiest of them all. And in my imagination, as I push aside the undergrowth, I run the film of our pornography again on the back of my eyes. Her breasts, her secret places enfolded in exciting black lace, the tease of elastic, the feel of nylon clad legs, the softness and the wetness of.. of her womanhood, for want of a better word.

So why my caution? Why do I want to look in at my clearing and to spy on her, to secretly watch her before she knows that I have arrived. I'm afraid of something and the worst part of the fear is that I don't know what of.

I am flat on the ground. I pull myself forward to peer in

at the clearing and promptly push my head into a clump of brambles which pierce the skin on the front and sides of my head, their thorns digging into my skull, so that I can feel blood trickling through my long black hair. My beard, of which I am now so proud, (it's a form of liberation and to hell with Wilkinson Sword) is matted with dust and sweat and probably other awful things too terrible to contemplate and to make things worse I have leant back against a big clump of nettles and they sting me right through my light summer T-shirt, like a whiplash across my shoulder blades.

She's there. I knew she would be. I watch her, fascinated and the sight of her makes me forget the pain and the tortures I have been through.

Once again I marvel at her tall, slender figure, which looks even more so when viewed from a prone position under a bush and even though I am several yards form her, the afternoon breeze carries the sweet delicate scent of her perfume to me and the smell of it makes me glow inside.

Today she is dressed in a skirt, navy blue, which, like black, is a colour that suits her well and another blouse so thin that I can see again the shape of her breasts perfectly outlined through the thin white cotton and I can even make out the lace and 'trimmings' of her bra and with a pang of ecstasy I wonder if I will be able to run my hands over the fabric soon and caress her nipples through it and with an even greater surge of lust I wonder if her knickers will be the same – sheer, lacy and revealingly tight and I know that before we leave I must find out and I have insane urge to bury my face in between her legs and to feel the softness of the material against my lips and to inhale her womanhood as I do so.

The thought is so vivid that I have to shift uncomfortably

and the pain of thorns in my head digs deeper when I do so.

She has on very little make-up I notice and she looks wonderful and natural – better than she ever did with eye shadow and mascara and all those other tricks that she seems to go in for.

I should let her know I am here. I should stand-up and breeze into the clearing, kiss her on the mouth and make some joke about hotel rooms being more comfortable for an assignation, but instead I continue to spy on her.

She is standing very still as she has been the whole time I have been watching her. She is facing me but obviously not looking at me, for she has no idea that I am there, watching. Oddly she has her handbag with her. It is at her feet and beside it is the straw shopping basket. I wonder what's in it? More wine, some of the delicious pâté, the French Bread? She still hasn't moved from the spot. She seems to be looking into the distance, her eyes focused on some distant point and then I realise her lips are moving, very slowly, silently, as if she is saying a prayer. And that makes me catch my breath.

I thought I was the only person who came here to pray. I thought I was the only one who felt the holiness of the place even though my angel has now gone from it; that I was the only one who knew that this was a sacred and blessed place because he had graced it with his presence. So it means more to her than she said, more than a seaside memory. She too feels the spirit that is here.

Her lips stop moving. She blinks slowly as if coming out of a trance and she looks around unhurriedly. She reminds me of a child waking from an afternoon nap – not that I have much experience of children but my cousin twice removed from Birmingham came to stay with us once and brought her three year old daughter and I remember she looked like this when she woke up from her nap on our sofa one afternoon.

'Fran, I do wish you wouldn't allow the child to sleep there,' my mother had said to my twice removed cousin. 'That fabric cost eight pounds a yard from Selfridges and I do not want to have to replace it *every* time you visit us because she has got toffee and Ribena over it.' She needn't have worried – we haven't seen Fran since; my father's comments about unmarried mothers being a burden on us all, probably didn't make her feel all that welcome either.

Mrs Watson sighs, blinks again and slowly, elegantly, sexily, lowers herself to the ground beside her bags. She makes herself comfortable, folding one leg under her, stretching out the other and then she opens her bag and takes a packet of cigarettes and a lighter from it.

I decide, as she lights up and blows smoke onto the breeze, that I should make my appearance. I toy with crawling back the way I came but the thorns and the nettles are frankly off-putting and as I am so close I decide just to emerge from the bushes and surprise her.

I struggle to my feet and like a whale emerging from the deep I push myself up through the brambles and the bushes and step into the clearing.

She looks at me in surprise.

'Good God Billy, what are you doing? You're covered in dead leaves and scratches and is that blood on your head?'

I raise a hand to my forehead and confirm that it is.

'Why didn't you come in the other way? Through the path, like a normal human being?'

It's a fair question and I am suddenly faced with the

embarrassment of having to admit that I was watching her, spying she might call it and I can see all kinds of complications arising from this.

'I… I was looking… looking for slow worms… or even adders.'

She looks at me as if I have gone completely mad and I wonder where on earth I got that from and then I remember watching a nature programme on BBC 2 last night.

'I am a bit of an amateur…' I can't think of the right word so I try, '…snakeologist.' And she doesn't look as if it matters what word I use. 'I'm always looking for things like that.' I finish pathetically.

'Good lord, she says. 'How revolting.'

And there is something in the way she says this that makes me look at her. I realise there is a steely glint in her eyes, which is quite hard to notice at first because she is not looking directly at me. She keeps glancing at me and then looking quickly away, which I find both disconcerting and rather worrying.

I drop to the ground next to her and hold out my hand to touch her but she quickly pulls her hand away and takes a long drag on her cigarette instead.

Feeling a bit foolish, I nod towards the shopping basket.

'Have we got some more of that pâté,' I say. 'I really liked it.'

'No,' she says quickly and a little abruptly. 'No we haven't.'

'Oh,' I say. 'Any wine..?

'No, Billy. Nothing like that this evening.'

There is something wrong, I'm convinced of that now. Perhaps she realises that I have been lying in the bushes spying on her – but I think if that was it, she would have said some-thing. There is what you might call an uncomfortable silence between us while she puffs on her cigarette in a rather dra-matic fashion and as much because I am getting tired of the smell of it as anything else I say, 'Is something wrong… You don't seem very happy?'

She crushes the cigarette out on the dry and dead grass be-neath her feet and I want to say something about the danger of fire when we haven't had any rain for so long but I decide just in time that this may not be the right moment to mention it.

Suddenly she looks at me and I am now certain that there is definitely something wrong – her eyes flash and al-most look angry and there is something else. I'm not sure what. Sadness?

'Why did you bring me here?'

I'm confused. 'What..?' I reply, uncertain of my ground.

'Why did you bring me here? To this place…Your clear-ing.'

'I thought you said you liked it here?'

'Maybe,' she snaps. 'But why here?'

'It's peaceful…It's special…' I am not sure what to say. I don't want to explain how I feel about this place. I can't tell her that it is holy, that it is all tied-up in my mind with God and the Angel and my special mission and that this is the place where I feel most at peace – and safe from the world which on the whole I have always found pretty hostile and not very understanding.

So I don't say anything. I just look at her. She has bent her head down towards the ground and I can only see the thick waves of dark black hair hanging loose over her shoul-ders. I can't see her face, I can't see her eyes…

Without looking up she says quite slowly.

'Do you bring all the girls here?'

'I'm sorry,' I say and I really don't understand what she means?

She looks up at me.

'I said, do you bring all the girls here?'

'W…what girls?" I stammer.

'Your girlfriends…do you bring them all here..? Is this where you make love to them?'

I'm astonished. What is she saying, why is she sounding like this, so harsh and so cold, like she was in the cricket pitch. I open my mouth but I'm not sure what I'm going to say and it doesn't matter as she cuts across me anyway.

'Is this where you bring them to have sex? Like you did with me?'

This is appalling.

'I… No. No…'

She has completely confused me and I am not sure now where this conversation is going but I'm beginning to fear the worst. I look at her hopelessly. Why is she being so… so horrid to me? I can't understand what's happened.

She hauls herself wearily and slowly to her feet, her long and beautiful legs unfolding beneath her and the action sends a charge through my testicles and I can feel my penis stirring.

She straightens her skirt slowly, deliberately and looks at me – a cool unblinking look, and something about the way she stares at me makes my heart thud and my mouth go dry.

'How many girls have you brought here?' She says in a low voice.

'I…haven't… What's wrong…? what do you mean?'

She takes a step towards me and suddenly I feel frightened.

'Did you,' she says very slowly and so quietly that I can hardly hear her, 'Did you bring her here... that night?'

My blood runs cold and I feel a little sick.

'Bring who?' I ask – but I know who she means. And she knows that I do...

She doesn't speak again but turns away and takes a pace or two across the clearing. She stops and looks up at the sky through the fringe of trees above, throwing her head back and sending her long dark hair flying in little whiplashes of evening sunlight and I wonder what she is thinking about. Still without looking at me, still staring into the darkling sky she begins to speak:

'They only ever told me that she was... that she was killed somewhere in the countryside, on a hillside, near a place called Butler's Farm. One of the policewomen, a few days later, said that I could go to the place if I wanted, you know to lay a wreath, to pay my respects... But I didn't go...'

She lowers her head now and turns to face me.

'...I said I didn't want to know where she died and laying a wreath seemed, well it seemed a bit foreign to me – the sort of thing they'd do in Italy or Spain, if you know what I mean.'

I do. I'd been on the European Music Group tour when I was at Cambridge and I was amazed at the little road-side shrines you could see everywhere, especially in the mountains. I hadn't realised what they were at first and when I did, I remember thinking I must never risk travelling by road again when abroad. But I don't mention any of this to her now.

'...And they wouldn't let me visit her at the undertakers because... because she was so mutilated. Because they found so little of her...'

I shudder and feel suddenly sick

'Isn't that appalling? They found so little of her that they filled most of the coffin with sand bags – to give it some weight, you know…'

I can't look at her and I don't want to hear.

'I have never wanted to think of her dead,' she goes on and her words are merciless, cutting through me, cutting into me, dissecting my soul. 'I don't want to think of her dead,' she says. 'Only as she was – bright and bubbly, excited about going to the disco and meeting her boyfriend…'

She puts a funny emphasis on the word boyfriend and it makes me feel uncomfortable. Does she mean me or does she mean Teddy? I have a sinking feeling that she means Teddy of course, and I want to scream at her that Diana was going to meet me. That was the plan. That's what she'd wanted to do. But I don't say anything, though I can see the two of us, Diana and me, by the stream again as clear as if I was there now and her saying to me to go with her to the disco. I shake my head to get her smiling face and her blonde hair out of my mind. Her mother is still speaking.

'She came downstairs that afternoon and asked me what I thought of her new skirt and I said, "What skirt?" – that's how short it was and she said, "Oh, mum tell me you're not getting old like all the other mothers!" And we giggled and I gave her a hug and I remember thinking that she could be my sister or my friend – we were so close. We didn't have barriers like some parents.'

No, I think. Some parents you can never understand and they can never understand you – even though you may seem so alike.

She flicks a stray strand of hair from her eyes.

'So I never saw exactly where it happened, you see...'

Her voice is now even quieter. I can barely hear her and there is a crack in her voice, a dryness like the grass and first fallen leaves under our feet.

'They never told me exactly where she died... But now I know,' she says. 'Now I know where she died. I didn't realise the other day that the farm down there was called Butler's Farm.'

'You can't be sure where it was,' I say. 'If the police never told you...'

She moves suddenly, strides towards me and I recoil in shock; to be honest I am a little afraid. But she brushes past me and goes over to where she has left her basket and her handbag. She squats down beside them.

'No.' She says. 'You're wrong. I know for sure – because I found something.'

She fumbles inside the wicker shopping basket but this time she doesn't surprise me with food and drink, she pulls from inside it a red, hard-back book – a notepad of some sort or...

'...A diary,' she says finishing my unspoken thoughts. 'It's Diana's diary. I am so stupid. I've kept that bloody room like a shrine for seven years. Thank God for Sydney. It was his idea. "Clear it out," he said, "You can move on and still keep your memories without a shrine. It's morbid." He was right, you know. So I did. And wasn't I stupid, because she'd hardly hidden this at all? It was under her mattress actually. Why do children think everything is parent proof if they put it under their mattress?'

She looks at me and I am not sure if she expects me to answer or not, so I don't.

'Paul used to keep mucky mags under his,' she goes on and I suddenly remember Pete's hidden collection on the wardrobe – am I the only boy in the world then who never collected porn? The thought makes me rather sad.

She smiles. 'I found them about a day after he put the first one there, when he was thirteen. He had quite a collection by the time he left home. It's a wonder he could get in the bed…'

Actually, I don't want to know about Paul's mucky magazines but I watch her and the smile leaves her face as she looks down at the diary. For some reason I am suddenly very frightened and a cold feeling is gripping my guts and moving up towards my chest and my mouth has gone very dry.

'Is this what you were looking for?' she says. 'When you went into her room; when you broke into my house?'

I can't speak and anyway I have nothing to say. I just look at her.

'Were you worried that she'd left something behind?' And she stares at me so that I have to look away – and when I speak, it is my turn to be croaky.

'I told you,' I say. 'I never went into her room. I never broke into your house.'

'You're a liar,' she says. 'You've always lied. You even lie to yourself. You see I thought…. Well, it never occurred to me that more than one person might have gone into my house. Into her room… '

'No.'

'Yes!' she shouts. 'How the hell else did you know what to write on the card that came with the roses? I played the record Billy. I heard the lyrics…'

And the anger in her voice makes me rock back on my

heels. Then she waves the book at me, stepping towards me, so that it nearly brushes against my face.

'Do you want to read it?'

'It must be private,' I say. Which is pathetic and hopeless of course.

She gives me an odd look.

'Well, I don't think she's going to mind now, is she?'

She starts to flick through the pages.

'Some of it is so beautiful,' she says in a funny voice. 'I didn't realise she was so fond of Shakespeare.'

'*A Midsummer Night's Dream,*' I say. 'She liked that one.'

'Oh, she was so young, Billy. Odd isn't it? Yet, in some ways she was very grown-up for her age. I suppose you know she'd been through quite a lot with her father's illness and I probably wasn't the best mother in the world, come to that... She'd learnt the tough way, I think – you know, how to survive, to get on, fend for herself. I let her down really...'

'No,' I say. 'She thought you were great. Honestly.'

'I know what she thought, Billy.' And she says this in a hard little voice. 'She thought I was a very groovy mum. But I think I let her down. If you were older you'd understand.'

And that makes me feel stupid and immature.

She taps the cover of the book with her red nails.

'There's a lot about you in here...'

I swallow. 'Is there? That's nice.'

'She was very fond of you...'

I am genuinely relieved to hear this.

'But she thought you were very strange.'

She looks at me and I'm not sure what to say. I think she wants me to say something but I can't think what, so I don't say anything but I am rather hurt that Diana thought I was strange. I mean at the time I may have had some small problems but I have never thought of myself as strange. But then I reflect that the blessed and the chosen are often misunderstood by those they have come to save.

'Your school life sounds like a total mess to me. How on earth could you let that priest..? With a cine camera…? Dear God. What were your parents thinking of.'

'I don't know what you mean?' I say. And I don't. What does she mean about a priest? The education at my school was, in my opinion, pretty well second to none.

'I got to Cambridge,' I say rather pompously. 'So I don't think the priests did that bad a job.'

'I'm not talking about your education Billy. I'm talking abut the mess they made of you. Poor Diana. I don't think she understood you at all, though she thought she did. You know, Billy – I rather wish she'd never met anyone from your school but if she had to, I'm glad that eventually she met Teddy. Despite everything, he was quite normal.'

I feel a flare of anger rush through my body. Does she mean despite my school? Despite the priests? Worse, despite my faith? Who is she to say such things? And how could she be glad that Diana met that… that brainless… yobbo! She must be mad! But I don't show my anger. I have control. I can, with some pride, say that I am always in control of my emotions.

'You were very silly,' she is saying, and she is suddenly spiteful. 'Why on earth didn't you just let her go when Teddy came along? He was obviously more suitable.'

This is too much.

'Suitable? Suitable?' I splutter. 'He… He was a bully… He was rough and… and common…'

'Common!' She repeats. 'Oh, Billy. Please stop showing yourself up for what you are.'

And then she stares at me, right into me and I feel she is looking into my soul.

'No. Diana couldn't work you out and I'm not sure if I can either. You see Billy, I think you're one of those very difficult people who is one thing on the outside and something else on the inside and who hides it rather well, and I think as you've got older, you've got even better and better at hiding what you really are.'

I want to laugh because this is all nonsense.

'She thought you were a child of nature. That's what she said.' And once again she taps the diary. 'She thought you had something of the 'wild' about you because you were always outdoors, always in the woods or by the stream or up here – I think she thought at first that you were some kind of hippy – communing with nature, loving the trees and the flowers. But that's not you at all, Billy. Not at all. Is it? You're not exactly mother nature's son, are you? More a suburban mummy's boy.'

I am shaken to my core. Such anger, such hate, such venom. How could I have loved this woman. This viper. But I say nothing, although the cold feeling in my chest is getting worse and I can hear the blood beginning to sing in my ears.

'Out here,' she goes on, 'Was the only place where you felt safe, wasn't it? Alone in the woods and the fields, here where we are now – this was where you were safe. This is where no one could find you, could find out about you, ask questions… *get to know you.*'

She stops speaking and her words hang in the air around me.

'That's rubbish,' I say at last.

She smiles and to my eyes it is a rather slow sinister smile.

'What did you get up to here, when you were at school? Alone… All on your own. What do you get up to up here, now?'

'I told you the other day… I don't come here so much as I used to, like when I was younger.'

'And why's that Billy?'

'Other things to do, I suppose… Other fish to fry.'

'Perhaps you don't come here so much now because of what happened?'

I'm shocked at this and I don't want to be here with her anymore. I just want her to go. She meant so much to me and now she is being cruel and spiteful, raking up things she shouldn't. For what seems like a very long time we look at each other and I can't think of anything to say – all I can do is listen to the breeze in the leaves and the birdsong that is suddenly very loud all around me.

And the she says, in a low and surprisingly calm voice.

'This is where she died. Right here. In this clearing…'

My mouth is dry. The world is spinning in my eyes but I manage to say.

'No… No, I'm certain it isn't.'

She opens the diary and for the first time I notice she has marked some of the pages with little pieces of paper. She turns to one of these and reads some of the page out loud in a clear voice and I can't help but realise that she has been trained – she has a wonderful speaking voice, when all is said and done.

'*He is a child of the wild, child of the night, child of the woods… And I know that's where he'll be – in his clearing.*'

She looks up at me.

She's right then, Diana/Emma did think I was a child of nature – and I am rather pleased at this – it gives me a certain mystery, I think. Hearing this I am more confident now, so I say.

'I don't see what that's got to do with... well, you know, where she died?'

She looks at me with cold eyes and I long for the passion in them that I saw when we made love.

'She wrote that on the night,' she says. 'When she got back from the disco after you'd run away.'

That hurts. I'd never thought of it as running away. Not that I think about it, that night, not very much but when I do, I prefer to think that I made a tactical exit in order to calm down what might have become a very ugly incident.

'Still,' I say carefully. 'It doesn't mean she actually came here. She was just wondering about where I'd gone to.'

And as I say this I get a sudden warm feeling because I realise that even then, after what happened at the disco, she'd gone home and she was thinking about me, she'd even written in her diary about me. She wanted to know where I was – she cared. But then the warm feeling vanishes almost as soon as it has come and I feel terrible. She was still thinking about me, she cared about me and... and... and then – *Oh, God did I do that awful thing to her?*

Emma/Diana's mother is watching me now. Looking at me with calm eyes, cold eyes.

'She came here Billy – after the disco, after she'd written this...'

'No,' I say.

She looks down at the diary and starts to read from it

again and this time she reads everything.

'*I must be mad! It's well past midnight and I am going to go out and find him. I can't believe that I really intend to do this. He's probably at home and I don't even know where that is but I just have this feeling he won't be. He is a child of the wild, child of the night, child of the woods... And I know that's where he'll be – in his clearing...*'

The words hang in the air, they fill the place where we are standing – my clearing in the woods at the top of the hill, the clearing that she is writing about – and now Diana's mother is looking at me, at the boy her daughter was writing about.

I return her look and I understand that she knows the truth, so now everything is clear to me: I have to save myself. Above all things *I have to save myself.* It is my duty if I am to fulfil what the Lord expects of me. I have been chosen and although I made a mistake I have been forgiven in the Lord's eyes and that is all that matters. He would expect me to save myself – nothing else will do.

Diana's mother turns a page in the diary and once again her clear actress voice rings out.

'*It's a bright night outside, the moon is out and I am really not afraid. I guess I should be, but I am not. I need to see him. I need to explain...*'

'Stop it,' I say suddenly. 'Just stop reading it...' I pause, lost for the right words and then I say. 'Please...'

She closes the book and raises her eyes to look at me. When she speaks her voice is quiet, almost gentle.

'What happened Billy?'

I look at the ground but she carries on, answering her own questions.

'It was very late but she came to find you... She walked

all that way in the dark, along country lanes, through footpaths, across fields all the way up to here, in the dark,
through the woods. Jesus, Billy – she must have been terrified. You owe it to her to tell me what happened…'

But I can't. I can't even speak. I just stare at the dried-
up grass and I focus on a small black beetle that's nosing its
way through the brown stalks. And I think, 'nosing' can't be
the right word because surely beetles don't have noses… I
almost jump when I feel her hand on my shoulder. She is
gripping it hard and pulling me round so that I look at her.

'Did you have a fight? Did you lose your temper?'

I am surprised, though she has grabbed me with some
force she doesn't sound angry at all. More resigned, you
might say, suffering quietly.

Finally I manage to say, 'No… I don't think we had a
fight?'

She lets go of me.

'What does that mean?'

'I don't know,' I say slowly. 'I really don't know what
happened. I don't remember an argument. I don't remember
her coming here. I don't remember anything. Honestly.'

It sounds pathetic so I add.

'It's true. It's just a blank…'

I look up at her I know she is thinking that I am a liar
and I can see the hatred in her eyes. And now I know it's all
going to come out, so I take a deep breath and begin.

'I remember coming here after the disco and I remember… I remember being terribly sad and very hurt.' And now
I try appealing to her better nature. 'You can't imagine what
it was like,' I say, and I try to put on my most hurt voice.
'They were awful to me, all of them. They made fun of me

and…laughed at me and everyone was looking and Diana said some terrible things about me, things that were revolting and just weren't true…'

'Oh, Billy,' her mother says and she sounds almost sad. 'She didn't mean to hurt you. It just happened in the heat of the moment…' She holds up the book. 'She felt awful about it afterwards.'

'Did she?' I'm not sure that I believe her. 'They were pointing at me and jeering me…all of them. And that stupid Teddy… I just wanted to be alone.'

I stop speaking and for a while she doesn't say anything and we stand there a few feet apart while the birds sing and the light begins to fade.

She sighs. It's a deep and heavy silence in the gathering dusk and I think the saddest sound I have heard so far in my life.

'You killed her Billy, didn't you?' And she says it slowly and I think a little reluctantly, like we'd both known it but neither of us had been quite ready to say it. Eventually I find my voice again.

'I don't know.' And I really don't. 'Like I said, it's all a blank. I really don't remember.'

'I don't believe you Billy.' Again she doesn't sound angry, just matter of fact.

'It's true,' I say. 'Really. You see… I… I had this vision. That's all I know.'

'Vision?' She sounds puzzled.

'Yes.'

'I don't understand.'

'In my head – I saw someone – but I don't think it was her…'

I stop, thinking I have said enough but although she doesn't say anything her eyes tell me she doubts every word I say. So I carry on.

'It's true. Someone… was here in the clearing… she came in over there.'

I point to where the trees had parted to allow the BVM into my clearing. Her eyes follow my pointing finger but she replies in a dull monotone.

'It was Diana, Billy.'

I shake my head.

'The only person who came here that night was Diana.'

'No. You see… these things happen to me… I… I see things.'

For a second she looks even more annoyed than she has been.

'What? What are you talking about you silly boy?'

'Don't call me that,' I snap. 'You don't understand. I see things… I have visions…'

I think she is going to laugh at me, she certainly gives me an odd look.

'I do… really.' I say quickly. 'I see what people would like to be and what they want to do… I saw you at a fun fair once when I knew you were at your home, and I've seen people from off the television here, here where we are now… and… and…' I was falling over myself now to tell her, to share what I had to live with every day with someone else and I knew that I was speaking faster and faster and that I probably sounded totally mad, but I didn't care.

'And I see…' I went on in a rush, 'I see holy things like saints and angels. And they speak to me. And my special angel, my guardian angel, he used to wait for me up here and watch over me. Sometimes I hear their voices and they tell me to pray or to make sacrifices because that's what I have to do because... well, just because...'

I tail off and I daren't say anymore.

'Because of what Billy?' she says in a quiet voice that doesn't actually sound like her at all.

I swallow and then I decide to share my secret.

'Because The Lord has chosen me. I am the chosen one...'

I see a sudden flash of confusion in her eyes – a fraction of a moment of uncertainty.

'What?' She almost whispers

'It doesn't matter,' I say, and it really doesn't – she wouldn't understand anyway and I have already said more than I meant to, more than I should.

And then she starts to laugh...

Yes. She actually laughs. I have told her the most precious secret of my life, I have let her know about my visions that so far only God, and my angel have ever shared with me and about what is expected of me and she laughs!

Then, just as suddenly her face clouds over and she sets her jaw firmly, her lips tightening into little thin lines of anger, her eyes blazing with hatred.

'Vision!' she snaps. 'Oh, please, Billy – give me some credit. If you're going to lie, lie well.'

'It's true!' I shout at her. 'I have visions. All the time... Holy, holy visions.'

She is spitting anger.

'You little bastard...' And she raises a hand as if she's going to slap me. But I don't take any notice. Now I'm angry too. Oh, ye of little faith, I think.

'Don't laugh at me,' I shout and my voice is so loud that it seems to echo off the hills and you could probably hear me in Leeford. A few birds, startled, crash into flight from the trees above us and small leaves flutter down on our head, like green confetti I think.

I take a deep breath and try to speak calmly now: 'Please. Please listen to me. That night. That night here in the dark all I know is that the Blessed Virgin Mary came to me and… and…'

What can I say? What blasphemy am I about to utter. How can I say what the BVM did? It's too horrific to recall and anyway I know that it can't be true. It can't be. The BVM could never do that. Never. It just can't be true – and I remember that's what I had thought then on that night, when I came to my senses, that it couldn't be true, that it was another vision and then a terrible thought occurs to me – supposing my visions are just some trick of my mind. Supposing they *are* simply *madness!*

And then I start to cry. I'm crying and somehow I'm down on my knees. I'm holding out my hands to Diana/Emma's mother and I have no idea how I end up here on the ground – how I end-up kneeling in front of her, holding out my hands to her, palms upward, in supplication.

'I'm sorry… I'm sorry…' I'm saying and she is looking down at me and there is no sign of pity in her dark eyes.

'Oh, my God,' she says quietly and she is backing away from me. She drops the diary onto the ground and she almost trips over her bags as she stumbles backwards towards the edge of the clearing.

'Oh, my God, she says again. And then she says the thing I have feared most for the last seven years or maybe for longer…

'You're bonkers… You're completely insane.'

I jump up. My heart will burst, my brain will explode.

'No,' I almost scream. 'No. Don't say that.'

I take a deep breath because I am sobbing. 'You're not the man in the Bow Tie and even he didn't say that.'

She puts a hand to her mouth and I can see fear in her eyes.

'What are you talking about? What man?'

'They made me see him. But I never told. I never said a word. My secret was safe between me and my God. The time wasn't right, you see. There will be a time when I am allowed to speak but not yet.'

'I don't understand,' she says, then more firmly she adds. 'Billy, I'm going now. I'm going home.'

'I'll come,' I say.

'No. You stay here. I want to go on my own. Just stay here.'

And I know then what she is going to do. She is going to go to my parents or worse to the police and she is going to tell them that I have gone mad and that I did something awful to her daughter.

'Now…' I say. 'Now it's going to have to end. All the pain, all the sacrifices I've made. You're going to ruin it, because you're going to say things about me… things that aren't true. You're going to ruin it all now. Aren't you? Now… Now…Now…'

I step towards her and she almost jumps back.

'Go away, Billy. Leave me alone!' and I see the sudden look of surprise in her eyes and then real fear as she backs away.

'You mustn't spoil it,' I say and I am almost crying now. 'I've had to wait before I begin my ministry.' I try to explain.

'Like Jesus. You know he had to wait while he grew up before he was allowed to preach and teach, before he could become our saviour. And it's the same with me.'

I stop abruptly. I have said more than I intended. More
than I have ever said about who and what I am. Time seems
to stop now. I cannot move. I cannot hear the bird song. I
cannot see the sun setting over the trees, what was an orange
ball of flame is a black void above my head and she, the
woman, is standing stock still, her mouth slightly open, staring at me. And then as if from very far away she speaks and I
can barely hear her.

'And Diana,' she whispers. 'What about her?'

'I'm the chosen one,' I say. 'And I was tempted, for forty
days...' and I add for the sake of accuracy, 'Or thereabouts.'

I cannot look at her, so I stare at the ground.

'The devil came to me and she tempted me – she offered
me things I wanted, sins of pride and of the flesh, and when
I wouldn't be tempted, then she tormented me, humiliated
me and... and...'

There is silence. All is silence... The birds are quiet. The
breeze has ceased. The world doesn't spin. My heart has
stopped beating. How can she speak when the oxygen has
been sucked from the air? But she does:

'..And then...' She says, so slowly you could count the
words. 'And then you killed her...'

Before her words can hurt me, a great wind begins to
blow, the leaves are clattered against one another, the boughs
of the trees bend under its strength, the dry grass bends and
the dust of the parched soil is whipped up in little stinging
spirals against my face and hands. Her long hair is dragged
into the air, her dress flattened against her body and she

seems to stagger under the force of it.

And through the blowing of the winds, the howl of the gale, the cracking of the hurricane's cheeks, the spouts and cataracts of dust, I hear a voice, bell clear, strident and forceful and it says:

'This is my son, in whom I am well pleased.'

And as quickly as it came the wind has gone, there is silence again, the sunset is vivid and red, the birds sing their evening song and everything is peaceful and the woman is looking at me, quite sadly I think.

'Billy,' she says and something in her voice reminds me of my mother when I was very small and she was trying to explain things that were too complicated for me to understand. 'I'm going now and you must stay here and wait for me to come back. I'm going to fetch someone to help you and we'll get all this sorted out and you can tell us all about what happened... Do you understand?'

Of course I do. I understand only too well and I really don't want her to go but she is already walking away, slowly, carefully picking her way through the grass and the fallen leaves. She mustn't go of course.

I look around desperately and my eye falls on the short, heavy log that I'd been leaning on when I watched her through the bushes and the brambles, that already seems like a lifetime ago...

I can move pretty quickly when I want to and I move like a panther now. I am across the clearing and the log is in my hand in a single bound. I am like Superman and Batman rolled into one. I leap, you might say, like the amazing Daley Thompson, who is an athlete we can all be proud of in my opinion. He makes it good to be British, or so my father says.

* * *

The tools are still here, under the Sycamore tree where I buried them. I have to admit that I did a good job all those years ago of making sure they were well protected against the elements. Even after so long they have not a trace of rust on them and the blades are as keen as they ever were. It's the oiled cloth I wrapped them in, I reckon. A less fastidious person might not have been so conscientious but I have always had an eye for detail.

I'm pleased to say that I have not lost my technique. I work methodically and accurately and I am perfectly confident that the pieces will be small enough to provide a hearty meal for the foxes once more. No doubt they will be pleased to see me back, scattering their free meal around their burrows.

There are one or two other items that will be less easy to dispose of – clothing, bags etc. but I have never been afraid of digging a good sized hole when called upon, and hard work never hurts anyone, as my father says. It will mean a late night but I'm not bothered by that.

There is the matter of the diary. A little part of me would like to keep that. A sort of keepsake I suppose for good times gone by. I'll have to think about it. I've got a few hours hard labour ahead of me with a shovel, so plenty of time to mull it over...

* * *

'...If it should thunder as it did before, I know not where to hide my head...'

Shakespeare, The Tempest

I stayed away from home for a while.

According to my mother (who gave me regular up-dates by letter) the only people who seemed concerned about the disappearance of Mrs Watson at first were Sydney Pontefract and Mrs Watson's son Paul – oh, and the members of the Drama Club, of course.

A few days after her disappearance Sydney P went to the police; they took all the details and told him not to worry, people went missing all the time apparently and usually turned up again when they'd 'sorted themselves out' – whatever that means. I gather S. P. wasn't too pleased with their attitude, but then, as my mother said, 'What can you do? They're in charge, when all is said and done.'

Fortunately, no one seemed to be aware of my friendship with the missing woman and to be frank I wanted to keep it like that. I wasn't feeling too well and one of the reasons I decide to go away was to, what they call, *get my head straight*. In fact, I went to Bognor Regis and spent most of my time wandering along the beach and sleeping rough near the pier. At this time I started to suffer from very bad headaches and I found by concentrating on the sound of waves breaking on the shore I could tune out of my own mind and my head pain and feel free of any feelings of… of… well, guilt I suppose, and it was only then that I got any peace from certain nagging voices that seemed to be whispering at me day and night, day and night – endlessly, relentlessly.

Yes – it was strangely comforting to be in Bognor. And it was here that I finally came to realise that I was not in any way responsible for what had happened.

You see, I have been sent here on a mission – that had been made clear to me many years ago, as I believe I may

413

have alluded to before in these notes. Everything I do is steered by powers greater than me – by the heavenly father you might say. So, although I may not understand or even approve of certain actions I have taken today and in the past, it is not for me to question them. They are *ordained* and it is my duty to *obey*.

Time went by – ten days passed and Mrs W still hadn't been seen. Apparently the story gradually spread beyond the D Club and became the main topic of village gossip which got more excitable as the days passed and Mrs W still hadn't returned.

At first the buzz was that she'd probably gone away for a few days' break or was visiting friends somewhere but the fact that Paul hadn't heard from his mother and that she'd never mentioned going away soon led to more romantic ideas – she'd eloped, or more likely, being a former actress, she'd gone in to a clinic to get over her drug addiction. My mother told me when I phoned home one evening, that Mrs Woods, the butcher's wife, knew for a fact that Mrs W was going through cold chicken – and no one liked to point out to a butcher's wife that she meant cold turkey.

The centre of rumours, the source of what you might call the village jungle drums, was Mr Tidyman in the village shop (of course he would be!). Mr T seemed to be in the 'know' – though how he could 'know' anything was beyond me, as he hadn't even met Mrs Watson.

He put forward various theories ranging from her visiting friends abroad to her having had a nervous breakdown and admitting herself to a home for the insane. None of these ideas were based on anything factual but if you ask me he probably drank quite a lot of his own *Blue Nun* or possibly he indulged in a can or two of the *Watney's Pale Ale* of an evening.

The best idea he came up with was that she had been leading a 'double life' and in reality she worked for the soviet government who had recalled her at sudden and short notice, spiriting her away in a black limousine in the middle of the night. Mr Tidyman actually claimed he saw the car in the High Street while he was drawing his curtains one night. He lives above his shop of course, so he often looks out for Soviet spies in black limousines of a night-time.

Actually, irony aside, this was one crazy idea too far and a lot of people began to reckon that Mr T was spinning a few too many yarns in order to boost what my father called 'footfall' through the village store. My father knows these retailing expressions because he has often been called upon to value shops for rating purposes, so he's quite at home with the jargon.

And then things began to move with the police. This made me very nervous and although I had been thinking about going home I decided to stay put in Bognor. I had become by this time quite an aficionado of the pin-ball machines in the pier amusement arcade. Quite a wizard in fact! So it was no hardship to stay where I was.

The police moved quite quickly this time because even they had to admit that two weeks was quite some time 'to sort yourself out' without letting your son or your friends know where you were. And for the next few days panda cars cruised the area and by the end of the third week, door to door enquiries began to take place.

Soon enough even the press arrived, or at least Monica Lewis did, who wrote under the name of 'Girl Friday' for the

Leeford and District Times. She spent a day chatting to a few people and getting interviews that she carefully took down in shorthand in a blue notebook – I know this because shortly after I came home again, she interviewed my mother in our living room.

In fact, my mother wasn't in the article when it was published – well, not by name – she was described as a concerned member of the Local Amateur Dramatic Society, which made her furious, especially as she had given '*Girl Friday*' coffee (the expensive Gold Blend stuff) and a chocolate Digestive. However, a 'distraught' Sydney Pontefract did make it into the page two story and was tactfully described as a 'close friend' of the missing woman. The story even made the Nationals a few days later – well, the bottom of page five in *The Daily Mail* to be exact.

And I think this was when I started to become a little nervous and I realised I would have to go home and *sort* things out.

You learn from experience, let's face it. The whole business seven years ago with Emma/Diana has taught me a lot. Even a hint, a flicker of guilt, a look in the eyes, a word dropped in the wrong place can lead to DISASTER – so I have learnt that when it comes to keeping certain things private it is important to, what I call, *divert* attention. I mean what happened, happened! And nobody regretted it more than me – but the attention generated by such things can draw one in and get one involved in a way that can lead to all kinds of what I call, *repercussions*.

I had to prevent these repercussions as I had done before in the (let's use the word '*case*' as we are dealing with police matters) in the *case* of Diana/Emma.

At that time I had the rather brilliant idea of pointing the finger (as they say amongst the criminal classes) at one Teddy Edwards – a deeply unpleasant individual as I have made clear in these notes and who, in my humble O deserved everything that came his way in the manner of imprisonment, interrogation and public humiliation. The satisfactory thing about this solution had been what you might call the 'double effect' of diversion *and* revenge – a kind of poetic justice if ever there was one.

Well, I figured what worked once was sure to work again and I happily decided to repeat my previous (as we're still in police mode here) *modus operandi*. All I had to do was work out how to adapt it to the current situation.

So, I went for a walk to my stream one afternoon and sat on the grassy bank under my tree, crossed-leg, staring into the water to think things through.

It only took me about five minutes and my idea was crystal clear and pleasantly dead simple.

I put my plan into immediate effect…

* * *

As an old friend of the family the least I could do was to go round to see Paul and offer to help in any way I could, in the current terrible circumstances in which he found himself.

The fact that Diana/Emma had never ever introduced me to Paul and that I only vaguely remember him as a tall youth in a black suit that didn't fit him when I saw him at her funeral was a bit of a draw back, but I reckoned I could get away with it. Of course, a lot depended on whether he had any idea about the relationship between me and his mother.

I figured that if she had let on he wouldn't be too happy about it – I mean it would be like me discovering that Ian Shane was having sex with my mother and the thought of that painted a terrible picture in my mind's eye. I had this picture of my father standing over the two of them as they thrashed around in my parents' new *Slumberland* bed (with *unique posture springing*) and him saying, 'You see, that's what I mean about the country going to the dogs.'

It was odd to be back in the little front garden in front of the scruffy front door again and to know that she, the Cleopatra of the Maltings, wouldn't come to the door.

It took ages for the door to be opened and when it did a gust of stale smoky air, with a tang of old fried food wafted over me. Paul looked terrible. He was very pale, his clothes hung limply off his tall body and his hair, which was very long, looked greasy and straggly. He blinked at me, like he hadn't been out in the day-light for a long time. I stared at him and he stared at me and then he said:

'Oh, I thought it might be the police. Can I help you?'

'I'm Billy,' I said.

He looked at me and I noticed that his eyes were quite dilated and to be honest I think I could smell a hint of marijuana in the air as well as old cooking but I may have been wrong as I have never indulged in drugs – even in Cambridge where they were all at it, especially the Dons.

'Who?' he said at last.

'Billy... er... we didn't ever actually meet but I was erm... I was Diana's boyfriend for a while.'

'Oh, he said and blinked again. 'The one who liked fifties rock?'

'No.' I said firmly. 'Not that one.'

He suddenly grinned and looked much better.

'Oh,' he laughed. 'You were the weird one.'

I was quite offended at that but in view of the purpose of my visit I managed to keep smiling and say nothing. 'Stiff-upper lip old son, never fails,' my father would have said.

'What can I do you for?' he said at last, getting his words backwards which he may have meant to be funny but you can never tell when someone is clearly a drug addict.

'I've come round to see if I can be of any help, you know, because of your mum and everything. I... I met her quite a few times with Diana and I, well, you know. I was sorry to hear...'

I think this took him aback a bit.

'That's kind,' he said. 'That's very kind... It's been a rough couple of weeks... er look, do you want to come in.. tea or something?'

'Thank you,' I said immediately. 'I think that would be lovely.'

He was probably thinking I would refuse politely, say a few nice words and be on my way but instead I stepped into the house.

'We in the kitchen?' I said and I strode off down the corridor while he closed the door, looking a bit startled to be honest.

'It's good to be back again,' I thought to myself. 'Happy memories.'

The kitchen was shocking – even worse than usual. At least Diana's mother made some effort to tidy-up, clearly Paul did not. There were dirty dishes everywhere, not just in the sink which was overflowing with them but on the table, the worktop and even the floor! He'd left a pile of his dirty clothes by the washing machine – not in it – and the room was grey with old smoke and stank of decaying food most of which seemed to be falling out of the overflowing swing bin.

Unconsciously, I walked over to the bin and pushed the lid down as hard as I could.

'Sorry,' his sad voice said from behind me.

I turned round and he was standing in the doorway grinning. 'Bit of a mess, I'm afraid.'

I grinned back. 'No. No – seems all right to me,' I said, adopting a 'matey' voice which I guessed was the right tone and seemed to mimic his.

I think he was quite surprised that his late sister's boyfriend should appear out of the blue just a few days after his mother had vanished, but I explained to him that although I'd been away for a while, I'd recently bumped into his mother a couple of times.

'My parents had a party and your mum was there – you know, she and my mother were in...' I quickly corrected myself, '...are in the amateur dramatic club together.'

I couldn't see any point in elaborating or being much more truthful than that – I'm sure he didn't want to know the details.

He poured boiling water into two mugs and threw a couple of tea bags into them. Frankly, this is not in my humble O how you make tea – a warmed pot is required, loose leaves and freshly drawn water straight from the tap are the fundamentals of good tea; still I was relieved that the boiling water probably killed most of the germs on the otherwise pretty grubby mug.

'It's nice of you to call round,' he said.

'For old times sake,' I said, putting on what I hoped was a

sincere and yet somehow sympathetic look. 'I just want you to know that although I haven't been in touch very much and although we've never had the chance to meet I am always here if I can help, you know, until they find your mum...'

I sort of regretted the way I'd phrased this as it made it sound like they were going to find her dead, which of course they might well do, but I was obviously anxious that he shouldn't know that I knew that, if you follow me.

The offer definitely touched him and he asked me if I wanted a biscuit to go with what he called my 'cuppa' – naturally I accepted. Needless to say the biscuit was stale.

Despite the sordid atmosphere we got on well, I think, and we started to chat about things. I was careful not to say too much about either his mother or his sister though obviously that's what he wanted to talk about. I just had to be careful not to 'give the game away', as it were – so I kept my answers pretty vague and I even said when the subject came up, that yes, I did used to know Teddy Edwards, we were at school together.

'Didn't she ditch you for him?' he said.

I was stung to the quick but I kept on grinning like the proverbial C C, while I thought of an answer. Eventually I said, 'Well, we all move on, don't we, eh? Times change, seasons come and go.'

Which I thought made me sound quite man of the world-ish.

'I heard,' he said (and I wish he hadn't), 'That something happened at the disco that...' he hesitated, it obviously still hurt. '...That last night, you know – between you and Teddy.'

We were on very dangerous ground now and I needed to set a few parameters.

'Not really,' I said. 'We were just larking around…'
Then I added in a quiet and serious voice. 'Though I wish
I'd stayed on instead of going… maybe if I had, if I'd not left
her there… things… things would have turned out *very dif-
ferently* if you follow me. Very different.'

There was a silence and he looked at me.

'Yeah,' he said at last. 'Yeah. I reckon you'd have seen
her home safe and sound. I can tell that. I mean, you can't
blame Teddy, that was established eventually, but she should
never have gone home alone.'

I sighed with relief. Dear old Paul. We'd become quite
pally.

'Want another?' he said looking at my mug.

'Another cuppa. Lovely,' I said, getting into the spirit.

He made the tea and we got chatting about this and
that. He was amazed to find that I too had a deep interest in
music and some practical experience in the business.

'Didn't your mother tell you?' I asked.

'No,' he said. 'What you into?'

'All the classics like *The Stones* and *Floyd* but more and
more I'm into *Genesis* and especially *King Crimson*.'

He looked suitably impressed.

'You're a breath of fresh air,' he said. 'Round here music
means hymns in Church and *Two Way Family Favourites* on
a Sunday afternoon. Christ, I miss London. I've only been
stuck here for a fortnight and I can't wait to get back.'

Naturally, we got onto his career at *Abbey Road* about
which by the way, I was dead jealous and I wasn't afraid to
tell him how impressed I was.

He nodded and looked serious.

'Yeah, it's all right,' he said, feigning modesty. 'But it's not all you might think it would be though. I mean, I mainly make coffee – you know, for the engineers and the artists, and fetch sarnies and stuff.'

'The artists?' I said, trying not to sound as envious as I felt. 'You must have met some big names?'

He grinned.

'Floyd…' My heart missed several beats… '…Alan Parsons, McCartney…' My heart missed several more. '…All in the last two months as it happens,' he went on not noticing that I had turned green.

'Wow,' I said. 'McCartney and the Floyd. That's fantastic.'

He lit a cigarette and stared into space through the cloud of smoke, while I was dreaming of four guys who changed the world asking me for ham sandwiches and coffee.

I watched him exhale thick blue clouds of smoke, sitting at the kitchen table in that house where she used to sit and smoke, and it made me feel a little odd and I was uncomfortably reminded of things and people I wanted to forget. So I took a deep breath.

'I saw her on the day she went missing,' I said suddenly.

His dreamy eyes focused sharply on me. He blew the last of the smoke out in a hiss.

'Who?'

'Your mother.'

'Christ! Why didn't you say?!'

'I didn't know it was that day. Not until recently.'

He stubbed the cigarette out in the filthy ashtray and turned suddenly bright eyes on me.

'Where? When? What happened?'

'Nothing really. I was on the bus in Leeford at the end of the High Street and I saw her walking along the pavement, she turned left into a side street. That's all.'

'What street?' he asked, suddenly animated.

'I…I don't know what it's called… opposite Timothy White's…'

* * *

I'll say one thing for Paul Watson, when he wants to, he can get things done. He was on the phone to the police before I'd even finished speaking or so it seemed to me. There was a particular detective he asked for and he was put straight through. I hadn't realised until then that the hunt for Diana's mother was quite so, now what's the word, I think the papers would say 'High Profile' but it must have been because things began to move really fast.

Detective Sergeant Hoyle and a couple of uniformed PCs were with us within the hour and after asking me several questions, the answers to which I kept as vague as I could, they drove both Paul and myself into Leeford in the back of what I know from *Softly Softly* and other police dramas is called in police parlance a 'jam sandwich' but is a marked police car to you and me.

Needless to say, I was able to show them the exact street that I had supposedly seen Mrs W. turn into and I can honestly say that no one could have looked more surprised than myself to hear that Geraldine Road was where Sydney Pontefract lived. I suspect D S Hoyle shouldn't have told us that, but it kind of slipped out in his excitement.

Paul went quite pale, standing there on the corner with me at his side and his lips set in a little thin line of anger when he heard what the Sergeant said.

'Who's that?' I asked him as innocently as I could.

'Some slimy ex-actor she once worked with,' and he sounded furious. I got the definite feeling that Paul didn't like Mr Pontefract and this was confirmed when he added:

'He's been wheedling his way into her good books for the last few months and *into her bed.*' He hissed.

'I'm so sorry,' I said, patting Paul gently on the back. 'I had no idea her friend lived here. I guess she... I guess she must have been visiting him.' And I tried to make that sound as suggestive as I could.

I saw Paul tighten his hands into little fists of anger, not at me I hasten to add but at the thought of what Mr P was doing to his mother.

'I've made a lot of trouble for everyone,' I said quietly and as humbly as I could. 'I'm sure if they'd asked Mr Pontefract he would have told them that she'd been to see him...Just before she vanished.'

Paul looked at me in surprise.

'They did ask him,' he said flatly. 'But he said he hadn't. Don't you get it? Don't you see what this *means*?'

I looked even more innocent.

'No,' I said blandly. 'Does it mean anything?'

Paul looked at me pityingly and so did Sergeant Hoyle.

'Never mind, son,' he said. 'You did your bit to help and whatever happens now, you've moved this investigation forward and I'm very grateful.'

I have become horribly good at lying.

The police offered to drive us to our homes but I said to drop me off with Paul so he could have some company for the evening and later on I even went off to the local shop and came back with a couple of tinned *Fray Bentos* steak and kidney pies and some *Heinz* baked beans that I heated up for us, and I also bought a bottle of cheap whisky, that Paul drank most of.

I think you could say we were getting along rather well…

* * *

After all this I decided it was time to go away again – well actually, I went up to London to *Abbey Road Studios*. Oddly, it was Paul's idea – or so he liked to believe. He was desperate not to lose his job as the studio runner but he had to stay down here to 'sort things' as he put it.

By now the police had taken Mr Pontefract in for questioning and there was even more interest from the national press, so Paul did indeed have to 'sort things.'

As I say, fortunately he had this brilliant idea of suggesting to the studio that I fill in for him while he was away. It saved them the bother of recruiting and they were dead keen when he told them how brilliant I was and what a fantastic C. V. I had. (I reckoned they were never going to take up any of the references so I was fairly free with them) and Paul said he would personally vouch for me…

…So there I was.

I am definitely perfecting the art of 'quiet persuasion' I reckon and if all else fails perhaps I should consider the diplomatic corps.

It's been hard work at *Abbey Road* but if I say it myself I've made a few good contacts and I think I have rather impressed the management with my willingness to work hard, my intelligence and my natural flair. I gather that Paul was never too keen on doing late nights, so of course, I have made it my business to work as many hours in the day and night as I can – my very own *Hard Day's Night* you might say, but then I have always been blessed with the ability to manage on very little sleep. As I may have mentioned at the start of this little 'memoir', I got plenty of practise at broken nights and going with very little rest from an early age.

Unfortunately not only was Paul bad at working long hours but more seriously it seems that Paul may have had what they call 'sticky fingers' – in the sense that his petty cash receipts and his weekly float suffered from several discrepancies.

These discrepancies I 'found' when I was reviewing the system after I took it over, and I must say I felt compelled (reluctantly, of course) to bring it to the attention of the management, just to make sure there was no misunderstanding and that they would not think I was to blame.

I haven't seen Paul since I got home but I rather suspect he won't be pleased to see me as I reckon by now he will have been informed by letter that our temporary job 'swap' has taken on a more permanent feel to it, or as the studio manager put it to me: 'He's out and you're in!'

* * *

Where was I? Oh yes, I haven't been home for a while but I'm back now for a much needed rest. I would have liked to have gone elsewhere but ultimately where else can you get board and lodging, free meals and your laundry done at no charge? My parents have always been very obliging about this, so here I am for a fortnight's holiday.

But I have been nervous since returning to be quite honest – not because of the Paul situation, I hasten to say (I reckon if we meet I can bluster it out), more because I have laid certain ghosts to rest while I have been away but now I am home for a short break I find that those ghosts are walking again. I am reminded of Shakespeare – after I met Diana I made it my business to read Shakespeare who, as you may recall, was not an author I had thought a lot of when I was younger – the line that springs to my mind recently though, is from *Hamlet* – nowadays I think a lot about *Macbeth* and about *Hamlet*.

'*What art thou that usurp'st this time of night…?*'

I hope never to know the answer to that question but since I came home, phantoms do seem to abound at what the singer calls, '*the midnight hour!*'

* * *

It is the end of my first week's holiday, Friday afternoon and I have spent the day walking, visiting my old haunts – the woods, the fields around Butler's farm but not the clearing. I am now spending a little time outside of the school.

It is the middle of September and the boys are back, fresh for an Autumn term but I am here late in the afternoon and by now the day boys have gone home, only a few boarders hang around outside in small groups, chatting under a darkling sky while they wait for the bell to ring for boarders' tea in the dining hall – I stare at them over the low wall.

I could go in I suppose. No doubt the teaching staff will welcome me as one of their more successful former pupils. I mean, quite frankly they don't get a lot of their pupils into

Cambridge, so I will almost certainly be greeted as a returning hero. I imagine that they will invite me in for tea, perhaps introduce me to the boarders as an example of what hard work and dedication can achieve and perhaps they will even invite me back to address the whole school at assembly tomorrow.

I am just begin to enjoy this little daydream and I have expanded it to include some of the details of the speech I will make, along the lines of 'buckling down', 'living by one's faith in God', 'obedience,' 'honesty' etc. when a couple of sixth formers spot me staring at them over the wall and one of them trots across to where I am.

I am expecting him to say something along the lines of, *'Aren't you the chap who went to Cambridge and then became something big in the music industry? We all know you. You're a school legend. Oh, do come in and tell us all about it. We'd all love to meet you.'*

Instead he raises two fingers in a v-sign and says, 'Why don't you fuck off, wanker before we call the old Bill.'

I am shocked. Has everyone at this school become like Teddy Edwards now?

I try to think of a suitably withering reply but I am too shocked so I turn on my heel and trudge away across the field. I glance back, somewhat sadly over my shoulder, disappointed at what things have come to.

The boy is still there.

'Fuck off,' he shouts. 'Go and do your perving in the bog at the back of the station with the rest of the queers.'

Well, frankly!

I trudge home and the blackness in my heart is reflected by the sky above my head. For the first time in what seems like months heavy rain clouds are blowing in across the setting sun and the air suddenly feels uncomfortably sticky and damp. I reckon a storm's brewing.

By the time I am home I am damp with sweat and I decide to take a long, cool shower.

My parents are in the kitchen. My father is sitting at the table sipping a whisky and soda while my mother cooks dinner. Father has changed out of his office clothes which is to say that he has taken off his jacket and tie and rolled back his shirt sleeves and put on a pair of red leather slippers and he is reading The Telegraph. *The Archers* is on the radio and it seems that Phil is having problems with a difficult calving and there is a real risk that Syd Perks might be having an affair with the barmaid at The Bull. I'm not surprised. My mother has long said, that 'Polly is a flighty kind of girl.' And my mother is something of an expert in radio series such as this and the marvellous and much missed *Mrs Dale's Diary*.

'Rissoles,' my mother says when she see me.

I am a little confused but then I realise she means that's what we're having for dinner.

'Have I got time for a shower?' I ask.

'Fifteen minutes,' my father says. Which might sound odd as he is not actually doing any cooking but then he likes to eat at seven thirty sharp and it is now a quarter past and my mother would never let him down on that front – after all, 'He puts the bread on the table,' as she likes to say. I am often tempted to point out that technically she does that but I know that she is speaking metaphorically, of course.

I dash upstairs and throw myself into the shower and once in my bedroom I indulge in a quick burst of *Meddle* from the incomparable *Pink Floyd* on my new Philips tape deck while I pull on a pair of jeans and a clean T-shirt.

Barely thirteen and a half minutes since coming in I am strolling down the stairs ready for dinner. But when I walk into the kitchen I know at once something is wrong. The radio has been turned off, there is no sound of sizzling rissoles in the frying pan and looking around I see that they have been plated and are in the oven. My father has folded up his copy of *The Telegraph* and it is lying in front of him on the table beside his placemat, my mother stands with her back to me, staring out of the kitchen window.

I look from one to the other.

'What's wrong?" I say.

My father won't look me in the eyes but stares at his neatly folded newspaper instead.

'There was a phone call… while you were in the shower…'

That's all he says but his tone makes me shiver.

He coughs and looks up at me.

'It was a Sergeant Hoyle. He'd like you… like us to go to the police station. They've sent a car for us.'

The world suddenly lurches, tips to one side on its axis and I feel I am going to lose my balance. Just when everything was settling down, just when I felt I could move on…

My father stands heavily as we hear the sound of a car in our driveway.

'Come on,' he says. He looks, I think, suddenly quite old and he doesn't seem so… so commanding as he once did and for some reason I'd like to reach out and take his hand but I don't, we've never been into that kind of thing in my family. After all we're not Americans.

'You'd better both bring your coats,' he says. 'It looks like rain.'

* * *

The air in the interview room is blue with cigarette smoke even though we have only just stepped into it. D S Hoyle indicates a table with five wooden chairs around it, three on one side and two on the other.

'Have a seat,' he says.

And my parents and I sit in a line – see no evil, hear no evil, speak no evil – facing the two empty chairs.

'Sorry, about the smoke,' he says, waving a hand through the fug and he goes over to a little window on the other side of the room and tries to open it but it is stuck fast. He grunts, turns to face us and shrugs.

'Bloody thing,' he says and then he lights a cigarette from a pack in his jacket pocket. The door opens and his colleague who we met outside, D C Gold, totters into the room impossibly clutching three polystyrene cups of coffee, most of which he is sloshing onto the floor and over his trousers.

He plops the cups onto the table that that has been stained by a thousand other cups before it and my father and mother stare warily at the luke-warm, brown liquid.

'Three coffees,' he says. 'I don't know who wanted sugar, so I sugared them all.'

My mother finds a tissue in her handbag and dabs at the little brown pool that is creeping over the table and getting dangerously close to the edge of it and to dripping onto her new summer frock from Alders.

My father clears his throat.

'Well,' he says and his voice sounds dry and brittle. 'You wanted to see us. So what's all this about?'

D S Hoyle blows a cloud of smoke into the thick air and crosses to us. He drops a thick manila folder that he has had tucked under his arm on to the table and it lands with a thud, sending little ripples through the puddle of spilt coffee.

I am oddly calm. I guess I should be shaking with nerves, my stomach should be churning, I should at the very least have trembling hands but now that the crunch has come, as it were, I simply feel calm – numb you might say.

Is this what it has all been about? Is this what I have come to, my own little crucifixion in a smoky interview room in Leeford Police Station? Surely after all the efforts I've made, I deserved a little better than this. I should go down in a blaze of glory, shouldn't I? Where are my stations of the cross? Where is my moment of public humiliation and lasting fame?

The words, 'Why have you forsaken me?' spring to mind but I sit here, outwardly calm, watching the stocky figure of D S Hoyle. And then I realise something odd: it is D S Hoyle who looks nervous. It's him who has sweat on his upper lip, whose hands shake and who looks pale.

'Well, thank you for coming in so quickly,' he says at last. 'We'd have sent a car only we're a bit short staffed right now...'

It's a new kind of policing I think, where they ask suspects to make their own way in for a grilling. It'll never catch on.

D S Hoyle dabs his brow with a filthy hanky and I can feel my mother wince – how she'd love to get that into her twin-tub.

'Well,' he says again. 'I'm afraid this won't be easy and I apologize in advance...'

That is unusual I reckon. I mean do the police always say sorry before they arrest you for murder? I seems odd but then I haven't been in this situation before. D S Hoyle still seems nervous and hesitant and I want to say, 'Get on with it man. I did it. I confess. Don't put yourself and my parents through this torture!' And then I think that's probably just what he wants. He wants me to break; it's a kind of psychological warfare – modern policing at its very worst or best, depending on how you look at it, I guess. And once again, I think of Dr Ellerman and his Marxist conspiracy theories.

'It's like this…' D S Hoyle is saying and I try to concentrate on his words, hoping he won't see the fear in my eyes.

'We were contacted by the Birmingham force a few days ago. They were making enquiries following the suicide of a member of the public…'

He paused to take a puff on his cigarette and my mother takes the opportunity to speak.

'I don't understand,' she says and her lips are thin and frightened. 'What's that got to do with us? You said when you called that this concerned Billy… our son.'

'That's right, Madam. I'm afraid it does.' I swallow but stay as cool as I can. He picks up the folder from the table and 'tuts' in annoyance when he sees that the edges of it are soaked with spilt coffee. He turns to D C Gold: 'Bloody hell, Jim – get some tissues and mop that up will you.'

Jim looks a bit fed-up that he is being sent away just as things are getting interesting but as he turns to go my mother reaches into her handbag and produces two whole packets of *Handy Andies* – that's my mother for you, always prepared for any eventually – it's what makes her one in a million, my father always says.

'Jim' gratefully opens one of the little plastic pouches and mops up the spillage and dabs at the corners of the brown manila folder while we all watch him as if he is some kind of magician doing a very clever party trick. He drops the wet tissues in the bin and wipes his fingers on the last one left in the packet and then scrunches the package up and throws that away too.

'Finished..?' D S Hoyle says grumpily, which I think is a bit rich seeing as how he'd told him to do it in the first place. Jim nods.

'Yes. Ta.' He says affably.

Which is dreadful English and I see my father wince.

'Right, where was I?' D S Hoyle says. 'Yes… well, let me explain. When the house of the er… deceased…' He looks at us, as if to check that we knew what the word means and then carries on. 'When the house was cleared-out by neighbours… well, parishioners actually…'

'Parishioners?' my mother says in a surprised voice.

'Oh, yes. I should have said, the… er… deceased was a parish priest, a Catholic parish priest. When they cleared the house, certain… certain items were found – items of a delicate and rather disturbing nature…'

My father suddenly looks rather pale and he awkwardly clears his throat.

'I say, Sergeant…' he says and lowers his voice. 'Pas devant les enfants, what…?'

D S Hoyle looks blank, clearly French is not his strong point. D C Jim Gold leans forward happy to show off his linguistic ability or perhaps just to show-up his boss.

'He means, not in front of the children, Sarge…"

'I know what he means, *constable*…' snaps D S Hoyle,

though he obviously doesn't. He looks at my father. 'I'm sorry sir, but what children..?'

My father rolls his eyes in my direction.

'I'm twenty-one, father.' I groan.

'Yes... but...' my father says hopelessly. 'Even so, old boy... ladies present and all that...'

Sergeant Hoyle looks mystified. He probably thinks he's stepped into the middle of a 1930's schoolboy yarn. My father, who has very high values and strong opinions and a great love for the way things used to be, can to some people appear a little *old fashioned*, possibly even *pompous* at times. Sensibly Sergeant Hoyle decides not to pursue the point but carries on instead.

'Anyway,' he says firmly and suddenly his voice takes on a grim and serious tone. 'Anyway, I'm afraid that what was found, was a rather large collection of photographs. Many of them were highly indecent, undoubtedly bought mail-order from certain covert businesses on the continent – there's a lot of this stuff in Amsterdam, as it happens...'

'Such a wonderful place for flowers,' my mother sighs. 'Such a shame.'

'Most of it was of...'

'...Tulips especially,' my mother says.

D S Hoyle hesitates and looks at my mother wondering maybe if she is completely mad and then he starts again, 'Most of the material... well, it was of *kiddies,* I'm afraid...'

We all look at him. My mother's mouth opens but she can't speak, my father rocks back in his chair as if he has been punched. I look at the Sergeant; this isn't what I was expecting and I don't understand... What is he saying? What does he mean? What's it got to do with us?

My father finally speaks.

'I...I... You mean, children... in the... in the pictures?'

'Yes,' D S Hoyle says and his voice is low. 'Kids, being made to do things...'

'But I've never heard the like...' My father says and he is almost whispering.

'It happens I'm afraid – it's all too common.'

'Good God,' my father says. 'Does it? I had no idea...'

D C Gold, 'Jim', leans forward, 'It's not talked about much but I'm afraid it's out there all right... Your Mrs Whitehouse and the like going on about the telly and all that – makes me laugh! What's she know?' And he adds, 'The real world is a horrible place, worse than anything they can dream up on BBC Two.'

There is a silence while we think about this and then D S Hoyle says, 'I'm sorry to have to drag you into it...' He looks at my mother who still hasn't spoken and is now tearing a *Handy Andy* into little pieces without looking at it.

'I really am sorry...' he repeats watching the little pieces of white tissue fluttering to the floor of the interview room.

Finally, my father says, 'But what's this got to do with us?'

'I'm very sorry,' D S Hoyle says again. 'Look,' and he swallows on a dry mouth, 'Look, I'm afraid not all the photographs were, you know, bought. Seems he took quite a lot of them himself. Not posed. No one forced to do anything, but you know, telephoto lenses through school changing rooms, kiddies in the park, lavatories. Stuff like that...'

I think my mother will be sick.

'I still don't understand,' my father says.

I'm so confused now. This isn't what I thought would be happening. I am suddenly out of my depth.

'This has nothing to do with us. Why involve us?' My father asks more firmly and I can tell he is getting annoyed.

D S Hoyle turns to look at me. He seems to wait a long time before he says anything.

'I thought you might… like the support of your family around you…'

'I'm sorry…' I say.

'The suicide… the priest… You knew him. He was a teacher at your school.'

He looks from me to my father and mother but they don't respond. I remember P. G. Wodehouse writing that one of his characters looked like a stunned mullet or some such fish, on a slab and that's how my parents are now – they stare at D S Hoyle with bulging eyes and they open their mouths in little gulping movements but no sound comes out.

'That's why we got involved,' the sergeant goes on, oblivious it seems to the fact that he has just destroyed my parents' neat, ordered, respectable world. 'The Brummies tracked him back to our patch, asked us to look into things and we found out that he taught at your school – for quite a while actually, until he was moved to a parish, Redditch it was – five or so years ago that would be now.'

'Good Lord.' My father still looks terrible and he has turned very pale. 'A priest..?'

'Yes.'

'And he took photos of… of the boys.. in… in Billy's school?'

'In the changing rooms mainly.' D S Hoyle hesitates. 'And elsewhere. And of course it may well have been more than just pictures. You know…'

Clearly my parents don't know – or if they do they certainly don't want to. D S Hoyle waits for them to speak but they don't, they stare at the damp table top instead. He looks to his constable, hoping perhaps that he will lead the next part of the delicate conversation but Jim Gold doesn't seem to want to be involved either. Instead he concentrates on writing a long and complicated note in a little black book which he has pulled from his jacket pocket.

There is a long moment of stillness and we are all lost in our own thoughts. And I am remembering the drama club and the film club and a sunny afternoon in the holidays and a blonde wig and a short smock that was more like a dress and Greek Gods who were never appeased and I think of the boxes of film on dusty shelves in a room at the top of the school, films that went back through generations of schoolboys…

Then D S Hoyle lights another cigarette and makes the air even thicker than it was and the dull light from the little window seems grey now and not so bright as that from the little fly stained light bulb that hangs from a broken fixing in the ceiling.

At last the miserable policeman speaks again. His voice is quiet, measured.

'We're asking the kids…'

He catches my father's eye.

'That is the 'pupils' from that time if… if he, if this man ever did anything to them that was… er… inappropriate, as it were.'

'Inappropriate!' My father snaps and he takes us all aback with his raised voice. He grasps the edge of the table as if he will haul himself to his feet: '*Inappropriate*! I'd like to kill him..!'

And his words hang thickly in the thick air.

Then D S Hoyle looks at me, level, steady blue/grey eyes – like James Bond I think, as described by the incomparable Mr Fleming.

'Billy…' Says D S Hoyle. 'I have to ask you this. Did any of the teachers at your school, any of the priests ever… ever… in anyway at all… did they ever touch you or do anything…'

He tails off. So I finish the sentence for him.

'Inappropriate..?'

'Yes,' he says.

'No,' I say. 'No, they did not.'

My mother suddenly squeezes my hand and I can feel her rings digging into my palm and my father breathes a long sigh of relief.

'Good lad,' he says quietly as if I have been successful in an exam or won the one hundred yards at sports day.

'Were you aware,' the sergeant says, 'Of any teacher doing anything… *inappropriate*… to any other boy.'

'No,' I say again, firmly.

He seems disappointed.

'Are you sure?'

'Positive,' I say and then I add. 'May we go now? I think my mother is upset.'

And it's true. She is crying quietly and I am pretty sure she is going to draw blood from my hand with her rings at any second.

D S Hoyle glances at Jim Gold and he sighs.

'Could you organise a car please Jim?'

Jim snaps his book closed and trots quickly from the room.

'Well, I'm sorry to have troubled you,' D S Hoyle says. 'Please, if you'd like to wait in the front, the car will pick you up as soon as possible. In the meantime if I could ask for your discretion while we complete our investigations, I should be grateful.'

My parents and I stand, my father ram-rod straight, my mother rather slumped on his arm, looking older than she did. They lead the way to the door and my father pointedly doesn't say goodbye. He has clearly taken all of this as something of a personal slight against us, against the family – his family.

'These questions have to be asked, you know,' D S Hoyle says at their retreating backs as if he has read my father's mind – and he sounds a little offended.

My father stops dead and for a second he stands there with his back to the sergeant and then he turns slowly to face him.

'Maybe,' he says with great dignity. 'But not of people like us, Sergeant. Not of people like us.'

And then he leads my mother through the door and down the corridor. I half expect him to come back and add, 'I mean, I am churchwarden, you know.' But he doesn't.

I pick-up my jacket from the back of the chair and go to follow them but suddenly D S Hoyle springs to his feet and he reaches the door before me. I think he is going to hold it open for me – but instead he bars my way.

'I didn't like to say anything,' he says quietly and there is a sudden and unpleasant edge to his voice. 'But you should know that *most* of the photos were of you.'

I stand looking at him but there is nothing I can say.

'Yes,' He goes on. 'And most of them were taken not in the school but in some wood or something like that, there are trees and bushes...'

The world tips again, the axis wobbles once more just as it had done before in our kitchen. I feel very, very sick.

'He followed you around,' he says. 'He was always with you. Christ man, in some of them you hadn't even got all your clothes on. You were much younger, lying there in your Y-fronts, writing in an exercise book! What was that all about?'

I can't speak but I am back in the clearing on a hot summer day, my wet clothes smelling weakly of urine where they are drying on the bushes and then I see again a flash of gold and blue. My angel. Except it wasn't my angel...

'He followed you everywhere Billy. I'm sorry to say this but I don't believe you weren't... you weren't a victim of his. That's how these people are. They can't help it... He was a bad man...'

'So you say,' I reply tersely. 'Obviously.'

I move towards the door again but he reaches out to hold my shoulder.

'Wait. You should see this...'

He leaves me and goes back to the table, opens the manila folder and shakes out a piece of crumpled notepaper carefully wrapped in polythene. It has been partly burnt and the edges of it are charred but I can see there is writing on both sides of it. He comes back to me and hands it to me.

'Don't unwrap it,' he says, 'It's evidence.'

I glance at it and there is something familiar in the handwriting but I don't take much notice and I don't really want to look at it.

'He was more than a photographer, your teacher,' growls D S Hoyle. 'I think he was a killer. We think he killed that girl...'

I look up at him. My heart starts to race, my breath catches in my chest. I feel as though I am on top of a some high slope staring down into emptiness.

'Girl..?' I say as calmly as I can.

'Your friend, Billy. Diana. Diana Watson.'

'No…' My voice sounds not like my voice at all, it is thin, strangled…

'Read it!' he says, tapping the paper in my hand. 'Read it.'

And reluctantly I look down at Father Martin's words:

I think I've made the right decision. Explanations could only confuse things. Who's going to believe that I don't remember what happened, that I'm confused between reality and what happened in my head – so I don't know if I am guilty of… well, of what's happened, or not.

My guess is she was strangled – I mean it's hard to tell, she was pretty beaten-up but there are bruises on her neck and I might have done that – I just don't remember. I'm pretty handy, I suppose – I have strong wrists – in fact, I reckon I can hold my own with most people when it comes to… to things like taking the top off a bottle, for instance.

As I say, I think I've made the right decision. Better not to say anything, not even to suggest that I know where she is, because my only alibi is that at the time I was… Well, where I was…

I mean let's face it, who's going to believe me? Anyway, the whole thing's difficult and frankly, confusing. It could have been me, I suppose: I was jealous. And, truth to tell, I have never really understood girls. I mean, I haven't exactly had any 'experience' of them. Have I?

So as tragic as this is, I'm going to keep this to myself because

I don't really know what happened and I do not have the sort of alibi that I probably need for the police to be satisfied with my innocence. I keep a lot of things to myself. I always have. I've always had to.

Control. Everything is about control, isn't it?

I mean there aren't many who could have done what I have done with the knife and the other tools.

So, I have disposed of… Well, I have done what I had to do. It was distasteful, of course, but necessary.

And now I can dispose of the memory, forget it all. That's the trick. Just forget the whole thing… And pray for her. Yes. I must pray for her. Of course.'

'The Brummies found it.'

His voice makes me start and I have to drag myself from the horrors of what I am reading and look at him, at his smug, sallow face, his pasted on sincerity.

'It's from some kind of diary they reckon,' he goes on. '…But he'd burnt it. This was the only bit that survived.'

He is puffing on another cigarette and I want to say something to him about New Smoking Material but I can't be bothered.

'Control, he says,' D S Hoyle's voice is mocking and angry at the same time. 'Getting his rocks off watching kiddies – and he calls it control…'

He drops his cigarette on the floor and grinds it hard beneath the toe of his pointed black Chelsea boot.

'They should cut their balls off…' He lights yet another cigarette and throws the empty packet across the room into a metal waste bin. It 'clanks' noisily, like one beat of a death knell. 'I know I would, I'd chop their balls off – but we're too soft now…'

He looks at me.

'So now we know what happened to her, Billy. To that poor girl. No wonder her mother's topped herself... That poor woman – and we haven't found her body, either. Can't lay either of them to rest properly. It's a crying shame.'

We look at each other, both of us seeing her mother in our minds.

Then he speaks very slowly, spelling it out for me. 'I can't believe he didn't touch you, that he didn't do anything – he was obsessed by you Billy... He must have done something to you....'

He waits for me to speak but I stare at him dumbly.

'He watched you and the other boys at your school, took photos of you in the bogs and the changing rooms even in the woods...And he was a killer, Billy. The little fucker killed your friend,'

The expletive makes me shudder.

He takes a sharp breath. Steadying himself, pushing back his anger and his zeal.

'Look,' he says more calmly. 'It might help you to tell us... We can get you support, you could see someone.'

I stare at him and then I suddenly want to laugh and I have to swallow back my giggles.

'A man in a bow tie?' I say. 'No thank you.'

He looks puzzled but carries on.

'Billy, there's a photo of you on the ground. You look ill, your eyes are closed – if he'd done something to you... I know it hurts, but you must tell us...'

And his eyes are passionate, fervent burning with the need for revenge which he probably calls justice. I am remembering the cat and finding myself lying neatly – folded

you might say, in a genuflection after I passed out and I am
remembering footsteps along a dark track late at night and I
am remembering something else, bushes parting like curtains, spotlights wheeling through the night and the gentle
touch of the BVM's hands on my body and the awfulness of
what happened…

'Are you all right,' he's saying and he sounds suddenly
concerned. 'You've gone white. Here, sit down…'

And he pulls a chair over.

'Sorry,' he says. 'I didn't mean to upset you… It's just…
It's just… well, I've kids of my own, you know…'

Has he? For some reason I'm surprised. He doesn't look
like what I'd call a family man. I take a deep breath and push
the chair away.

'I'll be all right,' I mutter. And then I think, I'm always
all right, aren't I?

So is this what it has come to? After all I have been
through, was my angel nothing more than a tawdry drama
teacher in a dog collar? And at that moment I see life for
what it is – nothing but a series of let-downs and bitter dis-
appointments. What have I been chosen for? For this? For
this humiliation? A boy in a Greek dress, eye-candy for some
old lecher, a laughing stock for everyone else, for all the other
boys who knew what I didn't know because they were in the
other world, the not my world.

'Are you all right?' D S Hoyle says again.

'Yes,' I say at last.

He stares at me.

'You must tell me what happened, Billy. You really
must – for the sake of his other victims, you must tell me,
did he touch you..? Did he do anything?'

'That's nonsense,' I say. 'It won't help anyone, even if I had anything to tell you. He was just a sad old man, that's all...'

And now my head is full of memories, sweeping over me – I am bursting the banks of my mind.

'...He was a sad old man,' I say. 'Who sweated a lot and didn't bath enough. He was a sad old man who took snuff because he thought it made him look theatrical and he wanted us all to know that he was once in what he called 'Rep', as if anyone cared... As if anyone cared!'

D S Hoyle looks puzzled.

'Rep?' he repeated. 'As in the theatre?'

'He never stopped telling us about it.'

'Really?' He picked-up the folder and flicked through some type written pages. 'Not according to this. Went straight from his school to a seminary... Trained as a...' he hesitates over the alien word, '...As a Jesuit.' He pronounces it Jes-oo-it.

I stare at him.

'Father Martin?' I say. 'No. No, I don't think Father Martin was Jesuit material.' And for the first time that evening I have something to smile at. 'Definitely not, I'd say.'

Now it's D S Hoyle's turn to look puzzled.

'Father Martin?' He says. 'Who's he?'

I look blankly at him.

'No,' he says. 'Our suicide is a James Rogers. Father James Rogers... Didn't I say?'

He waits for me to respond but I can't. So he speaks again.

'Father Rogers, he was the man with the camera, the one who was following you around... Nasty little shit.'

I have no more to say to him. Frankly, I can't take any more shocks. My world is not the world it was. Suddenly good is bad and bad is good. Priests lust after little boys? It's not possible. The Church would never allow it, what would The Pope say? It could never happen, least of all with Father Rogers, that perfect well ordered man I always admired. My God – that mind – I wanted a mind like that – I wanted to be like it with its small red ticks and crosses and its acerbic little notes in the margins of my book.

And I glance down at the page wrapped in polythene, the neat hand writing, the perfectly measured margins, the red ink… And then I feel terribly low, depressed, you might say.

It seems that things change all the time; what we think something is, is not; what you seem to be, you're not – and we move on, we keep moving on, even when we don't want to – and there is no order. It's all random. It's all chaos and opposites. Things move on and I can't keep pace.

I realise then that I have collided with the other world, the 'not my world' and it is somehow forcing its way into my own private and personal world, into my life, into my soul. It's like my father said: these things happen but they shouldn't happen to people like us, not to people like me.

Everything is reversed in this other world. Here good is bad, order is chaos, right is wrong – and I hate it. So I don't speak any more. I don't look at this unkempt, uncouth, chain smoking Detective Sergeant because he is part of that world, the other world. I turn on my heel, turn away from him and his sordid little job and his sordid little crimes and I go outside to find my parents.

* * *

Later, as we are driving home in silence in the back of the police car, it suddenly dawns on me: so, I didn't kill the girl. It wasn't me. She must have come to find me and she… she took advantage of me, physically, like she was always trying to and Father Rogers must have seen her and lost his temper or something terrible like that. And HE KILLED HER. And I didn't remember. I didn't recall it because I was in a holy state, in one of my visionary moments. Or maybe I just fainted, like with the cat.

And suddenly I want to laugh out loud and shout out that I didn't kill her. God has saved me. I have been saved. But I don't say anything, rather I hunch down in the seat and let the warmth of the car envelop me because the nights are starting to get cooler now; Autumn is on its way.

We are nearly home when I realise something else: her mother didn't have to die. I didn't have to… to do what I did. There was no need after all, because I hadn't hurt her daughter and I had nothing to feel guilty about or to hide away from after all.

For a moment I panic and a great wave of sorrow and horror washes over me for the first time, for the first time in my life really, soaking me from head to toe. But I have to get a grip. I have to call on that iron self-control that always sees me through – somehow.

So I won't dwell on this. I daren't dwell on this. I have to keep my focus. I have always been good at self-discipline. Father Rogers is right, an iron-will is the secret to survival; some things are much better forgotten, put away into some dusty corner of my head where they cannot be annoying or get under your feet, as you might say, metaphorically speaking.

So I do this now. I put the thought of her death away in the attic of my mind and I close the door on it, very firmly...

We arrive home and my mother leads us straight into the kitchen and makes us cocoa. It is warm and comforting sitting here, sipping cocoa – especially as it has begun to rain outside, torrential pouring rain, slamming against our windows but we are safe indoors in the warmth of our own home – the storm can't reach us here, thank goodness.

Acknowledgements

Many thanks to Vanessa Neuling, who unstintingly supported me and encouraged me – and edited my many drafts with
vigour, and enthusiasm. Thank you.

I am very grateful to Margaret Wishart who read this intelligently and carefully and gave me many helpful comments
and much support.

I am deeply grateful to my children Will and Jess for
reading this and for speaking intelligently to me about it and
for just about putting up with me when I was moody and ill
while writing it.

This book would not have been written without my
wife Alison and my brother Duncan, who believe in me as a
writer and who support me in all my crazy ventures with
their love and with their money! There are not enough words
to say to you both what I feel.

Credits & Links

Cover design and illustration by Deana Riddle,
bookstarter.com

Author's photo by Georgia-Rae Sacre
www.otherpublishing.co.uk

Book design by Maureen Cutajar
www.gopublished.com

Published By The Other Publishing Company,
www.otherpublishing.co.uk

Also by Michael Cameron

In Harm's Way – (with Sean Hogan)
Published by Arrow Books

The Brinkmeyers
Published by The Other Publishing Company

Enjoy these titles from fine ebook retailers everywhere

Read an extract from
Michael Cameron's new book:
The Brinkmeyers

I am Hymie Brinkmeyer, 50 years old on a good day. Younger, some days. Older, quite often. New York, U.S. of A. by birth. Now live in the UK. I married my very own English rose – Maggie. (I'm a lucky man). Settled here in Queen Elizabeth-land to bring-up our kids – Kevin (now 17) and Karen (now 19). I work hard. I play hard. I pray to my God and I talk to Him regular.

We live in a digital world, so I thought 'hey, what the heck!' I'll start a blog. I have something to say. I have read other blogs and I don't believe you need to go on about sex and drugs or swear to be interesting. I'm in oil. I used to be in rubber – now that's interesting!

I'm middle aged but who says this blog thing can only be for young people?

We can share our experiences. Sharing I like and I want you to share with me; so you are welcome to my Blog. Tell me what you think of it. Talk to me about it. Shees! Someone please talk to me!

Am I alone?

God should get a PC. I know he is all seeing and all knowing but I am worried about the lack of communication with his creations. Since the tablets of stone business he has said so little. There are ways to reach his people BUT writing to us he ignored, the telegraph he ignored, the phone he ignored and I have never heard him on radio or TV.

God, get a PC! Email us. Start a web site.. It's a digital age. You need to bestride your universe with a cell phone in one hand and a lap top in the other.

You'll like the new technology – Digital TV, DVD, MP3, CD. I see you with an iPod! (Come to think of it, I see everyone with an iPod – on the subway it looks like mankind has evolved little white ears, with wires on. Soon we won't need flesh and blood – we'll download ourselves from the internet). Nowadays it's entertainment in a box, easy stimulation for the senses – a brave, bright new digital world.

God, let me ask you, have you surfed the web? There's a whole universe in there. It'll broaden your horizons!

A question of copyright

Of course God wrote The Bible. But does God consider that to be all his own work or does he share the credit with others? And which part does he consider to be most his own work? The Old Testament or the New?

Being Jewish, I have a natural affinity with the Old T. I see his hand at work here. The New T. has too much human interference, in my opinion.

Still, think of the copyright he could collect! He should claim. I have a lawyer. Very good on claims. God, call me if you want his number.

God's own country

Independence Day. I miss the U.S.A. Today and Thanks Giving, that's when I most miss my home.

In Queen Elizabeth-Land they don't carry the flag like we do. There is not so much patriotism. I like the British but they are either reserved or violent. They don't have much in between those two states of mind. And they do not have faith in their own kind, like we Americans do. I'm not saying we are always right but we BELIEVE we are always right – which helps us, and gives us the confidence to lead the world.

God Bless America!

Blind spots

It seems we all have blind spots. I raise this because I am thinking about Maggie, my wife. She has a blind spot about anything mechanical. The guy in our local filling station has just told me this story...

First you need to know that my wife is a woman very sassy and very clued-up on so many things. Ask her what shoes go with that handbag? This woman will tell you. Where do you get a face lift for less than 10K? – She knows! What's in my bank account? It's a cinch. But put her in a situation involving mechanics and she falls apart.

I bought her this car – it's not a Roller but it has style for a woman running round Guildford. Second week she goes out in it and she calls in at the filling station. The little red light is up that says to her she needs to put oil in the engine. So she buys a can of oil. Anyway forty minutes later the guy in the pay-booth starts to worry. She has had her head under the hood of the car all this time. He goes out to her and asks her what the problem is. She looks up at him, all red and oily, and tells him I have bought her a duff car. 'What kind of a car,' she says, 'only gives you a hole this big to pour in the oil.'

The guy looks in the bonnet and sure enough there is my wife trying to pour the oil into the little hole where the dip-stick goes… See what I mean… a great lady, but a blind spot!! You got to laugh.

More blind spots

Me? Yeah. I got blind spots too. I don't deny this. I just don't need to tell anyone about them. I deal with them in my own way. I have a little tendency to eat things that are bad for me… Which is possibly a vice and not a blind spot at all. But I do not feel fat. I feel a little uncomfortable around the middle but not always. Some of my pants fit better than others. The ones I bought in America fit better than the ones over here. They are better cut…

Perhaps I mean bigger!

Even more blind spots

To continue on the theme of blind spots. Mine, if you like.

I believe my kids can do no wrong. And this is foolish as I should know by now that if Kevin is busted one more time for possession, then we must assume he has a problem. Also I have to admit that Karen is pregnant, unmarried and as far as I know she has no idea who the father is but it's not the same guy who got her pregnant last time. Of that she is sure – but I still think of her as my little bunny…. (Which euphemism she seems determined to prove… in her breeding habits at least!).

Another blind spot….

I believe I am welcome at my golf club because of the jolly figure I cut at the bar and because I am good competitive player but I know that really it is because I have money and buy drinks after every game. Also…. I think I am a firm but fair employer but actually I just fire any bastard who gets in my way!

Is that enough blind spots for one man? I should become Catholic. I would take to confession, like a duck to water.

ABOUT ME
I am Karen Brinkmeyer.

I was called by Karen Brinkmeyer by my so-called parents. I prefer Karrie or Karrie B. I'm 19. I live in a shit place called Farnham which is in the South of England. I am a writer/artist/poet but mainly I write. I am starting a novel and this blog is to show my notes about it and how it grows from what you might call an embryo to the finished thing and how I get it published and what the critics/readers etc. think of it when it is published.

Stay in touch with my progress. Updates every day, and lots of snippets, bits and source material as I accumulate them.

More about me: I am a single mother of one – a baby boy – Cleo, age 1 year and 3 months and I am pregnant with a second one – due in 6 months. I believe in freedom to choose how we live our lives.

I have chosen not to have a partner because:

A) I like my freedom
B) Most men are a penis with an ego attached
C) I will not be told to shave my armpits by a gorilla who scratches his balls and thinks he has a right to fart in bed.

A bit more about me:

I hate capitalism and want to protect the environment from crap-producing, exploitative businesses who are destroying the world and exploiting poor people everywhere. I hate MacDonald's, Hollywood, Rupert Murdoch's trash press and most commercial television and, of course, food manufacturers who are filling our kids with processed junk and robbing developing world farmers of a decent living.

The Manifesto by which I live my life:

Give Africa a chance.

The Afghan war is interventionist and exploitative – I protest against it.

Every one deserves freedom but only the kind of freedom they want – not the one imposed on it by so called democracies like the UK and the USA and NATO and all that shit.

My country did not go to war in my name!

Bob Geldoff and Jamie Oliver, Barrack Obama and Oprah should be made joint presidents of the entire world – oh, and Will.I.Am – 'cos he's cute and intelligent.

Police powers need curbing.

Drugs are bad for you but the right to take them is good for you.

AIDS is spread by ignorance – (the ignorance of corrupt governments, mainly)

Also –

I believe all politicians are liars – except Obama (and he doesn't count as a politician really, 'cos he's more like a saint or something) .

My country will not fight another war, even for our friends like America and… and… (Check this – what other friends do we have?) when a new generation (mine) takes over.

Somewhere in Farnham, Surrey there is a little bit of rebel insurgency – and I'm leading it. I see myself as a kind of urban (well, strictly speaking, suburban) guerrilla!

Through my art I will fight!

Read on.

My Dad

My Dad says he misses the USA. He is American and I was born there, so was my brother, but we have lived in the UK for the last 12 years because my Mother wanted to come home. She is English and we always do what she wants. My Dad has been homesick since Monday – because that was Independence Day. He does this every fucking year and also at Thanksgiving. He will be over it in a week. He always is.

Dad is very emotional. I guess this is because he is Jewish. My Mother is the ice queen – English and cold.

So, I am half Jewish, half English. That means I have emotions but I hide them...

THE BRINKMEYERS

published by The Other Publishing Company

For more details visit
www.michaelcameron.co.uk
or
www.otherpublishing.co.uk